YVONNE WOON grew up in Worcester, Massachusetts, USA, in an old stone colonial house surrounded by woods. It was here that she first developed a taste for the macabre, and she has been writing mysteries ever since.

Yvonne attended the prestigious Worcester Academy prep school in Boston, where, like Renée, the length of her skirt was routinely measured. She first began thinking about Latin and the Undead while studying in the library of Columbia University, New York, where she obtained a Masters of Fine Arts in fiction.

www.yvonnewoon.com

LIFE ETERNAL

YVONNE WOON

USBORNE

For my mother,
a mysterious woman.

First published in the UK in 2012 by Usborne Publishing Ltd., Usborne House,
83-85 Saffron Hill, London EC1N 8RT, England. www.usborne.com

Copyright © 2012 by Yvonne Woon

Published by arrangement with Hyperion, an imprint of Disney Book Group,
114 Fifth Avenue, New York, NY 10011-5690, USA.

A CIP catalogue record for this book is available from the British Library.

ISBN 9781409546726   JFM MJJASOND/12   02743/03
Printed in Reading, Berkshire, UK

It is the great myth of history.
That one can cheat death.

CONTENTS

Do you desire to be united as one; never apart both day and night? If this is your desire, I will melt you down and fuse you together, so that two become one, and while you live you will share a single life, and when you die, you will still be one in the world below, instead of two...

– Plato, *Symposium*

A LONG TIME AGO, we used to believe that people were made of two things – the body and the soul. When the body died, the soul lived on and was cleansed and reborn into someone new. The idea was explored by many, though namely in Western culture by Plato, and then René Descartes.

Descartes was a famous philosopher in his time. He was obsessed with death – he wrote about it incessantly. He even claimed to have discovered the path to immortality. He was going to reveal his secret in an essay he claimed would be his lifetime achievement, and which he worked on up until his death. He called it his *Seventh Meditation*. When he died, people believed that his death was a hoax, an experiment. They thought he had found a way to cheat death and become reborn.

That, of course, was never proven, and Descartes was never heard from again. All that remained were his papers. People combed through them, searching for the *Seventh Meditation*, but they only found six, none of which contained anything about the key to immortality.

After everyone had given up hope, rumours began to surface that they had found something buried beneath the foundation of his house. Descartes' *Seventh Meditation*. But the book was banned just before it was released. According to rumour, all copies were immediately burned, as were the men who had printed it. And before it could even be read, the book was gone, along with all of its secrets.

Extract from the *Seventh Meditation* by René Descartes

I. Of Death and the Soul

In these meditations, I will attempt to consider the idea of the Dead as Undead. Matters of the Body and Soul are ones that our faithful institutions of government and justice would like to keep hidden. Therefore, in accordance with the idea that knowledge should be accessible to all men, I will divulge in these writings the little-known facts about Life and Death.

Humans are made of two things – a Body and a Soul. Upon death, a person's body dies, after which point his soul is "cleansed" and reborn into a new person. This is why some moments feel as though we've lived them

11

twice; why a person can often have the same essence as someone who died decades before.

II. OF THE DEATH OF CHILDREN

The matter of Children is one that is particularly troubling to adults. All adults follow the rules stipulated in Part I of this Meditation. However, there is one exception. When a child dies, his Soul *leaves his body. Yet, in opposition to our customary education of the biological processes of Life and Death, the child does not die. Instead of "dying", as adult bodies do, the child's body lies dormant for nine days. On the tenth day it rises again without a soul. The child then wanders the world, searching for it. It is my supposition that this is nature's way of giving youth a second chance at life. They are what we call* Non Mortuus, *or the* Undead.

III. OF *NON MORTUUS*

The Undead *have no Souls. They cannot be killed by normal means, for they are already dead. Although they are still children, and appear harmless, this is a falsehood. The Undead have no human instincts. They do not eat, they do not sleep, they do not feel. With time, their bodies decay, and they must constantly seek ways to preserve themselves before their bodies die again and return to the earth.*

The observed characteristics of the Undead are those often associated with other dead creatures. Skin that is cold to the

12

touch. *A stiffness of the limbs. Breath that contains no human warmth. They have also been identified to have incredible healing powers, their wounds closing as quickly as they are broken. Fluency in Latin and Latinate tongues. A lack of complete sensation and emotion. Yet most notably, they are known to reanimate into the best versions of themselves. Stronger than their human form, or more intelligent, or more beautiful.*

Thus, their existence is a tortured and miserable one. They have but one purpose – to seek and obtain their missing Soul. They have twenty-one years to find it, twenty-one being the number demarcating the transformation from child to adult. If by their twenty-first year they do not find their soul, they begin to decompose at an accelerated rate until their bodies are completely destroyed. This, I have observed to be a particularly painful process. However, if they do find the person with their Soul, they reclaim it through the pressing together of mouths, otherwise known as Basium Mortis. *Through this act the Undead becomes human again, and lives a natural life. The victim dies from a failure of the heart, their corpse aged and withered without its soul.*

The danger of the Undead lies in this method, for they are also able to take Souls that are not theirs. This temporarily reverses the decaying process; however, it also results in the death of the other. The problem for humans lies in the dire handicap that we are unable to distinguish between the living

13

and the Undead. In my logic, it would thus seem that humans are doomed to fall under the mercy of these unkillable, soulless creatures...

IV. OF BURIAL RITUALS

Ancient civilizations discovered a way to prevent children from turning into the Undead. Before this period, burial rituals were not yet in existence. The dead were left to nature, which was the fate that all of Earth's creatures met when they died. The Egyptians were among the first to discover that by mummifying their dead and encasing them in pyramids, the children wouldn't rise again.

Later civilizations found that there were three things the Undead could not withstand without decaying: fire, geometric golden ratios and being underground. Since then, each society has discovered new ways of preventing the Undead from rising: by fire – funeral pyres and cremation; by golden ratio – coffins and pyramids; and by the subterranean – burials and catacombs. Each of these rituals was created for one sole purpose – to let our children rest.

Over time and transgression, the rituals became so ingrained in society that people forgot why they were performed. Soon, everyone – including adults – was buried or cremated, and no one remembered that children could rise from the dead.

V. OF LATIN AND ITS EXTINCTION

Latin is the language the Undead speak. In ancient times, before the founding of the Roman Empire, before people discovered burial rituals, Latin was only spoken by children. It was the one way to tell who was Undead and who was alive.

In Roman mythology, two children were the original founders of Rome. Their names were Romulus and Remus, and they were brothers. While this is a commonly accepted myth among educated society, what most are not aware of is that Romulus and Remus were Undead, having both drowned in the River Tiber before rising again.

Before the founding of Rome, knowledge of the existence of the Undead was not prevalent. Romulus and Remus gained followers by displaying their incredible abilities in large public gatherings. People were awed at their inhuman healing powers, their inability to be killed by normal means, and their advanced rhetoric and linguistic skills, and believed the children to be sent from the gods to found their city.

However, they quarrelled over who would be king. Romulus slew Remus by burying him alive. As the first king of Rome, Romulus instituted Latin as the primary language, teaching it not only to children, but to adults of the upper class who were involved in governmental matters.

Eventually the clergy adopted Latin. Since Latin came so naturally to the Undead, they believed it had to be a language sent from the gods. Meanwhile, Romulus was trying to find his lost soul, and worried that the other Undead in Rome would accidentally take it. He thus instituted burial rituals and funeral pyres to rid the city of the Undead.

With the spread of Protestantism and the reform of the Catholic Church, Latin slowly died out, replaced by the Romance languages. Many people forgot about the Undead and, consequently, the origins of Latin. Thus, it came as a surprise when an entire language ceased to exist. Of course, one realizes that a language can only become extinct when the people who speak it have been exterminated.

CHAPTER 1

THE LITTLE SISTER

A DIM LIGHT SHONE THROUGH the fog rising off the lake. Wading into the water, I swam towards it until a red rowing boat materialized from the mist. It creaked when a woman leaned out, squinting into the night. She was just close enough for me to see her hands tremble as she steadied herself. My limbs grew still. The ripples lapped against my lips as I sank lower in the water. Alert, the woman pushed the hood back from her face, letting her dull hair flutter about her cheeks.

"Who are you?" Annette LaBarge said, her voice carrying over the water. The beam of her flashlight passed in front of me, searching the surface.

I didn't dare move lest there was anyone watching us. No one could know I was here.

Her lips quivered. "Show yourself." Her eyes seemed to linger on me, though her gaze was out of focus.

I held my breath. A breeze skimmed the lake, making her boat drift. Switching off the light, she dipped her oars into the water and began to row away from me. The fog folded around her until there was nothing left but a wake, undulating behind her like two dark ribbons. Soundlessly, I followed it.

And then the water went still, and I was alone. I stopped, treading in place as I listened for the sound of her oars, but all was silent. Before I could look up, something swung down over my head. With a swift move of the arm, I grabbed the shovel from Miss LaBarge's hands and twisted it from her grasp, the water splashing around us as it slipped from my fingers and sank into the depths of the lake.

She stumbled back, bracing herself on the seat. Seizing the opportunity, I reached for the edge of her boat and curled my fingers over its wooden rim, raising myself out of the water. The boat tilted towards me.

"Stop!" she shouted, blinking into the darkness. "Don't come closer!"

Before I could speak, something in the distance

splashed. We both froze and turned to search the darkness. Whispers travelled over the wind. The water around us rippled with a nearby disturbance.

Miss LaBarge's eyes darted around the darkness, finally resting on me. "Who are you?" she asked. "Why have you followed me?"

Waves began to swell around us. "Be quiet," I said, my voice low as I watched the water slosh against the side of the boat. I had to take her now, before anyone could find us.

Through the fog came the sound of kicking, as if something were swimming towards us. Miss LaBarge turned, her scarf flapping against her face. "Who have you come with? What do you want?"

"Shut up," I said, grabbing the edge of her boat. The wood creaked beneath her as she backed away from me. "Stop moving!" I said, trying to control my voice.

Frantically, she fumbled with her flashlight as I tried to pull myself onto her boat; but the water was heavy on my clothes. Gasping, she kicked at my knuckles, peeling my fingers off the wood until I couldn't hang on any longer. Thrashing, I made one last attempt to thrust myself onto the boat, but it bobbed away from me, and I slipped back into the lake.

When I surfaced, Miss LaBarge shined her yellow beam into my eyes. I winced, my wet hair dangling at my shoulders.

"You?" she said, surprised. As she stared at my face, the moon reflected off her eyes, making them glow white. Before she could say anything more, something splashed in the distance; this time, closer. She glanced over her shoulder, her features contorting with fear.

I didn't have time to respond. Miss LaBarge dropped her flashlight into the basin of the boat and grabbed the oars. Rowing as quickly as she could, she disappeared once more into the mist.

I wiped my eyes and peered around the lake, trying to discern her position. Then came the sound of her breath, heavy and quick, in rhythm with her oars as they dipped in and out, in and out, in and out. I followed the sound, pushing through the swells until a small, rocky island appeared out of the fog.

The waves rolled off the lake and crashed onto the shore, carrying Miss LaBarge's tiny boat. I watched as she jumped into the water and trudged towards the beach, towing her boat behind her. When I picked up my pace, a dark figure rose out of the wave in front of me. Moments later, another emerged, followed by another – what seemed like dozens of dark, irregular shapes, small and slick. They crawled onto the beach, their movements abrupt and frenetic, and began to run over the rocks towards Miss LaBarge. I dived towards the shore, moving through the darkness until I saw her, swinging an oar wildly at the creatures as I approached. Above us, a shrill and deafening cry resonated through the night.

I awoke to the sound of the phone ringing. Sitting up in bed, I blinked. It was another wet August morning, so early the sun had barely risen behind the clouds. Relieved to find myself in my room, I slumped back into the pillows and listened to the rain tap against the windowpanes of my grandfather's house. I'd been having strange, dark dreams all summer, all the same in only one way: in each of them, I was desperately searching for someone.

On the pillow beside me sat one of my mother's old books on Monitoring history. My grandfather had given me a stack of them at the beginning of the summer, to educate me on what I was, what everyone in my family was: Monitors, people born with the innate talent to sense death, or more specifically, the Undead. Once trained, I'd be charged with the task of tracking the Undead and putting them to rest by burial, a task that had been haunting me ever since I'd found out about the undercover world of Monitors and the Undead.

I glanced at the book. Spread across the page I'd been reading last night was a passage on the Monitor migration to the Midwest, accompanied by a photograph of Lake Erie. When I'd seen it, a wave of panic had pushed against my chest, making my breath grow shallow. Suddenly, everything felt heavy, and I couldn't bear to look at the photograph any longer. That was the last thing I remembered before falling asleep.

The phone rang once more, then stopped. The clock on my nightstand read 5.42 a.m., which was early even for the mansion staff; the only people awake at this hour were the kitchen help. Outside, someone hurried down the hall towards my grandfather's bedroom. There were three loud raps on his door, fumbling, then voices.

Kicking off the sheets, I slid out of bed and peered down the hallway. My grandfather's door was cracked open, letting a thin line of light shine across the carpet.

I crept down the hall and waited by a linen closet.

"You found whom?" My grandfather's voice was sharp. "Where was she?"

Silence.

"Was she trailing one of them? Where was her partner?"

A shadow passed by the door, blocking the light. I strained to hear what was going on, but my grandfather's voice was muffled. He slammed the phone back into the cradle.

Without warning, the door flew open and my grandfather burst into the hall, pulling on his coat. Dustin, his estate manager, struggled behind him with my grandfather's briefcase and travelling bag. Ducking inside the linen closet, I crouched next to a hamper of dirty laundry and waited. When I was sure both men were downstairs, I slipped back into my room and went to the window.

A damp breeze blew in through the screen. From where I stood, I could see Dustin juggling the two bags and holding an umbrella over my grandfather as he ran out the front door and into his Aston Martin. Dustin deposited the bags in the trunk, and I watched as the car lurched down the driveway, turned, and sped out of sight.

I tried to go back to sleep but ended up drifting in and out of my dream, haunted by the face of Miss LaBarge, my philosophy professor at Gottfried Academy. "You?" she'd said, as if she'd been frightened of me. What had she meant?

A knock on the door pulled me back into the day. Outside it was still drizzling, the sun a faint orb behind the clouds.

I pulled on a sweater and opened the door. "Yes?"

Dustin entered, bald and droopy as an earlobe, balancing an elaborate platter of eggs, pancakes, sausages, and fruit. His suit was tight around his paunch. When he saw me, he froze. "My," he said, his forehead wrinkling as he studied me. "You truly *do* look older. Remarkable."

A draught came in from the hall, and I wrapped my arms around myself. "What?"

"Oh, come now. Don't tell me you've forgotten what day it is. I saw your light on and took the chance that you were awake. Breakfast in bed? I've brought you exactly seventeen items to commemorate the occasion."

My birthday, of course. I leaned against my bedpost as Dustin arranged the platter on my nightstand. I hadn't forgotten it, exactly; I had just replaced it. Now it was the day my parents had died, exactly one year ago. The day Dante had died, seventeen years ago. "I told you, I don't want to celebrate."

"Oh, yes, yes. It's a sombre occasion, I know," Dustin said, folding a napkin. "But your parents would have wanted you to enjoy yourself. You're seventeen. Quite the adult."

"Thanks," I said, giving him a meagre smile, but all I could think of was Dante. He was Undead – a person who'd died before reaching twenty-one, the age of adulthood, without a burial or cremation, and had thus reanimated. Until last year, he had been doomed to wander the earth in search of the person his soul had been reincarnated into, and take it back through a kiss.

Me.

Against all odds, we'd stumbled across each other – the first known soulmates in history. The only problem was that we'd fallen in love. The Undead only have twenty-one years after their first death to roam the earth before their bodies decay, and today marked Dante's seventeenth year. Soon he'd be gone for good. Closing my eyes, I shook the thought out of my head and looked up at Dustin. "Who was on the phone?"

Dustin grew stiff. "Oh, the phone, yes." Avoiding my gaze, he busied himself with the silverware. "Don't worry yourself about that just yet. First, eat."

The food looked syrupy and hot, but I had no appetite. It had been like this all summer. "Will you join me?"

Surprised, Dustin blushed. "I'd be honoured. I'll set up two places in the dining room."

After he closed the door, I noticed an envelope lying on my night table where the breakfast tray had been. With the beginnings of a smile, I picked it up. The return address read:

Eleanor Bell
18, rue Châtel
55100 Verdun
France

Below it was a mailing code.

1-11-1-33-7-13-58-1-8-2

I emptied the contents onto my bed. The seal was already broken, but I was so used to my grandfather reading my mail that I didn't care. My best friend from Gottfried, Eleanor, had been travelling around Europe with her mother all summer, and had been sending me postcards sealed in envelopes for privacy, each from a different town: Ascona, Switzerland; Grasmere, England; Utrecht, the Netherlands; Immenstaad, Germany; Frosses, Ireland. Waxy landscapes decorated the mirror over my dresser, a pathetic but welcome stand-in for Eleanor. This one was a picture of a shimmering lake, its blue water speckled with green islands. I flipped it over.

Renée,

Bonjour from Verdun! As in Verdun, France, which is where I am for the next few days. My mother has been dragging me to all of these remote lakes that are apparently famous in Monitoring history. She's also been really paranoid, like we're not safe. She's worried about pickpockets and thieves, but the places we've visited are practically off the map and pretty much empty, so I don't see who could steal our things. It's weird how obsessed she is. To be honest, I think she's actually worried about me. She still refuses to acknowledge what I am. It's like she thinks that by taking me to all of these Monitoring places she can somehow reverse what

happened. Anyway, it's hardly fun without you here.
Hope you have an amazing birthday.
Love,
Eleanor D. Bell

I read the last lines again, knowing exactly how she felt. Eleanor had been a Monitor, like me, until last year, when she was drowned and reanimated into an Undead. Now her Monitor parents could put her to rest at will. I knew that fear because I'd seen it in Dante's eyes, a momentary lapse of trust when he realized that I was a Monitor, and that somewhere within me I had a primal urge to bury him.

Placing the envelope next to the postcard, I picked up a pencil, and, following the mailing code, I began counting. I wrote down the first word of Eleanor's note, then the eleventh word after that, then the first word after that, then the thirty-third, and so on, until I was left with the following message:

Renée,
I am safe but empty without you.
Love,
D

I lingered on the letter *D*, feeling an aching hollowness within me. *Dante.* As I said his name out loud, my insides

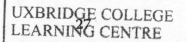

stirred, as if something inside had just come alive. I hadn't seen him since he'd kissed me in the field behind the chapel last spring and literally given me back my soul.

I shuddered, remembering that night. Dante and I had been brought to Calysta Von Laark's office. She was the headmistress at Gottfried Academy, our exclusive school where the Undead and Monitors were educated together. It was then she told me what Dante had known all along; that I was his soulmate, and were I to kiss him, I would save his life, restoring his soul to him, but transforming myself into an Undead. As she spoke, I realized how afraid I was of life without Dante; how tired I was from the constant pain I felt since my parents' death; how, after all I'd been through, I was not afraid of dying.

It was then that Gideon DuPont, an Undead student, entered the headmistress's office. It was Gideon who had stolen Eleanor's soul, transforming her into an Undead, in a cruel act of vengeance. I confronted him immediately, and Headmistress Von Laark attempted to apprehend him. But before Dante or I could stop him, Gideon had taken the headmistress's soul, her legs quivering before they finally went still.

Dante pursued Gideon outside, pulling him underground in a forced burial, which should have killed them both. I remember sitting there beside him, watching him die. And I knew what I had to do.

I kissed him. I gave Dante my soul to save his life. I died for him, and then ten days later, he gave my soul back to me.

I should have been alive after that. I should have gone back to the Renée I had been before the kiss, and Dante should have gone back to being Undead. But something wasn't right. I could barely even recall what happened that day in the field; I must have left him there like he'd asked me to, because the next thing I knew, I was surrounded by professors, who carried me to the nurses' wing. That was the last time I could remember the smell of flowers or the feel of the sun on my neck. Without Dante, everything was dull and colourless, a world made of cardboard. What did it feel like to drink a glass of cold water on a hot day? To taste the tartness of a summer peach? These days, I could hardly remember what it felt like to enjoy even simple pleasures like that.

My only comfort was the memory of Dante, and the hope that once I saw him, I would be able to understand what had happened to me, and what had happened to him. Was he alive? Was he Undead? Or somewhere in between, like me? He had been sending me messages through Eleanor all summer, each brief and devoid of any information other than that he was safe. I knew he didn't have a choice. He was in hiding; he had to be concise. But where did that leave me? Dante couldn't return to

Gottfried; the professors suspected him of killing the headmistress last spring, and even though he didn't, he could never tell them the truth – that he took my soul and gave it back – because they would still view it as murder. If he went back to Gottfried the Monitors would sense him, find him, and bury him. So how would I see him? And what if I never heard from him again?

I read his message one last time, touching the *D* with the tip of my finger as I imagined his voice seeping in through the window with the rain. Placing the postcard next to the others on my bureau, I went to the bathroom and turned on the shower, a little less upset that it was my birthday. While the water was warming up, I glanced in the mirror, my reflection catching me off guard. Dustin was wrong; I didn't just look older; I looked different, surreal – my eyes darker and deeper, my lips brilliant, my face angular and expressive and somehow sad. Had it happened overnight, or had I just not noticed until now? Steam wafted out of the shower, fogging the glass. *Dante*, I wrote on the mirror with one finger. I watched as the fog on the surface slowly thickened, until all I could see of my face was his name.

The mansion was unusually quiet as I made my way downstairs for breakfast. The rain pattered against the side of the house. "Hello?" I said, skimming my hands along the banister; but when I reached the dining room, it was empty. The chandelier was lit, but the table was bare. Water trickled down the windows. "Dustin?" I called out. I was wandering into the hall when I heard a muffled noise coming from the kitchen.

I pushed through the doors. From the corner of the room came the scratchy voice of an announcer. "The news of this chilling tragedy has left many of us in shock."

Huddled by the pantry were the entire kitchen and maintenance staff, as well as Dustin, who had a particularly sombre look on his face. In front of them sat a tiny television, set up on a stool. On the screen, a reporter dressed in a windbreaker spoke into the camera.

"This morning, a fisherman found the body of a woman washed up on a small island in Lake Erie. The woman has been identified as Annette LaBarge, a native of Vermont, and a philosophy teacher at Gottfried Academy, a private high school located in Maine. According to a close friend, Annette LaBarge had been missing for over a week."

I raised a hand to my mouth, accidentally knocking some pots and pans on the wall. The entire staff turned around at the clamour.

Stunned, I looked to Dustin, who was standing by the sink, too appalled to move.

"The victim was discovered on the beach, her mouth

stuffed with some sort of white cloth, which authorities believe to be gauze. Although the cause of death is still unclear, initial police reports indicate that her body was severely bruised and scratched, possibly by fingernails. These reports have aroused strong suspicions of foul play."

I stared at the screen, unable to believe what I was seeing. Behind the reporter was a familiar scene. A rocky beach, the coastguard, a thicket of trees in the background. A red rowing boat was tipped on its side near an area blocked off with caution tape.

"It can't be," I murmured, but no one in the kitchen seemed to hear me.

"The boat left on the island had been rented from a company just a few kilometres away. The man who was working there attested that Annette LaBarge was alone when she rented it late last Friday. Authorities still do not know why the woman rowed to the island on her own. No suspects have been identified yet."

Gauze in her mouth. My parents had died like that, too, their souls sucked out by the Undead they had been tracking. That was the danger with the Undead – some of them took souls at random to get a momentary burst of life. Miss LaBarge was a Monitor, just like my parents. Could she have died in a Monitoring accident? Is that what I had seen in my dream?

"The island, known locally as Little Sister Island, is a small and deserted outcrop in Lake Erie, where there have recently been a startling number of reported sightings of unidentified objects floating in the water. Are they sea creatures? Mythical beasts? Or something far more sinister than just the monsters of the tabloids?"

The camera panned away to a bumpy shot of the shoreline, where two uniformed men were carrying a heavy stretcher onto a patrol boat. "It can't be her," I whispered, my eyes darting across the screen, trying to wrap my mind around what I was seeing. How could I reconcile the body on the stretcher with Miss LaBarge, the woman who loved English Breakfast tea and Nietzsche; who was the only voice of reason when nothing else made sense, and the only professor at Gottfried whom I considered a friend?

"There must have been a mistake," I said, turning to Dustin. "I mean, are they even sure it's her?" He didn't answer, so I pressed. "Maybe they identified the wrong person. It doesn't sound like her. Monitors always work in pairs. Miss LaBarge would never have gone out alone."

"It's possible," he offered, but didn't look me in the eye.

The camera swept back to the scene on the beach. I shuddered as it lingered for the briefest moment on the zigzag of footprints scrawled in the rocky sand like a message.

We stayed glued to the television, waiting for some kind of explanation, but it repeated the same story before moving on to a commercial break and the daily programmes, which were almost offensive in their normality. Had what I dreamed actually happened? Had I somehow foreseen Miss LaBarge's last moments?

"Turn it off," I said, but my voice was so small that no one heard me. "Turn it off," I repeated. "Please."

When no one moved, I lunged forward and hit the power button. Stunned, the staff stared at me. Dustin reached for my arm, but I pulled away.

I can only remember snippets of what happened after that. Dustin rattling the knob on the library door after I locked myself inside; the feeling of dust on my palms as I pulled out all the philosophy books on dreams and death from my grandfather's collection and piled them around me; the roughness of the rug as I collapsed on the floor among them, too exhausted to do anything but feel them surrounding me like the scraps of people I had once known.

I stayed there until the hallway went quiet. All I could think about was my dream: the look on my teacher's face as she turned to me with her flashlight and said, "You," the water lapping against my face as I swam after her boat, the slick creatures that climbed onto the beach in front of me. If I hadn't woken up, what would I have done? What would I have seen? "Nothing," I said out loud. I was a Monitor; I could sense death, but I couldn't predict it. No one could. "It was just a bad dream." But still, I wasn't sure I believed it.

Dustin, apparently still hovering outside the library, responded through the door. "Renée? Are you all right? Will you let me in?"

I didn't answer.

"Everything is going to be all right, Renée," Dustin said, his voice gentle. "It was an accident. A Monitoring accident. She was probably killed by the Undead she was hunting. These things happen sometimes."

I stared at the light peeking in beneath the door, but didn't move.

Dustin sighed. "Well, I'm here."

I was still here too, I thought, but last night I had drifted somewhere else. Was it an accident? In my dream, it didn't seem like she was hunting anyone. It seemed like I was hunting her.

I didn't open the door. Instead, I sat against the wall beneath the window, listening to the rain trickle down the side of the house until I fell asleep.

When I woke up, the rain had stopped and the house was quiet. I rubbed my eyes and stood up, unlocking the door and nearly tripping over Dustin, who was sitting on the floor outside, dozing off next to a tray with a teapot, two cups, and a plate of butter cookies.

"Renée," he said, shaking himself awake. Hoisting himself up, he reached for the tray. "I thought you might need something to warm you up," he said, and carried it into the library.

He folded his legs into the small space beside me and sat down between the piles of books. There he adjusted his jacket and gave me a sad smile. "This is a cosy spot you've made. A nice reading selection," he said, gesturing to a pile of books by Aristotle. He used them as a table while he poured me a cup of tea, which was now cold. "You know, Annette LaBarge came to the house with your mother every summer when they were at Gottfried together," he said, gazing out the window at the wet, green lawn. "She was a lovely girl."

"It feels like everyone around me is dying," I murmured.

"That's what happens when you get older."

"But I'm not old."

"You're a Monitor. I used to be one too, you know, and look at me." Wincing, he adjusted his knees. "Time passes differently with us. Life, death – sometimes it all seems like a dream."

His words made me shudder. "A dream?"

Dustin nodded.

I wanted to tell him what I had seen in my sleep, and to ask him what it meant. I wanted him to tell me that it wasn't my fault, that it was a coincidence. But I couldn't. What if he told my grandfather? That would only add to my problems.

I studied his fleshy hands, the skin covered with age spots. "You were a Monitor?"

"I was." He leaned over and took two cookies from the plate, offering me one. "Go on."

I turned away, unable to look at it. "What if I don't know how to?"

Dustin furrowed his brow. "Don't know how to what?"

"Just go on."

"It will happen whether you know how to or not," he said. "After all, what else can we do?"

CHAPTER 2

THE COTTAGE

I WOKE UP IN THE library, my face planted in the middle of Nietzsche's *Beyond Good and Evil*, to the sound of a horn honking. After my conversation with Dustin, time had seemed stretched out, as though the forty-eight hours had been one unbearably long moment. I had wandered in and out of the library in a daze, hoping the news of Miss LaBarge's death had been a nightmare, but it wasn't. The seventeen-item breakfast that Dustin had prepared for me had sat on the kitchen counter until one of the cooks scraped it into the garbage. Even though the staff were going about their normal work, knowing that Miss

LaBarge was dead made the mansion feel draughty and deserted, as if everyone else had died along with her.

Miss LaBarge had an accident while hunting an Undead. That's what Dustin kept telling me. But the more I thought about it, the less sense it made. Why had she been there alone, when I knew that Monitors always worked in pairs? Or, more importantly, why had she been hunting at all? The little I'd gleaned from my mother's Monitoring books had taught me that all Monitors eventually specialized – burying, researching, judging, teaching, coffin building... There was an order to tracking and hunting the Undead; we didn't just go out and bury them. Especially not professors, like Miss LaBarge, who had dedicated their lives to teaching the Undead and Monitors how to coexist at Gottfried Academy. So why would she have travelled across several states to hunt one?

"Why?" I'd begged Dustin, when he couldn't give me an explanation. As if finding out the answer would somehow erase her mistakes.

Leaning over, I pushed the curtains aside and peered out the window. It was a crisp, blue day, so bright it made me wince. My grandfather's car was parked at the end of the crescent driveway, the doors open as Dustin struggled to carry in two stacks of papers, a briefcase, and a travelling bag.

I went into the hall just as my grandfather thrust

himself into the foyer, his coat-tails swooping in behind him. His wrinkled face was tanned, like his old leather briefcase.

"Did you hear that Miss LaBarge—" I started to say, but my grandfather waved his hand to quiet me.

"I'm aware of what happened." He took off his coat and draped it over the pile of things Dustin was balancing in his arms.

"Do they know who—"

"I don't know, Renée," he said, his face softening while he studied me. "I'm sorry." He took off his hat and dropped it on top of his coat. Dustin gave him a perfunctory nod before whisking everything away.

"Where were you?" I persisted, walking behind him.

"I'll explain later," he said, without turning around. "There are things I need to attend to now."

I stood in the doorway of his study while he sifted through the papers on his desk until he found the one he was looking for. Ignoring me, he picked up the phone and dialled a number written on the page.

"Yes, hello. Is this the LaBarge residence?" With one hand he loosened his tie.

"Who is that?" I mouthed.

"Yes, thank you," my grandfather continued, and, leaning over the desk, he shooed me out into the hall. As his office door closed, I could hear him say, "Jeffrey, hello.

This is Brownell Winters speaking. I'm so sorry for your loss..."

With nothing else to do, I slid to the floor and waited. I tried to listen in, but all I could hear were occasional phrases. "I see." "How odd." "Yes, I would very much like to see it, if it's not too much of an imposition."

His muffled voice faded in and out until the door opened.

"Oh, Renée," my grandfather said, bumping into me. "You're still here."

"Of course I'm still here. What was that about?"

Instead of answering my question, he rolled down his shirtsleeves and fastened them at the wrists with cufflinks. "Get dressed," he said. "We're going on a trip."

Vermont was green and rolling. I spent half the drive dozing in and out of sleep, my dreams permeated by dairy farms and grain silos, garage sales and lawn ornaments. The car sagged in the back with my grandfather's shovels and Monitoring supplies, which made a loud thumping sound every time we drove over a bump. He had brought them along just in case we encountered any Undead; though it seemed pretty unlikely that the Undead who killed Miss LaBarge would come to her childhood home. I had been trying not to think about where we were going, but everything around us reminded me of Miss LaBarge: the yarn stores and bakeries, where I could almost see her in a window, wearing an oversized sweater as she nibbled on a scone.

Her house was off a pastoral road riddled with potholes. It was a weathered wood cottage burrowed into a hillside, the roof almost completely overgrown with grass. There was one car in the driveway; otherwise, it looked deserted. Two of the front windows were broken.

We pulled up next to the house, in front of a small vegetable garden. "After we give our condolences to her family, I'll have to spend a few minutes examining her house to search for any information on the Undead she was hunting, per Monitor protocol," my grandfather said as we made our way up the stone path to the front door. "I'd like for you to join me."

"Monitor protocol?" I asked. "You do this for every Monitor that's killed?"

"I don't, but someone from the High Monitor Court does. I used to be a member, and now that I'm retired I only take cases that are especially close to me. Annette LaBarge was one of your mother's best friends. It's the least I can do to honour her memory."

Climbing roses curled their tendrils around the railing as if trying to pull the house into the ground. Swallowing, I gave my grandfather a brief nod and smoothed out my skirt, feeling unsure about what I was supposed to say or do once we went inside. "Just be yourself," my grandfather said, as though reading my mind.

Just before he swung the knocker, the door opened, and a stout man wearing a baggy sweater greeted us. "You must be Brownell," he said with a smile. He had the smooth face of a baby, but had to be at least forty years old.

My grandfather took off his sunglasses.

"I'm Jeffrey," the man said, holding out his hand first to my grandfather, then to me. "Annette's mother's nurse. She was too ill to make the journey, so I'm here in her stead. Please, come in," he said, and showed us into the front of the cottage. In the living room, a couch was positioned oddly next to a few overturned stools; a bland print of a landscape leaned on the floor in the hallway, as if it had been knocked off the wall; and a pile of broken dishes had been swept into the corner of the kitchen.

"The front of the house was ravaged when the police got here," Jeffrey said. "The windows were broken, the furniture was all over the place... They think it happened after her death; someone trying to steal her things. Thankfully there wasn't much here, and whoever it was didn't touch the back rooms."

"Where is everyone?" I asked, realizing we were the only ones there. "Her family? Friends?"

Jeffrey clasped his hands behind his back. "Annette

wasn't close with her family. I don't think any of them have been in touch for years. This cottage, which belongs to her mother, is really their only connection. Annette spent summers here, when she was away from Gottfried."

By my grandfather's foot was a shard of pottery. He picked it up and tossed it into a nearby dustpan, which contained the remains of a broken vase. "Remind me, what was her mother's name?"

"Henriette LaBarge. She's been living in a nursing home for twelve years." Jeffrey reached for a tin kettle steaming on the stove. It was dented and missing its lid. "Can I offer you tea?"

We nodded, and he took out two chipped mugs from the cabinet and dropped teabags inside. When he opened the refrigerator for milk, he winced at the smell.

This didn't seem like Miss LaBarge at all. Where were her books? Her photographs and tapestries and figurines? Her teacups?

"Twelve years?" my grandfather said. "That's quite a bit of time. I hope you won't take offence, but I was surprised to receive your message, especially since I've never heard about you before."

Jeffrey smiled. "With Annette gone, there's no one left to take care of the house, which is why I came. I contacted you first because Annette had your number listed as her emergency contact, though under the name of Lydia Winters."

I nearly dropped my mug at the mention of my mother's name. My grandfather frowned. "I see."

"I only arrived this morning, and barely had time to make the front rooms presentable again. The police have come and gone, so feel free to touch what you wish."

"I appreciate that. We'll be out of your way soon."

I followed my grandfather down the hallway. He opened doors here and there. A dining room. A bathroom. A coat closet. The ceilings were low and the rooms were small and dark. Still, this part of the house seemed far more welcoming than the front. There were pictures on the walls: watercolours, needlepoint, and photographs of Miss LaBarge as a child, jumping through a sprinkler and sitting in the garden playing with a shovel. I wasn't sure if I wanted to smile or cry.

"Pay attention, Renée," my grandfather said over his shoulder.

I frowned. "I am paying attention."

"Do you notice anything?" he said, his voice low.

"Not really," I murmured, shoving my hands into my pockets.

He turned around. "You're not even trying."

I let my arms drop to my sides in frustration. "Trying to do what?" I asked. I was trying as hard as I could to keep myself together, to appear normal.

"Don't you want to learn from her death?"

"Why does everything have to be a learning experience? Why does everything have to lead to something else? Why can't I just be?" I knew I sounded childish, but I couldn't help it.

Glancing down the hall, my grandfather took me by the arm and pulled me aside. Lowering his voice, he growled, "Who do you think broke into this cottage? Who do you think rooted through all of Annette's things?" His jowls shook. When I didn't respond, he answered his own question. "The Undead. Don't you want to find the Undead who killed a Monitor and then invaded her home? Don't you want to bury the Undead who would do a thing like that? If we don't, any of us could be next. *You* could be next."

I rolled my eyes. "Why would I be next—"

My grandfather cut me off. "Renée, you can keep fooling yourself into thinking you're a normal teenager. The truth is, you're not. You're a Monitor now. Start thinking like one."

I wriggled out of his grip.

"Now, what do you see?" he asked.

I crossed my arms and glanced at the decorations. It almost felt like I was in the creaky corridor in Horace Hall that led to Miss LaBarge's office. "There are more of her things here. It feels more like her."

My grandfather nodded and began walking. "Why do you think that is?"

I followed him until we reached the end of the hallway, where there stood a single door. On the floor was a mat identical to the one in Miss LaBarge's office at Gottfried. It said: WELCOME FRIENDS. I stepped before it, wishing that she would open the door, a plate of cookies in one hand, a book in the other. Only Miss LaBarge would have a welcome mat in the middle of her house. My grandfather stepped across it and opened the door. The room beyond was pitch black.

FRIENDS. I touched the word with my foot and then gazed at the walls. It was dark in this part of the house because there were no windows, and there were no windows because the back half of the cottage was nestled into the hillside.

"Because we're underground," I said with wonder, realizing that some people couldn't enter this part of the house. The Undead. "She was protecting her things. Or herself."

"My thoughts exactly," my grandfather said from within the room, and turned on the lights. "Oh, my."

He was standing in an office cluttered with books and papers. In the corner of the room was a desk, and above it was a map of the world, marked up with scribbles and circles. Tacked up next to the map was an assortment of newspaper clippings. Almost immediately, my grandfather and I were there, pushing aside the desk lamp and stacks of files to get a better look.

I felt my pulse flutter. On the map, Lake Erie, along with several other lakes, had been circled. I scanned the clippings. All of the articles had been published within the last year, but the stories varied. Some of them were about deaths, others about disappearances, and still others about strange sightings. The Loch Ness Monster. Bodies floating in the water. Two women mysteriously murdered in Utah. A woman vanishing from a bridge in Amsterdam. Judging from the way the papers were torn, it looked like some of the clippings had been taped and then moved around and re-taped to new locations on the wall.

My grandfather was leaning so close to the wall that his nose almost touched it, but he seemed just as baffled as I felt. "What were you up to, Annette?" he murmured.

I wondered the same thing.

On the far side of the room was a set of French doors that led to a bedroom. While my grandfather tried to piece together the wall of clippings, I slipped inside.

It was a cosy room, with tiny white lights strung around the ceiling, a heavy quilt on the bed, and a collection of Russian nesting dolls on the dresser. I went to pick one up, when I noticed a photograph leaning on the wall behind them. It was of a teenage Annette, sitting on a braided rug, hugging her knees beside two other girls. One was a slender blonde; the other a defiant-looking girl with a face just like mine. My mother. The girls stared into the camera, their eyes wide like deer, as if the photographer had caught them doing something in secret.

My mother's expression haunted me as I touched the edge of her lips, which were pursed in an O. The blonde beside her looked tall, like a ballerina, and familiar, incredibly familiar. Where had I seen her before? I reached for the frame to get a better look, but when I lifted it, something slid out the back onto the floor. It was a letter.

August 1, 2009

My Annette,

It was so comforting to hear news from Gottfried. It feels like ages since I've been back there, so long that I can't believe the world you described was once my life. I've been spending almost all of my time travelling in France, searching for the lost girl.

Half of the places I've been to were dead ends, but I think I've finally found something that might put us in the right direction. I found it on my last trip to Europe, though I was certain someone was following me. Robert thinks I'm insane from jet lag. He can't imagine how we're on anyone's radar, and I suppose he's right. We've been living out west for so long that even the idea of other Monitors has become a part of our distant past... Regardless, it serves as a reminder that we have to be careful. Anyway, I probably shouldn't write any more here. You understand.

It's been difficult having to keep it from Renée; I hate lying to her... I don't think she suspects anything yet, though every time I look at her, I have to suppress the urge to tell her everything about who she is and what we're doing. Once it's safe, I'll tell her everything.

Are you still planning to visit us later this month? The day you said you'd arrive is Renée's sixteenth birthday, and although I can't promise she'll remember you from the last time you visited, I'm sure you'd be a welcome surprise. We were thinking we could pick you up and go to that quaint coffee shop we went to the last time you were here. The sandwiches are the best in Northern California, and it's very private. It's also just outside the redwood forest, which is beautiful this time of year.

Until then,

Lydia

Lydia. The name dripped down the page in a long watery streak, and I realized I was crying.

Sitting down on the edge of Miss LaBarge's bed, I tried

50

to read the letter again, but couldn't, knowing that I was looking at my mother's handwriting. She had written these words. I could see the smudges in the margins from her palm. It was almost like she was still alive, speaking to me, except that the same phrases kept standing out. Travelling. Searching for the lost girl. California. My birthday. The redwood forest. This letter was probably the last one my mother sent before she was killed.

How come I hadn't even realized what was going on? We lived in the same house for sixteen years. We ate all of our meals together, we used the same computer, the same telephone. How could I not have even noticed that my mom had been travelling all over the world, looking for something? How could I not have known?

"Renée?" my grandfather called out.

"I – I found something."

Bounding in from the other room, my grandfather took the letter from me, muttering to himself as he read.

"What is it?" I asked, staring at the letter as if it were a strange relic.

The creases on my grandfather's face tightened. "I don't know yet."

I began pacing. I thought my parents had been killed by an Undead they were hunting; that they'd died in the line of duty. But was it true? It seemed like a strange coincidence that my parents had been killed by an Undead right after my mother sent this letter. Right after they had discovered something seemingly important. "Their deaths weren't just Monitor casualties, were they?" I said, the words coming out wobbly. "My mom was looking for a lost girl. She thought someone had been following her."

My grandfather held up a hand to silence me while he thought. Sticking out from beneath Miss LaBarge's bed was a rusty handle. I pushed it out with my foot, only to discover that it was the handle of a shovel.

"I wouldn't read too much into this, Renée," my grandfather said. "Your parents were travelling a lot for Monitor-related activities. Seeking out the Undead, Monitoring them. This is most likely referring to a similar episode that they were consulting with Annette LaBarge about."

"But she said she was looking for a *lost* girl, not an Undead girl—"

My grandfather cut me off. "Monitors often use vague words to communicate to each other, in case their correspondence is intercepted. Just like Annette protected her belongings underground. It's a precaution."

"But they were killed immediately after. And now Miss LaBarge is dead. What if she was out at Lake Erie looking for the same thing—"

"That your mother was searching for? No." He shook his head. "Lydia was killed by an Undead while performing her duty. She died honourably."

"I didn't mean that—"

"My daughter wasn't murdered," he said, as if it were painful to even say the word *daughter*.

"But Miss LaBarge hid the letter behind a photograph—"

My grandfather spoke over me. "Your parents were Monitors. Everything about their job was a secret, so it doesn't strike me as strange for your mother to have written a secretive letter."

He must have seen me shrink away from him, because he immediately composed himself. "I'm sorry," he said.

"Can I keep it?" I asked. "The letter. I just want to have something she wrote."

My grandfather hesitated, and then folded the note. "Of course."

"Thanks," I said softly. As I watched my grandfather collect the clippings from Miss LaBarge's office, I wondered if my parents had ever gotten the chance to tell her what they had discovered, and if so, what it was. But even if they had managed to talk, I feared that the secret of my parents' discovery had died along with my favourite teacher.

We arrived at the mansion late that evening after a long, silent car ride, and went straight from the car to the end of the dining room table, where the cooks had already laid out an arrangement of sausages, butter rolls, and vegetable pie. I used to love this meal, but today it looked like it was made of plastic.

My grandfather sighed as he stuffed a napkin into the collar of his shirt. He was still thinking about my mother and Miss LaBarge, I could tell. For a moment he looked like nothing more than an old man – sad, exhausted, and brittle. Seeing him like that, I realized that I had to tell him what I knew.

"I had a dream," I said as I picked at a bit of dry bread.

"A dream?"

"That I was chasing Miss LaBarge as she rowed a boat across a lake."

My grandfather stopped chewing. "I beg your pardon?"

"I dreamed it the night before my birthday. The night she was killed."

He put down his knife and fork. "You're telling me that you dreamed Annette LaBarge's death?"

I pushed my hair behind my ear. "Well, not exactly. Just the moments before. But I was chasing her, as if I wanted to kill her." I didn't even realize what I was saying, but once the words left my mouth, I knew they were true. Why else would I have been chasing Miss LaBarge like that?

Pushing his plate aside, he leaned on the table. "What aren't you telling me?"

"What do you mean?" I asked. "I just told you about my dream—"

"But nothing else!" he said. "I spoke with your psychiatrist, Dr. Porter. He told me you weren't very helpful when he met with you."

I pushed the vegetables around on my plate, suddenly defensive. "I don't know what you're talking about."

"The doctor said that you wouldn't even answer his questions."

"That's because he kept asking about my parents and my friends; about what we talk about on the phone. He even asked about my romantic life," I said, trying to control my voice as I stabbed a sausage. "He's a doctor. I don't see how that's any of his business." After chewing, I put my fork down. "Can you pass the salt?"

When my grandfather didn't move, Dustin came from the corner of the room and handed me the shaker. My grandfather eyed me as I sprinkled salt on my vegetable pie and took a bite. Still bland. I reached for the salt again, when my grandfather intercepted me.

"That is quite enough," he said, taking the shaker from me. "The food is already well seasoned. And you will answer all of the questions the doctors ask you. I hired them for a reason."

I stared down at my plate.

"It doesn't make sense," my grandfather said, wiping his

lips with his napkin. "You were dead," he said. "For nine days, you were dead. They found you on the green and took you to the nurses' wing, under my request, to wait for you to reanimate. I saw you with my own eyes." He paused to take a sip of water. "But on the day that you were supposed to reanimate, you disappeared. And when we found you, you were on the green again, not Undead, but alive. Completely alive." He studied me. "How did you survive?"

Outside, a maintenance worker was polishing the windows, the evening light blinking behind the motion of his rag. I could have filled in the gaps to my grandfather's story. I could have told him that Dante and I had the same soul. That I gave Dante my life that night, and ten days later he gave it back to me in a field of flowers. But then what? My grandfather would never understand. "I've told you everything I can already. I don't understand it any better than you do. What else do you want me to say?"

My grandfather shook his head. "There's speculation among the professors that you have some sort of immunity to the Undead. That you're a new kind of Monitor."

"What do you mean?" I said, swallowing.

"They think you're immortal." He paused. "But it doesn't make sense. No one cheats death like that."

Breaking his gaze, I picked at the food on my plate. "Well, I'm alive now. Can't we all just forget about it?"

"Forget about it?" he said, almost offended. "You're curious about Annette LaBarge's death, about your parents' deaths, but not about your own? This is your *life*, Renée. Don't you want to know how you survived?"

"Of course I do," I muttered.

"You're not yourself. You don't even look like yourself. And you're keeping something from me."

I glanced down the hall to where I could see the cooks shuffling in and out of the kitchen, pots clanking as someone did the dishes. Although I could remember the way the halls of the mansion used to fill up with the smell of simmering food around mealtimes, now I could barely smell it unless I lowered my face to my dish. "I don't know what you're talking about," I said. "Everything is fine." But the words fell flat.

I was definitely alive, not Undead, at least according to the doctors. Their tests had returned normal results: the glare of a flashlight shining into my eyes, my ears. A wooden stick pressed against my tongue. The cold shock of a stethoscope as it touched my back. What the doctors couldn't seem to measure or explain was how I woke up most mornings: groggy, disoriented, my eyes dry and heavy with sleep, as if I had just come out of a long afternoon nap and didn't know how much time had passed while I was sleeping. To be honest, since last spring, I wasn't sure that I had ever completely awoken.

"You haven't been seeing that boy, have you?"

I choked on my water. "What boy?"

"You know which boy I'm referring to."

"No, I don't."

"Dante Berlin," my grandfather said with force. "Have you or have you not been seeing him?"

My throat tightened at Dante's name. It had been so long since I'd heard anyone other than myself say those words; it almost felt as though Dante had become a figment of my imagination. "No," I said, wishing I was lying. "I haven't."

My grandfather's face hardened. "Good. If he comes near you, I'll bury him."

I shrank back in my seat. *No!* I wanted to scream, but I knew that I couldn't. I couldn't do anything at all.

My grandfather motioned to Dustin to take his plate away, and pushed out his chair. Just before he left the room, he stopped. "We're giving Annette a Monitor's funeral on Friday. I expect you to come. Death is your profession now. It's time you accepted that."

Every day was windy on the coast of Maine. I could tell by the craggy cliffs and small knotted trees that were swirled and twisted out of shape. When we arrived at Friendship Harbour on Friday, after a five-hour drive, a crowd of people was already gathered by the shore. They all wore black. Docked behind them was a large wooden boat painted with the name *Le Prochain Voyage*.

Brandon Bell, Eleanor's older brother, was standing by the side of the boat, handing out garden trowels to the guests as he directed them on board. Beside him was his mother, an elegant blonde. I recognized her immediately, not only because I had met her at Gottfried last winter, when Eleanor had disappeared, but because I had just seen her. She was an older replica of the third girl in the photograph in Miss LaBarge's cottage. Cindy Bell. Seeing her now – her sleek black suit and impeccable make-up – I could barely imagine the two women being friends. But if Cindy was here, it meant Eleanor had to be back from Europe.

Brandon's eyes lingered on me for a moment before he bent down to pick up a trowel.

"Thank you for coming," he said, handing it to me and averting his eyes. "The ceremony will take place just outside Wreck Island."

I had expected a warmer welcome, considering I was one of his sister's best friends.

"Where's Eleanor?" I asked, looking over his shoulder to see if I could spot her blonde ringlets. I wanted to tell her about my dream, Miss LaBarge's cottage, and the letter my mom had written to her.

Brandon looked puzzled. "She's not here," he said, as if it were obvious.

"What? Why?"

"Only Monitors can attend a Monitor burial."

"Oh. Right," I mumbled. Eleanor wasn't a Monitor any more; she was the enemy. "How is she—" I started to ask, but Brandon didn't let me finish.

"If you could move along, that would be helpful," he said, and handed the couple behind me two trowels.

"Yeah, okay," I said slowly, stung by how quickly he had brushed me off.

The deck was crowded with Gottfried professors and a handful of older people that I didn't recognize. Genevieve Tart and a few other girls from Gottfried were standing by the wine table in sleek dresses, chatting. When they saw me, they stopped and huddled together, whispering. Waiters dressed in black suits wove through the crowd carrying platters of hors d'oeuvres amid the low hum of talk. "*Monitoring without a partner.*" "*Careless mistakes.*" "*The Undead.*" "*She didn't even have a shovel on her.*"

No shovel? In my dream I had taken the shovel from her and dropped it into the lake. Could it have been real? I continued listening, but it was more of the same. It was odd hearing the word "Undead" spoken in public, but everyone here was a Monitor, so there wasn't any reason for secrecy. The only person not engrossed in conversation was Eleanor's mother, who was sitting alone by the mast, nursing a drink and looking out to the horizon. A waiter offered her a canapé, but she waved him away.

Beyond them, the waves crashed onto the rocky shore, where a woman was standing. She had plain brown hair and was wearing a dress that twisted around her in the wind like the trunks of the trees. Ducking beneath the lines that held the sails, I made for the side of the boat to get a better look, but people crowded past me, blocking my view. When I looked at the shore again, the woman was gone.

"Miss LaBarge?" I whispered, staring at the spot where I thought I had seen her. The salty air blew through my hair, and I blinked. It couldn't be, I thought, letting my eyes wander to the open casket on the other side of the boat. I was so disturbed by her death, and by the letter my mother had written to her, that I was seeing things.

"Renée," a boy said from behind me, and I turned. Brett Steyers, a friend from Gottfried and Eleanor's former boyfriend, stood there in a navy suit, his sandy hair blowing in the sea breeze. "Where have you been hiding all summer?"

I gathered my own hair as it tangled in the wind. "At my grandfather's," I said, forcing a smile.

"I bet," he said.

I furrowed my brow. "What's that supposed to mean?"

"Nothing," he said, tracing the lines in the wooden deck with his shoe. "So when did you find out about all of this?" His gaze drifted across the other Monitors, and I realized that he and I had never before spoken of the Undead.

"Last winter," I said softly. "You?"

"Last spring," he said.

"Are you still in touch with Eleanor?" I asked.

Brett shoved his hands into his pockets, shaking his head ever so slightly. "What about you and..." He let his voice trail off. Everyone knew that the Gottfried professors were searching for Dante.

Looking away, I watched a gull land on the deck and peck at a discarded hors d'oeuvre. "No," I said.

"People are saying he and his friend Gideon killed the headmistress last spring," Brett said.

I shuddered. He wasn't a murderer. I wanted to scream it into the wind until everyone knew the truth, until it sank into their bones. But how could I possibly explain everything, let alone prove that he wasn't dangerous?

"And they say that Dante's on the run. That he left for Canada." He searched my face for an answer.

"Dante would never kill anyone," I said defensively. "As for Canada, I wouldn't know."

A few paces behind him were April and Allison, the twins from my Horticulture class, along with a few other kids I recognized. I waved at them, but instead of returning the gesture, they turned away. I frowned.

Brett followed my gaze. "Don't worry about them," he said, and took a crab canapé from one of the waiters.

The boat slowed, and the captain lowered an anchor into the water. The chain unravelled for what seemed like minutes, until it finally grew taut. My grandfather's voice boomed from the back of the boat. "Would everyone please convene at the bow?" he said.

The crowd formed a tight circle around Miss LaBarge's casket. Brett and I stood near the back.

"So, is it true?" Brett asked, his voice low.

"Is what true?"

"You know."

I shook my head. "No, I don't."

Brett glanced around us. "That you're some kind of... immortal?" He said it in jest, as if he didn't believe it, but I knew his question was sincere.

My face grew hot. Now I understood why Brandon and the girls from Horticulture had acted so aloof. Is this what it would be like when I went back to school? "I – I don't know what you're talking about."

An old man in front of us turned around and scowled. Brett gave him a polite smile, and leaned over me. "All of the Monitors are saying that Gideon took your soul, and you died, but instead of reanimating as an Undead, you just woke up. Alive."

I bit my lip. I couldn't tell him the truth. I couldn't tell anyone the truth, or Dante would be buried and I would become a specimen.

Brett studied me with wonder. "It *is* true; I can tell."

Before I could come up with an appropriately vague response, my grandfather stepped into the centre of the circle and cleared his throat. The boat grew quiet.

"Monitors! Friends. Thank you for joining us on this cloudy occasion." His white hair waved in the wind. "Annette LaBarge was a mysterious woman. A solitary woman." He paused, letting his words hang in the air. "Some of us are here because we knew Annette the philosophy professor. Others, Annette the student, Monitor, and later, colleague. Still others, Annette the caretaker and friend."

The boat swayed. Two women in the front were weeping.

"As Annette would say, 'We cannot control the actions of others. All we have are our reactions.' So I implore you: let us learn from her death. Let us react. Let us find the Undead who killed her and put that creature to rest."

My grandfather took the pocket square from his jacket and wiped his temple before continuing with his eulogy. I gazed at the open casket, which was close enough for me to see the tip of Miss LaBarge's nose. Was death ever fair? If Miss LaBarge had died naturally, would that have been easier to bear? Or would it always feel as if life were being taken from us?

A gust of wind blew a stack of napkins into the water, speckling the surface with white squares. Above us, a flock of seagulls cawed.

My grandfather opened a prayer book and read a passage in French as I looked at the swells of water sloshing against the side of the boat, at the seagulls roosting on the mast, and at the sky, which seemed larger and more dramatic over the ocean. I thought about how all these details seemed that much more beautiful, knowing that Dante still existed, and that he loved me.

My grandfather closed the prayer book and motioned to two men, who hoisted a barrel of soil up from below the deck and set it beside the casket. My grandfather touched Miss LaBarge's forehead with his thumb, and then, grasping his trowel, he plunged it into the barrel of soil and sprinkled the dirt over her body.

A line formed along the side of the boat, and, one by one, everyone followed. Brett stood behind me, and we inched forward until it was my turn.

I hesitated before stepping up to the casket, where Miss LaBarge was resting with two coins over her eyes. They made her look expressionless and somehow inhuman. Soil and flower petals were sprinkled across her body.

"Go on," Brett said, giving me a little nudge.

Dipping my trowel into the barrel, I leaned over her, my hand quivering, and touched her forehead.

Surprised by how cold her skin was, I jolted, spilling the soil everywhere. Everyone looked in my direction, and I bent down, mortified, and tried to scoop the soil up from the deck.

"Just leave it, Renée," my grandfather said, pulling me up by the arm.

I walked to the edge of the boat, feeling lost. On the bench across from me sat Eleanor's mother, hugging her knees as her blonde hair blew around her face. Our eyes met for the briefest moment, before we both looked away. After my parents, after Dante, I still didn't know what to do when confronted with death. That's the thing nobody tells you. It never gets easier.

The captain opened a latch, pulling open a gate in the handrail at the edge of the deck. With some effort, my grandfather and three other men shifted the lid onto Miss LaBarge's casket, closed it firmly, then lifted the sealed box to the edge of the deck and slid it into the water. The splash was much smaller than I had expected, and I leaned over the railing and watched as the casket trembled on the surface for a moment before sinking into the sea, a tiny trail of bubbles rising behind the box as if Miss LaBarge had let out one last breath.

*   *   *

That night my grandfather and I returned to the mansion in silence. I tried to sleep but kept being shaken awake by the prickling presence of Dante, as if he were in the room with me, his cold breath tickling my lips. Kicking off the covers, I went to the window, my head throbbing with distorted images: the tip of Miss LaBarge's nose as she lay in the casket; Brett chewing a crab canapé, the crumbs clinging to his chin as he asked me about Dante.

I pressed my fingers against the pane of glass, now cool from the night air, and imagined I was touching Dante. Cracking open the window, I let the chilly air flutter against the top of my nightgown. Outside, the trees that lined the driveway flexed and bowed in the wind, their shadows shifting across the pavement. I watched them, waiting for Dante's face to emerge out of the darkness, until the sun rose over the horizon.

The mail arrived early. I jolted awake at the chimes of the doorbell, my neck stiff from falling asleep in an armchair. Through the window I could see a lanky mailman standing on the front stoop, adjusting the bag on his shoulder as he admired the façade of the mansion. Downstairs I could hear Dustin shuffle to the door and greet him.

After pulling on a cardigan, I ran downstairs. Dustin was standing in the foyer, signing something on a clipboard.

When he was finished, the mailman handed him a single letter.

"What is it?" I asked, watching Dustin turn it over before shutting the door.

He jumped. "Oh, Renée," he said, composing himself. "How convenient. It's for you."

Hoping it was from Eleanor, I took the letter from him and immediately knew it wasn't. The envelope was made of a heavy paper, the colour of bone. My name was inscribed in fine print. The return address read: *Gottfried Academy*. I tore the seal open.

Gottfried Students and Parents:

We are deeply saddened to report that the Gottfried community has lost another one of its members. Annette LaBarge, alumnus and celebrated philosophy professor, has passed away. She was a friend, colleague, and mentor to many of us at the Academy, and our hearts go out to her family and loved ones.

This tragedy has forced us to evaluate the larger picture of our recent history at Gottfried. After the unfortunate loss of a student, Gideon DuPont, and Headmistress Calysta Von Laark, in an accident last spring, along with the unsettling events of two years ago when we lost an esteemed member of our student body, Benjamin Gallow, we no longer believe that

Gottfried Academy can provide a safe and healthy learning environment for our students. After careful consideration, we have made the difficult decision to close Gottfried's doors. The Academy will only remain open to provide services to a small number of students with special needs.

Should you have any questions regarding matriculation at our sister school, Lycée St. Clément, or lingering thoughts about the recent losses to our family, I encourage you to contact me or any Gottfried staff member. Individually and as a community, we remain committed to the health and future success of all our students.

Sincerely yours,

Professor Edith Lumbar

I looked out the windows at the mail truck disappearing behind the trees. Somewhere inside me I had known that Gottfried would have to close. I just didn't think it actually would. But when I looked down, the letter was still there in my hand, and none of the words had changed.

Dustin glanced at me before picking up a tray with coffee and scones. "I'm so sorry, Renée."

"Did you know about this?"

Dustin's face dropped. "Oh, no. I – er – why don't you

talk to your grandfather?" he said, and hurried into the hallway, carrying the platter to my grandfather's study. I followed him.

Dustin knocked. "Come in," my grandfather said, taking off his reading glasses when he saw me.

"Is it true?" I demanded, handing him the letter.

He took it from me and skimmed it.

"Yes," he said. "And no."

I shook my head. "What?"

"You will not be returning to Gottfried," he said, tossing the letter aside. "But I will be."

I must have looked confused, because he continued. "I will be resuming my position as headmaster. Gottfried is going to be a disciplinary school for the Undead, where we can monitor them in privacy, and, as necessary, put them to rest without risk of exposure. The Academy is returning to its roots – the way it began, under Dr. Bertrand Gottfried and his nurses."

My chair creaked as I sat back. So that's what the letter meant by "special needs". But where would I go? Where would everyone go? I couldn't return to a normal school now. Not after everything I knew, after everything I had seen and done. I thought about Eleanor, about the Board of Monitors and the chimneys and Grub Day. They were the only things that had helped me rebuild my life after I'd lost my parents. They had *become* my life. How could

I move on from Gottfried now? I felt a stab of sadness. Gottfried was the only school where the Undead were educated alongside Monitors and Plebeians. If Gottfried couldn't succeed, what hope was there for me and Dante?

"You will continue on to Lycée St. Clément, Gottfried's sister school, and an academy solely for Monitors."

From the foyer, the clock chimed nine times. "A Monitor's academy?" I repeated. How would I see Dante? How would I tell him what was happening or where I was going? It would be hard enough to see him at Gottfried, but at least there, he knew where I was. And there was the distraction of other Undead students. We could have met off campus. We could have found a way. But at a Monitor's academy, there wouldn't be any Undead to muffle Dante's presence, and the entire student body along with the professors would be able to sense him. Would be *training* to sense him.

"Many of your classmates will move to St. Clément with you. It won't be a difficult transition," my grandfather continued. "Of course, those who are Undead will remain at Gottfried. And the rest, well, who knows. I suppose they'll go to a *normal* school—"

I cut him off. "Where is it?"

"Montreal, Canada. It's just across the border, really. Not far at all."

"Canada?" I should have been upset, but instead, all I

71

could hear were Brett's words: *People are saying he left for Canada.* Was there a chance that they were right, and Dante was already waiting for me in Montreal?

"You're upset," my grandfather said, leaning back in his chair, his wrinkled knuckles turning white as he gripped the armrests. "The limiting of Gottfried to only Undead students was not my decision. But the events of last year are impossible to ignore when the welfare of both students and professors is at stake."

Trying to compose myself, I looked up at him. "Fine," I said, my voice weary as I grasped on to the only hope I had: that fate was on my side and Dante was somewhere in Canada. "When do I leave?"

CHAPTER 3

LYCÉE ST. CLÉMENT

"Six letters, ends with ry." Dustin tried to write it out for me, but his pen was dry. He shook it and then tried again. We were on an aeroplane, travelling to Quebec.

I blinked. While he dug through his bag, looking for a replacement, an image of a bird flashed into my head, as if it were engraved on the underside of my eyelids. Without knowing why, I was overwhelmed with the desire to find this bird. To have it for my own.

"Ah," Dustin said, emerging with a pencil in hand. He hovered over his crossword puzzle. "Now, where was I? Oh yes, number seventeen across—"

The answer seemed so obvious that I didn't even let Dustin finish his sentence. "Canary."

He counted the letters, and threw down his pen. "Now how did you know that? I hadn't even read you the clue yet."

"I don't know. I – I guess it was just on my mind." I averted my eyes to the little window, where I gazed at the clouds below.

"You must have inherited that gift from your mother. She was a master of crossword puzzles. Always used to sneak them under the table during breakfast."

"What was the clue?"

"Blank in a coal mine."

"Was I right?"

Dustin let out a laugh. "Yes, of course."

"A canary in a coal mine?" I said, turning the words over in my mouth. The saying sounded familiar, though I couldn't remember where I had heard it. "What does it mean?"

"You don't know?" His face wrinkled with surprise. "Miners used to bring canaries down into the coal pits to test for poisonous gas. Canaries are very sensitive to that kind of thing, and if there was any gas, the birds would die immediately, alerting the miners to evacuate." Dustin tilted his seat forward and back. "Isn't it marvellous?" he said. "At this very moment we're thousands of metres above the earth, shooting through the air!"

Despite how gloomy I felt, I couldn't help but smile as I watched him fiddle with the buttons on his armrest. Dustin loved aeroplanes. The compartmentalized meals, the in-flight magazines, the flight attendants in their prim outfits, pointing front, back, side, side.

"Beverage?" an attendant asked, pushing a cart down the aisle.

"I'll have a club soda, please," Dustin said, and then changed his mind. "No – make that a cranberry juice." As she filled a cup with ice, Dustin interjected, "Actually, could you change that to a tomato cocktail?"

He turned to me, looking pleased. "Lovely," he said, as if the flight attendant couldn't hear him. He shook a bag of peanuts with delight. "Everything is in miniature!"

Picking up Dustin's magazine, I flipped through it, glancing at the ads until I stumbled across a map of North America. I spread it out on the folding table. "Have you ever been to Lake Erie?" I asked, staring at its blue shape.

The smile faded from Dustin's face. "Yes."

"What's it like?"

"Cold. Wet."

"Were they close?" I asked. "My mom and Miss LaBarge?"

He loosened his seat belt. "When they were your age they were inseparable. Except when your father was around, of course."

Finding Montreal on the map, I laid my hand down on the page. The width of one index finger – that was how far away my grandfather's house in Massachusetts was from the city. Two index fingers – that was how far away from Montreal Miss LaBarge was when she died. Four index fingers – that was how far away my parents were when they died. I spread out my hand across the page – that was where Dante could be. Anywhere. And every day we were apart felt like a lifetime lost.

"Do you ever feel like you're running out of time?" I asked Dustin.

He stared at the ice cubes in his drink. "Always."

"So what do you do about it?"

"Nothing," he said. "I just try to enjoy the time I do have. That's all we can do, really."

The rest of the flight was quick; it seemed like we had just boarded when three chimes sounded over the intercom, followed by the flight attendant's voice, announcing in both French and English that we had begun our descent. Dustin leaned over me to look out the window. The blue sky faded as we entered the clouds, and was replaced by the tiny lights of buildings, the irregular spirals of roads. And then, through the mist, an island emerged.

* * *

Montreal was a castle of a city, surrounded by water on all sides, and connected to the mainland by bridges. After going through customs, we rented a compact car and set out for St. Clément, in the old part of town, Vieux-Port. We drove down a street called rue Notre-Dame, which was lined with uneven pavements and town houses capped with mansard roofs.

It was an overcast afternoon, the air warm and thick. I rolled down my window as we passed a group of cyclists, all wearing little hats. One of them turned to me as we passed, his hair pulled back into a messy knot. *Dante,* I thought as I pressed my nose to the window. But it was just a tall man with long hair. He winked as we turned down rue Saint-Maurice. There, we drove until we passed a narrow street with no sign. Slowing to a stop, Dustin looked over his shoulder, and then reversed until we were even with the unnamed street, which was really more of an alleyway. Dustin squinted at the stained brick buildings.

"If my memory serves me correctly, this is it," he said finally, and turned. The cobblestones were slanted, putting our tiny car on an incline.

A pair of pigeons flew out of our way and flapped around the alley as we squeezed past the trash bins that lined the kerb. The street ended at a sign that read PETITE RUE SAINT-CLÉMENT.

It was only slightly larger than the alley, but much

sunnier. Dustin took a left, and about a hundred metres down, pulled up in front of a large stone building with an arched entranceway. Etched over it in large letters was: LYCÉE SAINT-CLÉMENT.

A security guard sauntered towards us. Setting down my bags, Dustin fished around in his pockets for a piece of paper. Upon reading it, the guard uttered something in French to us, making hand gestures. To my surprise, Dustin seemed to understand. "*Merci, monsieur,*" he said, with what sounded like a perfect accent, and picked up my bags.

"I didn't know you could speak French," I said as we crossed a grassy courtyard surrounded by the school. In the middle was a fountain. Two girls were standing next to it, holding books as the water spouted behind them.

"Nor did I," said Dustin. "The last time I spoke it was a lifetime ago."

We entered one of the buildings on the far side of the courtyard, which said FEMMES. Unlike the Gottfried dormitories, this one was small and cosy. A plush carpet blanketed the lobby, which was furnished with overstuffed sofas. A bulletin board hung on one wall, cluttered with tacks and colourful fliers. Potted plants streamed over the window sills, and brass numbers and nameplates decorated each of the doors. Upstairs we found a maze of hallways lined with rose wallpaper, and crowded with girls hauling trunks, suitcases, and piles of books into their rooms. They barely paid attention to me as I squeezed past them.

My room was nestled into a sunny corner of the building with one other room, number 32, labelled with the name CLÉMENTINE LAGUERRE. Mine was number 31. I fumbled with the keys, pushing the door open just as Dustin, hauling the luggage, caught up with me.

The only word to describe it was lovely. An arched hallway led to a series of little areas: a sink and mirror, a bedroom with a real pot-bellied stove, and small balcony that overlooked the courtyard. There was even a beautiful old fireplace, which had been sealed years ago, according to Dustin, after a bad fire. But the most foreign thing of all was that I had the whole room to myself.

The only shared part was the bathroom, which connected my room and Clémentine's, and had a deep porcelain tub that could fit three of me in it. I fiddled with the knobs on the bidet, turning the right one around and around, but nothing happened. It must be broken, I thought, hitting it with my hand just as Dustin said something from the other room. Suddenly, water burst out of the tap, spraying my legs.

"What?" I shouted, jumping out of the way.

"I said, someone just slipped an envelope under the door. Would you like me to open it?"

"Okay," I said, struggling with the tap.

"'Promptly report to the gymnasium at 9 a.m. on Monday for your placement examination.'"

Wiping off my shorts, I went to the main room. "A placement test?"

"Yes," Dustin said, checking his watch. "Tomorrow." When he saw my wet clothes, he chuckled and dug through my bag until he found a towel.

"Tomorrow? But I don't even know what the test is on."

"I'm sure it will be fine," Dustin said. He pulled some sheets from my bag and stretched one over the mattress. When I tried to help, he swatted me away.

Of course he thought it was fine; he wasn't the one who had to take the exam. I blew a wisp of hair from my face before beginning to unpack. While we worked, Dustin taught me tidbits of French. "*La pelle,*" he said, handing me a shovel. "*Les pièces,*" he continued, handing me a bag of coins with the rest of my Monitor supplies. "*La vie.*" Life. "*La mort.*" Death. He unpacked my old philosophy books from Miss LaBarge's class, and glanced out the window. The sun was setting behind the buildings. "*Éphémère.*" And after dusting off my bookshelf one last time, he said, "*Cri du coeur,*" and hugged me goodbye, hurrying back to the airport to catch his flight home. After he left, I looked it up in my French dictionary. It meant *a cry of the heart.*

That evening I skipped dinner and spent the rest of the night alone in my room. I only ventured out once to carry my trash to the bins, but ended up getting lost in the maze of hallways as I tried to find my way back to my room. I ended up in a side hall that looked just like mine, except that the room number was 21, and the name on the door read ANYA PINSKY. It was ajar, revealing a messy clutter of boxes and clothes, the room half decorated with tall glass candlesticks and colourful charms. A girl with hair dyed a dark, unnatural red was holding a bundle of linens and having an argument with an older man in what sounded like Russian. When she saw me looking in, she squinted at me and then walked to the door and shut it.

The door beside it was painted shut with so many layers that I could barely see the seam of the wall. BROOM CLOSET, it read.

I tried to retrace my steps, making a few wrong turns until I finally found my door. Shutting myself inside, I sat on my bed and listened through the walls to the girls walking down the hall, speaking to each other in French. I didn't know who they were or what they were saying; I wasn't even sure that I wanted to know. They lived in a different world than I did. I could tell by the way they were laughing, by the fact that they *could* laugh.

Just as I was falling asleep, I heard the toilet flush from the shared bathroom, and sat up. "Eleanor?" I said, staring at the other side of the dark room before realizing that I was alone. If Dustin were here, he would tell me the word in French. Turning on the light, I picked up the pocket dictionary he'd left for me. "Alone" had eight entries. "*Seul. Isolé. Séparé. Écarté. Solitaire. Singulier. Sans aide. Perdu.*" Which kind was I? Left behind by my parents, by Miss LaBarge. Separated from Dante. Isolated from the people around me. Lost.

I was closing the book when the phone rang. Startled, I jumped.

"Renée?" a hushed voice said as I held the receiver to my ear.

"Eleanor?" I said, a little louder than I had intended, and then repeated, "Eleanor?"

I heard a breath on the other line. "It's really you," she said, uncharacteristically monotone.

"It's really you," I repeated, leaning against the wall. She must have been back at Gottfried, calling me from the room we used to share. "I feel like I haven't seen you in ages."

"I know," Eleanor said, her voice duller than I remembered.

"And your postcards – I don't know how I would have gotten through the summer without them."

"Well, it gave me something to do. My mom was driving me insane all summer. Anyway, how is it over there?"

I sighed.

"Same here at Gottfried," she said. "They've been calling each of us in to be questioned. About Miss LaBarge's death." Her voice didn't waver when she said Miss LaBarge's name, as if she were talking about a stranger rather than our philosophy professor.

"Questioned?"

"They know she was killed by a group of Undead, and want to see if any of us have information. I went in this morning. Your grandfather kept asking me if I had been contacted recently by a group of Undead."

"By a *group* of Undead? What does that mean? What group?"

"I don't know," she said. "He wouldn't say anything more specific. I was hoping you might know."

"I have no idea," I said, tracing the stitching on my comforter. "How is your mom doing?" I asked, thinking of the photograph I'd found in Miss LaBarge's cottage.

"She's fine, I think," Eleanor said, though she sounded confused. "The same as always. Why?"

"I thought she was friends with Miss LaBarge."

"Why would you think that?" Eleanor said. "She met her for the first time last year."

"What?" I said, sitting upright. "But I went to Miss LaBarge's cottage with my grandfather and found a photograph of her with your mom and mine when they were our age. It was framed in her bedroom. And I saw her at the funeral."

Eleanor paused. "Are you sure it was my mom in the photo? Every time I mentioned Miss LaBarge at home, she always forgot her name or messed it up, calling her DuFarge or something. I'm certain she'd never met her before in her life."

I frowned. "Well, I'm certain it was her in the photo. Unless your mom has a sister?"

"No. She's an only child."

I coiled the telephone cord around my finger, remembering the way Eleanor's mom had looked sitting alone on the deck of the boat. Why would she have lied about knowing Miss LaBarge?

"Have you heard from Dante?" I asked, breaking the long pause.

"No." She cleared her throat. "He hasn't sent me anything since your birthday. I'm sorry." I knew she meant it, but she sounded devoid of empathy.

I loosened my grip on the receiver. "At the funeral, Brett told me there was a rumour Dante was in Canada. Do you think it's true?"

Eleanor didn't respond for a long while. "I don't know where he is," she said stiffly. Her tone reminded me that she was Undead, and that funerals weren't the best subject matter; nor was Brett, her ex-boyfriend.

I immediately regretted saying anything. "Eleanor, I'm sorry—"

"It's fine," she said quickly, as if she didn't even want me to say what I was about to say. "The weird thing is that I don't really care. I know I should, but I can't feel anything. Not for Miss LaBarge's death, or for my break-up with Brett. Nothing. It's not right. I know it's not right, but I can't help it."

"It's not your fault," I said softly.

"It's not about fault any more. It's about dealing with it every day. Knowing that every day that passes, I'm a little less human."

I pressed the receiver to my cheek, trying to find the words that would explain how badly I wanted to help her, how badly I wished I could be with her right now. But all I could come up with was, "I'm sorry. I'm so sorry."

"It's okay," she said, her voice cracking. "I shouldn't have even brought it up. It's just a passing thing, I bet." But the words dissipated between us. "Tell me about you. I'm tired of me."

So I told her about my dream, about the newspaper articles in Miss LaBarge's cottage, the letter my mother had written to her, and how my grandfather thought Miss LaBarge and my parents had only been searching for the Undead when they were killed.

Eleanor paused. "Maybe he's right. I mean, that's what Monitors do, isn't it? Search for the Undead and bury them?"

"I don't think it's that simple," I said. "We don't just bury the Undead immediately, right?"

"You tell me," Eleanor said. "You're the Monitor now, not me."

"It's not like that," I said. "I'm the same; nothing has changed."

"Then how come you're at St. Clément and I'm at Gottfried?"

Shocked, I stared at the receiver. "Oh, I see. So it's my fault that I'm here and you're there? Do you actually think that I *want* to be here? That I *want* to learn how to bury people?" I was about to hang up the phone, when Eleanor cut in.

"Wait – Renée, I'm sorry. I didn't mean that. I know it's not your fault. It just isn't fair. I don't belong here with everyone else. I'm not like them."

"If it makes you feel any better, apparently all the other Monitors think I'm immortal," I said, carrying the phone to the bed.

"They've been saying that here, too." She lowered her voice to a whisper. "Have you told anyone else what really happened?"

I'd told Eleanor everything in a letter over the summer.

She was the only one who knew that Dante and I shared a soul.

"No. I can't. My grandfather suspects something, but he doesn't actually know anything."

"So, do you think immortality is really possible?"

"I don't think so," I said, staring at the beams lining the ceiling. "I mean, how could it be?"

Eleanor paused. "Yeah, you're probably right. But, you know, the whole Undead thing – I always thought that was a myth until I came to Gottfried and it happened to me. So maybe there are other things out there that we don't know about."

I recognized something in Eleanor's voice. It was the same kind of blind hope I had when I thought about Dante. Was Eleanor right? Could there be some other course for her future, and mine? "Maybe there are. Anything's possible, right?"

The line went quiet.

"Are you still there?"

"Yeah... sort of."

"Are you okay?"

Her voice cracked. "I don't know."

"I don't know if I am, either."

"Can we not hang up yet?" she whispered. "It gets so lonely here at night."

"I know," I said, and, pulling the blanket up, I talked to

her under the sheets, listening to the sound of her breathing on the other end of the line until I fell asleep.

The gymnasium was dingy and old, the floors a faded orange. I was wearing my dress-code clothes – black stockings, a pleated skirt, and a pressed oxford shirt – for the first time since Gottfried. Two boys ahead of me held the door as I entered, my shoes squeaking against the rubber floor. Sitting on two folding chairs in the middle of the gym were a man and a woman, both in suits. They directed us to the locker rooms to wait.

The long wooden benches of the locker room were already crowded with girls when I walked in. Some were chatting, others checking their hair in mirrors above the line of sinks off to the right. In the corner were a group of girls I recognized from Gottfried. I pushed through the crowd towards them, but when they saw me coming, they dispersed, avoiding my eyes. I froze, realizing they had been talking about me. Finally, Greta, an athletic girl who had lived on my floor last year, gave me a half-hearted wave. Turning away from them, I clutched my things to my chest, and was about to go to the toilets, when above the din I heard someone say, "I'm sorry, Clémentine."

I turned around, curious to see who lived in the room across from mine.

Clémentine LaGuerre was petite, with dark brown skin so smooth it looked buttery. Her short hair was oiled and elegantly parted on one side like a flapper. A group of girls surrounded her as she pinned it in place with a single hairpin. She met my gaze in the mirror, her eyes a startling green.

"Who are you?" she said, speaking to my reflection. Her voice was soft and lyrical, a mix between a French and a Caribbean accent. The girls beside her stopped talking and stared at me.

"Renée."

"Renée *Winters*?"

I nodded, surprised she knew my name.

"So you're the one who can cheat death," she said quietly, her face impossible to read.

"And you're Clémentine. You live across the hall from me."

"I know where I live," she said, her voice calm but firm. Behind her, two girls in matching cardigans laughed. "So did you or did you not survive the kiss of the Undead?"

Somewhere in the room a locker door clanged shut. The girls scrutinized me, waiting for me to answer. But I was sick of being stared at by strangers, of being asked the same question over and over again. They weren't there that night; they didn't know what happened. What gave them the right to pry into the most private moments of my past? By their looks I could tell that it didn't matter what I said; they already believed I was immortal. So why not let them?

Clémentine put a hand on her hip. "Well, is it true or is it not?"

I shrugged, trying to look nonchalant. "I'm alive, aren't I?"

The room erupted in whispers, but Clémentine said nothing, her eyes glued to my reflection.

"Prove it."

I hesitated, my face in the mirror staring back at me, bewildered. Was she serious?

Clémentine crossed her arms. "Go on."

At the back of the room was a stairway with a sign that said it led to the swimming pool. I walked towards it. The Undead couldn't go underground – it would put them to rest, like a burial.

I paused dramatically at the top step, and felt everyone hold their breath as I descended.

Behind me, the girls murmured, "But how? What happened?" Until they were interrupted by the locker room door swinging open.

A graceful woman entered, her cheeks hollowed out with age, her neck thin and curved like a swan's. She was wearing a wool skirt suit, her hair coiled into a bun.

"Girls?" she said with a thick French accent. "It is time."

We filed out into the gymnasium, where she handed us each a pencil and a map of the school grounds. The boys were nowhere to be seen, and I assumed they were to perform the test separately.

"*Bonjour,*" the woman said, flexing her neck as she spoke. Standing beside her was a childlike man with a pudgy face that seemed to engulf his eyes. "I am Madame Goût, and this is Monsieur Pollet," she continued, pronouncing the name *Po-lay.*

"Poll*et*," the man corrected, accentuating the *t.* He sounded American.

She ignored him. "We will serve as your placement exam proctors. This exam will determine your class rank by testing your talent, speed, and strategy."

She turned to Mr. Pollet, who continued. "We have hidden nine dead animals around the St. Clément campus. Your task is to mark the exact location of each animal on the map we have provided for you. We expect the list to be numbered in order, and we will collect it at the end of the exam."

"What kind of order?" a freckled girl asked.

The woman frowned. "Why, any order you wish."

I glanced around at the other girls, relieved to discover that I wasn't the only one confused by these instructions.

Mr. Pollet continued. "You may find and identify the

animals by any means necessary. There are only three rules. One, you must return in exactly one hour. Two, you may not touch, move, or relocate the animals. And three, you must work alone."

Madame Goût took over. "Are there any questions before we begin?"

I felt myself starting to panic. I had too many questions. One hour? To find nine dead animals hidden around campus, while every other girl was doing the same thing? It seemed impossible.

"No?" she asked, flexing the tendons in her neck as she peered around the crowd to make sure she wasn't missing anyone. "Okay. Ready yourselves," she said, watching the clock on the wall. When the hands hit nine o'clock, she said, "Begin!"

Everyone dispersed. Some of the girls meandered around, unsure of what to do. Others set off in one direction with determination, and the rest followed the decisive-looking ones. Clémentine glanced at me, and with a smile, slipped out the door and into the daylight.

I was the only person who didn't move. I didn't do anything until everyone had emptied out of the gymnasium. "The clock is ticking, mademoiselle," Madame Goût warned.

Now that there was silence, I could think. I walked to the centre of the gymnasium, where there was a circle painted on the floor. Not completely sure what I was doing, I stood in the middle of it and closed my eyes.

Taking small steps, I turned around in the circle until I felt the air shift, as if it were moving out of my way. The tiny path that it left was cool and seemingly devoid of anything. I imagined myself walking down it, marking the number of paces on my map. Twelve paces straight, four paces to the left, up ten stairs. Eleven paces to the right. Down three stairs. Two paces to the left. There, I drew an X. And without realizing what I was writing, I scrawled the word CAT in big wobbly letters.

Puzzled, I stared at it. I had no idea how I knew it was a cat, but now that I saw the word on the page, I was certain that was it. Next to it I wrote #1.

I repeated the process. This time when the air shifted, the path seemed a little narrower. I followed it, counting the paces. Marking it with an X, I wrote SHEEP, #2. I continued on, the empty paths in the air growing thinner and thinner. CROW, #3. BOAR, #4. SQUIRREL, #5. POSSUM, #6. RAT, #7.

When I got to the last two I wavered. Their paths were so narrow that they barely seemed to exist. FISH, I wrote, feeling a little unsure of myself, and then crossed it out and replaced it with CARP, #8. Glancing at the clock, I realized I only had five minutes left until the exam was up. But no matter how hard I tried, I couldn't identify the last animal.

As the second hand made its final rotation, Clémentine burst through the doors in her white tennis shoes, and handed in her list. How could she have finished? Giving up, I drew a simple X where the last animal rested, and labelled it #9.

After a series of written tests on Monitoring history, we finally finished the exam. I spent the rest of the day in my room, listening to the girls in the hall laughing and talking about their summers. Part of me wanted to go talk to them, but what would I say if they asked me about my summer? That I'd spent it indoors, seeing doctors and therapists? That I'd spent my nights pacing by the window, wondering when I would hear from my Undead boyfriend?

Suddenly the bathroom door burst open, and a plump girl with rosy cheeks fell into my room. "Oh, sorry. Wrong door," she said, staring at me. "Hey, are you that girl who can't die?"

Sitting up, I glared at her.

"Sorry," she said, rolling her eyes, and popped back into Clémentine's room, where faintly I heard her talking, probably about me.

I didn't venture out until dinner. The dining hall had the feel of a medieval kitchen, with long wooden tables and three cooks standing behind a counter, flipping meat in skillets. The whole room was crowded and steamy. Even though there were plenty of empty seats, it still felt like there wasn't one for me. Clémentine and a group of her friends whispered as I passed them. Over the noise of clattering plates, I could hear Brett laughing as he joined a group of boys by the wall. Finally I spotted some girls from Gottfried sharing a table with a few people I recognized from my floor. I made my way towards them.

"Is anyone sitting here?" I asked.

April looked up at me. "Oh, Renée. Um – no," she said, and pushed over just enough for me to squeeze onto the end.

"Thanks," I mumbled.

After a solid moment of silence, conversation resumed.

"So you had Undead at Gottfried. I mean, in your classes. What were they like?" a prim Korean girl asked April's twin, Allison.

"They're like us," Allison said, picking at her salad. "Except they can speak Latin."

"Do they look different?" the girl pressed. "Clémentine said that they look like corpses. That their eyes are cloudy."

My stomach tightened. "You've never met one before?" I asked, gazing at the St. Clément girls on the other side of the table. They shook their heads as if it were obvious. "Well, Clémentine doesn't know what she's talking about."

"But she's met the Undead before. With her dad."

"So have I," I said. "And she's wrong."

A couple of girls across from me went rigid, as if I had insulted their religion.

"But aren't they angry and uncontrollable?" said a delicate brunette, her eyes wide beneath her glasses. "That's what Clémentine said. That they're animals."

"I don't see how they can stand it," her friend said, playing with the straw of her soda. "Knowing that a murderer is lurking inside them." The other girls nodded in agreement.

I stopped eating. "Not all Undead take souls at random. And besides, any of us could kill someone. It's not like we're perfect. Humans kill each other all the time. As Monitors, we're going to learn how to kill the Undead. That doesn't bother you?"

There was an awkward stillness as everyone gazed at me. I looked to the girls from Gottfried for support, but only April gave me a sympathetic glance before looking away. The rest of them were too cowardly to even look me in the eyes, even though they had been close with the same friends I'd had at Gottfried. "Allison, are you still in touch with Eleanor?" I asked.

"She's different now."

"She's had a hard time. It's not her fault."

"I never said it was," Allison said, offended. "But she's

Undead now, and I'm a Monitor. That's not my fault, either." Putting down her fork, she stood up. "You know, I'm not really hungry any more." Without looking at me, she turned to her sister. "I'll see you back at the dorm."

The table went silent as she gathered her things, and I realized that none of them were comfortable with me there. "Right," I said, crumpling my napkin in my fist. "I guess I'll go." And picking up my tray, I walked down the aisle, refusing to look back. I paused when I spotted Anya Pinsky sitting by herself in the corner. Smiling, I walked over to her table and sat across from her.

She looked up from her brisket. "Did I say you could sit?" she asked, pronouncing every consonant immaculately. Her dark red hair was pulled into a low bun.

"Sorry. I thought you were alone."

"I am," she said.

"I was just trying to be friendly."

"I don't need any friends," she said.

"Now I know." Just as I moved to the end of the table, the main door of the dining hall opened, and a tall, ebony-skinned man sauntered down the aisle, carrying a folder of papers. He was wearing a dark green suit, the kind only a tall person could pull off. His hair was greying.

A hush fell over the crowd as he stood at the head of the room and put on his glasses.

"Hello," he said in a French-Caribbean accent, his voice

deep yet wavering, as if he were singing the words. "As many of you know, I am Headmaster LaGuerre, and I'd like to welcome you all to Lycée St. Clément."

Everyone clapped. From where I was sitting, I could see the back of Clémentine's head near the front. Her last name was LaGuerre, too.

"You are all Monitors," he said, and smiled. "It makes me proud to say those words. Some of you come from old Monitoring families, others are new to our community, but we are all united by our shared talents: the unique ability to sense death, and the primal urge to seek it out and bury it."

The room went still as he gazed around us, his words pulsing beneath the silence like electricity.

"In your time at St. Clément, you'll make new friends, discover new skills, and eventually you'll specialize in one branch of Monitoring. However, most importantly, you will learn how to control and use your powers. The purpose of our calling is to police the Undead, and to put them to rest only when completely necessary. All life is precious, even second lives."

I wanted to turn to April's table, but resisted the urge.

"Monitoring is not a safe calling. Every day you will be risking your lives for the betterment of humanity." He paused dramatically. "In your classes you will hone the three basic Monitoring skills: *intuition*, sensing the Undead;

evaluation, judging the Undead; and *execution*, putting the Undead to rest. But classes aren't a replacement for real experience. You need to learn how to look after yourselves, and now is the perfect time to start." He motioned towards the doors. "The gates are always open. You can come and go as you please, and at your own risk.

"That said, we do have two rules. First, I ask you to keep what you learn at St. Clément to yourselves. You are not to discuss the existence of Monitors or the Undead to anyone outside of these walls; nor shall you blatantly display your talents to anyone outside this community unless the situation is life threatening. Should the public find out about the existence of the Undead, they will try to bury them all. History has proven this to be true over and over again.

"And second, I ask you to carry around some sort of protection at all times. A small shovel is preferable, as it can be used as both a blunt weapon and a burial tool; but a box of matches, a roll of gauze – any of these things will suffice. It is our job to start training you to act and think like Monitors." He reached into his jacket and pulled out something wrapped in a cloth. He unfolded it and held up a small trowel and a pair of gloves. "As you can see, we professors take the same precautions as you."

The room was completely silent as he wrapped up his tools and slid them back into his pocket.

"Finally, I'd like to name this year's top rank. For those of you who are new to St. Clément, the top rank is the student who scored the highest in the placement exam, which the entire school takes. That student is thus the best Monitor at our academy."

He looked down at a piece of paper. "Renée Winters."

It took me a few moments to realize he had said my name. When I did, I was so surprised that I dropped my fork into my lap. I picked it up and brushed myself off, feeling my cheeks flush as all heads turned in my direction. How could I have gotten first rank when I hadn't even finished the exam?

"Renée, would you come to the front?" the headmaster said, gazing around the crowd, unsure of who I was.

I stood up and walked to the podium, my shoes loud against the wooden floor. People whispered as I approached the front of the room. The headmaster beamed and took out a small brooch in the shape of a cat.

"The cat is the mascot of St. Clément, and the symbol of Monitors all across the world," he said as he pinned it to the collar of my shirt. "Now you and the cat are one."

"Thanks," I said, trying not to blush.

"Congratulations," he said. "And welcome to St. Clément." Under the noise of everyone clapping, the headmaster added, "Could you meet me in my office Monday afternoon after your classes?"

"Sure," I said, giving him a curious look. But he only smiled. I was about to return to my seat when he stopped me.

"And now Renée will lead us in the recital of the Cartesian Oath."

I felt a wave of nausea pass over me as the entire dining hall rose, their benches scraping against the floor.

"Drafted by our ancestors in the spirit of René Descartes, the Cartesian Oath is the sole pledge all Monitors must take in their training. It is our constitution, our ethical standard, our *déclaration des droits de l'homme.*"

Ethical standard? I was the last person who should be reading this aloud. I shook my head at him, but he merely smiled and handed me a roll of paper. "If you would please repeat after Renée."

I could feel the girls from my floor glaring at me. Trying to will my hands to stop shaking, I unrolled the paper.

"Go on," the headmaster said softly.

I cleared my throat. "'As a Monitor, I swear by O-Osiris'–" my voice cracked – "'god of judgment and the afterlife, that, to the best of my ability, I shall bury all deceased humans within ten days of death, to prevent reanimation, even if the deceased is my son, daughter, sibling, friend, or – or... or lover,'" I said finally, apologizing to Dante in my head as I listened to the drone of my classmates repeating my words.

"'If I should sense the presence of an Undead, I shall seek him out and evaluate his rate of decay,'" I continued. My eyes rested on Brett's as I watched him mouth my words and give me an encouraging smile.

"'Should he be desperate, dangerous, or close to complete putrefaction, I shall endeavour to capture him and bring him to the High Monitor Court for examination and trial.'"

Clémentine stared at me from the centre of the room, her face wrought with jealousy.

"'I shall never bury an Undead until he has proven himself guilty of murder or has – has—'" The headmaster nodded at me to continue. "'Has threatened my life.'"

When the voices stopped, I unrolled the paper even more and continued. "'When I do bury an Undead, I shall do so promptly, painlessly, and in accordance with Monitor ritual, with no vengeance or brutality.

"'I shall never announce myself to Plebeians or Undead. And finally, I understand that every being on Earth has the capacity to cause pain, even Monitors, and that I will use my power and training with the caution and consideration given to my own life.'"

There was a lull in the room as we uttered the last phrase. Without a word, Headmaster LaGuerre gave me a slight bow indicating that I could sit down, and the hum of conversations recommenced.

After dinner, everyone parted around me as we filed out of the dining hall. I tried to blend in, covering the pin on my collar with my scarf. The lobby was crowded with girls, all clamouring to look at something on the bulletin board.

"What's going on?" I asked a girl standing near the perimeter. She started when she saw me, as if I'd frightened her. "It's the class rank list. They just posted it, along with our class schedules."

Just then Clémentine LaGuerre stormed through, glaring at me as she pushed past my shoulder and up the stairs. I made my way to the front and flipped through a folder of schedules until I found the sheet with my name at the top. It read as follows:

WINTERS, RENÉE: JUNIOR YEAR SCHEDULE
History of Monitors
Strategy and Prediction
Child Psychology
French
Advanced Latin

I scanned the class rank list until I found my name. *Winters, Renée.* Number one. I stared at it, still incredulous. Out of curiosity, I looked for *LaGuerre, Clémentine.* She was number two.

CHAPTER 4

ROYAL VICTORIA HOSPITAL

IT WAS A BRISK SEPTEMBER MORNING, the sun spilling into the halls as I climbed up the three flights of stairs that led to History of Monitors, my first class of the semester. The room had beamed ceilings and pigeons roosting on window ledges, their chests puffing as they slept. I envied them. My weekend had been sleepless, and with no one to talk to, the days had become languid and distorted, like a dream. I took a seat, watching Mr. Pollet fiddle with a projector at the back of the room, his underarms damp with sweat.

There were only nine others around the table, including

Anya, Clémentine, Brett, and a few boys I didn't know. When the bell rang, Mr. Pollet straightened himself out and took his place at the blackboard.

"Montreal is a city underground," he said, dabbing his pink forehead. "It's the only city built by Monitors, for Monitors, and is therefore the only Monitor safe hold in existence, the only Monitor fortress."

He crossed the room to switch off the lights, and turned on the projector. "Monitors first emigrated here from France, with the dream of designing a place where they could study the Undead in an enclosed environment. Thus, they chose to settle on an island, where they built a network of tunnels underneath the city to keep them safe from the Undead, who cannot go underground."

He pressed a button on his remote control, and the first slide appeared. It was a photograph of a normal city street. On the pavement was a small hut that looked like an outhouse.

"An entrance to the tunnel network," he said, and clicked to the next slide, a photograph of the stairs inside leading down under the earth.

He clicked ahead. A tunnel entrance beneath a building. A staircase in the back of an alley. A wooden hut on the side of Mont Royal, which marked the centre of the city.

"And conveniently, they all connect here."

He showed a black-and-white illustration of a sprawling

gothic building with castle spires and pointed alcoves. "This is the Royal Victoria Hospital, just after it was built by the Monitors. Of course, at the time it was called Hôpital Saint-Laurent."

Something within me began to throb with anticipation, as if years of effort had led up to this moment. I was suddenly overwhelmed with the need to know what rested behind its walls. Not the patients or the doctors and nurses, but something else...

"In the early days, when Monitors ran the city, the Royal Victoria was one of the first hospitals in North America to treat Undead children. Later, during the 1890s, the hospital was taken over by the Plebeians, but this sketch was drawn during the time of the Monitors."

I blinked and the image was in colour.

"Tunnels from all across the city led directly to the hospital supply room. That way, if there was ever an Undead attack, the Monitors could easily access supplies like gauze, ointments and scissors in the hospital."

I blinked again, and the flags on the building's spires seemed to move in the wind.

"After the Monitoring community began to die out, we slowly lost control over Montreal."

I blinked once more, and the classroom around me seemed to collapse into itself.

"Today, Montreal is no longer run by Monitors, nor is

the hospital. In fact, most people here are not even aware that we or the Undead exist."

That was the last thing I heard before everything went black.

The next thing I knew, I was in the image, standing in the grass on the lawn in front of the hospital. It was a crisp autumn day, a slight breeze making the flags on the spires billow. I was holding a bouquet of flowers.

Four ambulances were parked in the driveway outside the hospital as I walked towards the entrance and through the double doors. In the foyer was a reception area lined with nurses sitting behind a counter. Smiling, I leaned over to get their attention.

"May I help you?" a young nurse asked. She was plump, with round cheeks and lots of freckles. She wore a white-and-yellow uniform.

"Yes, I'm visiting the patient in room 151," I said, holding up the flowers.

"Is the patient related to you?"

"My sis— I mean, brother. He's my brother," I said quickly.

The nurse gave me a sad smile. "I'm so sorry," she said as she typed something into her computer and directed me towards the paediatrics wing.

The hallways were sterile and fluorescent. I looked through the window of the door before opening it, to make sure no other visitors were inside, and then turned the knob.

A little boy lay sleeping in a hospital bed. He looked about five and was very thin. He shifted under the sheets as I closed the door. Flowers lined the window sill. I set my bouquet on the sill amongst them and approached the bed, checking the floor on either side. It was covered in creamy linoleum. The gap between the frame and floor seemed just big enough to fit my arm in comfortably. Kneeling down, I rolled up my sleeve and reached under the bed.

I couldn't feel anything at first, but after patting around, my fingers grazed something cool and bumpy. Engraved metal. Relieved, I opened my bag and took out a piece of paper and a stick of graphite. I slid the paper under the bed until it was covering the metal spot, and, quietly as I could, I rubbed the graphite over the paper to make a print of the engraving.

Just as I finished, the door clicked open. I shoved the paper in my pocket, stood up, and leaned over the sleeping boy. I didn't even know his name. A nurse was holding the door open with an elbow, her back turned to me as she laughed and chatted with someone in the hall. The boy shivered and clutched the sheets to his chest. Gently, I pulled up his blankets and tucked him in. Above me, the lights flickered and slowly darkened until the room, the boy, and the nurse's laughter all faded away.

I woke up in a strange room, my face cold and wet. A well-dressed man stood over me, holding a spray bottle.

"Ah, here she comes," he said, his voice gruff. "Sorry to spray you with water, but we tried ammonia several times," he said, putting the bottle aside. "It seems you have a weak sense of smell."

"It comes and goes," I said, sitting up. I was lying on a worn leather couch. The room around me was made almost entirely of mahogany – the floors, the walls, the furniture. Several diplomas and certificates hung above a desk. A medical coat was draped over the back of the chair. On its breast pocket was a name tag that read DR. NEWHAUS.

"Am I in the hospital?" I asked, bewildered. Without thinking, I patted my pockets, looking for the paper that I had rubbed against the floor.

"You're at St. Clément," the man said, taking a seat in a chair next to the couch. His face was dull, fleshy, and somehow expressionless. As he stared at me, I noticed that one of his eyes was crooked, as though it was sliding off towards the side of his head. "My name is Dr. Newhaus. I'm your psychology professor, though we haven't met yet, and I'm also the school doctor." Opening a briefcase, he pulled out a stethoscope and a flashlight.

"You gave us quite a show," he said as he listened to my breathing.

"What do you mean—" I began to ask, but he quieted me.

"How strange," he said, lowering his stethoscope. "You have a slightly irregular heartbeat."

"It's just a murmur," I said quickly. The doctors this summer had noticed it, too. "I've had it for a while," I lied.

Leaning towards me, he listened again, the stethoscope cold beneath my shirt. "This is quite different," he said. "It almost has the cadence of an Undead—"

I cut him off before he could finish. "What did you say happened to me?" I asked, squirming away from him.

He removed the scope, draped it around his shoulders, and crossed his hands in his lap. "You collapsed during history class and seemed to have had a kind of fainting spell."

I glanced at the clock above his desk. It had been a few hours since the start of class. "What do you mean?"

"I was hoping you'd be able to tell me." His expression was so placid that it made me uneasy.

I stared at the paisley patterns in the rug to avoid his gaze. How had I dreamed of the hospital when I'd never actually been there? It seemed alarmingly similar to my dream of Miss LaBarge.

He studied me with one eye while the other wandered off to the right. "I unsettle you," he said, his lip curling into a frown. "It's this." He motioned to his eye. "I don't blame you; it makes most students uncomfortable."

"Oh, no. I, um—" I stammered, feeling suddenly guilty. "It's not that. It's just, well..." He waited for me to finish, but I let my sentence trail off.

His expression softened. "Just a moment ago, you were patting your pockets. Did you lose something?"

The rubbing. The dream had been so vivid that when I woke up, I thought I might still have it in my pocket. "Oh, it was just...nothing."

He raised an eyebrow, but then let it drop. "Do you have any pre-existing neurological conditions or a history of brain trauma?"

"No."

"Have you ever fainted like this before?"

"No."

"Do you remember anything that might have triggered the event this morning?"

I thought of the slide of the hospital, of how I was overwhelmed with the need to know what was behind the building's walls. "No."

Lowering his pad, Dr. Newhaus tried to meet my eyes,

111

but I looked away. "I'm not your enemy," he said. "I'm here to help you."

"I've had a lot of bad doctors in the past."

"I understand," he said. "So have I. That's why I decided to become one."

He smiled, one eye resting on me, the other on the trees swaying outside the window. He seemed trustworthy.

"Can you remember what happened before you fainted?" he said. He crossed his legs, revealing mismatching striped socks.

For some reason, they put me at ease. "I remember Mr. Pollet telling us about the founding of Montreal and its tunnels. I remember him showing us slides of a bunch of old buildings. The last one I saw was of the Royal Victoria Hospital, before everything went black."

He shined a flashlight into my eyes and asked me to count backwards from ten. When I was finished, he asked, "And you don't remember anything in between then and now?"

Wringing my fingers together, I thought about my dream of Miss LaBarge, about all the sleep I'd lost, and all the mornings I'd woken up in sheets drenched in sweat. But at least those dreams had happened at night. Passing out in class was different; it was abnormal, intrusive, and frightening. "I had a dream," I said, looking at my feet. "Or something like one. I'm not really sure."

"Of what?"

"Of the Royal Victoria Hospital. I was walking through it to a certain room, looking for something. Everything was so clear and detailed, like I'd been there before."

"Have you?"

I shook my head.

"Can you describe what you saw?"

I told him about the hospital waiting room, about going to the paediatric ward and entering the boy's room and making a rubbing beneath the bed.

He looked unnerved. "That's startlingly accurate," he said. "The layout, the interior of the hospital – that's all correct. Are you sure you haven't been there before?"

I nodded.

The doctor frowned. "Have you had other dreams like this?"

I swallowed. "At night, yes. In each of them, I'm searching for something."

He took notes as I told him about the nightmares I'd had all summer. When I was finished, he made me stand up and walk across the room. He then tested my balance, my vision, and my hearing.

"Physically, everything seems to be fine, though your body is exhausted and sleep deprived. I'm going to schedule you for some tests, just to make sure everything inside is okay." He leaned forward. "But if I may speak candidly, you've been through a lot in the last year, and I think you'd benefit from a little help. I'd like you to consider coming in to see me regularly."

I wiped off a dusty mark on my stockings, which must have been there from when I fell out of my chair.

"You can think about it if you'd like. In the meantime, these may help you get some sound sleep." He jotted something down on a pad and tore off the prescriptions for two kinds of pills.

"What are they?" I asked, trying to sound out the names in my head.

"One is an anti-anxiety medication. The other is an antidepressant."

"But I'm not depressed."

"That may be," he said, in a way that made me think he was humouring me. "However, for now, this medication should put an end to these dreams of yours, and hopefully help you relax and get some much needed sleep."

"But what if I don't want to stop them? What if I'm seeing them for a reason?"

"And what reason would that be?" he asked, puzzled.

I let my hands drop into my lap. "I don't know."

I spent the rest of the day undergoing tests and scans of my brain. When they all came back normal, Dr. Newhaus reviewed my chart one last time and let me go. By then it was already late afternoon, the shadows shifting over the courtyard as the sun sank in the sky. Classes were over, and students poured out of the buildings. Keeping my head down, I clutched my bag to my chest and hurried through the columns that lined the perimeter of the campus. A group of girls was sitting on the stoop of the dormitory, Clémentine LaGuerre's voice ringing above the others.

"Apparently she had some sort of seizure in class today," she was saying, popping her gum as if to punctuate her sentence. "I heard from one of the fourth years that she wasn't even that good of a Monitor at Gottfried," she added, turning to April and Allison and three other girls who had lived down the hall from me last year.

I hid behind a column and watched them. "She was good," April said, looking to her sister for approval.

"Well, she wasn't *that* good," Allison corrected. She was only distinguishable from her sister by the mole on her chin and her haughty tone. "She just made a big show whenever she found a dead animal. I bet in reality she was only a little bit above average." The other girls nodded in agreement.

"So how did she do it?" Clémentine asked, her voice calm. "How did she survive the kiss of an Undead?"

I leaned closer, trying to hear Allison's response, when her eyes met mine. Her face dropped and everyone turned.

Swallowing, I raised my chin and pushed through them, using all my courage to act like I didn't care. I was almost at the doors when Clémentine slipped off the ledge, her legs bare and smooth beneath her wool skirt. "So are you going to answer my question? Or are you keeping it a secret because you know you're a fraud?"

A fraud? Her words tripped me mid-step. Maybe they stung so much because somewhere inside me I agreed with her – I didn't know how I had gotten first rank, and I didn't know what was happening to me. All I knew was that it was real – it was all real, and it was separating me from the person I loved the most – Dante. Slowing, I turned around. "Or maybe the truth is too painful to relive," I said. "But of course you wouldn't think of that because all you care about is your own ego."

A hush fell over the girls as Clémentine struggled to respond, but I was already through the doors and up the stairs to my room. Opening my dresser, I rummaged through my underwear drawer until I found a half-burned candle left over from Eleanor's stash last year. Even though it was still light out, I lit the wick and set it on my desk, feeling suddenly better as I stepped back and stared at it, imagining I was still at Gottfried.

Before the wax could even melt, a gust of wind came in through the window and blew the flame out. Except it didn't feel like wind, exactly. Approaching the candle,

I held my hand up, letting the black smoke coil around my fingers. The breeze had a smell to it, a taste, a wetness, as if it were the long cold breath of someone I had known in a previous life. Dante.

I ran downstairs, bursting through the doors to where the girls still stood on the stoop. Clémentine put a hand on her hip. "You have something to say to me?"

But I barely heard her. She couldn't feel it; none of them could. When I made it to the school gates, I stopped and balanced at the edge of the kerb, feeling the breeze lick at my ankles.

I could feel Dante before I could see him. A prickling sensation climbed up my legs, making them move, and suddenly I was winding through the Montreal streets, following a thin strand of air as it swirled past people on the pavement, coaxing them out of the way.

My skin tingled as I passed a butcher's, a fishmonger's, a veterinary clinic, and a funeral home. Animals, humans, soulless and empty, I could feel all of them – some intensely, some weakly; their presences grasping at me like the fingers of a ghost. Disoriented, I spun around, the lights of the crossing changing from green to yellow to red as I glanced down one street and then the next, trying to figure out which one led to Dante. A throng of people in suits pressed past me as the walk sign blinked white.

I had to find a way to filter it all out. Letting my hands

drop to my sides, I closed my eyes and concentrated on Dante, remembering the way his presence felt – its weight, its texture, the way it seemed to absorb me...

"Are you okay?" a balding man with a briefcase asked, tapping me on the shoulder.

Frustrated, I brushed him off and closed my eyes. Unbuttoning my cardigan, I let the breeze lap against my chest until everything around me – the cars, the people, the traffic lights and the yelling; the wisps of the dead beckoning me – blurred into white noise.

I found myself outside a looming cathedral, its arches chiselled with saints, their faces darkened by the elements. Running up the steps, I pushed at the doors until they parted with a gasp. Tea lights lined the entrance. A handful of people were scattered about in the pews, their heads bowed. Windows stained the light red, blue, purple, gold. No one looked up when I followed Dante's presence down the left side of the cathedral to an alcove behind the altar.

Dozens of faded tapestries hung from the walls, each displaying an old map. I approached one that illustrated the path from earth to the afterlife, with a square-sailed ship travelling towards a frayed edge and beyond. In the still air of the church, the tapestry billowed.

"Dante?" I whispered, passing my hand over the heavy cloth, the material coarse beneath my fingertips. But it was just a draught that had blown in. I followed the current to a door that opened onto to a lush, tangled cemetery, its walls overgrown with flowering vines.

The wind blew patterns into the yellow grass until it rearranged itself into a path. I took a step, the grass flattening beneath my shoes, and then another, around a dry fountain and towards the corner of the yard, where a boy was bending over a grave.

Stopping behind a tree, I watched him, suddenly nervous. Was it him or someone else? This boy looked older, taller, more like a man – far older than seventeen years. His shoulders curled as if they were too wide for his body; a white-collared shirt stretched over them. His long dark hair was pulled into a messy knot, a stray lock falling in front of his face as he stood up.

Trembling, I waited for him to turn around. And when he did, he was both familiar and strange – his pensive eyes and ashen cheeks as pale and angular as stone – they were all exactly as I remembered, though somehow sad, like a statue that looked all the more beautiful in person.

A branch cracked beneath my foot, and Dante's gaze met mine, his lips forming my name.

"Renée?"

He took a step towards me and then stopped, as if he were too scared to come any closer – as if I weren't real. Suddenly I felt like I was seeing him for the first time; like we were meeting each other all over again in Crude

Sciences, shivering as our fingers touched beneath the table.

After months of feeling numb, of tossing in my sleep and waking up to another day without smells or tastes, without music or laughter or warmth, it seemed impossible that Dante was now here, stepping towards me. And without knowing why or where it was coming from, I started to cry.

Closing my eyes, I let myself collapse into him, feeling his cool skin against mine, my chest rising and falling with his, breathless, as if my soul were flitting in and out of me. "You're here," I said, listening to the irregular sound of his heartbeat. "You're still here."

Quiet, still, we stood like that – one person instead of two. I pulled back and studied his face, touching his nose, his cheeks, his eyelashes – each a vague reminder of someone I had loved in another life. How much time had passed between us?

"You look different," I said, my voice cracking as I stared at his eyes, which almost looked cloudy.

"So do you," he said, wiping my cheek.

Now that I was with him, it was as if a film had been rubbed off. I could smell the garden air, sticky and sweet. I could feel the warmth of the sun on my shoulders. And when I raised my lips to his, I almost felt complete again. He put a finger to my mouth just before we touched.

"How did you know I was here?"

"What?" I asked, confused. "I thought you were—" and that's when I realized he hadn't been waiting for me. I took a step back, hurt. "So you aren't here to see me?"

"Of course I am. Why else would I come to Montreal, where there are hundreds of Monitors searching for me? I just didn't know how to get to you. If I got any closer to St. Clément, I was worried someone would sense me. So I came here, looking for a place for us to meet. I thought a cemetery would help muffle my presence." His eyes wandered across the headstones. "That way if someone sensed me, they would assume it was just the graveyard."

"I felt you," I said softly. "But I don't think the other girls could. Or the doctor."

Dante's face hardened, a wrinkle forming over his eyes. "Doctor? What do you mean?"

I told him everything: about my summer with my grandfather and the doctors; about the way everything seemed dull and meaningless without him; about how I had changed. I told him about my dream of Miss LaBarge and how it came true, and then about the placement test, and history class, and how I'd made a rubbing of something beneath the hospital bed.

When I finished, Dante ran his hand down my face, his eyes worried as he searched me. "Are you okay? Is everything okay now?"

In the distance, a wind chime clinked together, its sound cascading in tiny notes like water droplets falling onto a roof. I nodded and touched his fingers. "Are you? Where have you been? I was so worried."

Instead of answering, Dante pressed on. "What did the doctor say?"

"He gave me some sort of medication that will stop the dreams, but I don't know if I want it. This will probably sound crazy, but I think the dreams might be useful."

Dante gripped my hand. "You're not thinking of—"

"Going to the hospital to see what's under the bed," I whispered, finishing his sentence. "The dream I had before Miss LaBarge died was true. What if this one is too?"

"No," Dante said, his voice abrupt. "You can't."

I shook my head. "Why?"

"Because it isn't safe. You don't know where these dreams are coming from or why you're having them. You just said that you dreamed of Miss LaBarge directly before she died. What would have happened if you had woken up in time to have gone there?"

"I could have saved her."

"Or you could have died too," he said, louder than he intended. Lowering his voice, he pleaded, "I almost lost you last year. I can't risk that again. Please, promise me you won't go to the hospital."

I hesitated. Before I could respond, something rustled

near the back of the cathedral. We both froze, listening to the metal gate of the cemetery creak open and clatter shut.

Before I knew what was happening, Dante led me behind a large headstone beneath the willow tree and pulled me on top of him as we both fell into the grass.

I buried my face in his neck as we waited, listening to the sound of footsteps. "Who is it?" I whispered into Dante's ear as he peered around the side of the stone. He smelled of cedar and dried leaves, of a cold winter night in the woods. Grasping the collar of his shirt, I held him closer. When he turned to me, our lips were centimetres apart. "The groundskeeper," he said, his cool breath mingling with mine.

Dante ran his hand along my back, his hands climbing up the crests of my shoulder blades as the footsteps grew distant. When his fingers grazed the space between my shoulders, a sharp pain shot through my body. Unable to stop myself, I gasped.

"What was that?" Dante said, stopping abruptly. His hand fell to his side.

Just as quickly as the pain had started, it ended. Dante's face was furrowed into a frown. Had he felt it too? "I don't know," I said, trying to compose myself.

Giving me a sceptical look, he slowly placed his palm between my shoulders again. I couldn't help but wince as the same prickling pain shot through my neck. Gently, he took off my cardigan and pulled down the back of my shirt.

"You have a mark here," he said, tracing the lines of my vertebrae. "How long have you had this?"

"I didn't know I had one," I said, his gaze making me uncomfortable. Squirming away from him, I sat up. "It's probably nothing."

"It's not nothing. I have the same ones. Look," he said, and led my hand to the small of his back.

I ran my fingers across his spine until I felt them. Tiny indentations, barely visible, leading all the way up his back. They were as shallow as crease marks left from sleeping too long in the sheets; so subtle that I wasn't surprised I had never noticed them before. Unable to help myself, I pulled my hand away. "What are they?"

Dante touched a freckle on my arm. "I like to think of them as age spots."

"I don't understand."

"I've been getting one every year, on the exact same day. The anniversary of my death."

"The marks count how long you've been dead?"

Dante averted his eyes, as if apologizing for what he was.

Grasping the bottom of his shirt, I pulled it off him, watching his shoulder muscles roll under his skin as he let his arms drop. I reached around him and eased my fingers up his back, counting each mark like a knot in a lifeline. They stopped in the middle of his shoulder blades, one vertebra short of where my mark was.

"There are only sixteen—" I said, and then stopped. I had just turned seventeen, which meant that Dante was missing one spot.

As if reading my mind, he said, "I didn't get one this year."

"What happens when you run out of space?" I asked, placing my hand on his neck, just above the last mark. My fingers fit perfectly.

Dante gazed out at the gravestones peeking through the grass.

Stunned, I pulled away and stared at the space left on Dante's back, counting how many marks could fit. Suddenly I felt weak. Five years. That's how much time he had left.

How do you measure someone's life? By the scope of their accomplishments, or the number of people they've touched, or by the width of a hand? None of it seemed fair. None of it seemed like enough.

"But it doesn't make sense," I said. "Why didn't they just disappear? You became human when you took my soul. And then you gave it back to me, becoming Undead. Doesn't that mean that you should start afresh again, and have another twenty-one years?"

Dante shook his head. "All I know is that I was never fully alive even after you gave me your soul. And you—"

"I'm not, either," I said, my voice cracking. "But I don't understand. Why?"

"We were underground when you gave me your soul; we were both already buried, which made the transfer incomplete."

"Which means what?" I asked, but he didn't reply. "Tell me what you're thinking," I pleaded. "Just because we have the same soul doesn't mean I know what's going on in your head. I'm not inside you. You have to tell me."

Dante let out a sad laugh. "That's just it, though. I think you are."

"What?"

He closed his fingers around my hand, holding my fist in his. It fitted perfectly. "I think a part of your soul is in me now."

I shrank back and raised my hand to my face, my fingers grazing my cheek as if I were touching a stranger. I had spent the entire summer trying not to think about my *symptoms*, as the doctors called them. The small changes I had been noticing in myself. The fact that I barely had an appetite and couldn't sleep like I used to. That I couldn't smell cooked food until it was right in front of me. That I felt severed in some way, as if a piece of me were missing. Could he be right? Is that why my senses were dulled;

why nothing had meaning or beauty until I was around Dante?

"But we still saved each other," I said in awe. "I have one of your marks now, which means that you have one extra year to live. Can't we just keep sharing our soul?"

Dante suddenly looked angry. "And you have one less. Are you suggesting that we kill each other every year?"

I swallowed. When he put it that way, it did sound a little extreme.

"Can you even fathom what that could do to us? What kind of existence that would be? Even after dying once, you've changed more than you know. I can see it in your face, the way you stand, the way you speak."

"What's that supposed to mean?" I said, sitting upright. "Do you think I look *old*?"

He shook his head. "No," he said, his voice softer. "You're surreal." He ran his hand down the pale side of my wrist, feeling my pulse. "I took your life. And now a piece of your soul is gone. It's in *me* now. You're a little more Undead, and I'm a little more alive."

The sun set behind the cathedral, mottling the light around us as though the sky were a stained-glass window. Pulling my knees to my chest, I looked up at him, watching the shadows move across his face as he leaned on the gravestone. "Why is that so bad if it keeps you alive?" I asked quietly.

"Because if we keep sharing our soul, it will only get worse. You'll become more Undead. You'll become wasted and miserable like the rest of us, and then we'll both die."

"But you'll live longer. We'll have more time together," I pleaded, unable to understand why he didn't agree with me.

"At what cost? Neither of us will be fully human. No one has ever done this before. Anything could happen. We could both die the next time we kiss."

"But what else can we do?" Angry tears blurred my vision, and I turned away from him. "You can't die. I don't know what I'd do without you."

"We'll be okay," Dante said, running his hand down my leg. My skin trembled beneath his touch. "We'll keep looking. We'll find a solution."

When I didn't say anything, he took my hand and held it to his chest. "Listen to me," he said. "I won't lose you. I'll find a way."

I nodded, wanting to believe him. Curling up beside him on the grass, I listened to the birds flit through the trees towards the cathedral beyond, its rose windows flickering with candlelight. Voices carried through the cemetery, singing a hymn, and it was the first time in months that I'd heard music and harmony instead of just noise. Dante moved towards me, entwining his limbs with mine as if piecing our broken soul back together. I closed my eyes. As night fell, I pressed my ear against his chest and listened to the irregular rhythm of his heart beating in tandem with mine, the muscles within me stirring with warmth, as if finally awake after a deep slumber.

When the church bells chimed eleven, Dante sat up. "I have to go."

I brushed my hair away from my face. "Why?"

"The Monitors do a sweep of the city every night at midnight. I have to be far away from here when they do." Taking my hand in his, he led me to the gates of the cemetery.

"When will I see you again?" I said as he slipped through to the other side.

He narrowed his eyes as he glanced at the cathedral door behind me, making sure no one could hear us. "It isn't safe for me to stay here, but I'll come back as soon as I can. Two weeks? Maybe sooner. Will you be able to sense me?"

I grasped the iron bars and nodded. "What will you do in the meantime?"

"Try to find a way for us to be together," he said, wrapping his hands around mine.

"Me too," I whispered. Letting my hand slip from his, Dante disappeared into the night.

The walk back to St. Clément seemed much longer than the walk from the school had been. The streets were wide and empty at night, with an occasional smoker loitering outside a bar. I retraced my steps until I made it to the junction by the campus. It was quarter to midnight. I was about to cross the street to the alley that led to St. Clément when a pair of people stole down the pavement, weaving around the street lamps so they wouldn't be seen. I crouched in the shadows beneath an elm tree and watched as they turned left. They were wearing long dark coats that shielded their faces. A few moments later, another pair emerged, followed by another. The Monitor sweep.

I waited while each pair broke off in a different direction. When they had all disappeared, I stepped out to the kerb just as a grey Peugeot pulled up to the traffic light. The driver was a woman with a plain face and dull brown hair, her neck wrapped in a thick knitted scarf.

"Miss LaBarge?" I uttered, watching her face glow red, then green as the light changed. She fiddled with a knob on her dashboard and then looked straight ahead, neglecting to see me.

"Wait!" I yelled, but it was too late. Running into the middle of the street, I watched as her car disappeared around a corner. I caught a glimpse of her licence plate, which was from Quebec, but I didn't see it well enough to commit it to memory. I must have been imagining things, I thought. Miss LaBarge was dead; I saw her coffin drop into the Atlantic Ocean. What was happening to me? I rubbed my eyes, and pulling my gaze away from the spot where the car had been, I ran the rest of the way back to my dormitory.

After I reached my floor, I made the same wrong turn on the way to my room. Spying the broom closet again, I cursed under my breath and was about to turn back when I heard shrieks coming from Anya Pinsky's room. I crept towards it.

The door was cracked open, and inside, Anya was sitting on the floor with her back to me, half sobbing, half screaming into the phone in rapid, high-pitched Russian. Pausing, she took a few deep hysterical breaths, said one last word into the receiver, and then slammed it into its base.

All was still as she caught her breath, hiccupping a few times. Then, without warning, she picked up the phone and threw it across the room. I gasped as it hit the wall.

She whipped around, her face swollen and red. Mascara was smeared across her cheeks. "You," she barked, wiping her face with her sleeve.

The dial tone beeped in the background.

"Come here."

She looked so crazed, it took me a moment to realize

that she was addressing me. Without responding, I turned and started to walk back to my room.

"Why are you always here, lurking at my door?" she said, sticking her head into the hall. "Do you think I want to talk to you?"

I kept walking.

"You think you're interesting or something because you didn't die?"

I took a breath, trying to convince myself it wasn't worth it to turn around.

"Because you had a fit in the middle of class? What's your problem, anyway? Are you some kind of freak?"

I looked down at my hands, and realized they were clenched.

"Why aren't you answering me? Did your parents never teach you English?"

At that I spun around. "I never said I was interesting," I yelled, louder than I meant to. "And of course I can hear you. Everyone can hear you." It felt surprisingly good to shout at someone. Maybe this was what I had needed to do all along. "I don't *lurk* in front of your room. I get lost. And I really don't think you're in a position to be calling anyone a freak."

She glared at me. "What is that supposed to mean?"

I took in her bad dye job, her asymmetrical clothes, and her acrylic nails. "You look ridiculous."

"So do you!" she said, waving her hands wildly. "And you're possessed!"

Catching our breaths, we stood there in silence, unsure of what to do next. Behind me, I could hear a group of girls gathering in the hall.

"A witch arguing with a liar," Clémentine said, as she put a hand on her hip. She was wearing slippers, her short hair held back with a series of bobby pins. The girls behind her started to whisper.

Before I could formulate a response, Anya's voice cut through the hallway. "July thirtieth. Have you forgotten?" she said, her eyes dark and steady. "Because I haven't."

Confused, I glanced at Anya and then at Clémentine, who was glaring back at her. Her friends seemed just as baffled as I was.

Clémentine let out a nervous laugh. "Is that a threat?"

"Yes," Anya said plainly.

"What's she talking about?" Josie, one of Clémentine's friends, asked, her lips thin and pursed in a pout. I recognized her from class.

Clémentine began to look uncomfortable. Prying her eyes away from Anya, she turned to her friends. "I have no idea," she said, though I could tell that wasn't true. "Come on, let's go."

After everyone had left, I turned to Anya. "What was that? July thirtieth?"

"Oh, nothing," she said, her face bearing the hint of a smile. "Just a little secret of Clémentine's that I happened to stumble across this summer."

"You're blackmailing her?"

"No," Anya said, a tiny wrinkle forming on her forehead. "I'm not asking for anything in return. Only that she leave me alone."

"But isn't that still—"

Anya cut me off. "Do you really think I look ridiculous?" Curling a lock of red hair around her finger, she studied me.

I considered how to answer. "No," I said, lying.

She gave me a sceptical look. "Why did you say it, then?"

"I was angry."

She wiped her cheek, smearing the mascara even more. "So you're apologizing?"

Her words caught me off guard. "No," I said. "Not until you apologize to me."

"But you insulted me first," she insisted, as if it were the truth.

I shook my head in disbelief. "That's not how I remember it."

"Fine. I'm sorry," she said, so quickly I could barely catch it. "Now you have to come inside."

"What? Why?"

"Because I apologized first, so now you have to make it up to me."

"I don't have to make anything up to you," I said, confused.

"You don't have to be rude about it," Anya said. "I'm not going to hurt you. I just need some help."

I hesitated, listening to Clémentine's melodic voice down the hall. "Help doing what?"

She waved her hand. "Oh, just something really small."

Anya's room was dingy and cluttered with charms and feathers and an odd collection of talismans. A few posters dotted the walls, but they all seemed a little off, either too small or poorly placed. One of the overhead light bulbs had gone out. To make up for it, Anya had lit a tall red candle encased in glass with a stencil of the Virgin Mary. A single cross hung over her bed. It was draped in neon beads.

I sat on the edge of the bed. "What exactly do you want me to do?" I said, fingering a string of charms hanging from her bedpost.

"Hold on," Anya said, sifting through her desk drawer until she found a pocket sewing kit. "Why did you collapse this morning?" she asked as she removed a needle from the kit and held it in the flame of the candle.

"I don't know," I said, not wanting to divulge that I had hallucinated.

"Come on. I'm not stupid," she said, handing me the needle. "Hold this for a minute."

"I don't want to talk about it," I said, taking the needle from her.

She opened her closet door and rummaged through her shoes until she found a chunky platform. "I already think you're weird, so it's not like anything you tell me will make me think worse of you. And don't even try to trick me with that cheating death story. I don't believe any of it."

After wiping the lobe with rubbing alcohol, she placed the platform shoe just behind her ear. "Hold this right here," she said, and I put my hands where hers had been. I was surprised at how relieved I felt, hearing those words. *I don't believe any of it.*

"Did it look that bad?" I asked.

"You fell off your chair, and then you started blinking. You were just blinking really fast for a long time."

I winced.

Anya bent down and took an ice cube from a miniature refrigerator on the floor. She rubbed it against her ear. "Don't worry," she said. "I've seen worse, but everyone else basically thinks you're possessed."

"Maybe I am."

Tossing the ice on the floor, Anya took the needle from me and shook her head. "I don't think so. Have you ever

136

seen a possessed person?" she asked, as if she had. "You're too normal."

Looking in the mirror, Anya held the needle up to her ear, where there were already four piercings. "Okay," she said. "Hold the shoe steady."

"Wait, what are you doing?"

"Piercing my ear," she said.

I backed away. "No. I'm not doing that."

"How do you expect to bury an Undead when you can't even watch me use a needle?" she said, and put my hand back into place. "You're not doing anything – I'm doing it. It'll be over in a minute. Just hold your hand steady."

"Are you sure this is safe?" I said as I tightened my grip on the shoe.

"Of course it is."

I braced myself, trying to stop my hand from trembling as I watched her in the mirror, her eyes red and fierce. She took a deep breath and began counting in Russian. "*Raz, dva. . .*" Just before she said "*tri,*" I pressed my eyes closed. The needle plunged into the sole of the shoe, and the entire room rang as Anya let out a deafening, high-pitched scream.

After the bleeding stopped and the silver cuff was in place, Anya opened a tin of almond cookies her father had sent her, and we sat on her shag carpet eating them until we were giddy on sugar. She tried to explain why she had been so upset earlier, speaking quickly in jarring bursts, and by the time she was finished, I still wasn't exactly sure what had transpired. Something to do with a boyfriend, or maybe an ex-boyfriend, and two other boys. One named Vlad, two named Dmitri. Or was it one named Dmitri, two named Vlad? They were Plebeians, unaware of the Undead, which meant that Anya couldn't tell them she was a Monitor. When she left for school, it made things a little complicated.

"I have a piercing for every break-up," she said, pointing to the line of studs in each ear.

I told her I understood, because I did. It wasn't easy dating someone when you were a Monitor.

"But how can you understand?" she said, fingering the new silver cuff that clung to her ear, which was now bright red and swollen. "Do you have a boyfriend?"

I hesitated. "No," I said slowly, taking another cookie.

She rolled her eyes. "Is he a Monitor?"

I paused again. "I can't really talk about it."

When she kept pressing me, I changed the subject to my blackout, and the dream I'd had of the Royal Victoria Hospital. Or the vision, as she called it.

"What was under the bed?" she asked.

"I don't know. I couldn't see it."

Anya looked disappointed.

"What if I'm seeing the future?"

She gave me a questioning look, and when she saw that I was serious, she burst out laughing. "I know people who can read the future, and you definitely can't."

"How do you know?" I said, taking offence.

"What's going to happen to me tomorrow?" she asked, her lips in a pout.

"It doesn't work like that."

"Oh?" she said, smug. "How does it work, then?"

"I think it was triggered by the photograph of the hospital."

"So you just have to see a picture of the future before it comes to you," she said sarcastically.

I rolled my eyes.

"If you want to see your future, I know a woman who can do that. She'll tell you what the visions are."

I leaned back against the wall. "I don't believe in that kind of stuff," I said, dismissing her.

Anya laughed. "How can you say you don't believe when you just thought *you* were seeing the future?"

"That's different," I said. I had been reborn, but I was now a little Undead. I didn't know how that future was going to affect me, but maybe this was it. The Undead reanimate as the best versions of themselves. Wasn't I prettier now, my features more mature? Wasn't I a better Monitor? Maybe I could see the future, too. "That's believing in myself."

It was nearly two in the morning when I returned to my room. I still couldn't get used to the fact that there was no curfew at St. Clément. Madame Goût was the girls' dorm parent, but her primary rule was that we didn't bother her. Otherwise, we could do whatever we wanted. While I brushed my teeth, I took off my shirt and examined the mark on my back in the bathroom mirror. If I raised my shoulders in just the right way, it almost looked like Dante's silhouette.

Before I knew what was happening, the door leading into the adjacent room burst open, and Clémentine barged inside, unaware that the bathroom was occupied. Letting the toothbrush fall to the floor, I grabbed my shirt and jumped back, trying to cover myself with my arms.

"Oh," she said, letting out a laugh as she looked at me. She was wearing a tight camisole, her face delicate now that it was stripped of make-up. "What were you doing?"

"Get out!" I cried.

"Smart enough to rank number one, but not smart enough to lock the door," she said, backing away.

I caught a glimpse of her room: dimly lit and velvety like a boudoir. A group of girls were splayed across her canopied bed, giggling. With force, I slammed the door shut.

CHAPTER 5

THE PROPHECY

SOUL SHARING DOES NOT EXIST. A soul may only inhabit one body at a time.

After days of searching through the narrow stacks of the St. Clément library for anything that might save Dante, it was the only answer I could find. Shutting that book, I pulled a thicker one off the shelf, entitled *The Art of Dying*, which the cover described as "*The most comprehensive study of death and its aftermath in current publication*". Checking the index, I flipped to the section on *Souls* and skimmed the page until I found the entry I was looking for.

Soul splitting does not exist. To split one's soul is to kill one's self.

Frustrated, I shut the book and shoved it back on the shelf. We were never going to find a solution. Sliding to the floor, I rubbed my face with my hands. The reality was this: I was searching for an antidote to death. I laughed at the irony that everyone thought I was immortal, when here I was, sitting on the floor of the library, trying to find the answer to immortality in a book. As if it were that easy.

I spread my fingers on the floor, imagining the wood was Dante's back. Four. That was how long he had left to live. Across the room, I heard a chair scrape the wood as someone sat down. I looked up to see Clémentine unpacking her books from her bag. She was alone and hadn't seen me. Quietly, I put the books back on the shelf and crept towards the exit.

It wasn't until the end of the week that I woke with the sickening suspicion that I had forgotten something. Sitting up in bed, I looked at the clock. It was eight in the morning. I wasn't late for class and I hadn't missed any assignments. I didn't have any plans or any friends, I thought miserably, except for Anya, who wasn't really a friend at all; and I wasn't supposed to see Dante for another week. The only other person I knew here was Dr. Newhaus... That's when I remembered.

Kicking back the covers, I jumped out of bed and threw on whatever clothes were lying around my room. And without looking in the mirror, I ran across campus.

The headmaster's office was in the main building, above the school archway. I walked down the hallway, my feet sinking into the plush carpet as I studied the old sketches of Montreal that hung on the walls. Dozens of boats and barges speckled the river and canals.

Between two sketches stood a lacquered wooden door with a nameplate that said: HEADMASTER JOHN LAGUERRE. I knocked, and when no one answered, I sat on a wooden bench in the hall.

Just then Headmaster LaGuerre opened the door. "Renée?" he said, looking at me.

I stood up and he smiled, baring impressively white teeth. "And here I was thinking you'd forgotten about me."

"Headmaster LaGuerre, I'm so sorry," I said. "I know it's early, but I only just remembered that you had asked me to come to your office, and I thought I should come immediately. I'm sorry I didn't make it sooner."

"That's quite all right," he said, and held out his hand. "Call me John. Please, come in."

He motioned to a green leather chair. "Have a seat." Up close, he was soft spoken, his accent gentle and less pronounced. "I heard you fell ill?"

"I'm fine now," I said, trying to smooth out the wrinkles in my skirt.

"Good," he said, unbuttoning his suit jacket as he sat down. "Good. So how are you liking St. Clément?"

I sat on my hands. "It's okay."

"My daughter, Clémentine, told me you'd met."

"Oh," I said, surprised she had mentioned me. "I guess we did."

Clasping his hands in front of his mouth, he studied me, and then laughed. "Why so timid?"

"You don't have any cats, do you?" I asked, glancing around his office, which, admittedly, looked nothing like Headmistress Von Laark's. It was a sunny alcove, finished with blond wood and floorboards worn smooth with time. The window sills held overgrown leafy plants, which, if I stretched my imagination, almost seemed to give off the faint smell of mint.

He gave me an amused look. "No. Why do you ask?"

"Because…" I said, glancing across his desk until I spotted a school folder, which had the crest of a cat. "Because it's the St. Clément mascot."

He shook his head. "To be honest, I'm actually very allergic. But that's between you and me. If the administration finds out, they might give me the boot." He winked and leaned forward, sifting through his documents until he found a piece of paper.

"The other day, when everyone was taking the placement exam, I stepped in to take a look. You were the only one in the gymnasium other than Madam Goût and Mr. Pollet. I observed you. You were standing in the middle of the gymnasium, writing."

He pushed the sheet of paper across the desk. It was the map I had marked up, identifying eight out of the nine animals.

"This is incredible," he said.

I felt my face turn red. Was it?

"I'm sorry," he said. "I'm making you uncomfortable. Let me explain. I called you in here to congratulate you because of your class rank. Though, to be honest, after watching you, and studying your results, the title of top rank doesn't even do you justice. The ability to locate death without moving, without taking a *single* step." He placed his finger at the centre of my map. "That is an ability that many of us strive for, but few ever achieve, even after years of training. How did you do it?"

How *had* I done it? I thought it might have had something to do with my being a little Undead, with my being a better version of myself, but that still didn't explain *how* I did it. At Gottfried, I had been at the top of my Horticulture class, and it was there my Monitor skills were first identified. But I never used to feel the air parting into a path, nor could I map the exact location of a dead thing without actually seeing it. I would just wander stupidly in one direction, where I would stumble across a dead animal and embarrass myself by screaming. Now it was different. It was as if the dead animals were items I had lost, and all I had to do was mentally retrace my steps to remember where I had put them. Only, I'd never known where they were in the first place. "I – I—"

The headmaster laughed. "Don't look so scared. I'm not expecting an answer. I just wanted to meet the girl who could map death."

I gave him an embarrassed smile. "I hope I haven't disappointed you."

A wrinkle formed between the headmaster's eyebrows. "Of course not," he said, and stood up. "Well, thank you for taking the time to meet with me."

I picked up my bag and made for the door, but then stopped. "May I ask you a question?"

"By all means."

"What was the last animal on the test?"

Headmaster LaGuerre crossed his hands. "A canary."

I must have looked confused, because he asked, "Is something wrong?"

"I don't understand. How did I rank first if I couldn't even identify all of the animals?"

"Because that would have been impossible," he said. "A canary has the lightest soul of all animals. Its soul is fragile, hollow, like its bones. It dies so quickly and so suddenly that it seems to barely have any life at all. It's as if it isn't even *present* in this world. No Monitor has ever been known to identify one correctly. The fact that you could detect its location was extremely impressive."

I broke his gaze, not sure how to respond to his compliment. I didn't feel very impressive, just confused.

A breeze blew in through the window, rustling the papers on the headmaster's desk. "You were the only one who made it past the fifth animal," he said, studying me as if he were trying to figure me out. "Most students only identified three before the time was up. Does that answer your question?"

A canary? I repeated in my head, remembering how I had blurted out that word on the aeroplane without knowing why. Was it a coincidence that the canary was the last animal on the test? No, I thought. Impossible.

"Is there something else?" The headmaster probed.

I shook my head. "Yes. I mean, no," I said, and forced a smile. "Thank you."

When I got back to my room, Anya was waiting outside my door, looking annoyed. She was dressed in a tight little ensemble that was more nightclub than dress code. Her red hair was pulled into two loose braids, her dull roots showing along her parting.

"Why aren't you ready?" she asked, taking in my haphazard outfit.

I fumbled with my keys. "Ready for what?"

"Seeing your future," she said, adjusting her purse, which was covered in tassels.

"Today? But I have to go to class."

"Yes, today," she said in disbelief. "And we don't have class. It's Saturday."

I glanced at my watch. So it was.

"So? Are we going?"

I was pretty sure we had never made plans, but no matter. It's not like I had anything better to do. "Okay."

The woman Anya knew lived in Mile End, the neighbourhood where Anya grew up. We travelled there by foot, winding through the city streets until we passed Mont Royal, the mountain looming at the centre of Montreal, swallowing the west side of the city in its shadow.

It was a hazy morning, the sky a thick orange as Anya led the way. We chatted as we walked. She was born in Russia but had been living in Montreal since she was ten. Her father ran a drugstore, and she used to help out on the weekends, stocking the shelves. That was where she first learned how to put on make-up and dye her hair, by "borrowing" items from her father's shelves.

Even though she had been at St. Clément for two years now, she had few friends there. "I have my own people. Russian people," she explained. But the way she talked about them was the same way I talked about everyone I'd once known in California: as if they didn't exist any more. They were in a different world, a world that didn't include Monitors and the Undead, and I couldn't tell them who I was or what I was doing.

Anya and I turned down a curved street lined with buildings that looked like tenement houses. The people who passed us on the pavement all seemed to be speaking Russian. "It's across from my hairdresser," Anya said. "See, there." She pointed to a weathered brick building streaked with water stains. Over the entrance was a sign in huge Russian print. Anya held the door for me, and I stepped inside. It was a spice shop. The dusty trail of cloves and nutmeg and paprika tickled my nose. Anya said something in Russian to the man behind the counter, who seemed to know her. He smiled as he responded, giving us each a honey stick before letting us through a back door that led to the rest of the building.

We walked up four flights of stairs until we reached an apartment with an etching of an eye on the door. "This is it," Anya said, and rang the buzzer. No one answered. Anya rang it again, and tried to peer through the peephole.

"Maybe she's out," I said, cringing as Anya knocked and then held down the buzzer.

"No, they're here. They're always here."

Moments later, we heard heavy footsteps in the hall, followed by the clicking sound of dead bolts unlatching. When it swung open, a hairy, middle-aged man wearing an undershirt stood there, appraising us. Anya said something to him in Russian. He looked at me, back at her, and then promptly shut the door.

"Zinyochka!" I heard him bellow within.

"What did he say?" I asked.

"We have to wait here for her to come meet us. If she decides to see us, she'll let us in. If not, we have to go."

While we waited, I peered out the tiny window in the staircase. A tall boy my age was wandering down the pavement below us, his broad shoulders moving beneath his collared shirt as he stepped into the street. "Dante?" I breathed, and stepped down a stair.

"What are you looking at?" Anya said.

I barely heard her as I watched the boy hail a taxi. Just before he ducked inside, he looked up. I pressed myself to the wall. It definitely wasn't Dante.

Before Anya could ask me anything, the apartment door opened, and a woman appeared in the entryway. She was thick-boned, with thinning hair and a heavy bosom. "Yes?" she said, her voice deep. Her hands were stained

150

a blotchy red. She wiped them on her apron.

Anya spoke to her in Russian. After she was finished, the woman looked me up and down. "Why have you come to see me?" she said with a thick accent.

"I've been having dreams that I think might be premonitions," I said softly.

The woman squinted at me. "Give me your hands."

After hesitating, I placed them in hers. She squeezed them as if giving me a massage, her fingers moist and strong. Letting my hands drop, the woman said something to Anya in Russian, and disappeared inside.

"She said okay," Anya translated, and together we followed the woman into the apartment.

The hall was dark and carpeted, with smudged windows that looked out on a fire escape and a brick wall. It stank of meat. We walked to the back of the apartment, through a maze of little rooms – one with a boy watching television, another with a sewing machine and two mannequins stuck with pins – until we made it to the dining room.

Zinya supported her weight on the back of a chair. "Will cost forty dollars. Okay?"

Anya dropped her bag on the floor, and with wild gesticulations she spouted a torrent of Russian words, which came out so quickly, I was surprised even Zinya could understand them. After haggling, Zinya finally turned to me and said, "Twenty."

I nodded.

A fly buzzed around the windows. Without warning, Zinya picked up a swatter and killed it. "Only one at a time," she continued, as it slid down the glass, leaving a brown streak.

"You go," Anya said, examining a set of porcelain figurines with distaste. When I hesitated, she repeated, "Go on."

I followed Zinya into the kitchen, which had a dingy linoleum floor and a ceiling fan. "Wash your hands," she said, sitting at a round table.

By the sink was a tub of beetroot soaking in water, and a coagulated bar of soap. I turned on the tap. Above it hung a black-and-white photograph of a rigid old couple.

"I tell you three things," Zinya said from behind me. "One about past. One about present. One about future. But nothing more. Past, present and future, they are always connected." She waved a hand. "Always. You understand?"

I didn't actually understand, but nodded anyway. What else was I supposed to do?

"Now choose a beetroot," she said, motioning to the tub.

Fruit flies circled around it. I waved them away, and after some hesitation, plunged my hand into the tepid water and selected a small, irregular bulb. It was warm, as if it had just been boiled. I brought it to the table, where there was a box of parchment paper and a bowl. Zinya pushed the bowl towards me. "Now peel."

I stared at the dirty beetroot in my hand, confused. I didn't even have a knife. "I'm supposed to peel this?"

She nodded as if it were completely natural.

"Right." I turned the beetroot in my palm, trying to find a good place to start.

It was a messy ordeal, the juice dripping down my arms as I inexpertly took off huge hunks of beetroot skin and tossed them into a bowl until I was left with the slippery, round interior.

"Good," Zinya said. "Good."

When I was finished, she laid out a piece of paper on the table beneath me. "Squeeze beetroot over sheet."

I did as she said. Dark pink syrup ran down the sides of my palms and dripped onto the paper.

Pushing my hands away, Zinya picked up the paper and folded it in half, pressing it down with her thick fingers as if she were kneading dough.

Setting it aside, she had me squeeze the beetroot over two other pieces of paper. I watched as she worked each sheet, folding them over and over, compressing them with her palm until there were three tight squares on the table in front of me.

"Past." She unfolded the first paper. It was coloured with a swirled pattern that almost looked like waves. She spread out the creases and turned it around, then grunted and turned it around again, tracing a smeared mark near the bottom of the page.

Shifting uncomfortably in her seat, she looked up. Her expression was different as she scrutinized me, as if she had seen something in my face that she hadn't expected. "Past is very dark."

I sat back in my chair, unimpressed. It was so vague that it could have applied to anyone.

She traced a shape in the middle of the stain. "There is woman in boat. You chase her." Zinya looked to me for confirmation.

I became alert. "Yes."

"You take her weapon, drop it in water. Could not protect herself. She die."

I felt so stunned that I couldn't move. Even in her broken English, Zinya's words had thrust me back into that hellish night, which was still so crisp in my memory that it could have been real. I felt the water, cool and still against my lips; I saw the fog part as Miss LaBarge swung the shovel down over my head; I felt the splintered wood of its handle as I pulled it from her grasp and dropped it, watching it sink into the black water of the lake. Could Zinya be right? Did Miss LaBarge die because her weapon was taken away? Could I have saved her? Leaning over, I looked at the marks on the paper, trying to see what she saw, but it was nothing but pink swirls to me.

Zinya rested her fleshy elbows on the table. When she looked up at me, her eyes were wet and somehow understanding. "We can stop if you like."

Sitting on my hands, I shook my head. She unfolded the second paper. "Present."

It revealed a series of concentric ovals, wobbly and smeared from the folds. She squinted at the page. "Your dreams. They are not future. They are now. Present."

A fly buzzed around the bowl on the table. Zinya shooed it away as I processed what she'd said. In my dreams, I wasn't seeing the future, I was seeing the present. But why? That meant that I never could have saved Miss LaBarge. That regardless of what I saw in my visions, I was helpless; I couldn't change them. What was the point?

Zinya unfolded the third square of paper and flattened it on the table. "Future."

The pattern was divided in half by a winding line. One side was completely white; the other was a mess of red dots that were smeared and splattered like blood. When Zinya saw it, her face grew pinched. She didn't say anything for a long time.

Finally, I cut in. "What is it?" I said, my voice frantic. "What does it say?"

"In your dreams, you are searching for something," she said, following the line travelling down the middle of the page. "If you follow, will end in death." She covered the clean half of the paper. "And life," she said, removing her hand.

My eyes darted across the two halves of the paper. "Death *and* life? It can't be both. Which one is it? Which one will it end in?"

She pointed to the bottom of the page, where the trail forked off to either side. "This is what is written."

"So what am I supposed to do?" I said, my chair scraping the floor as I collapsed back, frustrated. "Should I follow the visions or not?"

"Depends if you want to find what they lead to."

"What do you mean? What do they lead to?"

Wiping her hands on her apron, she hoisted herself up. "The answer to your soul."

I must have looked spooked when we left, because after Anya came out from her reading with Zinya, she stared at me for a long time before leading me outside in silence. "What did she say to you?" she said finally. We were walking back to school, down a brick street lined with tiny storefronts.

"She knew things that no one could have known," I

said, speaking to myself more than to Anya. "She knew about Miss LaBarge."

"I told you she was the real thing."

"She knew about my vision," I murmured to myself. "About the shovel."

Anya gave me a puzzled look. "What shovel?"

I barely even registered her question. "She said my visions were in the present. Which means I'm not seeing the future."

"I knew it. Didn't I tell you that?"

"She said that if I follow them, I'll find life *and* death."

Anya froze. "You might die?" she said, so loud that a couple walking in front of us turned around.

"Shh!" I said, though I wasn't sure who I was worried would hear me. Down the street was a quiet cafe. "Come on," I said, and pulled her behind me.

Inside it was warm and comfortably vacant, save for a few crouched men reading newspapers to the sound of grinding coffee. At the counter, I ordered a large tea and sat at a table in the back corner while Anya picked out a plate of biscotti.

"So you might die?" Anya repeated, after sitting down across from me.

"Zinya said I would meet *both* life and death. But that the visions will lead to the answer to my soul."

"What does that mean?"

Dante, I thought, my heart skipping as it came to life. She must have meant that the visions will lead to an answer for me and Dante to be together. But did she mean that one of us would meet life and the other, death? "I don't know. Do you think she meant the life and death part literally? That I would die and live?"

"She's a peasant. Everything is literal with her."

I traced the rim of my saucer, thinking about the visions. Something within me screamed, *Follow them!* It was the only thing that made sense: to see where they led me. Otherwise, I would never know. But what if Dante was right? What if they were dangerous?

"Who's Dante?" Anya asked, disrupting my thoughts.

"What?"

She broke a piece of biscotti in half, the crumbs sticking to the side of her mouth as she nibbled on an end. "You just said, 'What if Dante was right?'"

I frowned. I hadn't realized I was speaking out loud.

Anya licked the tips of her fingers. "Is he your boyfriend?"

"I – um – no, just friends," I said, worried that if word got back to my grandfather or any of the Monitors that Dante and I were still together, they would bury him.

"I like that name," she said.

"What do you know about the Royal Victoria Hospital?" I asked, trying to direct the conversation back to Zinya.

"Dante," Anya said, letting his name roll off her tongue. "Where do I know that name from?"

I coughed, choking on my tea, when I realized that she probably knew his name from hearing rumours about what happened last spring at Gottfried.

Anya stopped chewing. "Oh my god. That's who you're dating?"

I wiped my mouth with a napkin. "I – um – no."

"It's true," she said in awe. "You still see him. But how? It's so dangerous here." When I didn't say anything, Anya moved her chair closer. "Are the rumours true? Did he really plot to kill the headmistress?"

Worried my expression would betray my thoughts, I looked down at my biscotti, which I had broken up into crumbs. I hadn't told anyone what had really happened that night last spring, except Eleanor. I'd always liked having secrets, the kind I told my best friends under the covers with a flashlight. It was like I was spilling a part of myself into them, and for ever after we were connected. I now understood that *real* secrets were lonely. They planted themselves inside of you and expanded, until you felt like that was all you were – a lonely little secret, isolated in your experiences. "He didn't kill the headmistress, but other than that, I can't talk about it," I said. "I wish I could."

Anya studied me as if reading the true answer on my

face, and then sank back in her chair. "Don't worry," she said. "I won't tell anyone."

"Thanks," I said softly, watching the steam rise from my mug.

Anya paused for a moment and then clasped her hands on the table. "So what about your visions, then? Should we figure out a way to follow them?"

"I have to think about it," I said. Dante's voice echoed in my head, asking me to promise not to endanger myself. "What if it's exactly the opposite, and the dreams are actually a warning? What if I'm seeing them to tell me what I should be *avoiding*?"

Anya rolled her eyes as she put on her coat. "You dreamed of a bed in the Royal Victoria Hospital. What could be a safer place than that?"

She had a point. As we stepped out into the street, I turned to her. "Wait. I never even asked what Zinya told *you*."

Anya hesitated, and then began fidgeting with a tassel on her bag. "It's bad luck to tell someone else your fortune."

"But you didn't say anything about that when I told you mine—" I started to say, but Anya cut me off.

"I'm not telling you, Renée. It's bad luck." She pushed a red wisp of hair away from her face. "Maybe later I'll change my mind."

* * *

160

We didn't make it to the hospital for another week. As classes picked up, Anya and I were too busy with schoolwork to plan anything, and we decided to postpone our trip to the weekend. In the meantime, I waited, keeping my window open each evening, but the days and nights passed without a sign of Dante.

Before class on Monday I traced my finger around the perimeter of the mark on my back, twisting in front of the mirror to study the way its edges grew pink after a hot shower. I liked to know it was still there, to be reminded that a part of Dante was within me. After getting dressed, I walked two blocks away from campus to the *dépanneur*, a convenience store, where I picked up a copy of the daily newspaper and scoured the pages, searching for deaths, disappearances, mysterious sightings – anything that might have to do with the Undead. And even though I knew that if Dante had been discovered and buried by the Monitors, it wouldn't be in any newspaper, it made me feel better just to look.

A boy held the door for me when I got to Latin. "Thanks," I murmured, barely looking at him as I took a seat at the far end of the table. Just as I shoved the paper beneath the table, leaving it open at the obituaries so I could read when the professor wasn't looking, I heard a voice behind me.

"Any news from the outside?"

Brett pulled out the chair next to me and slung his blazer over the back. From his expression, I knew he was talking about Dante.

"No," I said, giving him a sad smile.

"I haven't talked to you in a while," he said, lowering his voice. "How is everything going?"

I shrugged. "I've been better."

"Yeah. I hear the girls gossiping at dinner. I wouldn't listen to them, though. People here, they don't know what it's like. Most of them have never even met an Undead. Just keep your head down and do what you have to do. Everything else will take care of itself."

"Thanks," I said, appreciating his words more than he knew.

Monsieur Orneaux, our Latin professor, was already seated at the head of the table, his back upright, his eyes dark and heavy. He was a gaunt man with hollowed cheeks and a rigid expression that rarely changed, regardless of what mood he was in. He seemed to dislike everyone, but held a particularly vehement disdain for women.

"Latin is a calculated language. A language of strategy, of ancient wars, of pagan gods and sacrifice, and later, of the clergy. It is a language that has always belonged to the afterlife." He had a way of drawing out each syllable, as if the words had turned sour in his mouth. "And as the language, so its people. The Undead are a miserable lot."

I didn't think I had to pay attention because, unlike last year, I was now practically fluent in Latin. I found myself knowing vocabulary I had never learned before; conjugating verbs without even having to think. So instead, I glanced down at the newspaper on top of my bag and skimmed an article on the deaths of two tourists in British Columbia.

The professor interrupted my thoughts. "What do the Undead fear most?"

As the class fell silent, a shudder crept through my body. All at once I felt cold and sweaty, my heart palpitating against my ribs, its beat quick and irregular. Fear – it was in me, overwhelming me, as if I knew what the professor was talking about...

"Hey, are you okay?" Brett whispered to me. "You look kind of pale."

Before I realized what I was doing, I blurted out the answer. "The Île des Soeurs."

All heads turned in my direction. Confused, I slid lower in my chair. What had I just said? Something in French? I barely even knew French, and whatever phrase I had said was one I had never known before.

Monsieur Orneaux studied me. "What did you say?"

I pulled at the neck of my shirt, which suddenly felt damp and far too tight. "I – I can't remember," I said. The words I had just spoken were gone, as if someone else had said them.

Across the room, Clémentine answered, an eyebrow raised as if challenging me. "She said, 'the Île des Soeurs'."

The professor studied me. "That is correct."

"What is it?" Brett asked, looking at me and then at the professor. I let my hair fall across my face, not wanting to reveal that I had no idea what I meant.

"It's the island just outside of—" Arielle began to answer, but Monsieur Orneaux held up a hand to silence her.

"Island of the Sisters, to Monitors," Monsieur Orneaux translated, "Or Nuns' Island, to regular Canadians. It is an island just outside of Montreal, known in Monitor history as the place where they used to send the Undead to be punished.

"It was a barbaric place. Run solely by female Monitors, who operated out of an old convent. They did terrible things. Torture, seclusion, exorcism. They bled the Undead with leeches, they probed them with medical equipment in an attempt to cure them of their evil..." Monsieur Orneaux's face remained utterly calm as he recounted all the ways the early Monitors attempted to "cure" the Undead.

"It has a reputation among the Undead, though few Monitors are aware of it." His eyes met mine, as if trying to understand how I had known the answer. "It's one of the reasons why the Undead rarely come to Montreal. Along with, of course, the fact that Montreal is historically a Monitor's city."

"I've heard of it," a boy with a French accent said. "The convent is still there; it's now abandoned. In primary school there used to be a rumour that it was haunted, though I never knew why. The story was that any child who passed through the gates would disappear for ever. We used to dare each other to go inside—"

Monsieur Orneaux cut him off. "That's enough. This is not a history course."

He was about to return to his lecture on Latin and what it told us about the Undead when Clémentine raised her hand. Monsieur Orneaux ignored her until she finally just spoke up.

"Why was it run only by female Monitors?" she asked, holding the end of her pencil up to her lips.

Monsieur Orneaux clenched his jaw. "Female Monitors are not my area of expertise. If you're interested in the Nine Sisters, go to the library in your free time."

Clémentine's back went rigid. "What do you mean, the Nine Sisters?"

Monsieur Orneaux blinked, looking like he wished he could take back his last words. "That's enough," he said again, raising his voice for the first time. "Latin. Back to Latin."

And picking up his class notes, he continued his

lecture on roots and verbs and declensions, the Undead, and how the way they spoke could teach us about how they behaved.

I spent the rest of the afternoon gazing out the windows of my various classes, hoping I would sense Dante.

"When you restrain an Undead, the most important step is to protect your mouth," Headmaster LaGuerre said in Strategy and Prediction, during a lecture about the art of burial. On the board he had drawn a series of diagrams of a Monitor attacking an Undead from behind, pinning him to the ground as he secured his arms and legs, and finally wrapping his head with gauze to prevent a kiss. On each of them, I mentally superimposed Dante's head, and shuddered. How could everyone else in the room be taking notes on this? Didn't they realize we were learning how to kill people?

"Renée?" Headmaster LaGuerre said. "Do you know what the primary cause of Monitor death is?"

Sitting up straight, I felt my cheeks flush. "I – um – no."

"Trying to speak to the Undead in the process of burial," Clémentine said, shooting me a smug grin.

I don't belong here, I thought. I don't belong here.

When the last bell rang, I made my way downstairs and

through the school gates. I had hours of homework to do, but I didn't care. I wasn't sure where I was going, exactly, only that St. Clément was the last place I would find Dante, which meant that if I wanted to see him, my best chance would be out in the city.

I only made it a few blocks before I caught a glimpse of a grey Peugeot, just like the one I'd seen Miss LaBarge in the other night. Or someone who I thought was Miss LaBarge.

"Wait!" I said, watching as the car turned down the street ahead of me. I pushed through the people on the pavement.

It all happened before I could move out of the way. I stepped onto the crossing, not realizing the light was still red. From the kerb, an old woman yelled at me to stop. The brakes of a car squealed, muffling her voice, and I turned just in time to see something metal hurl itself towards me. This is it, I thought; just as Zinya predicted. I am going to die before I can even say goodbye to Dante.

A sharp pain shot up my right side as a bicycle and a bouquet of flowers flew into the air. Covering my face, I fell over and landed on something soft.

After a long moment, I sat up. To my surprise, the ground beneath me groaned.

I was lying on top of a boy. A tall, lean boy. I looked closer. A cute boy. Yellow daffodils were crushed into the ground around us. He groaned again, and I jumped off him.

"Are you all right?" he said, wincing as he looked at his palms, which were scraped from the pavement. His bicycle was a few metres away, its front wheel still spinning.

I nodded. Save for what was probably going to be a big bruise on my right thigh, I was fine.

The boy's eyes travelled up to mine. He was clean-shaven, with olive skin and hair that reminded me of the best months of autumn. He wore a rectangular pair of glasses that made him look like a college student. "You saved my life," he said, with a slight French accent.

"I'm so sorry."

"About saving my life?" He smiled. He had three artfully placed freckles. One under his eye, one on his chin, one on his neck.

"Oh – oh, no," I said. "Wait, what do you mean?"

"I didn't see the red light. If you hadn't blocked me, I would have run it and been hit by that car."

"Oh," I said, blushing. "It was an accident."

He laughed and helped me up.

"You're warm," I said, accustomed to Dante's coldness.

He took me in. "You're the girl who can't die."

"You go to St. Clément?" I asked, surprised.

"I sit three seats down from you in Strategy and

168

Prediction. And in History and Latin. I held the door for you today?"

"Oh." I felt my face grow red as his features grew familiar. I was used to seeing only the side of his head.

He smirked. "It's okay. You're the famous one."

I looked away and brushed off my skirt. "Those are just rumours."

"Or maybe some of your immortality just rubbed off on me."

I smiled. "Then I guess you owe me one."

"Owe you one what?"

"I won't know until I want it." The words came out of my mouth automatically. What was I saying? Was I flirting with this boy?

"Deal."

"I'm Renée, by the way," I said.

"Noah Fontaine."

He held out his hand, and I hesitated, staring at it and thinking of Dante. "Oh, I'm sorry," he said, looking at his scratches and then wiping his hand on his jeans.

I looked at my feet and fidgeted with the buttons on my sleeve.

Bending down, he picked up his bag and the remains of the bouquet of flowers he had been carrying, which had spilled out around us, coating the road in crushed petals.

"I'm sorry about your flowers," I said.

"Oh, it's okay. She probably won't even notice," he said, holding up a wilted stem.

And even though I had no idea this boy existed until a few seconds ago, for some reason, as I watched him collect the loose flowers, my heart sank imagining the girl he had bought them for.

He stood up. "Do you believe in fate?" he asked.

"No," I said quickly, and then reconsidered. "Well, maybe."

"My thoughts exactly," he said. And with the grace of a cat, he picked up his bicycle and pedalled off, grinning at me over his shoulder before he vanished into the crowd.

CHAPTER 6

LES NEUF SOEURS

ACCORDING TO MADAME GOÛT, FRENCH was an irregular language, a secretive language; the language of Monitors. The last three letters of almost every word were silent, which had the strange effect of making all words sound alike, regardless of their meanings. Everything was about accent, pronunciation, performance; as if the entire language were a disguise, designed to make us blend in with everyone else.

The other girls called it romantic, but I thought it insincere. The Latin Dante spoke made his love for me feel ancient and timeless, as if it could never die. What I didn't realize until later was that French had depth, too; the trick was to hear the words that weren't spoken.

Our classroom was in the attic, where it was oppressively hot, *comme l'état de Vichy*, our professor joked, saying it would improve our throaty accents.

Madame Goût was a slender woman in her fifties who wore high heels and belted dresses. She had a gap between her front teeth and spoke with a thick French-Canadian accent. Her favourite word was "*Non*", which she said in a definitive kind of way, to make sure we all knew when we were wrong.

"There are too many tenses and cases in Latin. It makes you think too much," she said, gesticulating quickly. "There is no love in it, no emotion, no *joie de vivre!* With French, it just spills out."

The heat rattled through the radiator, punctuating Madame Goût's lecture. Next to me, Anya was taking notes, pushing her red braids aside when they got in the way of her pencil. As the professor wrote a list of pronouns on the board, I could hear Clémentine whispering to two of her friends.

Madame Goût must have heard, too, because she put down the chalk and turned around, her heels rapping against the floor. "If you insist on whispering in my class, I would rather you share it with all of us."

The sharp edges of Clémentine's shoulders shifted

beneath her shirt as she faltered. She looked starched and pressed, her collared shirt crisp as an envelope.

"Well, speak up," the professor said.

"We were talking about the Île des Soeurs. About the women who used to torture the Undead there."

Madame Goût raised a pencil-thin eyebrow. "Torture? Who told you that?"

"Monsieur Orneaux."

Madame Goût groaned. "Of course Monsieur Orneaux would say that. He is what we call *un homme, un vrai.* A man's man. Like most men, he is not interested in the endeavours of women," she said, waving her hand in the air. "He does not know anything," she muttered. "I have been telling them time and time again that he is not qualified to teach."

The room fell into an uncomfortable silence.

"The truth is that women were the founders of our entire Monitoring society." Madame Goût lowered her voice. "And the women you speak of are *les Neuf Soeurs,* or the Nine Sisters."

"Who were they?" Clémentine asked.

Turning to the blackboard, she erased all of the pronouns scrawled across it. She then picked up a piece of chalk and wrote down the following names in a swirling cursive:

Gertrude Fine

173

Marie Champierre
Victoria Limon
Joséphine Klein
Prudence Beaufort
Ester Olivier
Chrisette Longtemps
Alma Alphonse

"They were a secret society of female Monitors," she said. "A sisterhood." Smoothing out her skirt, Madame Goût went to the door and closed it. "It started in 1728 in Paris, as just a group of friends. Brilliant Monitors, young, incredibly smart, and all husbandless, which was very uncommon at the time. They called themselves *les Neuf Soeurs*, after the nine muses in Greek mythology."

"What did they do?" Anya asked.

"It is believed that they were behind most of the early Monitoring advances – Monitoring schools, hospitals, the convent on the Île des Soeurs. But most famously, they were the protectors of a secret."

Everyone grew still, listening.

"A secret? What kind of secret?" Clémentine asked.

Madame Goût clasped her hands together. "That's where the facts end. The rest we can only guess at. The prevailing rumour is that they had discovered the secret to eternal life."

My pencil slipped from my fingers and dropped to the floor. I felt Clémentine's eyes on me, watching my reaction. I tried to hide my surprise.

Madame Goût continued. "It has long been speculated that since children can defy death for twenty-one years, there might be a possibility that adults could defy death indefinitely. The myth of immortality has powerful allure."

Immortality. The word floated around my mind like a feather. This is it, I thought. This is the solution that Dante and I have been looking for.

"As the story goes, once *les Neuf Soeurs* found the secret to eternal life, they decided they could never use it. They were frightened by the power they held. Eternal life is perverse, unnatural. A world without death is even more frightening than a world *with* death. The beauty, the magic, the *éphemérè*... it would all be lost. So before they died, the *Soeurs* supposedly made a pact to let their secret die with them."

The room went so still I could hear the footsteps of the professor in the classroom across the hall as he paced.

"So that's it?" Clémentine said. "The secret is gone?"

The professor tapped her finger on the table. "Maybe. Maybe not. Maybe the secret was never about immortality to begin with; maybe it was about a family heirloom or a dirty rumour. It all depends on what you want to believe."

"I don't understand," I said, raising my voice over the sputtering heater. "If *les Neuf Soeurs* was a secret society, then how do you know so much about them? Or is it all made up?"

Madame Goût raised an eyebrow, as if she had anticipated my question. "Oh, but it's not. At first, no one knew anything about them." She stood behind her chair and leaned on its back. "Until they died."

"What do you mean?" Anya asked.

Madame Goût's expression grew solemn. "They were killed. Each found murdered at home in France in 1732. That was how their identities were discovered."

Madame Goût motioned to the list of names on the blackboard as a murmur rose over the class.

There was a long pause as we read the names on the board.

"There are only eight names here," I said, breaking the silence. "Who was the ninth sister?"

"Ah, yes. The ninth sister. I told you that each of the *Soeurs* was killed at her home. Well, only eight bodies were found."

"What happened to the ninth?" Clémentine asked.

"No one knows. Some believe she died. Others believe that she used the secret and is still alive, guarding it from evil."

Madame Goût paused. The hands on the clock above her crept towards noon.

"Who was she?" I asked.

"No one has been able to confirm her name or anything about her identity. Other than this." Madame Goût's heels clicked against the floor as she walked to her desk and removed a heavy book from the lower drawer. Flipping through it, she opened to a painting and passed the book around the table.

"This is the only painting we have of the Sisters. Many believe this was painted just days before their deaths. It is very famous; you will find it in all of the books about *les Neuf Soeurs*."

When it came to me, I traced my finger across each of the *Soeurs*, their black eyes boring through the page as they stood in a parlour, each wearing a plain house dress. They were of varying ages, some in their twenties, others not much older than me. On the far left was a girl with wild brown hair and narrow eyes. She looked the youngest. Half of her face was obscured in shadows. Perched on her arm was a yellow bird.

"The girl on the left," Madame Goût said. "That is the ninth sister. The lost sister. Many Monitors searched for her, but all they knew was what half of her face looked like, from the portrait. But after years of nothing, everyone assumed her dead."

"Who did it?" Anya asked. "Who murdered them?"

"I will leave that to Monsieur Orneaux to explain. I believe it's his area of expertise. Latin is, after all, the language of the Undead." Leaning over her book, she turned the page. "Now, back to *français*."

"The Undead?" I said. "They were killed by the Undead?"

"Ah, ah, ah," Madame Goût said, raising her index finger. "I never said that."

"How come no one ever tried to look for the secret?" Clémentine asked.

"Oh, but of course they have. It's one of the most controversial stories in Monitoring history. Many Monitors have lost years of their lives searching for *la Vie éternelle*, or Life Eternal, as many of us call their secret. It is the Monitors' version of the lost city of Atlantis. The Holy Grail. The Fountain of Youth." Madame Goût shook her head. "And you've seen how many of those have turned out to be true."

The class erupted in whispers.

"Quiet, please," she said, rapping her knuckles on the table. "That's enough *futilités* for today."

As she continued her lecture on pronouns and gender, I thought back to the plane ride with Dustin, when I had blurted out the word *canary*. Could that have had something to do with the Nine Sisters?

That evening in the dining hall, I was pouring myself a glass of milk when a voice tickled my ear. Caught off guard, I nearly dropped the carton on the floor.

"You seemed awfully interested in the Nine Sisters today," Clémentine said over my shoulder. "What I'm wondering is why someone who supposedly already defied death is so intrigued by talk of the secret to immortality."

"What do you want me to say? That I'm just a normal person and all the rumours are a lie?" I said, keeping my chin up as I walked to the condiments section.

Clémentine followed me. "No. See, I don't think you're normal, either."

"You don't know anything about me," I said, and shrugged her off as I walked towards the table in the corner where Anya was sitting.

"I know you have a secret," Clémentine said as I left her behind. "And I'm going to find where you buried it and dig it up."

When I got back to my room after dinner, it was so quiet I could hear footsteps coming down the hall, and then the sound of Clémentine's door unlocking. I was setting down my bag when a sudden cold breeze blew in from the windows. I ran to the other side of the room, hoping it was Dante, but of course it wasn't. Clémentine's words crept into my head. If she ever found out about

Dante... I didn't even want to think about what would happen.

Closing the window, I went to the bathroom and turned on the shower. While I was leaning on the sink, waiting for the water to get hot, I heard someone knock on Clémentine's door. I assumed it was some of her girlfriends, so it surprised me when I heard a boy's voice.

"Noah," Clémentine said. Her voice sounded different. Soft. Sincere.

Noah? I thought. The same Noah who hit me with a bicycle, who had flirted with me? The Noah who had spilled a bouquet of daffodils all over the street. He had bought them for Clémentine?

Pressing myself against the wall, I listened to him whispering to her, to her whispering back. To the sound of a bra strap snapping against skin. To Clémentine giggling. To the silence when they kissed.

Closing my eyes, I imagined that it was me in there with Dante, but Noah's voice kept drowning him out. And for reasons I couldn't explain, I started crying.

I wasn't jealous of Clémentine; it wasn't that. Or maybe it was. As I stepped into the shower, gripping the tile, I wished, just for a moment, that I could be her, that Dante could be Noah, and that when I went back to my room, he would be there waiting for me. But I knew I could never have that.

The shower curtain billowed as I reached over my shoulder and, with delicate fingers, touched the indentation on my back. The pain was shrill and shaky, like the high note of a soprano, but I held my finger steady until it calmed to a long, low ache. It was all I had left of him. And in five years, when he was gone for ever, I wouldn't even have this, unless I did something now to change my fate. As my hand slipped to my side, I hung my head back, letting the hot water cascade over my body until I couldn't tell if I was crying any more, and the bathroom was filled with so much steam that it was hard to breathe.

My room was cold when I shut the bathroom door behind me. Clutching my towel, I went to my desk and pulled my history book off the shelf. I flipped through it until I found the section on *les Neuf Soeurs*. The painting Madame Goût had showed us in class stared back at me from the page. I studied the shadowy girl with the canary, wondering who she was and what had happened to her. But the text didn't help. It only mentioned the few facts Madame Goût had already told us, and spent the rest of the chapter talking about their influence on Monitoring culture and society.

Had they really found the secret to immortality? I had to know. And if it existed, I had to find it. But where was I supposed to start? Skipping ahead, I spotted a photograph of a stone carving on the bottom of the page. It was a simple thing – a small bird entwined with what looked like vines – yet still, it was enough to make my chest seize.

My breath grew shallow as I leaned back in my chair, unable to believe what I was seeing: the same bird that had flashed into my mind on the aeroplane with Dustin. *The Canary Crest of the Nine Sisters*, the caption read.

My voice cracked. "Impossible."

Switching on my desk lamp, I looked closer, but I was right: it was the same bird I had seen when I'd blurted out the word *canary*.

Did this mean that the visions I'd been having, the information I'd suddenly known, all had to do with the Nine Sisters?

A crisp swirl of air blew in, turning the pages of my book. But hadn't I just closed the window? I stood up. The window was indeed still shut, yet the air was streaming in, coiling around my wrists, my arms, my chest, until I let out his name like a breath. "Dante."

Acting on an impulse, I ran to the wall and turned off the light. And standing in the middle of the room, I closed my eyes and took a tiny step to the right, and then an even smaller step to the left, until I could feel the stream of air reaching up my legs.

I threw my towel aside and got dressed as quickly as I could, combing my wet hair with my fingers as I ran down the stairs and out the door. At the school gates, a group of boys were joking around with a security guard.

"Renée," a voice said. It was Brett.

"I – I have to go," I said, and squeezed through them. I disappeared into the winding streets of Montreal.

I didn't know where I was going; my only guide was the chilly passage that connected me to Dante. It was hard to follow. I kept getting distracted by death that I sensed nearby: crowded markets, hospitals, and churches with modest graveyards. I made a left, followed by two rights, but then lost my way. I turned around and retraced my steps, holding my breath until I could feel him.

Eventually I found myself at the far end of the old port, at a fisherman's wharf. The air was raw and cold, like the inside of a freezer, and filled with sounds of the ocean at night: the chug of the water splashing against the dock, the boats swaying in the marina, their lines clinking against their masts like chimes.

By the pier was a wholesale shack filled with beautiful two-metre-long fish hanging from the ceiling, their scales reflecting the fluorescent light in oily shades of red, orange and purple. I felt their pull on me as if they were the Undead. A weathered man in rubber boots and gloves wheeled a barrel of smaller fish up the dock. Lowering my head, I walked past him, watching the moon's reflection ripple on the water, when a cold hand grabbed my wrist.

I knew I had found Dante from the way his presence enveloped me, seeped into me, filling my lungs with the scent of the woods clinging to his clothes, the pine so sharp that for the first time in months I could remember what it felt like to walk through a forest at dusk.

"Is it safe here?" I uttered, but Dante put a finger over my lips.

"Nowhere in this city is safe," he said, and pulled me into the shadows between two oversized boats, his hand on my ribs, his breath soft against the back of my ear, as we waited, hushed, for the last workers to leave.

The dock rocked beneath our feet as Dante led me to the end of the platform, where a small white boat called *The Sea Maiden* was docked. Its sails were rolled up.

"Whose is it?" I asked as Dante put one foot on the deck.

"Ours tonight," he said. Before I knew what was happening, he lifted me up as if I were weightless and carried me into the boat, my feet knocking a handle of the steering wheel, making it spin and spin. I clung to his neck, burying my face in his hair, in his shoulder, not wanting him to let me go.

"I miss you," I said, as if I were imagining all of this. "I miss you," I repeated, already anticipating when the night would be over and he would be gone.

He carried me to the middle of the deck, where a set

of stairs led down into the cabin. I held on to the collar of Dante's shirt, touching the curves of his neck as he stepped over a pile of life jackets and into the hull of the boat.

He tightened his grip and flipped on the light switch. Strings of tiny lights lit up the perimeters of the windows. A plush red bench lined the room, which was walled with panels of dark wood. Laying me down on the cushions, Dante stood back and looked at me.

I felt myself blush. "What?" I whispered, embarrassed.

He kneeled by my side. Picking up my right leg, he gently unlaced my shoe and slid it off. My toes curled as he moved to my left leg, slipping my other shoe off and placing it on the floor.

The boat creaked as he looked up at me, his eyes somehow desperate. His fingers tickled my skin as he ran his hands up my thighs, reaching beneath the pleats of my skirt. Something within me ached. I closed my eyes and felt him grasp the waist of my tights and peel them off, one leg at a time. I let out a shallow breath as he kissed my bare knees, the cool air of the marina making my skin prickle.

"Is this okay?" he asked, his voice soft.

Swallowing, I nodded, his question making me want him even more. "Don't stop," I said, my voice cracking as I unbuttoned my cardigan and slipped it off my shoulders.

He kissed my neck. And slowly, he unbuttoned my

shirt, his breath dancing across my skin until I was clothed in nothing but a bit of cotton and lace.

Sitting back, he took me in, his eyes roaming across my body, bare and pale in the evening light. *Beautiful*, he mouthed, as if his lips had acted without him. He lowered himself on top of me and moved his hands across me, tangling his fingers in my hair, feeling the smooth lines of my hips, my ribcage, my collarbone, until everything inside me went limp.

Forgetting myself, I lifted my head and pulled his face towards mine.

He turned away just before our lips met. "Careful," he whispered into my hair.

And even on that tiny couch, in a cramped cabin in the stomach of a boat, everything seemed to fit together, as if he were the inverse of me. The cavity of his chest, the curve of his waist, the weight of his legs on top of mine – they filled the hollowness within me, and I breathed him in until I could smell the wet air, the dusty cushions beneath us, the salt on his skin as his stubble grazed my neck.

We stayed up into the night, whispering, touching, as if no time had passed between us, as if the last two weeks had been nothing but a pause in the middle of a long, rolling sentence.

"I think I found an answer," I breathed over my shoulder, my voice barely audible as I told him about

Zinya's prophecy, the Nine Sisters, and the canary. "If the legend is true, then their secret could still be out there. If we find it, then we can use it to give you life again."

I waited for Dante to press himself against me and tell me we were saved, but he remained still. "But all of that is just speculation," he said finally. "How do you know the ninth sister didn't let it die with her, or that immortality exists at all?"

His voice hit me like a splash of cold water, and I felt myself grow stiff. "Because it has to. A vision of a canary flashed into my mind on the aeroplane. That has to mean something. Zinya said the visions would lead to the answer to my soul. What if all of my visions are clues leading to the secret of the Nine Sisters?"

"You promised me when we were behind the cathedral that you wouldn't follow your visions."

"I never promised," I said. "And besides, I'm a Monitor. I can take care of myself."

"Could Miss LaBarge take care of herself? Could your parents?"

Bewildered, I hugged my arms to my chest. "Why are you saying these things? Don't you even want to try?"

He reached out to me, but I pulled away.

"Of course I do," he said.

I searched his face, trying to understand why he was acting this way. "Then why aren't you happy?"

"I am happy," he said, as if I had hurt him. "I just don't want to get my hopes up about something that might not even exist."

"But that's all I have," I said. "When you're gone, it feels like a piece of me is missing. If I lose you, what's left?"

Dante put a hand to my cheek and guided my face to his. "You won't lose me," he said. "I would never let that happen. I promise you."

He tangled his legs with mine, his fingers stroking my shoulders, his lips pressed against the back of my neck. Outside, the wind was strong, making the boat beneath us tilt and sway, pulling our bodies apart and then pushing us back together until I drifted to sleep in his arms. Sometime around midnight, I stirred, hearing him whispering in my ear. "I love you," he murmured, thinking I was still asleep. But he didn't need to say it, because I already knew.

I awoke the next morning alone. Sitting up, I turned to the space beside me where the shape of Dante's body was still imprinted in the cushions. I touched it even though I knew it would be cold. I shouldn't have been upset; I knew that he would have to leave by midnight, before the Monitor sweep. But no matter how hard I tried, I knew I would never get used to his absence.

Out the window, it was a dull rainy day. I gathered my things, the boat creaking as I steadied myself and tried to put on my clothes. I was about to leave when I picked up my sweater. Lying on the floor beneath it was a note. It must have fallen when I first got up.

I unfolded it.

I promise.

I smiled and clutched it to my side, feeling that Dante was still with me as I climbed out into the drizzle.

When I got back to the dormitory I went straight to Anya's room. She opened the door just as I was about to knock, appearing in the doorway in a black jumper and purple tights. Her red hair was pulled into a loose braid.

"Oh good," she said. "You remembered this time."

We didn't have a plan when we set out. I figured we could just follow what I'd done in my vision: buy a bouquet of flowers, go to the reception area, and tell them we were visiting room 151. It wasn't anything brilliant, but we were going to a hospital. How hard could it be?

We travelled there by foot, Anya holding a wobbly umbrella between us as we traipsed through the puddles. The Royal Victoria Hospital was just as I remembered it: a sprawling lawn leading up to a massive stone building, the flags on the spires waving in the wind. Inside, the building had glossy floors and clean white walls. A line of nurses sat behind the reception area, typing. I walked towards them,

Anya's wet shoes squeaking behind me.

"Hi," I said to a nurse with big hair. "We're here for visiting hours." I placed the bouquet of flowers on the counter for emphasis.

"Who are you visiting?"

"Er – room 151."

"In which ward?"

"Paediatrics," I replied, a little too stiffly.

She typed something into her computer, and then frowned. "What's the name of the *patient* you're visiting?"

I gave Anya a panicked look. This wasn't supposed to happen. "Um—"

"Pierre," Anya said, cutting in. "He's my cousin."

I nodded. "Her cousin."

"Last name?" the nurse asked, giving us a suspicious look.

"LaGuerre," I blurted out.

After typing something else into her computer, she leaned back in her chair. "Pierre LaGuerre?"

It sounded so silly when she said it out loud. "There is no patient here with that name, and there never has been, according to our records."

I could feel myself start to sweat. "Oh, um—"

"What are your names?" The nurse's voice was stern as she picked up a pencil.

Anya kicked me just as I was about to answer. "Our

mistake," she said. "We must have gotten the wrong hospital."

The nurse stood up, but before she could respond, Anya grabbed my arm and pulled me towards the exit.

"Now what?" I asked, once we were outside.

"We go through the tunnels."

She led me to a mall, where we took an escalator down, down, down, until we emerged in the underground level. The halls were tiled in grey and lit with bright fluorescent lights that made me shield my eyes. People bustled around us, shopping, drinking coffee, heading towards the food court, which stank of hot oil.

I followed Anya as she wove through the tunnel system, taking a left and then right, past a Metro entrance, a perfume shop, and a huge grocery store, until we made it to a tunnel that had been almost completely blocked off by cement slabs.

"I think this is it," she said, stepping past a shallow puddle of orange water.

"How do you know about this?" I asked, sucking in a breath as I pressed myself against the side of the tunnel and followed her.

"All of the Russians here know about them," she said, leading me through a dank corridor lined with rust. "We were the ones who built them. Well, not me, but, you know, Russian immigrants. When I was little, my father used to take me through all the barricaded tunnels."

At the end was a narrow stairway that led to a single door. Anya pushed it open with her shoulder. It opened into a long storage closet in the hospital. Kicking away a box, I stepped over a mess of supplies – gauze, syringes, boxes of latex gloves – until I made it to the far door, lined with light.

"Let's use these," Anya said, and picked up a sheet of visitor stickers. Writing the name *Tanya* on one sticker, she peeled it off and stuck it on her shirt. She then wrote *Dasha* on another sticker and stuck it on my chest. Together, we crouched by the door, listening to the footsteps outside, and when there was a lull, we snuck out.

We found ourselves in the geriatrics ward – a drab place, its overhead lights buzzing in silence. It felt vacant and cold, as if it were inhabited by death. Trying to act inconspicuous, Anya and I walked towards the elevators. A bell dinged and we stepped inside.

It was crowded with two nurses standing by a patient on a stretcher. He was an old but robust man, his bare arms still muscular, his beard a deep grey. He wasn't dead, but sleeping; I knew because I couldn't sense him. Anya stared at him as I pressed the button for the third floor, which was labelled Paediatrics.

"You know, he was kind of good-looking," she said, when we got off.

I groaned. "He could be your grandfather," I said. "Your great-grandfather."

"I think older men are sexy," she continued. "Their chest hair. I love it."

I put my hand up. "Just – stop – no more. Let's focus," I said, eyeing a nurse as she talked on the phone.

Everything was just as I remembered: the drawings on the walls, the crayons and picture books in the waiting room, the hum of machines beeping, nurses chatting, shoes tapping against the floor. A line of bedrooms.

Then room 151. "Someone's in there," Anya said, peering through the window. Standing on my toes, I peered over her shoulder. A single bed stood in the middle of the room, and a boy was lying in it, the sheets tucked around his tiny legs.

I knocked. When he didn't move, I knocked again, louder, and turned the knob.

The room was still, save for the breeze from an air-conditioning vent, which blew up beneath a potted plant, making its leaves quiver. The same boy from my vision was asleep in the bed, his arms riddled with patches and tubes, as if he had been turned inside out.

Anya poked his leg, but he didn't wake.

"Don't touch him!" I whispered.

"Why not?"

"Just – watch him while I go under, okay?" I took out

a piece of notebook paper and a stick of graphite from my coat. The plastic tiles felt cold and slippery as I kneeled on the floor.

Pushing away a knot of wires, I slid underneath the bed, which was nailed to the floor, my body just fitting in the narrow space. I patted the ground with my hand until I felt something rough and cold, like metal. I traced its edges with my fingers: it was in the shape of a circle. And placing the piece of paper over the area, I rubbed the page with graphite to make an impression of the surface, hoping that I was doing it correctly.

I emerged with a sneeze. We both froze, waiting for the boy to wake up, but he didn't move.

"So what is it?" Anya asked, pulling dust out of my hair as we looked down at the rubbing I had made. It was an oval plaque of some sort, engraved with the following inscription:

to arrive there
follow the nose of the bear
to the salty waters beneath;

Beneath the words was a crest depicting a small bird. I felt my heart skip. "It can't be," I whispered, gripping the paper.

"What?" Anya said.

"It's a canary," I said, tracing its wings. "The crest of the Nine Sisters."

Before I could say anything more, the small boy shifted in his bed, making Anya and me jump. "Let's talk about this somewhere else," I whispered, and made for the door.

"So what is it?" she said as we waited for the elevator.

Glancing down the hall to make sure no one was looking, I took out the paper. "Some sort of riddle. A set of directions," I said, pointing to the first line: *to arrive there.* Suddenly, I looked up. "Maybe it's a set of directions to the secret of the Nine Sisters."

I looked to Anya, expecting her to be excited, but instead she said, "I don't know. It seems too easy. Why would it be beneath a hospital bed?"

I watched the dial of the elevator tremble as it moved down the floors towards us.

"The last line ends with a semicolon, not a full stop. Maybe it's incomplete."

Anya looked sceptical. "All of that stuff is a legend, though. We don't even know if any of it is true."

"It's a stretch, I know, but this exists, right?" I said, staring down at the page. "What else could explain this?"

"How are you so sure it belongs to the Nine Sisters?"

I pointed to the bird at the bottom of the page. "This is the exact same crest that's in our history book, under the Nine Sisters. I looked them up last night."

Anya shook her head. "It can't be. It has to be a fake, or a crest that looks just like it."

"Why? Why can't it be real?"

She gazed at the paper as if she feared it. "How could you have seen that in a vision?"

"Maybe I was meant to find it."

As she studied me, a smile spread across her face. "That is the most ridiculous thing I've ever heard."

"So what do you propose, then?" I asked, taking offence. "We just ignore it?"

She sucked on a lock of red hair. "Fine," she said. "Let me see it again."

The elevator dinged, and a down arrow lit up. Once the doors closed, I took out the rubbing.

"So we have to follow the nose of the bear to the salty waters beneath," I said, reading the final two lines.

"I don't know what that means," Anya said.

I crossed my arms. *The nose of the bear.* That couldn't be referring to a real bear. Maybe it meant an etching on a building, or a rock formation that looked like a bear... And *the salty waters* probably referred to the ocean...

"But Madame Goût said that the Nine Sisters vowed to let their secret die with them so no one would ever find it," Anya said. "So why would they leave a riddle leading to it?"

I didn't know, and before I could say anything more, the elevator doors opened to the ground floor.

"Renée?"

My eyes travelled up from the right leg of his trousers, cuffed as if he had just come from riding a bicycle, to his collared shirt, unbuttoned at the top, to his auburn mess of hair.

"Noah?" He was carrying a cup of coffee and a book.

He looked at my name tag. Quickly, I ripped it off and crumpled it in my hand, hoping he hadn't read it.

"What was that?"

"Nothing," I said, giving Anya a look. She did the same. "Why are you here?"

"Visiting my grandmother," he said.

I swallowed, staring at his dimples, at the dark red stubble on his cheeks. "I'm so sorry."

"No, it's okay. She's been here for a while. I like to come every so often to say hi, even if she can't hear me. I was actually on my way here when I ran into you on the street."

"You were?" I said, inexplicably relieved to realize that the flowers weren't for Clémentine, but for his grandmother.

"Who are you visiting?"

"Oh, um, no one, really."

"No one, really?" he said, letting out a laugh. "What are you doing here, then?"

As I searched for the right answer, Anya piped in. "Sampling the cafeteria."

"We were just leaving," I said, grabbing her arm. "We have to get back to campus for a..."

"Club meeting," Anya said, finishing my sentence.

He backed into the elevator. "A club? What club?"

"It's girls only. A private thing," Anya said, making my face go red with embarrassment.

"I hope your grandmother feels better," I said, just as the doors closed. Together Anya and I ran back to St. Clément, splashing through the puddles collecting on the flagstones, and into the dormitory.

CHAPTER 7

THE NAMELESS HEADSTONE

IT RAINED FOR THE NEXT few weeks, September washing into October with little change. I should have been happy about my discovery in the hospital, but I couldn't feel anything but dull. With Dante gone, time seemed to stand still around me; the mornings just as cloudy and dark as the evenings, as if the sun had never decided to rise. There was no wind, like the world was holding its breath along with me, waiting for him to return.

Anya and I spent the beginning of October huddled in the library, trying to decode the riddle. I looked up the crest of the canary dozens of times, comparing the photographs in the books to the one on my rubbing just to make sure. Despite the imprecision of the graphite, the similarities were unmistakable. The crests were the same. That's when I got the first tingling sensation that I might be right: the secret of the Nine Sisters wasn't dead; it was preserved in a riddle.

But what did it mean? I had already searched all of the indexes for anything about oceans, bears, noses, or any combination of them, but the clues were so vague that they rendered nothing. The more I studied the rubbing, the more I was certain of just one thing: the verse was only one part of a larger riddle. And in order to make sense of it, I had to find the other pieces.

"But how?" Anya asked, the bangles on her wrists clinking together as we walked to Strategy and Prediction, which was being held off campus.

"Maybe it will come to me in another vision," I said. "That's how it happened before."

The rest of the students loitered on the pavement by the school gates, which were matted with wet leaves. Parked by the guard's booth was a dark green van, with the St. Clément crest printed discreetly on the back.

Headmaster LaGuerre sauntered down the path in a light brown suit. When he saw us, he smiled and fished the keys out of his pocket.

I sat in the back row, in between Anya and a boy

named Harrison, who had a chubby face covered in freckles. The seats were dusty and rough. In front of me sat Noah and Clémentine, their heads bobbing together as we rolled over the cobblestone streets of the old port. I watched as she played with a lock of his hair and whispered something in his ear. He laughed, and I looked away, not wanting to admit that some part of me was jealous.

"As you probably realized from your placement tests, some dead animals are easier to sense than others," said Headmaster LaGuerre, glancing back at us through the rear-view mirror. "The French term that Monitors use to describe this is *force majeure*, or in English, *superior force*. Some dead animals have a stronger force than other animals, which makes them easier to detect.

"For example, other than humans, the animal with the heaviest soul, and therefore the greatest force, is the cat, which is why it is our school mascot. The cat is much like a Monitor, because it can detect death just as we can."

I thought back to Headmistress Von Laark's Siamese cats, who always pawed at Dante and Gideon.

"The same distinctions of force exist within humans. The sign of a Clairvoyant Monitor is being able to recognize these differences in weight. Death is everywhere. In order to do our jobs, we need to be able to distinguish between dead animals, dead people, and the Undead. After that, we find the Undead who are dangerous, and put them to rest."

"Who put us in charge?" I asked, thinking of Dante. "Why do we get to decide who lives and who dies?"

As I spoke, I felt a pair of eyes on me, which I assumed were Clémentine's. But when I looked up, I discovered they belonged to Noah.

The headmaster nodded thoughtfully. "Because a world without order would collapse in on itself. We're the only ones capable of sensing the Undead. It's not fair, I suppose, but it's not our task to solve the mysteries of nature."

The van continued along the St. Lawrence River to the grungy industrial area of Montreal. Headmaster LaGuerre glanced over his shoulder as he manoeuvred down the waterfront. "But water," he said, "water complicates everything."

Following the headmaster, we climbed out of the van and walked to the dock. Big windowless factories lined the shore, spewing a continual stream of black smog into the sky. Rusty pipes and corroded beams of metal stuck out of the river like the remnants of a flooded forest. It smelled like a mixture of salt and sewage, and for the first time, I was glad my sense of smell was partially muted.

"It is incredibly difficult to sense a dead creature when it is immersed in water," the headmaster said, stopping at the end of the dock. Behind him, a slew of rowing boats bobbed in the water. "And the deeper it is, the more challenging it is for us to sense its presence. Which is exactly why we're here. To practise our *intuition*."

I shivered as I studied the flotsam drifting along the riverbank: beer cans and wrappers and cigarette butts.

"This is where people dump things that they never want to be found again. Weapons, clothes, the dead... Death often resides in inconvenient locations, and as a Monitor in the world, places like this will be your office. Many of the cases you will encounter are of children who have drowned – and per the Cartesian Oath, you will have to find them and bury them before they float and reanimate."

A murmur rose over the class.

He gazed out at the murky water. "I have planted one dead animal out there," he said. "Your job is to locate it, identify it, and if possible, record its depth."

We paired up. Noah was working with Clémentine. I worked with Anya, her platform shoes wobbling as she climbed into a rowing boat.

After I settled in, she handed me the oars. "You row," she said. "I'll direct you."

"Why do you get to direct?" I said.

"Because I have weak arms," she said. "I'm not good at sports."

"But I'm better at detecting the dead than you are."

She looked offended at my statement, but shook it off. "All the more reason for me to practise."

"Fine."

"Fine."

As we rowed out, the headmaster stood on the dock and continued to shout out tips on sensing the presence of the dead beneath the water. I tried to pay attention, but Anya kept changing our course. "To the left more. No, now to the right. Oh, sorry, never mind, back to the left again."

Frustrated, I turned around. "Can you just pick a direction and stick with it?" At the periphery of my vision, I could see Noah put one of his oars down.

Anya pointed to the left. "More that way."

"That's wrong," I said. "I can feel it."

"So can I," Anya said. "Just because you're first rank doesn't mean you're always right."

"I'm right this time," I said, but was distracted by a splash.

Clémentine and Noah were a few metres behind us, their boat wobbling as Noah teased her with a net he'd fished out of the river.

"Stop it!" Clémentine said, shielding her face as she laughed. "You're shaking the whole boat!"

She winced as an oar fell in, splashing water into her face. Her voice was shrill as she screamed.

"Okay!" she said, smiling while she wiped her cheeks. "We have to get back to work."

"You work too much," Noah said, teasing her as he shook the water from his arms.

"Everyone else is already looking for the animal; we're behind."

"Oh, come on," Noah said. "It's just a class. Besides, how hard could it be?"

Clémentine adjusted her hairpin. "Everything worth doing is hard," she said, and picked up an oar.

Letting out a sigh, Noah's eyes wandered across the river as she rowed backwards. I felt his gaze linger on me.

Clémentine must have seen him staring, because her lips tightened. Quickly, I averted my eyes, and, under Anya's directions, we zigzagged away from them until we were close enough to hear the headmaster speaking to one of the boats ahead of us.

"Stop," Anya said. "I think it's right below us."

I couldn't feel anything and knew she was wrong. But I humoured her. Putting down the oars, I leaned over the edge of the boat and stared into the water, where I could see the headmaster's reflection as he rowed alongside a pair of girls.

I watched his lips move as he spoke. "It's customary to bury Monitors at sea – a place where their bodies can never be detected, even by fellow Monitors. Very few Monitors ask to be buried in the ground. The few that do are buried in the Monitors' section of the Mont Royal Cemetery."

Mont Royal Cemetery. I watched the reflection of the headmaster's face in the water. Suddenly I felt exhausted and miserable, as if I'd been searching for something but had failed.

Mont Royal Cemetery. I felt dizzy. I hated myself. I hated that I had failed.

My chest heaved, and I coughed. Slowly, I felt myself falling forward. There was a splash. And then everything went cold.

When I surfaced, I was dry and standing in a thicket of trees on the side of the mountain. In one hand I held a flashlight. Below me, the city was reduced to strings of tiny lights, and beyond that, I could see the St. Lawrence River, its waves glimmering in the moonlight.

I began to walk. Just a few metres away, there was a joggers' path illuminated by street lamps, which wound up the mountain. I stayed away from it. Instead, I chose to travel unseen, weaving through the trees until I reached the other side of Mont Royal.

Two teenagers were standing by a drinking fountain, holding hands. Unable to help myself, I stopped for a moment and watched them whisper to each other and laugh. They seemed so carefree, as if time didn't matter. The boy played with the girl's hair, touching her neck, and

I leaned against the trunk of a tree near them, my eyes so dry that they stung. When the girl leaned in to give the boy a delicate kiss, I looked away.

A tree branch behind me gave out, filling the silence with a loud crack. The couple froze and looked in my direction. Not wanting to be discovered, I crouched down and closed my eyes. I didn't want to be reminded of myself, to be reminded that I was there, invading their intimacy. Slowly, I receded into the trees behind me, and when I knew I was out of sight, I ran down the other side of the mountain, knowing that no matter how much I wished otherwise, I would always be that person peering from the woods, because I could never have what they had.

When I descended on the opposite side of Mont Royal, I found myself at the tall black gates of a cemetery. The mere sight of their iron tendrils made me relax. As I slipped inside, the air seemed to settle into a quiet stillness, the sound of the cars on the street fading into nothing.

I turned on my flashlight. The cemetery was overwhelmingly vast, with rows of headstones as far as I could see. Daunted, I walked towards a map – an intricate thing, as complex as a nervous system. After skimming the index, I found the section I was looking for and put my finger on it, tracing the path from where I stood to a tiny circle of land near the back of the grounds.

I set off. The sky was so wide that it felt like I was at sea.

I knew I'd found what I needed when I spotted a grassy area enclosed by a chain. The headstones here were smaller than most of the others I had passed, and far less ornate – many just rectangular stones overgrown with weeds.

Hopping over the chain, I shone my flashlight on each headstone, reading the inscriptions. There weren't more than two dozen of them, and they were all brief – just names and dates spanning the last two hundred years. I didn't recognize any of the names, and felt myself growing impatient.

As I neared the last stone I began to panic. It had to be here. Just as I was about to turn around, my foot hit something hard, and I tripped and fell into the grass. I groaned, feeling the rocky soil against my palms. I was about to hoist myself up when I noticed the headstone that had impeded my way.

It was low to the ground, flat, and so overgrown that I would have otherwise missed it. Stooping down, I pushed the weeds aside and shone my light on its surface. There was no name or date. Only the word SOEUR and the following inscription:

here it is laid to rest
where to only the best
of our kind it shall be bequeathed.

Engraved beneath the words was the crest of a small bird.

I read the inscription again, lingering on the first line. I heard my heart beat, irregular and quick, like the sound of something tumbling down the stairs. I had to find a shovel. On my walk here I had passed a worker's pickup truck on the side of a path. There could have been a shovel there. Standing up, I retraced my steps.

The truck was only a little way back. Beside it sat a collection of garbage bins and a few tools: a pitchfork, a rake and a shovel.

I hesitated before touching the handle of the shovel. I despised it. I didn't want to touch it. But tonight I had no other option. Its shaft felt rough and splintered as I ran my hand along it, growing accustomed to the quality of the wood. Lifting it over my shoulder, I carried the shovel back to the nameless headstone.

here it is laid to rest

I focused on the words as I planted the shovel firmly into the ground and began to dig. The moon moved lower in the sky. Wiping my forehead, I stepped back to look at my work. The hole was now about a metre deep; though, to go any deeper I'd have to lower myself inside and dig.

I began to pace around the hole. I could try. I could stick one foot in and see what happened. It wasn't even close to the six-foot mark, where things started to get dangerous... Slowly, I lowered my foot into the hole. As it went below the surface, a tingling feeling passed through my body. It quickly sharpened to a sting. My toes curled in my shoes, the muscles seizing before they went numb. Quickly, I pulled my leg back and collapsed on the grass. I couldn't. It was impossible. My body wouldn't let me. My eyes darted around the cemetery, looking for some other way. There wasn't one. Why had I not foreseen this? Why had I been so unprepared? My grip on the shovel loosened, and it dropped to the ground beside me with a soft thud.

When I woke up, I found myself surrounded by the mahogany walls of Dr. Newhaus's office. I was lying on a sofa, an itchy wool blanket draped over me. Rubbing my eyes, I kicked it off me and sat up. My hair was still damp from the river.

Dr. Newhaus was standing at the far end of the room, his back turned to me as he gazed out the window. When he heard me shuffling around, he faced me. He was wearing a maroon waistcoat over a shirt and tie.

"Miss Winters," he said, holding his fingers together, his lids heavy as one eye gazed at me, the other at the plant

210

on the window sill. "You've returned from the netherworld. How are you feeling?"

"A little groggy."

Before I knew what was happening, I had a thermometer in my mouth, a blood pressure cuff on my arm, and the cold nose of a stethoscope pressed to my back.

"Still irregular," the doctor said as he counted my heartbeats with his watch. "Though otherwise, everything seems normal." He stood, his knees cracking, and fetched me a towel from a supply closet. "You baffle me."

I thanked him and wiped my face. Dr. Newhaus took off his glasses. "Can you tell me exactly what happened?"

I told him about Strategy and Prediction, about the boat, about how when the headmaster mentioned the cemetery in Mont Royal, I blacked out and fell into the water.

"Do you remember anything after that?"

"I had another vision," I said. "I was digging up someone's grave, but I stopped halfway."

Dr. Newhaus squinted. "Whose grave was it?"

SOEUR, I thought, but instead said, "It was nameless."

He grunted. "It seems your hallucinations are being prompted by visual or aural stimuli. A photograph, a phrase..."

I said nothing. He was right, partly, but I knew it was more than that. It was a feeling, a strong feeling of fear, of dread, of hate, of disappointment.

"Could you detect any other connection between this vision and the one you experienced previously?"

I hesitated. There was the second part of the riddle, which I should have been more excited about, but I was preoccupied by something else. Why couldn't I have jumped into the hole? Why had my foot reacted in that way? Why had I not wanted to touch the shovel?

"Renée?" Dr. Newhaus said, trying to catch my gaze. "Any connection between your visions?"

"Um – no," I said, my mouth suddenly feeling parched. The only reason why I wouldn't have been able to jump into the hole was if I were Undead. But I wasn't Undead. I could go underground; I had been in the Montreal tunnels.

The doctor wrote something on his pad, and I wondered what it was. If my visions were those of an Undead, whose were I seeing? There were hundreds of them out there, but only one person made sense.

But no – it couldn't be. When I'd told Dante about my visions, he hadn't recognized them, had he? He'd even asked me where they had come from, and worried that they might be dangerous.

"Have you been taking the medications I prescribed for you?"

I stared at the rug, flattening its tassels with my toe. "No."

"Why not?" he said with disapproval.

"I – forgot."

"I see. Well, I would still encourage you to take them." Dr. Newhaus crossed his arms. "Have you considered my offer?"

I frowned, waiting for him to elaborate.

"To meet with me on a more regular basis."

"Oh, um...no, thank you. I think I'm fine now."

Dr. Newhaus seemed sceptical, but let it go. "Very well; it's your decision. But keep an open mind." Standing, he continued. "Well, I don't want to keep your young man waiting any longer. He's been very patient."

I froze. "Young man?"

The doctor nodded, handing me my bag as he walked me to the door. "He's been waiting for you outside."

Dante. But how could he be here at St. Clément? It wasn't safe. Suddenly becoming aware that my hair was wet and my clothes probably smelled like the St. Lawrence River, I slung my bag over my shoulder, thanked Dr. Newhaus, and slipped out the door.

But when I got to the hallway, Dante wasn't there.

"Noah?" He was sitting on a bench, reading.

I must have surprised him, because he jolted, dropping his book.

"Renée," he said, studying me through his glasses. "You move like a cat. Soundless."

Smiling, I bent down and picked up his book. Colourful drawings of heroes and villains filled the pages. All of the dialogue was in French.

"Comics?" I asked with a smile, and handed it to him.

"You say it with such disdain," he said.

I laughed. "What's it about?"

"Superheroes fighting the Napoleonic wars. But really it's about so much more. Life, death, violence, love, immortality. The meaning of our existence on earth." His tone was serious, but his eyes seemed to be teasing me. "I think you'd like it."

"Why do you say that?"

"Don't you have a super power, too?"

I shrugged. "Well, I can't read French, whatever that's worth."

"And her true tragic flaw is finally revealed," he teased, and stood up.

"Have you been here the whole time?"

He shrugged. "I wanted to make sure you were okay."

I picked at a piece of mud clinging to my shirt, not wanting to be reminded of the mortifying incident. "Thanks."

It was evening as we left the building and walked across the courtyard to the dormitories. Just as I was about to thank Noah and go up to my room, he turned to me.

"Hey," he said, "are you hungry? I know of a really great French deli."

"What about Clémentine?"

Noah's face dropped a little. "Oh, I think she's busy tonight. But she won't care."

Unable to help myself, I let out a laugh. Of course she would care.

But Noah didn't see the humour. "What's funny?"

"Nothing," I murmured.

"So what do you think?" He tilted his head to meet my gaze. "If you don't like French food, we can get something else."

I bit my lip, my face going soft with guilt. "I can't."

Noah stepped back. "Oh, okay."

"I'm sorry. I just—"

"No, it's okay. You don't have to explain."

Feeling grateful, I nodded, and was about to turn away when he said, "It's a boy, isn't it?"

"Excuse me?"

"I can tell by your expression."

I brushed my fringe away from my face. "I don't know what you're talking about."

"I knew you'd say that," he said with a wink. "Just thought I'd try."

He held the door for me, and after giving him a wave, I slipped inside. I passed Clémentine in the hallway, where I overheard her asking one of her friends if they had any dinner plans. I must have paused for a little too long, because Clémentine glared at me and asked me what I was looking at. Without answering, I squeezed by them, wondering why Noah had lied about her being busy tonight.

In my room, I showered the river water out of my hair, rifled through my closet for a dry outfit, and set off. I crept past the school gates and through the city until I reached the long curving path that led me to the base of Mont Royal. I pulled my coat closer to me as I climbed the mountain, passing the spot where I saw the girl and boy kissing by the water fountain. I could still remember the way they'd held each other, kissing as if it were an afterthought.

I was about to walk on when I heard something rustle in the leaves behind me. I froze. A rock tumbled down the hill. For a moment I thought it was the couple, back to haunt me with their happiness. A moth fluttered around a lamp, but otherwise all was still.

I continued until I found myself in front of the twisted gates of the Mont Royal Cemetery. I stopped in front of them, running my hand along the cold bars. Beyond them, tombstones stuck out of the ground in great winding rows that stretched as far as I could see. Dim lamps lit the path.

The gate creaked as I pushed it open just wide enough to squeeze through. Inside, the graveyard was just as I had envisioned it.

Frost laced the grass, making everything appear frozen in place, but when I stepped onto it, a headstone seemed to shift.

I gasped, backing against a tree as the ice seemed to crystallize up my feet and around my legs. Dante was here.

He was standing by a black marble tombstone carved into the shape of a pillar. All that was visible were the angles of his face, ivory against the shadows, like the planes of a statue.

"Renée?" Maybe it was the wind distorting his voice, but something about the way he said my name made me think he was just as surprised to see me as I was to see him.

Just before our arms met, I hesitated. It seemed strange that I would find him here, right after my vision.

"Is everything okay?" he said, his eyes searching mine.

"You scared me," I said.

"I wasn't sure you'd come. This cemetery is so far away from St. Clément that I was worried you wouldn't sense me. But you did."

I nodded as he wrapped his arms around me until there was no space between us. My visions couldn't have been his, I thought, burying my face in his chest. Everything felt right, now that we were together. Everything felt like it was in its place. Except that I hadn't felt him. I'd been too focused on finding the cemetery to notice his presence.

Extricating his arms from mine, Dante took a step back and studied me, his eyes dark and clouded like the sky. Maybe it was my own nervousness, or the fact that we were in a cemetery, or the fact that he never blinked, but something about the way he was staring made me uneasy. I tried to move towards him, but he stopped me.

"Let me look," he said, the words low. "Please."

My voice cracked. "At what?"

He didn't answer for a long while. "Sometimes I worry that I'll forget."

Beside us, a crow swooped onto a tombstone. My coat was unbuttoned, letting a chill creep beneath my clothes, but I didn't care. "Forget what?"

Dante's eyes travelled across me, but his mind seemed far away.

"Forget what?" I repeated, as some part of me began to panic. "Me? Us?"

He took a step closer. "No, not that. All of this. The *feeling* of being with you."

"Why would you forget?" I asked, growing anxious.

He let his hand drop down my arm, sending a shiver up my skin. "I don't know."

What was he saying? I touched a tombstone near us. The marble was cold and black. "Why did you choose this cemetery?"

Dante gazed around us. "It's the biggest in Montreal. I thought it would be safest."

"Have you been here before?"

Dante's eye twitched. "No."

I believed him. I had to give him the benefit of the doubt, though something about the way he turned away made me wonder. "Isn't there a section of this cemetery where Monitors are buried?"

"Monitors?" he said, betraying a hint of unease. "I don't know."

"I was just thinking that maybe the Nine Sisters might have been buried there. I know you're sceptical about them, but it wouldn't hurt to check."

Dante hesitated. "Doesn't that seem too easy?"

"I just want to look," I said. "Will you walk with me?"

In the distance, a car drove past the cemetery gates, its headlights shining across the headstones. Dante took my hand and slipped it into the pocket of his coat.

We walked to the fork in the path, and stopped at the map – the same one I'd seen in my vision. Barely taking any time to search, Dante put his finger on the small green area near the back of the grounds. "It's here."

I went stiff. "How do you know that's the right section?"

"Because it says so right here."

He pointed to a tiny line of text in the map's index that said *Founders*. I assumed it meant the founders of Montreal.

As we walked beneath the street lamps to the back of the cemetery, I watched the shadows change his face, darkening and distorting it until he looked like a stranger.

"What?" Dante said, giving me a confused look.

"Nothing," I said quickly, and looked straight ahead until I found myself standing in front of the same tiny circle of land I'd seen earlier today. It was framed with barren trees and separated from the path by a chain.

Slowing to a stop, Dante gazed around the frozen weeds at our feet. "They must be somewhere here," he said. Behind us was the same narrow aisle I had visited in my vision. I waited, expecting Dante to lead me down that row. But instead he pulled me in the opposite direction. "Maybe this way?" he said, bending down to look at the headstones as we walked.

I let out a sigh of relief. He hadn't been here before. It was all in my head. Leaning in to him, I pressed my head against his shoulder, silently apologizing for not trusting him. We walked like that for a while, meandering through each of the rows, Dante wiping the frost from the face of the headstones so I could read the names and dates. I gave each of them a brief glance, and then shook my head. We had almost made it through all of the aisles, when I turned to him. "I don't think it's here. We can go if you want."

"Are you sure?"

I nodded.

With that, we made our way back, our arms stretched over the headstones as we wove in and out of them, veering apart and then coming together in a dark waltz. I laughed as I skipped down an overgrown row a few steps ahead of Dante. I was almost at the chain when he called out to me. "Watch your step."

At his words, I froze, the smile fading from my face. Slowly, I looked down. Buried in weeds just below my feet was the nameless headstone, the same one I had tripped over in my vision. The word SOEUR peeked out just above the grass.

Suddenly I felt queasy. I put a hand to my head, my knees growing limp.

"Renée?" Dante said, just as I fell.

I landed on the frozen earth beside the crooked stone. Its inscription was barely visible through the frost.

"Are you okay?" Dante said from above me, bending down to offer me a hand. But I couldn't bring myself to look at him. Had he lied to me?

Rolling over, I stood up and brushed myself off.

"What's wrong?" he said, studying me. "You look sick."

I took a step away from him. "Did you see that headstone?"

"Of course. That's why I told you to watch your step."

I paused, trying to sort everything out. "But it's so dark. How did you see it from all the way over there?"

Dante gave me a confused look. "I was right behind you."

Was he? I couldn't remember.

"What's going on?" he said, his voice betraying a hint of alarm.

"I had another vision. I came to this cemetery, looking for a grave, but while I tried to find it, I tripped over a headstone. The same headstone you just warned me about." I squinted at him in the dark.

"What are you implying?"

"That my visions are yours. That I'm somehow seeing what you're doing." I swallowed. "That you've been lying to me about it."

Dante gave me a baffled look. "Lying to you about what? What do you think I'm doing that's so terrible?"

"I don't know," I said, shaking my head. "Digging up a grave. Looking for the secret of the Nine Sisters." But the more I spoke, the more absurd everything sounded. If he had been looking for the secret of the Nine Sisters, he would have told me.

"Is it really so hard to believe that I saw the headstone just before you fell?"

"I – I don't know," I said, and looked up at him, hoping the truth would be somehow etched in his face. "Tell me where you've been this whole time. Tell me what you've been doing. I feel like I'm walking in the dark."

"I've been in hiding," he said. "Moving around so the Monitors can't find me. You know that."

"But why won't you tell me any specifics?"

"I don't want to put you in any danger. If the Monitors here ask you questions, I don't want you to have to lie. It's better if you don't know where I am."

"So ask me to run away with you," I said. "I would say yes. You just have to ask me." My back went rigid as I leaned against the trunk of a tree and waited for him to say the words: *Come with me.*

But they never came.

"I can't."

I felt something inside me wither. It was too dark for me to see Dante's face, and I was glad. I didn't want to see what he looked like when he was pushing me away. "Why?" I said, my mouth suddenly growing dry.

"Because if we go somewhere together, I'll still die in five years. And you need to be at St. Clément. You need to train as a Monitor so you can protect yourself."

"Protect myself from whom?" I said, my voice cracking.

"The Undead? I can—"

"From me."

"But – but you wouldn't hurt me." The words got caught in my throat.

"Not now, but what if I change?" The wind whistled through the branches above us as I waited for him to continue. "The Undead have been known to grow uncharacteristically violent in the final stages of their existence. Maybe it's desperation, or maybe it's something less easy to control. I don't know. But you have to prepare yourself."

My hair blew across my cheeks. I didn't know what to say. The only thing I had been certain of was that Dante would never hurt me. It was the only thing that had given me hope these past months; hope that we would make it, that we would find a solution and be together for as long as time would let us. But I had been wrong, because he was hurting me now.

"And I need to stay here," Dante whispered. "I need to stay here and keep searching for a solution."

"But I've already found one," I cried, and then lowered my voice. "I think you know what it is."

Dante tilted his head as if he wanted to tell me something. "I..." He let his voice trail off in the wind.

I wanted him to say more, but he didn't. The wind quieted until everything became still. In the silence, I heard something rustle across the way, as if someone were stepping on dried leaves. I put a finger to Dante's lips.

"Do you feel that?" I heard a girl's voice say. It was the same voice I heard through the walls every night before I went to sleep. Clémentine. Had she followed me here?

"What?" another girl said. It was Arielle.

"An Undead," Clémentine said.

"We're in a cemetery," another girl said. "Everything here is dead—"

Clémentine cut her off. "No, this is stronger. It's coming from over there. Where the voices were."

Realizing she was talking about Dante, I dropped to the ground, pulling Dante with me behind a tall headstone. *Go,* I mouthed to him, hoping he would know to get as far away from Clémentine as he possibly could.

Before I could say anything more, he was gone, the shadows shifting around him as he moved soundlessly through the night.

The sound of Clémentine's footsteps got closer. "Stop being so scared," she said to one of her friends, who must have been hesitating. "We're Monitors. We can handle this."

"But I've never seen an Undead." I recognized Josie's voice.

The wind engulfed the rest. I heard Clémentine say something to the girls, but I couldn't make out what.

Someone responded. There was a brief argument. And then suddenly, everything went quiet.

I was beginning to think they had left, when, without warning, something sharp jabbed me in the side.

"Ow!" I yelped.

"Get up," Clémentine said from above me. "Slowly." She was holding a shovel against the back of my neck, the tip of it cold on my skin.

I did as she said.

"Now turn around," she said. "And keep your hands out so I can see them."

I closed my eyes, feeling Dante's presence disappear into the distance, and turned around.

"Who were you with?" Clémentine demanded from beneath the hood of her coat. A group of girls stood behind her.

"No one," I said quickly. "I am alone."

"That's a lie. We heard voices."

"Do you see anyone else? I'm here alone."

Clémentine studied me. "I heard a boy's voice. You were with a boy. An Undead boy." Her eyes wandered to the spot in the distance where Dante had disappeared.

"That was me. I was trying to talk to the dead," I persisted. I had to distract her. "This is the Monitor section. I thought I could contact one of them to ask about the Nine Sisters. There's no one else here but me."

"Then why could I feel you? Why did you feel like an Undead?"

"Because I died once. Remember?"

Clémentine looked me in the eyes, measuring whether or not I was telling the truth. I saw her falter, and before she could react, I grabbed the shovel and twisted it out of her arms. With more ease than I expected, I flipped it around and pointed the tip at her.

Her friends seemed to want to do something, but they were too terrified of me to get close. Now I was in control.

I pushed the tip of the shovel into Clémentine's neck. "Why did you follow me here?" I asked.

She raised an eyebrow, trying to maintain her cool. "Because I thought you were up to something. And I was right."

"Do you really want to know what I was doing?" I asked, holding the shovel steady.

Clémentine lifted her chin, but said nothing.

"Okay, I'll tell you. Or how about this? I'll show you."

"Fine," she said, though I could tell she didn't trust me.

"Bend down," I said.

She did as I said.

"Wipe away the frost from that headstone."

I watched the muscles in her neck tighten as she rubbed

her palm over the crest of the canary. The moon glinted in her eyes as she glanced over her shoulder at me. "Is this a joke?"

I turned the shovel around and held out the handle to her. "No. I came here tonight to find it."

Cautiously, she took the shovel from me, and we took a few steps away from each other. Breaking my gaze, she kneeled down and read the inscription.

"'Here it is laid to rest,'" she read, and turned to me. "The secret of the Nine Sisters is buried here?" she asked, as if she didn't believe it.

The grave before her was mounded higher than the others, the soil loose and scattered about the grass as if it were fresh. Or recently unearthed? I didn't know if the secret was there or not, but I did realize then that my visions were more than just wanderings.

"I don't know," I said. Whoever I had been in my vision – Dante or otherwise – had never made it to the bottom of the hole.

"You really don't know," Clémentine murmured, studying me before telling the girls to start digging.

I wanted to leave, to be anywhere but here, where everything – the headstone, the shovels, the girls tossing dirt over their shoulders – made my head spin. What was Dante going to tell me? Had he been here before, or was I losing my mind?

But I couldn't leave. Clémentine had sensed him. I could tell by the way her eyes darted towards the edge of the trees, as if she were searching for him. If I left, she might follow and find him. So I stayed, and as soil flung past me, and the hole got wider, deeper, I took a surreptitious survey of the cemetery, and let out a sigh of relief. I couldn't feel Dante anywhere.

CHAPTER 8

THE LIBERUM

WINTER CAME TO MONTREAL TWO months early. Or I should say, two months early to me. By the end of October I had only just gotten ready to take out my autumn coat, when the school started delivering a bundle of wood outside each of our doors in the morning for the pot-bellied stove. But no matter how close I sat to the fire, I couldn't get rid of the cold vacancy within me.

So instead I embraced it, and ventured out into the chilly Canadian air until I found my way to the edge of city. There, I wandered along the waterfront, where I could almost feel Dante watching me from the other side of the river. I spent most of my evenings there, pacing around the perimeter of Montreal, waiting for him to come to me.

Abandoned grain silos lined the opposite shore; lonely brown cylinders that rose behind the water. If you stood on a particular spot on the wharf and spoke over the river, your voice would bounce off the silos and echo back. At nightfall, when everyone had left, I approached the edge of the water and leaned on the railing.

It was scratched with graffiti: initials of lovers, etched in hearts. When the wind died down, I spoke.

"Did you lie?" I said, the words wobbly.

When they bounced back, my voice was low and round, repeating itself over and over: *lie lie lie lie.*

"No," I said into it again, and imagined it was Dante when it came back: *No. No. No. No. No.*

After that, I kept going back to the waterfront, speaking to myself through the silos. I was so intent on finding Dante that I barely thought about the riddle on the headstone. And to my surprise, Clémentine didn't remind me, even though I knew she'd been just as disappointed as I'd been after our run-in at the cemetery.

On that night, the girls had dug and dug, but there'd been nothing in the anonymous grave, not even a casket. Clémentine had said nothing as we walked back to the dormitory, our faces and hands streaked with dirt. She was quieter after that; she never stopped me in the halls or tried to embarrass me in front of her friends. At first I thought we had reached some sort of truce, but then I realized she was waiting, watching me closer than she ever had before, trying to figure out what I knew and who I had been with that night.

At first I didn't tell Anya what had happened, partly because that night confused me, too. That was why I went to the silos – with the hope that I would find Dante. But after a week of nothing, I gave up and told her everything.

"You went to the cemetery without me?" Anya said. We were sitting in Latin class, waiting for everyone else to show up.

"I was in a rush," I said. "Everything happened quickly."

She rotated the cuff in her ear. "What do you think it means?"

"What?"

"The riddle, obviously," she said in disbelief.

"Oh, I don't know."

She sat back, staring at me.

"What?" I said. "Why are you looking at me like that?"

"You've barely eaten anything for days," she said. "You're not interested in the riddle even though just a few weeks ago you were dragging me to the hospital with you. What's going on?"

The door opened and Clémentine and her friends walked in, followed by Monsieur Orneaux. I lowered my voice. "I'm sorry," I said, "but I can't talk about it."

Anya bit her fingernail. "It's about a boy," she said, studying me. "I've felt like this too. That's why I pierce my ears whenever I'm upset. It takes my mind off things I don't want to think about."

"I don't think I want to do that."

"Of course you don't," she teased, pinching my virgin earlobe as the professor sat at the head of the table and took out his lecture notes. "But maybe figuring out the riddle will distract you from your boy problems?"

"There was nothing buried beneath the headstone," I whispered as Monsieur Orneaux cleared his throat. "And I already checked the cemetery map – there's no body of salt water anywhere near there, and if there is a bear on one of the headstones, it could take years to find it. The cemetery is huge."

"Okay," Anya whispered. "You don't have to get testy about it."

That's when Clémentine raised her hand. Monsieur Orneaux tried to ignore it while he recited phrases from Seneca. But after a few minutes had passed, she decided to just speak up.

"Who killed the Nine Sisters?"

That woke everyone up.

Monsieur Orneaux narrowed his eyes, making his face look even more hollow. "I don't know anything about that. I teach Latin."

"Then why did Madame Goût say the murder of the Sisters was your area of expertise?" Clémentine said.

I put down my pencil, appreciating Clémentine's pushiness for the first time.

Monsieur Orneaux's face darkened as he leaned back in his chair, pressing his fingers together. "Madame Goût. I should have known." And without saying anything more, he stood up and wrote a word on the blackboard.

Liberum

"The group widely believed to have murdered the Nine Sisters call themselves the Liberum." He tapped his chalk to the blackboard, just over the letter *i*. "What do the roots of this word signify?"

Without giving us any time to respond, he underlined the beginning of the word. "*Liber* means *child*." He gazed at us. "As you know, only people under the age of twenty-one can potentially become Undead, which is clearly why the Liberum chose this word."

"It also means *freedom*," I said, my voice cutting through

the classroom. I felt a pair of eyes on me, and I lifted my chin to see Noah gazing at me, a pencil tucked behind his ear. He gave me a half smile, and then looked away when Clémentine leaned over and whispered something in his ear.

Monsieur Orneaux met my gaze for a split second, barely acknowledging me. He repeated, "It also means *freedom*."

"Who are they?" Noah asked.

"They are a brotherhood of Undead," the professor said, sitting down. "A secret brotherhood. Although we know they exist – for we've found their name scrawled in their abandoned abodes – no Monitor has ever captured one."

A brotherhood, I thought. A brotherhood to oppose a sisterhood.

"How come?" Clémentine asked.

"They're nameless. Faceless. Dangerous," Monsieur Orneaux said, his face solemn. "Desperate. More so than you could ever imagine."

A few people shifted in their seats. "What?" I heard someone murmur.

"All Undead can take souls at random to gain a bit of life," the professor explained. "But the Brothers have pushed it to the extreme. We believe they have taken enough souls to live far past their natural span of twenty-one years, and may have even survived for centuries, killing for life. As a result, they're shells – barely human except in form."

"How many are there?" Clémentine asked.

"We believe there are nine of them."

Just like the Sisters, I thought.

"But they're vagrant," Monsieur Orneaux said. "We don't know where they are. We don't know who they are. All we know is what they want."

"Which is what?" Noah asked.

When he answered, Monsieur Orneaux looked at me. "Freedom. They want to be human again. They want their souls back. Not just temporarily, but for ever. They want immortality, and they will stop at nothing to find it. That's why they killed *les Neuf Soeurs*. To find their secret."

"What?" I said. "But why would they kill people if they wanted information?"

"All eight of the Nine Sisters who were found dead had gauze stuffed in their mouths."

A murmur rose over the class. "Gauze?" I heard someone say. "Why gauze?"

"I don't understand," I said, remembering how my parents had died, how Miss LaBarge had died. "Isn't putting gauze in the mouth a normal way for Monitors to protect themselves from the kiss of an Undead?"

The class went silent as everyone stared at me.

"No," Monsieur Orneaux said. "It's known as a

method of torture that a select few Undead use on their victims."

"Torture?" I breathed. "What do you mean?"

"It's a simple gag, made cruel because it uses the victim's own weapon. The Liberum didn't kill the Sisters immediately; they systematically tortured them. The autopsy reports, along with many accounts of the crime scenes, indicate that each of the Sisters endured prolonged suffering before they finally met death."

"What?" I whispered, my voice so small I barely recognized it. "But my grandfather said—"

Monsieur Orneaux's eye began to pulse with irritation. "He was mistaken." Picking up his notes, he resumed his lecture.

Outside on the window ledge, a pair of pigeons ruffled their feathers and then swooped down to the fountain below. I watched them bathe in the water. Both my parents and Miss LaBarge were found with gauze in their mouths. Did that mean they weren't killed in a normal Monitoring accident, but that they were tortured and then killed?

The bell sounded, signalling the end of the class.

I lingered, lost in my thoughts, as everyone filtered out of the room. In the letter from Miss LaBarge's cottage, my mother had said that she'd found a clue that would lead them to the lost girl. *Lost girl.* My grandfather thought that had been a code word for an Undead, but the more I thought about it, the more I started to believe that she had meant the ninth sister. And Miss LaBarge had clearly been looking for something, too, judging from the clippings and the maps in her cottage.

Was it possible that my parents and Miss LaBarge had discovered eternal life, and were killed because of it? Or maybe they hadn't been killed. After all, hadn't I seen Miss LaBarge at her own funeral? Driving a grey Peugeot down the streets of Montreal? My chest trembled as the impossible suddenly became possible: maybe she and my parents had used the secret and were now immortal.

The sound of a boy clearing his throat thrust me back into the world. Startled, I spun around to find Noah standing by my chair.

"Hi," he said, his voice deep and smooth like the low notes of a cello.

Today he was the colour of apple cider – his wool sweater, his hair. Embarrassed, I averted my eyes towards the window. Outside, the courtyard was crowded with students hanging out around the fountain.

"Why do you always turn pink when I talk to you?"

I felt my face grow hotter. "There, now I'm red," I said with a self-conscious smile.

He laughed. "Do you want to get a coffee?"

"Oh, no," I said quickly, pulling my backpack over one

shoulder. "I'm really busy." Even though my only plan was to go to the waterfront and wait for Dante.

"Busy with what?"

"Oh – um – it's something personal."

"Fair enough," he said, pulling out my chair with a little bow.

I made my way into the hallway, Noah on my heels. After a moment I turned around. "You seem like you want to ask me something."

Noah was closer than I expected, his face centimetres away from mine. "Why do you say that?" His breath was warm as it tickled my nose. "Aren't I allowed to walk in the hallway with you?"

"Of course," I said, caught off guard.

"But you're right," he admitted, adjusting his glasses. "I wanted to talk to you. Is that so bad?"

I tilted my head, giving him a suspicious look.

"Okay, I'll confess I do have an ulterior motive."

"Which is?"

"I'll tell you over coffee," he said.

"I have a boyfriend, you know."

"And I have a girlfriend," he said. "How presumptuous of you to think that I was flirting."

I narrowed my eyes, trying to figure out if he actually had been flirting, or if that's just the way he was.

"So we're both taken," Noah said. "Now that that's

understood, we can just be friends. And as friends, I'd like to ask you to have a hot beverage with me."

I couldn't help but smile. "Okay."

Before I knew it, we were outside walking around the streets of the old port, just talking and laughing, something I hadn't done in a while. Noah was from Montreal. He'd grown up in Outremont, a residential neighbourhood on the other side of Mont Royal. His parents were professors and Monitors. "They're very opinionated," Noah stressed. "They love to argue about politics."

I didn't tell him much about myself; only the pertinent details: I was from California; after my parents died I moved in with my grandfather in Massachusetts. I preferred listening to Noah tell me about his life, which sounded sunny, happy. It reminded me of the way mine had been, a lifetime ago.

Listening to him talk about which cafe had the best coffee in Montreal, I realized that we didn't have to talk about matters of life and death. I could shed that Renée, even if just for a few hours, and stroll down the winding streets and debate whether or not hockey was better than basketball or why Madame Goût insisted on calling Mr. Pollet, *Monsieur Po-lay.*

We were about to turn in to a bakery, when I saw the flash of a woman's face across the street.

I froze as Noah went ahead, the bells on the door

ringing as he pushed it open. The woman now had her back to me. I watched as she walked down the pavement, waiting for her to turn around.

"Renée?" Noah said from behind me. "Are you coming?"

The cars stopped as the traffic light changed to red. Slowly, the woman turned, raising her face to mine.

Stunned, I looked away.

"It's her," I said to Noah, trying to control my voice.

"Who?"

"Annette LaBarge. My old philosophy professor from Gottfried. The one who died in August."

"What?" he said, letting go of the door. It swung shut, rattling the shade on the window.

He followed my gaze up the street, where Miss LaBarge was disappearing into a crowd of tourists.

"How could that be?" Noah asked.

"I don't know," I said over my shoulder, rushing to catch up with Miss LaBarge.

He ran after me. "But you're certain it's her?"

"Yes." I arched my neck to see over the crowd. Miss LaBarge was a few metres ahead of us, moving briskly through the city, her long skirt billowing around her ankles.

"Did she see you?"

"No. Or at least she didn't seem to."

"Wait," Noah said, stopping me just before I turned down the same deserted alley she was in.

"What are you doing?" I said, yanking my arm away from him. "We could lose her."

"Think about it," he said. "She clearly doesn't want anyone to know that she's here, or alive, or else she would have contacted someone. Right?"

Reluctantly, I nodded.

"Let's just slow down. Keep our distance. See where she goes."

So that's what we did. Staying a safe half block away, we followed her all the way to downtown Montreal, where it felt like we were moving forwards in time. Instead of the quaint stone buildings of the old port, we were surrounded by big glass high-rises and expensive designer stores. Everyone on the street was wearing a suit, talking on a cellphone, and walking quickly.

We followed her until she stopped in front of a large building. Tucked into the corner, near a bus stop, was a door covered with an accordion cage. Approaching it, she pulled the cage open, stepped inside, and shut it behind her.

"What is that?" I said as I watched her press a button. A sliding door closed, and she began to move downwards.

"It's an elevator to the underground," Noah said as she disappeared beneath the street.

"Then she definitely isn't Undead. She has to be alive

– I mean *fully* alive – if she's going underground. We have to follow her."

"There's another way down."

We ran into a family-run *dépanneur*. The store was a cramped place, its windows lined with boxed foods, cleaning agents, and a few bottles of cheap wine. Two Chinese women were working the counter, arranging plastic bags.

"Hi, Mrs. Cho," Noah said, rushing by them. "We'll just be a minute," he explained, a little out of breath.

The older of the two women nodded.

I gave them a grateful smile, but Noah pulled me along. "This way," he said, winding through the aisles of cereal and dishwashing detergent and tea until we made it to the back of the store. At the end of the aisle was a fogged-over glass door, just like the ones in the freezer sections of grocery stores, except larger, and fashioned like a proper house door. It popped when Noah opened it, breaking its suction. "Get in," he said, and closed the door behind us.

The room inside was frigid. It was long and narrow, and filled with bottles and bottles of beer. The dim light reflected off their coloured glass.

"Where are we?" I asked, and then crouched by the door and rubbed a peephole in the condensation on the window to look out. The women at the counter were busy fiddling with the cash register and didn't seem disturbed at all that we had just rushed past them and climbed into their freezer.

Noah's glasses were fogged. Taking them off, he squinted and wiped them on his shirt. "The beer refrigerator. A lot of *dep*s have them. Come on."

There was a narrow walkway in between the rows of cases. Noah walked down it. "This one's really good," he said, pointing to a dark stout. "Oh, and this one," he said, picking up a large red bottle with a corked head.

At the back of the room was a steel staircase. Moving a few boxes out of the way, Noah cleared enough space for us to walk down, and I followed him, the dust from the railing collecting on my hands.

"*Et voilà,*" he said, gesturing towards the murky tunnel at the bottom of the stairs. "The underground."

A brief moment of unease took hold of me as I looked down at him and remembered my vision of the cemetery, and the suffocating feeling of standing in the hole. That couldn't have been me, I thought. Shaking it off, I ran down the remaining steps.

We searched the maze of tunnels for nearly an hour, weaving between businesswomen and men in suits, mothers pushing strollers, and teenagers slurping milkshakes; but we never found her.

"You saw her, right?" I said to Noah, slowing to a stop. "I'm not losing my mind. You saw her too."

"I saw someone. But maybe it wasn't Annette LaBarge," Noah said. "Maybe it was just a lookalike. That happens a lot."

"Maybe," I said, gazing down the tunnel one last time.

"I never met her in person," he said. "I only saw the pictures in the papers. You'd know better than I would."

It was her, I thought. Or maybe it wasn't. I wasn't sure about anything any more. After all, how could it have been Miss LaBarge? I had watched her casket sink at sea.

Giving up, Noah led me back through a narrow tunnel to the St. Clément exit.

It was nearing dinner time when we made it back to school, but as we approached the gates, I slowed down. I didn't want to go back yet. To what? My empty dorm room? To the library books stacked on my desk; the same ones I had been poring over all semester? Looking at the ground, I kicked a rock down the street and watched as it rolled into the sewer.

"We never got that coffee," I said, stopping before we reached the gates. "You wouldn't want to get dinner with me, would you?"

Noah grinned. "Yes."

He brought me to an Italian grocery store, a short distance from school. Inside, everything was tiny and packaged in little tins or paper wrapping tied with ribbon. The men behind the counter wore white butchers' coats.

There was an entire corner devoted only to ravioli.

"What do you feel like eating?" Noah said, walking down the cramped aisles, a bounce in his step.

I bit my lip, embarrassed to admit what I was actually craving. "Pie?"

He gazed at me, a big grin spreading over his face. "Me too. And olives. Oh, and spaghetti," he said, pressing his fingers against a glass counter of prepared foods.

He zigzagged through the store, picking things off the shelves and piling them in my arms until I could barely see where I was walking. One hard salami. A wedge of cheese. A package of green figs. A container of pre-made spaghetti with pesto. And a slice of rhubarb pie from the bakery section, with a carton of vanilla ice cream to go on the side.

I kept laughing and dropping things on the floor as he took the items from me and placed them by the register.

While Noah joked with the cashier, I gazed out the window. The street lamps were off, but as I watched, something pale emerged from the darkness, approaching the storefront. I leaned forward, squinting into the night. A car passed, its headlights wrapping around the silhouette of a boy, his shoulders shifting as he moved towards me.

Slowly, the smile faded from my face. *Dante,* my lips mouthed as I watched the outline of his body, trying to make out his arms, his chest, his face.

"Renée," Noah said, leaning towards me.

Dante must have seen him standing beside me, because he froze.

The wedge of cheese slipped from my hands. No, I thought. Don't go.

As I made for the door, the figs slipped from my hands, but I didn't even stop to pick them up. "I'm sorry," I said to Noah as he bent over the fruit on the floor. "I'll be right back." And with that, I ran outside.

"Wait!" I yelled, but when I reached the pavement, Dante was nowhere to be seen. Desperate, I ran into the middle of the street, looking wildly in either direction. He was gone.

Through the storefront window, I could see Noah staring at me, confused. Stuffing my hands in my pockets, I walked back, when something caught my eye on the telephone pole next to where I had just seen Dante. A flyer was stapled to the post, its sides flapping in the wind. I flattened it out, my mouth dropping as I read the words scrawled in Latin over the advertisement in thick marker. I translated:

WAIT FOR ME.

"Are you okay?" Noah said as I stepped inside. "You look like you just saw a ghost."

"I think I did," I said softly, my mind racing. Had Dante left that note for me to find? How many people wrote notes in Latin around the city?

"Why did you run out there? What did you see?"

I paused, trying to feel for Dante's presence, but there was nothing; not even the slightest hint of him anywhere. Maybe it was just graffiti. Maybe I was losing my mind. Maybe he had never even been there in the first place. "Someone I haven't seen in a long time."

Wait for me, the wind seemed to say as we stepped outside. Even if Dante hadn't written it, I would wait.

We walked to a stone courtyard nearby and sat on the ground, surrounded by skinny trees, barren, save for a few lingering yellow leaves. Behind us stood a fountain with a statue of a boy playing the flute, filling the night with the quiet sound of trickling water. What did a flute sound like? I tried to remember, but couldn't.

Noah loosened the knot of his tie, revealing a freckle on his neck, and handed me a fork.

"*Bon appétit,*" he said, the street lamps illuminating his face.

As he poured me a glass of sparkling apple juice, I said, "At the end of class today, you said you had an ulterior motive for asking me to coffee. What was it?"

"I wanted to ask you what you were doing the other day in the hospital. With Anya."

"Oh." Immediately, I regretted asking.

I stared at my pie, which, despite my craving, still tasted bland. I could lie. I could tell him I was there visiting someone.

"You weren't visiting anyone," Noah said.

I clenched my jaw. Okay, that option was out. But I could still evade the question. Or I could just tell him the truth. I felt his eyes on me. He had just run across the city with me, chasing someone I thought was Miss LaBarge.

Reaching into my pocket, I touched the piece of paper on which I had written both parts of the riddle. I told him about my visions of the hospital and the cemetery, how I had gone to each and found this riddle. I omitted Dante and Clémentine. "The grave was there, just like I had seen it in my vision."

"You're joking," he said, his eyes searching mine.

"No," I said softly.

"It can't be," he said, a glimmer of a smile masking his unease. "I thought the immortality part was just a legend."

Taking the paper with the verses out of my pocket, I handed it to him. He unfolded it and spread it out on the ground and read the inscriptions.

to arrive there
follow the nose of the bear
to the salty waters beneath;
here it is laid to rest
where to only the best
of our kind it shall be bequeathed.

Noah didn't say anything for a long while. "You really found these? You didn't just make them up?"

"Why would I make them up?"

The smile fell from his face. "I don't know," he said.

Inching towards him, I leaned over the paper. "I've been trying to figure out what it means, but I haven't been able to get anywhere. It must mean somewhere in the cemetery, but there isn't any water there except for a drinking fountain."

He held the verses up to the light, reading them to himself again, before turning to me. "But of course it isn't buried in this grave. Look." He pointed to the line: *here it is laid to rest.* "When this line is isolated on a tombstone, it would lead you to believe that the secret was literally buried in that plot. But when you put it next to the riddle from the hospital, its meaning changes."

"The tombstone isn't marking anything," I realized, squinting at the page.

"Exactly," Noah said. "It's not buried in the cemetery. It's a trick, done on purpose to make people searching for the secret think it's buried there. But it's not. It's in salt water. Maybe in the ocean. The problem is that you're missing the last part, which I would guess is actually the first part, if you look at the punctuation."

"How do you know there's only one part of the riddle left?" I asked. "What if there are more?"

"I don't think there are," he said. "If there are three riddles, with three lines each, then there are a total of nine lines. One for each of the Sisters. All the tombstone riddle tells us is that the secret can only be found by Monitors," Noah said. "The phrase *the best of our kind* must mean that only the best Monitor will find it." Noah's eyes fell on me. "That's you."

Pulling my knees towards me, I shook my head. "No, I'm just ranked number one at St. Clément. There are lots of older, better Monitors than me. I couldn't even figure out the riddle without your help."

"All Monitors work in pairs..." he said, his gaze resting on me.

Blushing, I looked at my food, which I had barely touched. I should have felt flattered, but instead I was overwhelmed with guilt. "And you have Clémentine," I said softly.

"Right," he said, and we sat in an uncomfortable silence, Noah slicing more cheese as I glanced around the courtyard, wondering if, somehow, Dante was watching us right now.

"What we have to do is start looking for a body of salt water with some sort of bear near it. One that only Monitors can find."

"Or alternatively, that the Undead can't find. The Undead can't sink in water," I said, unable to meet his eye as I remembered the dead man's float lecture from gym class last year, and how we learned that once a person dies and reanimates, he floats to the surface. "It's got to be buried underwater somewhere."

"You might be right," Noah said, his hand grazing mine as he passed the piece of paper back to me. "What do you think it leads to?"

I imagined following Miss LaBarge to a small house where she was in hiding. When she opened the door, my parents were behind her, their eyes watering as they ran to me and wrapped me in their arms. "What took you so long?" they asked. I thought of Dante, of meeting him out in the open, on the streets of Montreal. I imagined him pinning me against the wall of my dorm room and kissing me. I thought of us ten years from now, falling asleep next to each other, our chests rising and falling in unison. I thought of the way he would look when he was older; I could almost see it. I picked up a fig, twirling its stem in my finger. "Happiness."

Noah studied me through his glasses, as if he could see a different side of me. Suddenly he said, "I like you."

I was so taken aback that I didn't know what to say. I loved Dante. He was my soulmate. "I'm sorry," I said softly, "but I— "

"No, I'm sorry," he said, shaking himself out of the moment. "I just meant that I don't know anyone else who would do this with me."

I rested my cheek on my hand, not sure what he meant.

He leaned back on his palms. "Chase a woman around underground. Buy one of every item in a gourmet grocery store and eat everything straight out of the box, while sitting on the ground in a random courtyard. And then for dessert, show me a set of cryptic messages that might lead to the secret of the Nine Sisters."

"I've barely eaten anything," I said. "And you make it sound much more exciting than it is."

Noah let out a laugh. "That's definitely not true. I don't know any girls who would break into a hospital through a private tunnel entry, sneak into a hospital room while someone is sleeping inside, and crawl under the bed to retrieve an engraving."

I wanted to tell him that I had seen Clémentine in the cemetery the other night, looking for the same thing I had been looking for, but for some reason I didn't. Maybe it was because I liked the way Noah was looking at me, as if there were no one else in the world. It reminded me of what I could have with Dante.

"You know I don't do this kind of thing every night," I said. "Most of the time I'm in my room alone, wishing I had a different life."

"I don't believe that."

"It's true," I said. "I'm not doing this for fun."

"What are you doing it for, then?"

Dante, my heart cried. "A wild dream, I guess."

I shivered. Noah took off his coat and draped it around my shoulders. "No, please," I said. "I'm fine." But he wouldn't let me refuse. Touching its lapels, I pulled it around me. It was still warm from his body.

"You look good in that," he said, gazing at me, his eyes like melting chocolate.

"Noah," I said gently.

Before I could go on, Noah completed my sentence. "You have a boyfriend – I know, I know. But a friend can still give a compliment, no?"

"What about Clémentine?"

The smile on Noah's face faded.

"I'm sorry," I said, wishing I hadn't mentioned her. "It's private; I shouldn't have asked."

"No," he said quickly. "It's fine. It's just hard to explain."

Leaning forward, I hugged my knees. "I know the feeling."

"When I first met her in class, I knew there was no one like her. She has this amazing sharp wit, and there was something about her that bit into me and wouldn't let go. She would challenge me when I was wrong; she would always push me to be better, stronger, smarter. She'll never settle for anything less than what she wants. I loved that about her."

"Loved? Past tense?"

"I still love her," he said. "But not in the same way. When we're together she wants to do couples' things. Watch movies, go out for expensive dinners. But she doesn't want...*adventure*. She doesn't want to have fun. That edge that she used to have, I only see glimmers of it now. We've been together for a year, and she only wants to work, to be the best." He paused, picking at his spaghetti. "She always says that everything worth doing is hard."

"She's right," I said, surprising myself.

"But should a relationship be hard?" Noah asked.

Around us, pigeons cooed from the tops of the buildings, but it just sounded like noise. The moonlight filtered through the water of the fountain, but no matter how long I stared at it, I couldn't see its beauty. And the food that I'd thought I wanted now sat in front of me, untouched. Maybe things would be easier with another boy, but Dante was the only person who understood how delicate life was, how quickly it vanished. He didn't care if I was the best Monitor in school, or if I was fun enough or wild enough; he just enjoyed my company. He knew how to make a single Latin word sound like poetry, how to make the past come alive and the present feel like it passed far too quickly. He made me *feel*. Without him, the world was nothing but a paper background.

I felt Noah waiting for me to respond, but I didn't know

how to tell him that I wasn't looking for adventure; I was looking for a way for me and Dante to grow old together, so we could watch movies together, go out for expensive dinners. I yearned for the same things Clémentine did; I just knew I could never have them.

CHAPTER 9

MAL DE MER

I DIDN'T REMEMBER GOING HOME that night; I just remembered Noah. How he kept finding ways to brush his hand against mine. How our shadows angled together as we walked beneath the street lamps. How if I closed my eyes, I could almost imagine that he was Dante.

Before I knew it, I was back in the darkness of my room, alone. I took off Noah's blazer and draped it over the back of my chair. But in the dark it almost felt as though Noah was there, sitting with me. Even though I knew Dante couldn't see me, I quickly tucked the coat into my closet, ashamed that I even had another boy's blazer in my room. And pressing my back against the door, I shook Noah out of my head, picked up my towel, and went to the bathroom to take a shower.

But when I turned the knob, the door was locked.

"Occupied," Clémentine called out. Through the door, I heard a chorus of giggles.

I threw my towel on a nearby armchair, and was about to collapse onto my bed when I heard one of them mention Anya's name.

Crouching by the door, I listened.

"I don't even understand how she got into this school." Josie's voice was full of spite. "You should have seen her the other day, trying to find the dead animal in the river. She had no idea what she was doing."

Another girl chimed in. "She can barely speak French or Latin. She can't sense a dead thing when it's on her plate; she can't dig a proper hole or even build a makeshift pyre; but she still ranked number four. Can you believe that?"

I glared at the door, but the truth was, they were right. If Anya had any talent as a Monitor, I hadn't witnessed it either, and I had no idea how she'd ranked number four, or how she'd been placed into the top Strategy and Prediction class.

Clémentine's voice rose above the others. "I heard she tried to commit suicide a couple of times. Obviously, it didn't work. How is she going to kill the Undead when she can't even kill herself?"

At that, I gave the door a firm kick and stormed out of my room, taking my towel with me.

Walking down the hall, I knocked on Anya's door. I could hear heavy metal blaring from inside. I knocked twice more, louder, and eventually the door opened.

Anya stood before me in an oversized collared shirt and shorts, a towel draped over her neck. Her hair was held up in all sorts of odd angles with pieces of tinfoil, and smeared with a reddish paste.

"Oh, hi," she said, looking at me and then my towel.

Her sleeves were rolled up, showing the insides of her arms, which were covered with irregular white scars that looked like burn marks. They appeared to have been there for a while. I had never noticed them before; she always wore long sleeves.

Anya must have caught me staring, because she immediately rolled down the cuffs of her shirt.

"Are you okay?" I asked.

"I'm fine," she muttered, and looked down the hall.

"Can I use your shower? Clémentine and her friends are in my bathroom."

While Anya sat on the bed and flipped through a magazine, I shut myself in the bathroom and turned on the tap, listening to Anya's music blaring in the background.

Standing under the hot water, I couldn't stop thinking about what Noah had said. Should relationships be hard? The question didn't even seem to apply to Dante and me. It didn't matter if it was easy or hard – with him gone, it felt like a piece of me had been carved away. Did that mean that I didn't have a choice? Water trickled down my face, collecting on my lashes. What if Dante had lied to me about the cemetery? What if he had been there before, and all of my visions had really been his? What would I do then?

As steam clouded the room, I pressed my eyes closed and tried to feel the warmth of the water, but the more I concentrated on it, the more tepid it felt. I turned the temperature up, letting it beat down on my back, and then turned it up again and again, waiting for something to happen as the water pooled about my feet and the skin on my fingers wrinkled.

By the time I emerged, Anya had changed the music to a mellow folk album.

"You were in there for a while," Anya said as I sat next to her on the couch, the steam following me.

She was sitting cross-legged, stringing something onto a piece of twine. Her hair was still pressed in pieces of foil.

"What are you making?" I said, rubbing my head with my towel.

"A charm necklace," she said. "For you."

Beside her, a buzzer went off. She hit the top of it and stood up. "Time to wash the dye out," she said, and threw the necklace into my lap. "Be right back."

While she washed her hair out in the sink, I studied the necklace. The frayed twine was strung with dozens of different dried beans, some as small as a pea, some as large as a quarter. Most of them had a white spot in the middle, which made them look like eyes. In the middle of the necklace hung what seemed to be a white rabbit's foot. I touched it. The fur was delicate and soft.

"So what do you think of it?" Anya said from the doorway.

"It's – nice," I said. "What's it made of?"

"Mung beans, black-eyed peas, fava beans, kidney beans... They're supposed to bring you health."

"And the rabbit's foot?"

"Oh, it's not a rabbit. It's a cat."

Letting the necklace drop into my lap, I said, "What? Why? Where did you—"

"It's from an herbal store I go to sometimes. It's for protection. It's supposed to give you nine lives."

"Oh," I said, examining the necklace again, trying not to feel queasy. "Thanks."

"And here," she said, picking up a mug from her nightstand and carrying it to me. "This is for you."

The mug was warm when I took it from her, the liquid inside murky and a brownish-green. "What is it?"

"It's tea," she said.

I swirled the cup around, but the contents were so viscous that they barely moved. "Really? What kind?" I said with a grimace.

"Oh, it's just an herbal thing. Good for the cold season."

I glanced in her mug. The water inside was a pleasant peach colour. A normal teabag dangled from a string.

"Why aren't you drinking any?" I asked.

"Oh, I already had some."

"Right," I said, taking a sip. It tasted like water from the bottom of a flower vase, and was oddly gritty.

She watched me, pleased. I told her about how I saw Miss LaBarge while I was with Noah, how she and my parents had died with gauze in their mouths. When I was finished, Anya's forehead was furrowed, her wet red hair dangling over her shoulders, leaving water marks on her shirt.

"Maybe they found the secret of the Nine Sisters and became immortal," I said. "Maybe that's why I'm seeing Miss LaBarge everywhere – because she's still alive. And maybe – maybe—"

"Your parents are still alive then, too?" Anya offered, finishing my sentence.

I fiddled with the hem of my shirt, nodding.

"I don't know," she said. "It doesn't seem right. Your parents were searching for the 'lost girl' when they wrote Miss LaBarge the letter, right? So that means they couldn't have found the secret. They were probably just searching for it, like us. And after they died, Miss LaBarge took what they found a step further. She was looking for something having to do with lakes or water—"

"Which is kind of what we're looking for," I said, thinking about the saltwater riddle.

"Exactly. Which means she hadn't found it either. And then she was killed."

I spun the beans on the necklace, unable to accept what she was saying. Why couldn't Miss LaBarge be alive? Why couldn't immortality be real? Why couldn't my parents still be alive? "But that doesn't explain why I keep seeing Miss LaBarge."

"You keep having weird visions," she reminded me. "Couldn't she be one of those, too?"

"But Noah saw her. Not just me."

"He never met her when she was alive, did he? He could have been mistaken. It could have just been someone who looked like her."

I sat back, frustrated. "Fine," I said. "You're right. They're dead. They're all dead. Does that make you happy?"

"It's better this way," she offered. "If your parents had

been alive all this time, and hadn't contacted you, that would be even more disturbing."

I gazed at the lamp until it burned a yellow orb into my vision. As much as I didn't want to admit it, she was right. If my parents were alive, they would've found a way to contact me. And Miss LaBarge – maybe I had been seeing things. "You can't know for sure, though," I said. "The only way to be certain is to follow the riddles. Maybe they'll all lead us to them."

It could have been a trick of the light, but Anya seemed to grow uncomfortable. "Yeah..." she murmured, and took a sip from her tea. "Drink up," she said, staring at my mug. "You've barely touched yours."

I ignored her. "Noah thinks there's one piece left of the riddle, the first piece, which will tie the clues together. We have to find it."

"You told *Noah* about them? As in Clémentine's Noah?"

I shrugged. "He chased Miss LaBarge with me. What else was I supposed to do? Besides, he helped."

"Barely," Anya said, sipping at her tea. "You know, I've been thinking about the riddles, and we're asking the wrong questions."

"What do you mean?"

"The Sisters vowed to let their secret die with them. So why would they hide the riddles?"

"You already asked that," I said. "And I still don't know."

"Well maybe we should figure it out. Think about it. The hospital room. The headstone. The riddles we've found so far haven't been hidden in major historical landmarks or encrypted in pieces of art. They're in places that would be important to an individual – a headstone, a hospital bed."

I leaned back, crossing my legs on the couch as I considered what she was suggesting. "The ninth sister," I said. "You think the ninth sister hid these in places that were meaningful to her."

Anya nodded.

"But why?"

"I don't know," Anya said, tapping her nails on the arm of the couch. "But we can guess a few things about her. Judging from the portrait of the Nine Sisters, she had to have been around our age in the 1730s, when the other Monitors were killed. She had ties to Montreal, which we know because of the headstone. And she was associated with the Royal Victoria Hospital."

As the first snow began to fall over St. Clément, dusting the shingles of the buildings in a thin layer of white, the wind blew through to my bones, rattling around inside me as if I were hollow. Anya and I searched for the ninth sister, going through as many records as we could in the St. Clément library, pulling dusty tomes out of the shelves one by one, and scanning every page. But before 1950, the information was slim and disorganized.

When that didn't work, I took to wandering the streets of Montreal, hoping that something I saw would set off another vision; though, really, I was looking for Dante. I found traces of him everywhere – a used Latin book left on my usual table at the coffee shop, a note scrawled inside that read: *I'm searching*; a message traced into the frost on a window: *I miss you*; graffiti etched into a mailbox near the corner store: *Remember us*. Every time I saw one, my heart trembled in my chest, and I had to force myself to look away so that I didn't draw attention to myself. Anya came with me at first, but as the holidays approached, her father asked her to help him at his store, which left me on my own. Sometimes Noah would join me, catching up with me after class, and together we'd walk down the snowy cobblestones, gazing up at the gargoyles that guarded the roofs. Every time I felt a cold breeze blow through an alleyway, I froze, staring at the empty street, waiting for Dante to appear. But he never did.

I didn't realize what I was doing. I thought I was just filling the time while Dante was gone, but as the weeks passed, every day pulled us further apart. I didn't know what was happening until I found myself looking forward to bumping into Noah, and then making plans to bump into him. When we were together, it felt like the pressure had been lifted from my chest. To be able to walk with someone and not talk about anything.

It was on one of the rare days when I wandered alone that I found myself on the waterfront, staring at the abandoned grain silos.

When the tourists had cleared, I approached the railing. Gazing across the water of the St. Lawrence River to the opposite shore, I cleared my throat. "Where are you?" I said, and without waiting to hear my echo, I continued. "Why do you always disappear? Why haven't you come to find me?"

My voice cracked and I paused, pushing my hair behind my ear as I tried to compose myself. When my questions bounced back to me, they were jumbled and confused, the words laying themselves on top of each other, each question repeating itself and merging with the next into incoherent mush. Just like the way I felt.

Where are you? I heard finally, my voice fading as it bounced off the walls of the silo. *Where are you?*

Tired, I leaned against the metal railing, empty of questions, of answers, of energy to even ask any more, when I heard a voice. Not from the echo, but from behind me.

"I'm right here."

My body grew rigid as his cold breath tickled my ear. I spun around. "Dante?"

I saw the cuff of his shirt first, followed by the collar, the lock of hair dangling by his chin, the pen tucked behind his ear. "You're here," I said, gazing at the stubble on his cheek, at his thin lips as he said, "I'm sorry it took so long."

"You left me those notes," I said, my eyes darting around us to make sure no one was watching.

Dante nodded. "I've been trying to reach you for weeks," he said. "But I haven't been able to find you alone."

I bit my lip, feeling suddenly guilty. "That night in the cemetery. You never finished your sentence."

Dante was silent for a minute. "I wish I could tell you what I'm doing," he said. "But I can't. I can't put you in danger."

I stood back. "Okay," I said slowly. "But what do you mean? Are you saying you *had* been to the cemetery before?"

Before he could answer, a voice called out to me from the distance. "Renée?"

I jolted at the sound of my name. Dante spun around, his eyes darting around the waterfront.

Noah, I thought. Not sure what to do, I turned to

Dante. "He wasn't supposed to meet me today," I said quickly.

"Who?" Dante said, narrowing his eyes.

"A Monitor. You have to go," I said, and glanced over my shoulder. From across the street, Noah waved at me, but I didn't wave back. "I'm going to go and distract him," I said, taking Dante's hand. Above us the seagulls cried as they wove around each other.

"Wait," Dante said, holding my wrist. "Tell me you believe me. That you believe I would never hurt you or anyone else."

"I do," I said, my eyes darting to Noah. If he found Dante, he would tell the professors, and it would all be over.

"Say it out loud," Dante said, his brown eyes pleading with me. "Please."

"I believe you," I said, confused. "You would never hurt me or anyone else."

A look of relief passed over his face, and he loosened his grip on my arm. "I love you," he said. "Now go."

Slipping away from the cold swirl of Dante, I ran to Noah. "What are you doing here?" I said, blocking his path.

"I got out of class early and came to find you," he said, a little perplexed. "Are you okay? You're acting kind of nervous."

"I'm fine," I said, staring at the reflection of the silos in

269

Noah's glasses, as Dante walked down the wharf, keeping his head lowered.

Noah must have seen him too, because he said, "Who was that?"

"Who?"

"That guy you were talking to."

"Oh, he was just a stranger asking me for directions."

Noah stepped back. "You're lying. I saw the way you looked at him. You seemed upset."

I followed his gaze down the street, where Dante was disappearing into a crowd. "I can feel him," Noah said, squinting. "He's an – an—"

Undead, I thought, though Noah never finished his sentence. Instead, he turned to me. "It's him, isn't it?" he said in disbelief. "Your boyfriend is an Undead."

"No," I said, shaking my head. "He's just a friend."

Noah backed away from me. "That's why you never talk about him. That's your big secret?"

"No—" I started to say, but he cut me off.

"How could you not tell me?"

"Tell you what?" I said, going rigid. "It's not your life, it's mine. You have a girlfriend, remember?"

"Don't bring Clémentine into this," he said, his voice so firm it was unfamiliar.

"Why not? You're with me every day. Does she know? Is that why she's so rude to me?"

"I know you don't like her, but Clémentine would never date an Undead while training to be a Monitor. It's not right," he said, his voice low.

I stepped away from him in disbelief. "So now Clémentine is my moral standard? What does she know about love? About loss? What do *you* know about it?"

Noah seemed to shrink back at my words, and I immediately felt guilty for hurting him. "She had to bury her brother last summer. He was an Undead. Her father made her do it. She hasn't told anyone for the same reasons you haven't told anyone about your secret, I'm guessing. Though her decision was very different to yours."

July thirtieth, I thought, remembering what Anya had said to Clémentine in the hallway earlier this year. That's what she'd been referring to. My eyes wandered from the waterfront to Noah, but when I looked up at him he was already gone.

When I returned to my room that night, it was all I could do to lie in bed with the blankets off and windows open, letting the cold air seep in, as if it were Dante's presence wrapping itself around me. I needed something to remind me of him; to bring me back to him. So I did the next best thing. I called Eleanor.

"You sound depressed," she said, after I had told her

everything. "Maybe you should see a doctor."

Eleanor's suggestion caught me off guard. "What? I'm not depressed," I said, as I curled up in an armchair by the window, watching the street lamps flicker to life as night fell over the courtyard.

"You've been having visions. Hallucinations. And you're seeing another guy? What about Dante? He's your soulmate."

"Noah is just a friend." I whispered so Clémentine wouldn't hear.

Eleanor didn't say anything for a long time. Through the walls, I could hear Clémentine yell something, her tone angry. Maybe she was on the phone with Noah.

"I've been going to therapy, and it's really helping me... understand myself," Eleanor said. "And understanding myself helps me control myself."

"Therapy?" I said. "But you're fine the way you are. You don't need to see a doctor."

Eleanor lowered her voice. "I've been having a lot of thoughts lately. Bad thoughts."

I frowned. "What do you mean?"

"About life and death. About me and what makes me different. About the things I want."

I waited for her to go on.

"I'm so scared," she said, the words quivering through the receiver. "I don't want to die."

"You won't," I said automatically, not wanting to even think about it.

Eleanor let out a cold laugh. "Renée, you know I'm Undead. I only get another twenty-one years. That means that unless a miracle happens, I'm almost middle-aged."

"No," I said. "We're going to find a way out. The Nine Sisters. The visions. The riddles. When I find the last one, you'll—"

But Eleanor cut me off, her voice firmer than I had ever heard it before. "There is no answer, Renée. You're in denial. I'm going to die. Dante's going to die. We're all going to die."

I swallowed. "No," I said. "You're just upset. There's a solution, I know it."

I heard Eleanor take a deep breath. "The other day I was walking to the Megaron, and I saw one of the maintenance worker's sons smoking behind the bushes when he was supposed to be watering the plants. He only looks a little older than me. I couldn't stop staring at him. I kept thinking, why does he get to have a full life when I don't? What makes him more deserving than me?"

"He's not," I said.

"I wanted to take his soul, Renée. I wanted to go up to him and just take it."

I went quiet.

"Are you still there?"

"I'm here," I said. "It wouldn't help you, though. He doesn't have your soul."

"I know," she said. "I wasn't thinking. I was just so angry. I felt like I had no time. Taking his soul would give me more time."

I felt the same way. Dante only had five years left, and although I never would have admitted it to Eleanor, ever since Latin, when the professor told us about the Liberum living long past their lifespans, I had been trying to suppress the one thought that I knew was too terrible to consider: if the Liberum could take souls to extend their lives, so could Dante. "I know how you feel," I said. "But I wonder if it'll always feel like we have no time, even if we live until we're eighty."

"Not me," she said. "When I was little, I used to put on make-up and picture the way I would look when I was older. But when I try to imagine it now, I can't."

I smiled, remembering the way she put expensive lotion on her face every night when we were at Gottfried. "You were obsessed with wrinkles."

"I still am," she said. "Only now, I want them."

Eleanor's words echoed in my head as Headmaster LaGuerre drove us to a small wooded area outside of Montreal. It was an overcast November afternoon, the trees bare and frostbitten. In front of me, Clémentine's head rested on Noah's shoulder as we crossed a planked bridge. I studied her slender neck and the short waves of her hair, trying to imagine what she would look like in twenty-one years, what Noah would look like. By then, Eleanor would be dead.

Noah and I hadn't spoken since our fight at the waterfront, and even though I felt terrible about what I'd said, I was still angry. What gave him the right to make judgments about my life? And worse: what if his judgments were right?

We parked on a shoulder and carried our tools to a clearing in the woods, now dusted with snow.

"In order to be a great Monitor, you must treat burial rituals as an art form," the headmaster said. "You must read the soil just by crumbling it in your fingers; dig the deepest holes, craft the most durable coffins, and wrap the dead as if you were draping a mannequin in delicate silk.

"The object of today's exercise is to build a funeral pyre. You will work alone, gathering your supplies from the forest. At the end of the class we will ignite them." He unrolled a cloth bag and handed each of us an axe. "The characteristics of a good funeral pyre are as follows: first, it must ignite quickly and stay ignited. Second, it must be sturdy enough to hold the weight of a human without collapsing. Third, it should generate as little smoke as possible. Drawing attention to a funeral pyre is never in our interest."

When he was finished, we dispersed, running to the trees to collect as much wood as possible. I passed Anya chopping off the branches of a birch tree; Brett, who was working at a decomposing pine; and April and Allison, who seemed to be working together despite the headmaster's instructions. To my right, Clémentine sauntered through the trees, swinging her axe at the underbrush to make a path.

I gathered only dead wood that I foraged from the forest floor, and piled it at my spot in the clearing.

Across from me, Noah rolled up his sleeves, broke a branch over his thigh, and began to weave his wood together, his hands moving quickly as if he were working a loom.

I wasn't exactly sure what I was doing when I bent down and stacked the wood in pairs, threading them together until I had formed the base of a winding staircase.

Clémentine worked next to me. Her jacket was strewn on the ground, and her shirt was marked with sweat as she tiptoed around a pile of sticks that seemed to collapse in on itself every time she tried to set a new piece of wood on top. Frustrated, she threw a branch to the ground and took a big gulp from her water bottle. When she glimpsed my half-finished pyre, a look of shock flashed across her face, but quickly hardened into a glare.

Ignoring her, I wiped my hands on my skirt and traipsed off into the forest to collect more tinder.

On the way back, I passed Anya, who was sitting on the ground surrounded by sticks and twigs and leafy branches, looking dejected. Her face was streaked with dirt.

"Are you okay?" I asked, stooping next to her.

She threw her hands in the air. "No matter how I arrange them, they always fall over. It's hopeless."

I waited until no one was watching, and with swift motions, arranged her sticks into the beginning of a cylinder. "Like this," I said, before going back to my place.

By the end of class, Noah and I were the only ones who had finished pyres that could support the weight of a person; all of the others collapsed. Mine looked like a spiral staircase that climbed around a pedestal. "Lovely," the headmaster said, prodding the bottom level to check its foundations. But Noah's was exquisite. It was hundreds of thin sticks latticed around the centre platform like the inside of shell. He looked nervous when the headmaster stood up, his face wide with shock as he ran his hands across the joints of the wood.

"Remarkable," he said. "*Tout simplement remarquable.*"

And with that, the headmaster struck a match and lit the pyre. The flame caught immediately, travelling around the structure like fingers. But when he held a match to mine, nothing happened.

I raised a hand to my cheek, confused, as the headmaster struck another match, and then another.

"Your wood is wet," he remarked, touching a branch and rubbing his fingers together.

"What?" I said. "But I specifically chose dry, dead wood. None of it was wet."

The headmaster didn't respond. Instead, he struck another match, and then another, until the wood finally ignited. But as the fire spread to the rest of the pyre, the clearing was engulfed in thick, black smoke.

Moving away, everyone started to cough and swat at the air.

"Why is this happening?" I said. "I don't understand."

The headmaster picked up an axe, and with three rapid swings, he took the pyre down, the wood collapsing outwards until the fire went out and the smoke cleared. In the middle of my pyre was a messy pile of damp leaves and weeds, hissing as the smoke curled out of the embers.

"But I didn't put those there," I said. "I never put wet leaves in my pyre."

I glanced around the clearing, but no one seemed to care. As everyone began to pack up, my eyes rested on Clémentine, who gave me the beginning of a smile before bending over to pick up her water bottle. It was empty.

I threw my tools on the ground and was about to go over to her, when I saw Noah a couple of metres away. He had picked up Clémentine's coat but was frozen in place. He must have seen her look at me, because he studied her, his face twisting with disgust as he realized what she'd done. Dropping her coat at his feet, he turned and walked back to the van.

Clémentine sat in the back row, and Noah just in front of her, as we drove back to school. When there was a lull in the headmaster's music, I could hear the low hum of their arguing. As we wound through the streets, I felt a thin strand of cold air wrap itself around my ankles and then break free as we turned a corner.

"Did you feel that?" I asked Anya.

"Feel what?" she said, looking up from her book.

I held up a finger to silence her, and closed my eyes, trying to find it again, but there was nothing.

"Never mind," I said, and gazed out the window, staring at the faces of the people on the street, hoping to see Dante. When we got back to St. Clément, it was raining. As I walked across the courtyard with Anya, I felt a hand on the sleeve of my coat. Hearing Clémentine's voice near me, I whipped around. "Don't touch me." I was face to face with Noah.

He stepped back, retracting his hand. "Sorry, I didn't mean to bother you."

"Oh," I said, crossing my arms over my chest. "I thought you were..." I stopped short before saying her name.

"Ah," he said, understanding who I was talking about. "I see. Well, I just wanted to—"

"You don't have to apologize for her. I can take care of myself."

Noah pushed a lock of hair out of his face. " – apologize for my behaviour," he said. "I shouldn't have said all those things. I don't know anything about the guy or how he treats you. I was just caught off guard."

Biting my lip, I nodded. "I'm sorry, too. I didn't—"

"Don't worry," he said. "I know."

The mist speckled his glasses, the water catching on the rust stubble climbing up his cheeks. "I also wanted to ask what you were doing on Friday."

"Friday?" Even though I had no plans, I pretended to think about it so as not to appear pathetic. "I don't know. I'll have to check."

He hesitated, as if he were nervous. "Would you..." he said slowly, "have any interest in coming to my house for dinner?"

"Your house? Like with your parents?" I said, both flattered and confused.

"Yeah," he said, with an amused smile. "Haven't you ever been to dinner with someone's parents?"

To my embarrassment, I hadn't. At least not to a boy's house. Dante didn't have any parents, and before that... well, I could hardly remember life before that. The thought of having dinner with Noah's parents was so traditional, so normal, that it was almost strange.

"I go home every Friday, and even though my parents are delightful people, I don't know if I can take an entire evening alone with them this week. Having you there might actually make it fun." I must have looked a little uneasy, because he added, "Take pity on me?"

"But what about Clémentine?"

Noah's dimples disappeared as his smile faded. "What about her?"

"She's your girlfriend. Shouldn't you be bringing her?"

He scratched his head. "Right, well...we've been fighting." He shoved his hands into his pockets. "The point is, I'm asking you."

I bit my lip. "Oh, that's nice, but—"

"Great," he said with a huge grin. "I'll take that as a yes. I'll meet you at the gates at six."

That Friday, I spent an hour trying on clothes in front of the mirror in the bathroom, the thick fabrics tickling the mark between my shoulders, before I finally settled on an outfit that said "Just friends".

"What are you doing in there?" Clémentine yelled through the door. I was tempted to tell her that I was getting ready to go to dinner with Noah, but then decided that was too cruel.

Noah's parents lived in a beautiful brick town house in Outremont. We took the Metro there. It was crowded, and Noah's hand kept slipping down the metal railing, touching mine.

His father answered the door, wearing an apron over his work suit. Comfortably plump, with full cheeks and a swirl of brown hair clinging to the top of his head like a toupee, he looked nothing like Noah. He was holding a glass of red wine. "Ah, hello!" he said with a smile, his face flushed as he gave Noah a hug, the wine sloshing out of his glass. He wore a heavy ring on his pinkie finger.

"Dad, this is Renée."

"Luc," he said, squeezing my hand and then beckoning us inside.

The Fontaine house was a cosy mess – all oriental carpets and stacks of political magazines and books. A large aquarium stood on one side of the living room, filled with tiny spotted fish that looked like they were made of newspaper.

The sound of clattering dishes came from the kitchen,

followed by a tall woman who entered the hall holding a cutting board of charcuterie.

"Ah, and this is my Veronica," Luc said, turning to Noah's mother and placing his hand on the small of her back.

She looked just like Noah: tall, angular, effortlessly elegant. Her legs seemed even longer because of her high heels. "It's a pleasure."

As we followed her to the dining room, she said over her shoulder, "I hope you like meat." Before I could respond, she corrected herself. "Oh, but of course you do. You're a Monitor, no?"

The table was already set. Noah pulled out a chair for me, and in a sloppy bow, laid my napkin across my lap. I laughed as he sat next to me. His parents shared a knowing look as his mother passed around the cutting board, atop which sat an elaborate spread of pâté, sausage and paper-thin slices of roast beef. She then disappeared into the kitchen.

On one side of the room was an ornate fireplace. Above the mantel hung two tiny trowels, both mounted on wooden plaques. The first said *Noah*; the second said *Katherine*.

"That was my first trowel," Noah said over my shoulder. "I was four when my parents gave it to me."

"Is this how you grew up?" I asked. "You always knew what you were?"

"Every family is different," his father said, filling my glass with wine. "Here, we are very open. We are what we are. What's the use in keeping secrets from each other?"

I watched as Noah spread a bit of pâté on a piece of bread and took a bite. He laughed at something his father said, and then looked at me. I hadn't caught the joke, but I laughed anyway. This was what my life would have been if my parents hadn't died. If I could fall in love with Noah. But something was off about all of it. Why was I here, and not Clémentine? Was I really that special to Noah, or was he interested in an idea of a girl that he thought was me?

The door swung open and Noah's mother returned carrying a silver platter and another dish. Noah's father put his hand on her hip as she removed the lids, revealing potatoes roasted with rosemary and thyme and a rack of lamb, its ribs sticking out of its centre like a piece of modern art. I should have been overwhelmed by the aromas, but I couldn't smell anything. The more I stared at the food, the more it looked almost waxy and unreal, as if there were a filter between me and everything else.

"So Noah told us you ranked number one at St. Clément?" his mother said, serving each of us. "Very impressive."

Noah's father clucked and picked up his wine. "Yes," he said. "And what kind of Monitor are you?"

"Um – I don't know."

"I assume you are planning to join the High Monitor Court when you finish school?" Noah's mother asked, crossing her legs.

Before I could answer, Noah cut in. "She can do whatever she wants," he said. "She's good at everything."

I felt myself blush. "Then why wouldn't she?" Noah's father said. "It's the most coveted job in our society."

"Maybe she doesn't want to be a High Monitor," Noah offered. "Maybe she wants to do something else."

I tried to get a word in, when his mother's laugh stopped me. "But everyone wants to be a High Monitor. Noah, if you just apply yourself, one day you could—"

"I don't want to talk about this now," he said, trying to control his voice.

"Noah told me you're both professors?" I said, changing the subject.

Noah's mother smiled. "*Oui.* I am a scholar in *français* and the Romance languages, and Luc is one of the most celebrated historians in Canada." She rubbed her husband's arm. "Actually, your father just started doing research for a new book. It's very different."

Noah spooned a heaping pile of potatoes onto his plate. "What's it about?"

His father leaned back in his chair and swirled the wine around in his glass. "A forgotten female scientist who had a peculiar obsession."

Noah's mother gave him a coy smile before going to the kitchen to bring out more wine.

"Go on," Noah said.

"*Bon*," his father said, clasping his stubby hands together. "Her name was Ophelia Coeur. And she was obsessed with water."

Ophelia Coeur. The name sounded familiar somehow. "Who was she?" I asked, trying to remember where I knew her from.

"She is the Marie Curie of Monitors. The Mother Teresa of Monitors. The Christopher Columbus of Monitors!" his father said, spilling his wine as he gesticulated.

"But what did she do?" Noah pressed.

"Many, many things. She was the first person to study the effects of water on the dead."

I frowned. I definitely didn't know her name from that.

"She started her career as the school nurse at St. Clément, then moved to the Royal Victoria Hospital in 1894 just after it was taken over by the Plebeians, where she rose to become the head nurse of the children's ward."

"The Royal Victoria?" I repeated, my eyes darting to Noah's. "The children's ward?"

"*Oui*. She revolutionized the entire hospital."

I coughed, my mind racing. Noah gave me a knowing glance. "Then what?" he asked.

Noah's father dunked a piece of bread into his sauce and stuffed it in his mouth. "After a few years, Ophelia Coeur quit nursing and dedicated her life to science," he said, his words muffled as he chewed. "She went to every body of water in North America to study drowning victims and the way the flesh and soul reacted to being submerged in different kinds of water. She was the first person to figure out that water has a 'muffling' effect on dead beings."

Noah's mother leaned over and wiped a speck of food from Luc's chin. He smiled at her and squeezed her hand.

"She spent most of her time studying the Great Lakes, with special attention to Lake Erie. She claimed that the water in that lake muffled the dead even more than usual."

"Lake Erie?" I said.

"*Oui...*" Luc said, clearly confused by my interest. "She was the first one to set foot on many of the islands in the lake. Some of them were even named by her."

Little Sister Island. That was where Miss LaBarge had been found, dead.

"But I believe her greatest contribution was when she identified all of the lakes that had briny properties, or properties that mimicked those of salt water. That was, oh, in the early 1900s—"

"Where was she buried?" I demanded, and then shrank back when I realized how urgent my tone sounded.

Noah's parents didn't seem to notice. "Probably at sea, like everyone else," Noah's mother said, nibbling on a string bean.

"Oh," I said. A part of me expected the nameless headstone to be hers.

"Actually, I wasn't able to find any records of her death," Luc corrected. "But back then, our records system wasn't what it is today. Even now, though some of her research papers have been preserved in the archives, we know very little about her background. She was very private about her past. She rarely made public appearances, and only published her scientific findings sporadically. All we know about her past was that at some point in her childhood she was badly injured in a fire."

By then, both Noah and I had stopped eating.

"It's odd, *non?*" Noah's mother said, gesticulating with the carving knife.

"How do you know about the fire?" I asked.

"Because much of her face was covered in burns."

"Do you have images?" I asked, a little too eagerly.

Noah's father seemed a little taken aback by my abrupt request, but then smiled. "There's a spark in you," he said, and winked. "I like that. After dinner, I'll bring one out."

I felt Noah's foot touch mine beneath the table, and I blushed.

It was a long, hearty dinner. One course and two bottles

of wine later, Noah's father was a little pink in the face, but otherwise just as lucid as when he had answered the door. We finished the meal with a platter of soft cheeses, which Noah's mother ate as if they were dessert, scooping up the Camembert with one finger and licking it off like frosting. His father smiled, admiring her.

"So, are you interested in history, then?" Noah's father said to me through a mouthful of blue cheese.

"It used to be my favourite subject," I said slowly.

I must have looked confused, because Noah's father said, "Ah, well I just thought since you were so interested in my new book."

"What are you interested in?" Noah's mother asked.

"I – I don't know," I said. "Maybe teaching the Undead? Helping them in some way?"

Noah's mother let out a laugh as if I had made a joke. When she realized I was serious, she said, "Help them? But why?"

I froze. "What do you mean?"

"Well, they have no souls; they cannot be helped."

I felt Noah trying to catch my eye, but I refused to turn to him.

"That's not true," I said. "At Gottfried—"

At the mention of my old school, Noah's mother groaned. "Oh, that place. We've been trying to get them to shut it down for years. Teaching the Undead to be human.

Impossible! *Enfants terribles*. That's all they are."

I clutched the cheese knife, my knuckles white as I opened my mouth to respond. Noah cut in before I could. "A lot of her friends are at Gottfried," he said. "She's very close with them."

Incredulous, I wiped my mouth with my napkin. So he thought my opinions on the Undead were just biases that I had towards my friends?

"Sometimes I wonder," I said impulsively. "Are Monitors really saving humans from the Undead, or just killing people?"

Noah's mother coughed and put down her spoon as the table went quiet.

"There's an art to what we do," she said finally, her voice less friendly.

"But how is it different?" I said, trying not to sound too argumentative.

"We're civilized. We have courts and schools, we have a system. The Undead, they're—"

"They're what?" I said, anticipating what she was going to say. "They're monsters? They're murderers?"

"Okay!" Noah's father said. "Are you ready to see the portrait?" He glanced between me and his wife, patting a napkin to his head nervously.

"Sure," I said, trying to compose myself.

Grasping the arms of his chair, Luc hoisted himself up

and disappeared into another room, returning with a large envelope.

"Are you okay?" Noah whispered.

I picked at my cheese. Why hadn't he said anything when his mother talked about the Undead like that? Did he agree with her? "I'm fine."

Noah's father pushed the plates out of the way, slid a portrait out of the envelope, and placed it on the tablecloth in front of us. It was a faded black-and-white sketch from the shoulders up, its lines dulled from age.

A woman stared back at us, her eyes wide and black. Or *was* it a woman? It was hard to tell. She looked more like a creature: an anomaly of nature, beautiful in her deformity. Scalloped white welts climbed up her cheeks, layering themselves on top of each other in an odd, sloping pattern, like the feathers of a bird. Her expression was grim and focused, as if she were studying me. Her lips were pursed, somehow giving me the impression that she knew something I didn't.

"This was drawn after her first scientific publication. She must have been in her thirties or forties."

She looked much younger than that, I thought, though it was difficult to guess her age. "She's...terrifying," I said in awe.

"*Oui*," Noah's mother said, resting her head on two fingers. "*C'est incroyable.*"

"They look like waves, no?" Luc said, touching her scars with his fingers. "I think this will be the cover of my book."

"What will you call it?" I asked. "Your biography."

"*Mal de mer.*"

Seasick.

Before we left, Noah ran upstairs to collect a few clean shirts for school. Halfway up, he peered down at me through the balcony railing. "Well, come on."

On the walls lining the stairway were photographs of Noah and his sister growing up. A five-year-old Noah standing in front of St. Clément in an oversized shirt and tie, as if he were already preparing to attend. A ten-year-old Noah posing in front of a cemetery with his sister. A sombre thirteen-year-old Noah holding a shovel beside a small plot in the backyard. "That was my first pet," Noah said, suddenly standing behind me. I thought I felt him touch a lock of my hair, but I must have imagined it, because in no time he was on the second floor, leading me down the wallpapered hallway that led to his bedroom.

"Do you think Ophelia Coeur was the ninth sister?" I asked when we were out of earshot.

"She worked at the Royal Victoria—" he said.

"She could have put the riddle in one of the rooms she

worked in," I said excitedly. "And Lake Erie – that's where Miss LaBarge was found dead. Maybe she knew about the riddle," I said, thinking of the letter my mother had written to her about "the lost girl". "Maybe the last part of the riddle is hidden on Little Sister Island, and Miss LaBarge was going there to check on it."

When I finished I was breathless, brimming with the possibility of our discovery.

Noah's eyes were wide as he studied me. "There is one problem, though."

My smiled faded. "What?"

"The dates. My father said she began her career as a nurse in the 1890s. The Nine Sisters were killed in the 1730s. That's more than a hundred years off."

"What if..." I paused, thinking. "What if she used the secret and is immortal?"

Before he could respond, his mother's voice echoed from downstairs. "Noah? Can you help me sort your laundry?"

"*Un moment!*" he said, and turned the knob to his room.

When I stepped into his room, I immediately felt younger. It was filled with primary colours. Faded posters of rock bands were taped to the walls, handfuls of wrinkled ties were draped over the bedposts, and a dozen plastic figurines of Mexican wrestlers lined his nightstand.

Noah tried to hide his embarrassment as I gazed around the room.

Turning away from the stacks of CDs and comic books on his desk, I smiled. "I like it."

While Noah rummaged through his closet, I sat on his bed playing with a telescope that pointed out of one of the windows, and tried to figure out what made his room so different from Dante's. It wasn't just an excess of things... This room had had a childhood. I couldn't even imagine what Dante was like as a child. He had never told me about it.

"Why didn't you say anything earlier?" I asked him. "When your mom was talking about the Undead?"

Noah shrugged. "I come from an old Monitoring family. They're my parents; they're always going to think like that. It's not worth trying to change their minds."

"So you don't agree with them...?"

"I think the Undead have their reasons to do what they do. But we're Monitors. And we have to do what we do, too," he said, emerging from the closet with a handful of shirts on hangers.

I sat up straight. "Which is to kill them?"

"Which is to *Monitor* them, and bury them if they seem harmful," he said, pushing his hair away from his forehead. "Why bother asking me questions if you don't want to listen to my answers? I'm not a villain."

"I'm sorry," I said. "I didn't mean it like that."

"It's okay," he said, stuffing his shirts into a bag.

I picked up one of the plastic figurines. "I wish we had known each other when we were kids," I said, sitting on his single bed, which was so small that I was certain Noah's feet hung off the end when he slept in it. Noah was easy to know. He had a breezy life; he got what he wanted and was good at most things he put effort into. "I bet you were fun."

"I was the same," he said. "I would have liked you."

Tracing the stitches of his comforter, I allowed myself to wonder for a brief moment what would have happened if I had met Noah one year earlier. The only reason I was looking for the ninth sister was because of Dante. Because I *needed* to find her, not because I wanted to live for ever, or go on some sort of mythic quest. But without that, would Noah and I have even been friends? What was there between us except this mystery and the intrigue that goes with discovering something no one else has ever found before? Of course he thought I was exciting. The problem was, I knew the Renée he liked wasn't really me. "Maybe in a different life," I said.

When I got back to the dorm I flipped on the light and sat down on my bed, feeling more lost than I had in a long time. My coat still felt warm on the side where Noah had leaned against me on the Metro ride home.

"How did you do it?" a voice behind me said.

I nearly fell off the bed.

Clémentine let out a spiteful laugh. She was sitting at my desk, her slender legs folded into the chair like the limbs of a doe.

"What are you doing in my room?" I asked, catching my breath.

She leaned forward, her face stern again. "I want to know how you did it." The utter calmness of her voice was disquieting.

"You can't just come in here," I said.

"Don't treat me like I'm stupid," she snapped. "I know where you were tonight."

"What are you talking about?"

"I'm talking about how you stole my boyfriend. How you stole first rank from me. How you survived a kiss from an Undead."

"I didn't steal anything from you. I earned first rank. And Noah and I are just friends."

"Then what the hell is this?" she shouted, holding up the blazer Noah had lent me the night after we saw Miss LaBarge. I kept forgetting to give it back to him.

"Did you go through my closet?"

She gave me a steady look. "I've been watching you in

class. You're not that smart, and you don't act like an immortal. You're always so cautious, so *scared*. But why would an immortal be scared?" she asked. "Unless, of course, you're scared because you know you're just like the rest of us."

"Why do you care?" I said.

She didn't even bother to dignify my question with a response. Instead, she picked up a stack of pictures from my dresser. "Who were you with in the cemetery that night? You were with an Undead. I could sense him. I could hear his voice." When I didn't answer, her face contorted with anger. "Who was he?"

"There was no one there except for me."

Calming down, she raised an eyebrow. "I bet he wouldn't be so happy knowing that you had dinner with Noah's parents. I bet he wouldn't be so happy if I told my father that you were meeting up with an Undead at night."

"What do you want?" I said. "What are you trying to gain by going through my things? By threatening me and accusing me of doing things you have no proof of?"

"I want you gone. I want you out of my life." She met my gaze and then glanced down at my photographs.

Enough, I thought. I stood up and tried to grab them from her, but she held the pictures out of reach.

"Oh, are these your parents? What happened to them, again?"

I wanted to scream at her; to rip the pins out of her hair, lock her in the bathroom, and make her listen while I invited Noah over and kissed him on the other side of the door. I wanted her to know what it felt like to lose everyone she loved.

I heard the slap before I realized what I had done. Pulling my arm back, I watched as Clémentine pressed herself against the wall, holding her cheek.

"Get out of my room," I said softly, and opened the bathroom door.

"I'm going to find out who you were with that night in the cemetery, Renée."

"Get out," I repeated.

"I'm going to find him, and I'm going to bury him." With that, she finally left.

CHAPTER 10

WANDERLUST

I STAYED AWAY FROM NOAH after that. Or at least I tried to. November hardened to a colourless December, the city grey and lifeless like stone. When I felt Noah staring at me in class, I forced myself to look the other way. When he caught up with me in the hallway after the bell had rung, I brushed him off, saying I had to meet with a professor or do a group project. I knew I was hurting him from the way his face dropped, from the way his eyes searched mine for some kind of explanation, as if he had done something wrong. What else could I do? Clémentine's words haunted me, and I knew it was only a matter of time before she found out about Dante. But keeping my distance from Noah was harder than I thought, as I discovered in Strategy and Prediction.

"Renée?" the headmaster said, interrupting his demonstration on mummification and the art of wrapping a body with gauze. "You're unusually quiet today." We were standing in a frosty meadow a few kilometres outside of Montreal.

"Oh, um, I'm just not feeling well."

I glanced over at Noah, who was studying me as if he were trying to figure out what I was thinking. Snow swirled around my feet as I sent him a silent apology and averted my eyes.

After class ended, I sat in the back of the van with Anya, where we quizzed each other on our French vocabulary while the headmaster drove us back to campus. We were walking back to the dormitory when Noah called out to me across the courtyard.

I pretended I didn't hear him, and picked up the pace.

"You're not even going to stop?" Anya asked.

I shook my head and made for the dormitory doors, but he caught up with me and grabbed my arm.

"I don't understand. Why are you ignoring me?"

Letting the door go, I stepped back and glanced around the courtyard to make sure Clémentine wasn't around. "There are other people you should be chasing after," I said quietly. Anya was standing awkwardly by the stoop, pretending not to listen.

His shoulders collapsed a little.

"What do you want from me?" I asked.

"I don't know," he said finally, his eyes a watery brown through his glasses. "I just want to be around you. Why does it have to be more complicated than that?"

A few girls walked by, staring at us and whispering. I wondered if they were going to tell Clémentine that Noah was talking to me.

"Because life is complicated. If people see us together, they'll think things that aren't true."

"Since when do you care what other people think?" Noah took off his hat, his hair a matted mess beneath it. "You know me. You know the truth. That's all that matters."

Beside us, the fountain was coated in a glossy layer of ice. A year ago I might have thought it was beautiful, like melted bronze against the afternoon sun, but now it was nothing but water and stone. I had spent the last months waiting for Dante, barely paying attention in class. I had even shunned one of the only people at St. Clément that I enjoyed being around: Noah.

"Renée?" he prodded. "Are you okay?"

Catching my scarf as it fluttered around my face, I said, "Anya and I are going to a cafe to study. Do you want to come?"

His face softened in relief. "Sure."

We went to a cafe just a few blocks from school. Anya wiped her boots on the mat outside. While Noah held the door for me, a gust of wind, harsh and biting, blew between the buildings and took my scarf with it.

I grabbed at the air, watching my scarf swirl away and catch on the boxy shelter of a bus stop. I chased after it and pulled it down from where it hung on a wall of thick translucent glass. My reflection mimicked me as I wrapped the scarf around my neck. But when I adjusted my hat, the reflection didn't move.

I held my hand up to the glass and stepped closer until my nose grazed its icy surface. There was a person on the other side, his face like mine but ashen. His hair was pulled back in a knot.

"Dante?"

I took a step back in surprise and darted around the glass wall, dragging my fingers across the siding. But when I got to the other side, the only person there was an older man, tall and wrinkled, his grey hair gathered into a ponytail. He winked when he saw me staring.

"Oh – I'm – I'm sorry."

"Renée?" Noah called from down the street, his voice distorted by the wind.

Holding my hat down with one hand, I ran back to the coffee shop.

Streams of Christmas lights decorated the front window. I stepped inside, welcomed by a line of long glass countertops filled with cakes and pastries coated in frosting.

We were supposed to be studying for our history exam, but quickly abandoned the task to discuss Ophelia Coeur and the last part of the riddle. In the process, we devoured an entire plate of Hungarian cookies, dusting our books with crumbs and confectioner's sugar.

"But the dates don't match with Ophelia Coeur. So if she isn't the ninth sister, then who is?" I said.

Noah stirred his coffee. "I don't know. There are so many things that match with her. The scars on her face could have made her harder to identify when everyone was looking for her. The research on water, specifically islands and salt water..." He shook his head.

"I know," I said, tapping my fingers on the table.

Anya slid her finger through the excess sugar on the plate and licked it. "Well, it wasn't *that* certain. The girl in the portrait is practically unrecognizable anyway, so the burned face doesn't really matter. And how many nurses were at the Royal Victoria Hospital? So many."

Noah leaned back in his chair. "True," he said, taking a sip of coffee.

Anya continued. "I'll admit that the Lake Erie connection is weird, but that's just one fact that fits. The rest don't necessarily mean anything."

"So now what?" I asked.

Anya tried to cover her nose as she sneezed, but was too late, and blew confectioner's sugar across the table.

"We'll keep looking," Noah said, offering her his napkin. "We'll find the last part of the riddle."

"But how?"

Noah shrugged. "Maybe you'll have another vision?"

I rested my head on my palm. "I don't know. It's been months since my last vision. They might have stopped."

"Or maybe it will come when you least expect it," Anya said. "Isn't that how it works?"

Later that week, when Dr. Newhaus walked into Psychology, he said nothing. He merely glanced at the clock above the door, turned off the lights, and made his way to the back of the room. There, he flipped a switch. A projector cast a square of white light onto the screen in front of us. After a few moments, the following words came onto the screen, the film yellow and grainy:

The Death of Children
Interviews by F. H. Newhaus
October 1998

In the middle of the frame, a hand held up a small

white board with SUBJECT 003 written on it. When it dropped, we were looking at a classroom. All of the desks were empty, save for one in the front, where a boy was sitting, playing with a collection of rubber bands strung on his wrist.

Someone off-screen coughed. "How old are you?" Dr. Newhaus's voice resonated from behind the camera.

The boy remained still, as if he hadn't heard the question. Dr. Newhaus repeated himself, his voice slightly sharper.

"I don't remember," the boy said, fidgeting with his shirt. A map of the world was tacked to the wall behind him.

"Are you seven?" Dr. Newhaus asked. The boy made no reply. "Are you seven years old?"

The boy shook his head. "Much older."

"Why did you try to run away last week?" Dr. Newhaus asked.

"I don't like it here."

"At this school?"

The boy shook his head.

"You don't like it where?"

"I don't feel right," the boy said.

"Can I ask you to look at the camera when you answer?"

The boy looked up for the first time, staring at something

just left of the camera. A murmur floated through our class. The boy's face was hollow and aged, his eyes heavy, as if he were an older person stuck in a young body.

"What did you do yesterday?"

The boy didn't answer.

Dr. Newhaus repeated himself. "What did you do?"

"I took someone's soul." His voice was barely a whisper.

"Whose soul did you take?"

"My brother's."

"Why would you do such a thing?"

The boy hesitated, biting his finger.

Dr. Newhaus repeated his question.

"Because he wouldn't tell me where he hid my toy truck."

"But why would you kill him over that?"

"Because I wanted to know." The boy said it as if it should have been obvious.

"Why not just ask him?" Dr. Newhaus asked.

"I did, and he didn't tell me. So I found out myself instead."

After a moment of focusing on him, the film cut out. A hand held up a sign that read: SUBJECT 005.

Back in the same classroom sat a small boy. He was younger than the previous subject, no more than six years old. He was cross-legged on the floor, his hair a mop, his face covered in freckles. His eyes were growing hazy around the edges, just like Dante's.

"How old are you?" Dr. Newhaus asked.

The boy thought about it, sucking on his finger. "Twenty," he said finally, his voice boisterous.

"I see. That's quite old for such a small person."

The boy didn't answer.

"How many years have you been in school?"

The boy thought. "Ten."

"Can you tell me why it's bad to kiss people on the mouth?"

The boy looked at him as if he were confused.

"Is it bad to take someone else's soul?"

The boy didn't seem to register the question. "I'm hungry," he said instead.

"I don't think I have any food here except for a few butter biscuits. Would you like one of those?"

The boy hesitated. Without warning, he sprang up towards the camera, his limbs thrashing as he leaped towards Dr. Newhaus. Someone screamed. The camera trembled and then fell to the ground, focusing on the legs of a chair. Loud voices. A chair scuffing against the floor, and then an abrupt crash.

Two pairs of legs swathed in stockings crossed the frame. And then someone – presumably Dr. Newhaus – picked up the camera and steadied it, focusing on two nurses who were restraining the boy in the chair, while he kicked at them. They held him until he calmed, and remained by his side when silence resumed.

After a long pause, Dr. Newhaus said, "Why did you do that?"

The boy remained still.

"Why did you do that?"

His eyes darted quickly to the left.

"Look at me," Dr. Newhaus said, his voice sharp.

Before Dr. Newhaus could ask him another question, the boy kicked out of his seat, pushing the chair over as he lashed out at the nurse to the left. Setting the camera down, Dr. Newhaus jumped into view and pinned the boy to the floor.

"Okay, that's enough," Dr. Newhaus said, only his legs visible as he threw his suit coat on the floor and bent over the boy. "Let's get him back to his room."

The clip ended, and a hand held up another sign: SUBJECT 067. A girl sat in front of us. She was prim and obedient looking, like an elder sister. She sat on the edge of her seat with her knees together.

She gazed out the window, focusing on something far in the distance. "I still can't believe that I did it."

"What did you do?" asked Dr. Newhaus.

"I did what they asked me to do."

"Which is what?"

"I killed someone."

There was a long pause.

"Whom did you kill?"

"I killed a boy, a small boy."

"How did you do it?"

"I followed him, and then I captured him, and then I buried him." She blinked.

"Does what you did bother you?"

"Monitoring is my job," she said.

"But does it bother you?"

"I've been training to be a Monitor for my entire life. This is what I'm supposed to do."

"What are you looking at?" Dr. Newhaus asked, his voice gentle.

She looked at her knees, where her hands were clasped in a tight knot. "I'm not looking at anything."

"Could I ask you to look at the camera?"

"I'd rather not."

The film cut out again. We watched several more, the change of light in between each new subject making me wince. In the shadows I could see the whites of Noah's eyes as they travelled over me. I met his gaze. For the briefest moment, he held it, and then looked away, the projector humming behind us until the film turned white. Dr. Newhaus's voice boomed out from the darkness as if he were still off-screen. "I showed you this because you have to understand what you're being asked to do. You have to understand who you are.

"What can we glean from these interviews?" he asked, turning on the lights.

"Why were their eyes like that?" Brett asked. "I've met Undead before and they weren't like that."

Dr. Newhaus rewound the projector to the second Undead boy, paused it, and approached the screen. "You mean this?" he said, pointing to his irises, which had just begun to blur into the whites of his eyes. Just like Dante's. "As the Undead age, they decay and lose their senses. In other words, he is going blind."

"What?" I murmured, though only Anya could hear me. Dante was going blind? He hadn't told me.

Dr. Newhaus motioned to the image of the Undead boy. "As you'll remember, he had been in school for ten years at that point. But still, he had no idea what I was talking about when I asked him why it was bad to take someone's soul. This is why the very young Undead are so dangerous. When a child dies and reanimates before he reaches the maturity level to fully understand right and wrong, he will never be capable of learning the difference. This boy was six years old when he died. He will always remain six mentally, regardless of how many years he remains on earth. These Undead children are wild, unteachable, amoral. They take what they want without shame or guilt. And as you witnessed, they're agile."

The conversation wandered from the boy to the Monitor girl who had just completed her first burial. "She's just like us," everyone kept saying. But I wasn't interested in her.

Quietly, I raised my hand. Through everyone's voices, Dr. Newhaus called on me.

"Yes, Renée?"

The class grew still.

"In the first interview, the Undead boy said that he took his brother's soul because he wanted to know where his toy truck was," I said slowly, parsing it out in my mind. "He said his brother wouldn't tell him, so he had to *find it himself*."

Clémentine was about to interrupt me, but Dr. Newhaus held out his hand, letting me finish.

"What did he mean?" I asked.

Dr. Newhaus clasped his hands together. "All of us know that when an Undead takes a human's soul, the Undead also gains a temporary spurt of life."

Everyone nodded.

"However, there is a controversial theory that asserts that more gets exchanged in an Undead kiss than life. A handful of Monitor researchers believe that when the Undead absorbs a person's soul, some of the memories of that person become lodged in the Undead. In other words, the Undead boy in the interview took his brother's soul in order to *absorb* the information he needed."

I gripped the armrest of my chair. Absorb memories? It sounded sickeningly familiar. Beside me, Anya whispered, "Are you okay? You look a little red."

I took a breath, and then another, my chest feeling suddenly constricted. "I'm fine," I said quickly; though, the more I thought about the memories and absorption, the stranger I felt. I began to sweat, and pressed my lips together. It felt as though a secret were about to burst out of me. My throat grew dry, as if stuffed with gauze. I swallowed.

"This phenomenon is called—"

"*Wanderlust*," someone blurted out, finishing Dr. Newhaus's sentence.

I looked around to see who had answered, when I realized that *I* was the one who had said it.

"Yes," the doctor said, studying me with surprise. "Would you care to explain to the class what it is?"

A wave of nausea crept over me as I shook my head. I couldn't explain because I didn't know what the word even meant. It had come from nowhere.

"It's originally a German word, which translates literally into a desire for travel. However, in the Monitoring world it refers to the soul's desire to wander from body to body. Which is exactly what it does if given the opportunity.

There are two kinds of Wanderlust. What you saw in the first interview with the boy and the truck was the most common kind, where trivial or isolated snippets of information are transferred." He held up a finger. "Though it doesn't always work properly, because the information that wanders is random. The Undead boy in the interview never actually found his truck. He took a chance, and now that piece of information is lost for ever."

"What's—" I said, my voice cracking. "What's the second kind of – of—"

"Wanderlust?" the doctor said.

I nodded miserably.

A glimmer of excitement passed over his face. "I'll show you."

He fast-forwarded the film and a hand appeared on the screen, holding up a sign: SUBJECT 043.

A girl sat in the same classroom as before. She was wearing an oversized sweater, and hugging her knees. After a moment she looked up at the camera. My classmates shifted in their seats as they studied her. She looked about my age, though her hair was dull and brittle like straw. Clouds obscured her irises, making her pupils appear grey; her eyes were out of focus, as if she were staring at nothing.

"How old are you?" Dr. Newhaus asked off-screen.

"Seventeen," she said, biting her nails.

"And how long have you been dead?"

She moved her fingers, counting, and then started over again, as if she had lost track. "Nineteen years."

"How do you feel?"

"Parched. Dull. Empty."

"And how did you feel after you killed your last doctor?" He said it gently, but the question seemed to agitate her. She squirmed in her chair, looking from the camera to Dr. Newhaus, to the floor.

"I didn't mean to kill him. I just wanted to talk to him. We were good friends. He was the only one who understood me. I just couldn't stop..."

"Why did you put gauze in his mouth?" Dr. Newhaus said softly.

"It was right there," she said. "It was in his office. I didn't bring it myself."

"I know," he said. "But why did you put it in his mouth?"

The girl wrung her hands together. "Because I didn't want to kill him; I just wanted to be close to him. I heard a rumour that gauze stops the soul from being completely transferred if you do it right. But I didn't."

"Who told you that?" Dr. Newhaus said, his voice noticeably firmer.

"People say that the Brothers use it to take information from people."

There was a long pause.

"Were you trying to take information from your doctor?"

"No," she said flatly.

Dr. Newhaus waited, and eventually the girl corrected herself. "I just wanted to know if he felt the same way about me as I did about him. That's all."

"What happened next?"

"I kissed him and he – he collapsed, and I realized what I'd done. But then I felt...full."

"Can you elaborate?"

"I felt like I had absorbed him. I could remember things in his past. When he embarrassed himself in primary school, or when he had his first kiss. The first time he fell in love. The anger he felt when his father died."

"Could you remember other things? For example, what he had for dinner the previous night?"

The girl shook her head, looking like she wanted to cry, but couldn't.

Dr. Newhaus turned off the switch, and the screen went dark.

"The transferring of more detailed memories," he said as he turned on the overhead lights. "After taking her doctor's soul, she absorbed experiences associated with high emotion – embarrassment, fear, love, happiness... This is a rarer form of Wanderlust; one that tends to occur in teenage Undead, rather than young children."

315

"And the gauze?" Anya said from beside me. She was thinking of the Nine Sisters, though all I could think about was my parents and Miss LaBarge.

"I believe," he said slowly, "and mind you, none of this has been scientifically proven yet, that the act of inserting gauze in the mouth of a victim before taking a soul may be a method that the Undead use to take information or memories from their victims without killing them immediately. Or, in other words, when done correctly, inserting gauze in the mouth prevents the entire soul from being taken in one kiss."

My breath grew shallow as I turned Dr. Newhaus's words around in my head. Gauze? Was that why the Sisters died with gauze in their mouths, why my parents and Miss LaBarge died the same way – because the Undead had tried to get information from them?

Dr. Newhaus continued lecturing about how the Undead cope with death, but I was no longer paying attention. How had I known the word Wanderlust? How had I known any of the answers I'd been blurting out in my classes all semester? I was still lost in my thoughts when the bell rang.

Out of the corner of my eye I could see Noah gazing at me as Clémentine whispered something to him. Throwing my books in my bag, I gave him a quick glance, and left.

I ran across the courtyard, back to my room, and I slammed the door.

All semester I had been wondering where the information in my head was coming from. Where the visions were coming from. Could it be from Wanderlust?

Pacing across the rug, I thought back to what Dr. Newhaus had said in class: when the Undead takes a human's soul, there were two kinds of possible transfers — information and extended memories. It seemed I had a little of both.

Hadn't I exchanged souls with Dante last spring?

When we kissed, hadn't I relived his memories of when we first met in science class, of when we first kissed in the Latin classroom, of when we were called into Headmistress Von Laark's office for the last time?

Hadn't I also relived events that I'd never actually experienced before? His sister getting pneumonia. Flying in an aeroplane with his family. Crashing into the water. Dante drowning.

Like a burst of cold air, the truth wrapped itself around me. I leaned against my bedpost in shock. When we exchanged souls last spring, I had absorbed some of Dante's memories. I had been reliving Dante's past and unknowingly absorbing information he had once learned. That was how I knew what Wanderlust was, how I knew about the Île des Soeurs, how I knew that canaries were used in coal mines. Because Dante knew all of those things.

I don't know how long I stood there going over

everything in my head. If I had absorbed Dante's memories, did that mean that my visions belonged to him, too?

Dr. Newhaus had said that Wanderlust was about absorbing *memories*, but my visions weren't Dante's memories. I was seeing them long after our kiss, and it seemed like they were happening now, not in the past. Then again, we were soulmates; everything worked differently with us.

"*My sis*—" I'd said to the nurse in my vision of the hospital, just before I'd corrected myself to say brother. Dante had had a sister. And the cemetery. Dante had been there right after my vision; he'd known exactly where the Monitor section on the map was, and he'd noticed the headstone just before I tripped over it.

I thought back to the night before my birthday, when I had my first vision. Had Dante chased Miss LaBarge through the waters of Lake Erie? "*You?*" she'd said. Could she have been talking about Dante? In the vision, I'd had long hair. Dante did, too. Was it possible that he'd taken her shovel and then killed her?

Unable to control myself, I began to tremble. No. Maybe I was seeing him in my visions, but he couldn't have killed anyone. I had to believe that he would never hurt anyone. He'd told me himself that he wouldn't, that he wouldn't hurt me... Except he had. I was hurt now. And Miss LaBarge was dead. What explanation could he possibly have?

Outside, the day faded to night, and tiny snowflakes floated in through the open window on a cool, swirling breeze. Standing up, I lowered the pane and went to splash my face with water. But when I turned the knob of the bathroom door, it was locked again.

"Go away," Clémentine yelled from inside, though this time her voice was different. There were no girls in the background whispering or giggling.

She blew her nose. Quietly, I pressed my ear to the door, only to hear the soft sound of her crying.

"I can hear you," she yelled suddenly. "Go away."

Stunned, I fell back. And without thinking, I slipped on my coat and scarf, getting ready to leave. I didn't care where.

When I opened the door from my bedroom to the hall, Noah was right in front of me, his arm raised as if he were about to knock.

"Noah," I said, jumping. "What are you doing here?"

He looked red and flustered, his brow gathered into a tiny wrinkle. When he saw me, his face softened. "I just wanted to see you."

I scratched my head, confused. Behind me I could hear Clémentine turn the tap on in the bathroom.

"You seem upset. Are you leaving?" he asked, betraying a hint of panic as he surveyed my coat and scarf.

"I – I'm fine," I said, unable to think coherently enough to form a proper response. "I'm just going for a walk."

"Can I come?"

I glanced at Clémentine's door. The last thing I needed was for Clémentine to find out that Noah was here, talking to me. "Okay."

"Okay."

We walked in silence, both lost in our own thoughts as the traffic lights changed soundlessly in front of us. As we waited on the kerb for a car to pass, Noah turned to me. "I broke up with Clémentine for good."

His words took a moment to sink in. "I'm so sorry." I didn't know what else to say.

"Thanks."

He didn't offer anything more, and I didn't ask.

The city was different at night. Without any destination we meandered down the streets, past sex shops and head shops, tattoo parlours and peep shows. The windows of the storefronts were smudged and cracked and glowing neon.

As we passed under the awning of an all-night cafe, I stopped. Through the glass I spotted someone wearing a tan suit coat that looked incredibly familiar.

"That's Dr. Newhaus," I said.

Our psychology professor was sitting alone at a table, staring down at a plate of food, deep in thought.

It was a smoky French bistro, the kind that served cheap wine. A television was on, tuned to a hockey game.

There were barely any people inside, save for two older men smoking cigars, and a group of college boys heckling a waitress.

"I wonder why he's out so late alone," I murmured, watching him pick at his food.

"Do you know about him?" Noah asked from over my shoulder.

"Know what?"

"He was one of the best Monitors in his class. My father told me he was fearless; always the first to volunteer, and later the first one on the trail of an Undead. They used to be friends a long time ago.

"Eventually he got married and had a son. Apparently I was friends with the kid when we were both younger, though I can't remember any of it."

"You don't see him any more?"

Noah shook his head. "He died when he was ten. Fell out of a tree in their front yard."

I raised my hand to my mouth.

"In his grief, Dr. Newhaus decided that instead of burying him, he would wait until his son reanimated. That's when he and my father started drifting apart."

"What do you mean?"

"Dr. Newhaus decided to homeschool his son. The rumours are that his wife wanted to bury the boy, but Dr. Newhaus couldn't bear it. Supposedly that was what eventually destroyed their family – not the death itself, but Dr. Newhaus's inability to cope with it."

"What do you mean, it destroyed their family?"

Inside the restaurant, a haggard waitress carrying a tray was standing behind Dr. Newhaus, speaking to him, but the professor was lost in his thoughts and didn't seem to hear her. Only after she touched his arm did he turn around.

"His wife divorced him, leaving him to care for his Undead son alone." Noah shrugged. "You know how it ends. Folly after folly, and eventually he had to bury him. Bury his own son. Can you imagine?"

I gazed at Dr. Newhaus through my reflection in the window. "When did all of this happen?" I said, my voice cracking.

"A decade ago, maybe more. That's when he became a psychologist."

"I want to go," I said, tearing myself away from the window. "I don't want to be here any more." Though I wasn't sure if I meant here at the cafe, or here in Montreal, or here in general. Everything was too complicated.

"Me neither," Noah said, his breath dissipating into the night. I followed his gaze down the street, where the block lights of a cinema stuck out over the awnings. "Hey. Do you want to see a movie?"

The only thing showing past midnight was a black-and-white film about a man who plotted to murder his wife. I shuddered as I stared at the dull colours of the movie poster, which seemed to mock me. But before I knew it, I found myself waiting as Noah bought two tickets, a bag of buttery popcorn and two large sodas. We were the only people in the cinema, and took seats right in the middle.

"This is a classic," Noah said. "You're going to love it."

It wasn't until the movie started that I realized it was entirely in French, with no subtitles.

"They're talking so quickly I can barely understand them," I whispered to Noah as he passed me the popcorn.

After a moment of confusion, he realized what I was saying. "Oh no," he said. "I forgot."

Clearing his throat, he leaned towards my ear and began to translate, his voice deep and accented. I slid down in my seat, laughing despite everything and sipping my soda as our thighs pressed against each other. Somewhere in between a woman crooning in scratchy French and the fly that landed on the projector lens, I fell asleep, my dream a chaotic swirl of murder and betrayal, of me and Noah in black and white, smiling as we ran, hand in hand, into white light.

Hours later, a man with a broom and dustpan nudged me awake. I blinked. The screen glowed white, and popcorn was strewn about our feet. Noah's head was resting on my shoulder, his hand sweaty and wrapped around mine.

"Renée," he murmured in his sleep. He was dreaming of me, just as I had been dreaming of him.

I realized then that for the first time in months, my dream had been my own.

CHAPTER 11

THE NAME IN THE MAILBOX

DECEMBER IN MONTREAL WAS DARK and bleak, with winds so strong they could blow a person over, and snow that buried parking meters and bicycle stands. From the windows of our classrooms the city looked post-apocalyptic and abandoned. For me, it was real. The world I thought I had known, the world coloured by Dante, was gone now, and everything felt vacant and meaningless. Every morning it was harder to get out of bed. The prospect of facing the day seemed too exhausting to bear. I couldn't focus on studying for my exams, and every time the voice inside me screamed, *Search for the ninth sister!*, I silenced it. Eternal life doesn't exist, I told myself. The Nine Sisters were nothing more than a group of smart women who protected a secret about literature or politics. Immortality was a legend. And even if it wasn't, what was the point in searching for it? The only reason I wanted to find their secret was because of Dante, because I wanted to be with him for eternity. But I didn't know if I wanted that any more.

After the night in the cinema, things changed between Noah and me, though it happened so quietly that it was hard to catch. We still went on walks together, wandering through the slushy streets after classes to get a bite to eat, or studying for exams with Anya, on a rickety table at the coffee shop, an espresso machine whirring in the background. On the surface, everything appeared the same. I didn't tell Noah about Dante, but something about the way he studied me when he thought I wasn't looking made me think he understood.

"Hey, maybe the ninth sister was a doctor," he'd say in the middle of a study session, when he saw me lost in thought as I stared out the window at the snowplough on the street. "Maybe that's why the riddle was hidden at the Royal Victoria."

I shrugged. "Maybe."

"Or maybe she was very sick," Anya said, "and hid the riddle beneath the bed where she was treated."

Noah scratched the stubble on his chin. "I guess anything's possible. We could check hospital records. What do you think, Renée?" he said gently, trying to catch my gaze.

"Yeah," I said, trying to smile. "That sounds good."

"Great," he said. "Friday after class? Maybe after, we can all get dessert at my parents' house. Take it easy, you know?"

"Easy," I murmured. Should relationships be easy? No, I used to think. Everything worth doing took work and time, but for some reason, when I'd woken up next to Noah in the cinema, none of that seemed clear any more. I needed to talk to Dante. I needed him to tell me that he hadn't killed Miss LaBarge, that there was some reasonable explanation.

Before I knew it, exams were over, and as the snow swirled outside my window, I packed a single suitcase and dragged it across the courtyard. While I was waiting to hail a taxi, I heard shoes crunch in the snow behind me.

"You were just going to leave for three weeks without saying goodbye?" Noah said, his cheeks a deep red.

"I thought you were still in exams," I said as a taxi pulled over to the kerb and popped its trunk.

Noah shook his head. "I was sitting in my room when I saw you step outside. You looked like you were about to be blown away."

I laughed. "Definitely not with this thing," I said, lifting my suitcase.

"Here, let me get that," he said, but I pulled it out of reach.

"I can do it," I said, and with some difficulty, I pushed it into the trunk.

"Right," he said, shoving his hands into his pockets. "Of course you can."

The exhaust from the car fogged in the cold as we stood there, not quite looking at each other. "So, I guess I'll see you when you get back?" Noah said, as if he had meant to say something else, but had changed his mind.

"Yeah," I said, because what else could I say?

He forced a smile. "Great."

"Great."

Noah made to open the door for me, but I beat him to it, our hands touching as I reached the handle. "Oh, you don't have to—"

"Right. Sorry."

After I slammed the door, he brushed away a little circle of snow from the window so that we could see each other. He waved goodbye. And I was off.

When I got to the airport, I checked my bag and boarded a rickety little aeroplane with only one bathroom and one stewardess.

The looming buildings of Montreal shrank into white

as we ascended through the clouds.

A dishevelled college boy in a baggy sweater was sitting next to me. He was reading Dante's *Inferno*. He smiled when he saw me staring at his book. "Do you know it?" he asked, his gaze wandering from my face to my stockings.

I pulled down my skirt. "No," I said quickly, and put on my headphones.

Massachusetts was masked by a white flurry when we landed. Dustin met me at the airport with a takeout cup of hot chocolate and a big hug, and insisted on carrying my suitcase to the car.

Barren trees frosted in ice formed a canopy over the roads as we drove west to Wintershire House, the tyres squeaking as they pressed into the snow.

Dustin asked me about Montreal and St. Clément as he navigated. Tinny Christmas music played softly in the background. We passed frozen ponds, churches with Nativity scenes out front, and white colonial houses buried in snow, their owners shovelling tiny trails to their front doors.

The street lamps turned on one by one as we drove up the driveway to my grandfather's mansion. Burlap sacks covered the topiaries, now dusted in white. My grandfather's car was nowhere to be seen.

"He's travelling on business but will be back for dinner," Dustin said as he hoisted my suitcase out of the trunk.

And sure enough, when I ran down the stairs an hour

later, my grandfather was standing in the dining room, slinging his dinner jacket over the back of the chair.

"Ah, Renée. Welcome back." He always said *back* instead of *home*.

"Thanks."

Dustin served us a robust meal of pot roast and spaghetti puttanesca. My grandfather tucked his napkin into the collar of his shirt and picked up his knife and fork.

I stared at the pasta, remembering the night at the grocery store with Noah when I had seen Dante on the street. *Wait for me,* he'd written on the flyer.

"Eat," my grandfather said. "You look gaunt. Gaunt and tired. I take this to mean St. Clément is keeping you busy?"

I picked at my food but couldn't bring myself to eat it. "You never told me that dying with gauze in the mouth was rare for Monitors," I said. "How come?"

He coughed.

"May I get you some water?" Dustin said from the corner.

"No, no, that won't be necessary." Wiping his mouth, my grandfather met my gaze. "I see they're teaching you a lot at that school."

"Why did you make it seem like the way my parents and Miss LaBarge died was normal, when you knew it wasn't?"

"I didn't want to upset you any more than I already had."

"But you knew that they were probably killed by the Liberum. How could you keep that from me?"

He seemed surprised that I knew about the brotherhood of Undead. "I wanted to protect you. If the Liberum killed your parents, there was good chance they could kill you too. It was easier to keep you ignorant of them, in case you got it in your head to go out and find them. I wouldn't put that type of foolish attempt at heroism past you."

He picked up his fork and began cutting his meat, eating it in big, quick mouthfuls.

"What else do you know that you haven't told me?" I asked, watching him chew.

He took a sip of sparkling water. "Excuse me?"

"You must know other things, being the headmaster of Gottfried. You never even told me about the High Monitor Court. You didn't tell me about any of it."

"If I may remind you, this summer you were not all that inclined to listen to anything I said. You showed no interest in engaging with the world outside your head." He pulled the napkin out of his shirt.

"You're leaving?" I asked. We had only sat down a few minutes ago.

"Yes," he said. "I've finished my meal and now I must get to work."

"But—"

"If I may make a suggestion, I think you should change the focus of your studies. I am paying your tuition so that you can hone your skills as a Monitor."

"But isn't learning about the Liberum necessary if I'm going to hone my skills?"

"No. The task at hand is for you to develop technical abilities as a Monitor, not to play detective. We have actual detectives for that." Pushing his plate aside, he stood up and nodded to Dustin to clear the table.

The next week passed by in a flurry. Dustin took it upon himself to teach me how to cook. Every time I tried to talk to my grandfather about anything – the Liberum, the Nine Sisters, my parents, Miss LaBarge – Dustin would whisk me away to the kitchen, arm me with a rolling pin and an apron, and put me to work, as if he were trying to distract me.

We started with mince pies, the flour of the crust dusting the counters and floors so that inside looked just like outside. After that we made wild mushroom soup and stuffed artichokes, and I graduated to roasting and carving a chicken. First, cut along the breast; next, sever the thighs; and finally, dismember the wings. The cooking part was tedious, but dismembering the chicken was easy, even a little enjoyable, though I didn't want to admit it.

"You're a natural," Dustin said, examining the carcass.

But all I saw when I stared at the bird was the crest of the canary. No matter how hard I tried to ignore it, the secret of the Nine Sisters kept haunting me. My parents, Miss LaBarge – they'd been killed while searching for it. If I were braver, I would continue what they'd started. I'd comb through my visions, find the missing clue that led to the ninth sister, and dig up her secret. I would make sure that the Undead who killed my parents and Miss LaBarge would never find it. But therein lay the problem. What if the Undead who'd killed them was Dante?

At nightfall, when the kitchen staff had retired for the day, I went to the huge lazy Susan by the refrigerator and stepped inside, just like I had done last winter, and pulled on the hook on the back shelf. The ground wobbled and then began to rotate until I was thrust into the room on the other side of the wall. The First Living Room, where my grandfather kept all of his Monitoring books, tools and paraphernalia, was adorned with a heavy chandelier, hard antique sofas and animal busts, which followed me with glassy eyes as I scoured through a book on modern Undead theories. I meant to search for information on the

Nine Sisters, but when I turned to the index, I found myself flipping to *W*, and scanning the list until I found the word *Wanderlust*.

After an hour, I collapsed on one of the sofas, my neck sore and my fingers dusty. I hadn't found anything. Upstairs, I heard the taps turn on, the water beating against the ceiling. My grandfather was taking a bath. Running my hands along the carved wood of the armrest, I listened to him hum as the taps were turned off. There was one other place I could check, but I didn't have much time. Slipping back into the kitchen, I tiptoed down the hall and through the second door on the right.

A single table lamp illuminated my grandfather's office in a narrow cone of light, where papers scrawled with handwritten notes were strewn about his desk. As I lifted them to check beneath, a file slid out, its contents spilling to the floor. I bent down to pick them up when I noticed that they were articles and postcards, each stuck with pinholes and pieces of tape. Some passages were circled with marker, illegible notes written in the margins in handwriting that I recognized from my last year at Gottfried: Miss LaBarge's.

The papers suddenly felt incredibly delicate beneath my fingers as I realized they were the clippings from her cottage. Before I could get a better look at them I heard a noise through the ceiling. Freezing, I listened to the drain emptying through pipes in the wall, and my grandfather's footsteps as he walked down the upstairs hallway.

Gathering the articles in my arms, I stole down the long corridor and into the library. Snowflakes swirled around the windowpanes as I sat at the desk and picked up the first clipping.

It was a yellowed postcard with a photograph of majestic black rock formations jutting out of the earth like towers. At their base was a dark valley swathed in moss. BREAKER CHASM, VERMONT, the caption read.

I had to go there, I thought suddenly. I had to go there now. The grandfather clock began to chime, taunting me. There was no time, I thought. No time. I had to get to Breaker Chasm. Soon it would be too late.

I looked at the hands of the clock. They pointed to 9 p.m. I blinked and the hands had rotated backwards to 1 p.m.

More time, I thought urgently, and blinked again. The hands spun faster. In an instant, I felt tired, the room blurring as my eyelids grew heavier and heavier, until I could no longer muster the energy to keep them open.

When I woke up, I was sitting on a train. Afternoon sun streamed through the windows, which revealed a landscape of evergreens coated in soft, fluffy snow. The trees sped past the window as I pulled a piece of paper from my pocket and unfolded it. An address was written on one side: *15 Knollwood Drive.*

Over the intercom, the conductor announced that the next stop would be Breaker Chasm. Eagerly, I looked out the window. We were nearing the base of a mountain, where a tunnel had been bored through the hillside. Suddenly worried, I pressed my face against the glass to look at the train tracks. There was only one set, and they led directly into the tunnel. I couldn't go there; I would die.

I stood up and walked briskly down the aisle. The train wasn't very crowded; most of the other passengers were sleeping or listening to music. I tried not to disturb them as I made my way to the exit door. Trying to be discreet, I pulled the handle, but the door was locked.

I glanced out the window again. We had almost reached the mouth of the tunnel. Quickly, I slid open the door leading to the next car and stepped outside. The cold December air blew past my face as I straddled the narrow platform connecting my car to the next. The noise of the wheels on the tracks below me was deafening.

The train rattled as the front of it entered the tunnel. I inched towards the edge of the platform. Beyond it was just the snowy ground, rushing by much faster than I had expected. I waited for a clearing in the trees, and just before the car entered the tunnel, I jumped.

It was painless. I landed in the snow and slid a little way down the hill until a patch of underbrush broke my fall.

There, I watched as the mountain swallowed the rest of the train, leaving behind a curl of black smoke.

I travelled the rest of the way by foot, trudging through the knee-deep snow as I skirted around the mountain and followed the train tracks until I reached a small town, the sun setting behind the peaks of the houses. A sign stood on the side of the road. Written in friendly cursive were the words: BREAKER CHASM WELCOMES YOU!

It was a quaint town – quiet. As I walked down the road, the street lamps clicked on above me. Most of the stores were closed, except for a single gas station. I approached it. Inside, behind a register, sat an overweight man wearing a checked shirt. He was eating something out of a styrofoam container. Rolls and rolls of scratch tickets hung on the wall behind him.

He stopped eating. "Cold night," he said, stirring his food.

I ignored his comment. "Can you point me towards Knollwood Drive?"

"Are you heading to the farm?"

"No," I said. "Why do you ask?"

"I've got lots of kids coming in here looking for one of those farms."

I didn't respond. Instead, I leaned over the refrigerated case, picked out as many bottles of water as I could carry, and put them on the counter. "I'll take these," I said, searching through my pockets for change. The man gave me a strange look, but then rung them up and pointed me in the direction of Knollwood Drive.

I walked for what seemed like hours, past frozen fields and barns, until I reached a tin mailbox. A little way down the drive was a yellow farmhouse with a big yellow barn. There was no street sign, but on the side of the road I spotted dozens of small footprints embedded in the snow. I placed my bag of bottled water on the ground. Crouching over, I brushed off the mailbox so I could read the number, and then slipped a piece of paper out of my pocket and compared the addresses. Both read: *15 Knollwood Drive.*

Holding the joints in case they squeaked, I opened the door of the mailbox. Inside was a piece of paper. A single name was written on it: *Cindy Bell.*

I folded the note into my pocket. Before I left, I opened a bottle of water and poured it out on the ground behind me to melt my footprints.

I awoke to a loud crash, followed by the sound of things clattering to the floor.

Blinking, I opened my eyes. The morning sun was burning the back of my neck as it shone through the window of my grandfather's library. I must have slept through the night here, my head resting on the pile of clippings on the desk.

Rolling my neck, I sat up and looked at the postcard of Breaker Chasm that had fallen out of the stack. I flipped it over to see if anything was written on it, but it was blank.

Cindy Bell. That was Eleanor's mom. Why had her name been written on a slip of paper in a mailbox?

My thoughts were interrupted by a deep thump in an adjacent room. Then shouting. Tucking the postcard into my pocket, I ran out to the hallway.

I followed the voices to my grandfather's office, where I found him standing across the room from Dustin. Both of their faces were red and flustered.

"We should have done something," my grandfather yelled, not noticing that I was standing in the doorway. "Why didn't you tell me it was this bad?"

Dustin was about to respond when the floor creaked beneath me. Turning in my direction, both men went silent.

The room was a complete mess. A platter of breakfast was strewn across the floor, the eggs, hollandaise sauce, jam and pancakes all smeared into the wood among silverware and broken dishes.

"What happened?" I asked, wincing as I took it all in.

On top of all this lay dozens of loose papers, which looked like they had been purposely knocked off the desk.

They were now matted to the ground, sopping up the syrup and coffee. Even more incredible was that Dustin wasn't trying to clean it all up, as he normally would have.

I glanced between him and my grandfather. I had never seen them fight before; I had never even seen Dustin angry.

"What is going on?" I demanded.

Before my grandfather could answer, the phone rang. He picked it up and growled, "Yes?"

He looked at me. "It's for you."

"Me?"

He nodded. "I suggest you take it in the Red Room."

"Okay," I said slowly, and went to the small room down the hall, where I picked up the phone. "Hello?"

All I could hear was steady breathing on the other end of the line.

"Hello? Who is this?" I repeated.

"It's me," a thick voice said.

"Eleanor?" I said, sitting down on a bench. She sounded different. Sombre.

"Tell me what to do," she said, pleading into the phone.

"Do about what?" I asked, suddenly frightened.

"She disappeared," Eleanor said. "She must have run to the lake in the middle of the night while I was sleeping."

"Who disappeared? What lake? Where are you?"

"I'm in the bathroom," she said. "I'm in the bathroom of the ski lodge in Colorado."

I let out a sigh of relief. At first I thought she was in trouble, but it couldn't be that bad if she was with her family skiing. I tried to steady my voice. "Are you okay? What happened?"

There was a long pause.

"They found my mom this morning by the lake. She's dead."

After Eleanor hung up, I sat there on the bench for a long time, the receiver resting on my collarbone.

The only information I could glean from her was that her mother left the ski lodge in the middle of the night, unbeknownst to Eleanor, and was found by the mountain patrol at the foot of a lake, dead, with gauze stuffed in her mouth. It had snowed several centimetres that night, covering all tracks except for those of the rescuers.

Gauze. A lake. Just like Miss LaBarge.

I thought of the photograph I had found in the cottage, of Miss LaBarge and Cindy Bell as young girls. I thought of Miss LaBarge's funeral, and how Cindy Bell was sitting all alone on the boat, lost in her thoughts. Had she been searching for the secret of the Nine Sisters, too?

Dropping the phone, I ran upstairs to my room. There, I searched my dresser until I found the postcards Eleanor had sent to me last summer when she was travelling in Europe with her mother. I'd kept them with me, rereading Dante's embedded messages whenever I felt particularly lonely. But this time, I looked at the photographs on the cards. Each one was of a lake.

Backing onto my bed, I flipped through the pictures again, amazed that I'd had these cards all along, but hadn't realized what they suggested. Eleanor's mother had been searching for the last part of the riddle in Europe, and had brought Eleanor along with her.

Cindy Bell had been searching for the last sister, too. She must have gotten the first two riddles from Miss LaBarge, and was searching in the lakes for something buried in salt water. Until someone killed her.

Had she found anything? I wondered how close I had been to finding the secret before I'd been distracted by Noah and my search for Dante, and if the Undead who killed Cindy Bell would find it instead of me. Why hadn't I tried harder? People had died for this secret, people were still dying, and I had chosen to do nothing.

I wiped my eyes and shoved my hands into my pockets. That's when I felt it. The weathered photograph that had prompted my vision. *My vision,* I repeated, my stomach twisting into a knot. Last night I'd had a dream of going to a farmhouse in Vermont and taking a piece of paper with Cindy Bell's name on it from the mailbox. Now she was dead. And before Miss LaBarge died, I'd envisioned that I was chasing her to an island. Except this time I knew where the vision had come from.

I steadied myself, feeling like I was going to be sick. Had Dante done this?

Reluctantly, I slipped the postcard of Breaker Chasm out of my pocket. My vision was of Vermont, not Colorado, where Cindy Bell was found. That must mean something. Maybe Dante hadn't killed her. Maybe he was just...just...what?

Closing my eyes, I tried to recall a memory of the boy I fell in love with, any memory that would remind me that the Dante I knew would never hurt anyone. But as I did, the memories crumpled like flimsy photographs. I had to know what Breaker Chasm was; I had to know what he had done.

My grandfather was still in his office, stuffing a briefcase full of papers. In front of him, Dustin hunched down, cleaning up the mess.

I stepped around him and held up the postcard. "What is this place?"

Taking it from me, my grandfather put on his glasses and squinted at the image. "Where did you get this? Did you go through my office?"

When I didn't respond, he threw down his briefcase.

"Did you take Annette LaBarge's file from my desk? I've been looking for it all morning."

"I just stumbled across it," I said, stepping back.

Taking off his glasses, he stormed out the door and into the library, where the rest of the clippings were scattered on the desk. I watched as he shoved them into his briefcase.

"Where are you going?"

"Business," he said.

"What was Miss LaBarge looking for in Breaker Chasm, Vermont?"

"I don't know," he answered. "Which is why it's important that I keep things in order. You can't just take things like this and leave them about the house. What if they'd gotten thrown out? Misplaced? We would have lost the only clues we have." He snapped his briefcase shut. "This isn't a game. People are dying. *Monitors* are dying. I don't think your friend Eleanor would be amused by whatever half-hatched theory you've come up with. So I would suggest you save your childish endeavours for the dormitories."

That night, it started to snow. I ate dinner alone, sitting at the end of the long dining room table while Dustin stood in the corner, his hands clasped behind his back.

"If I may, Miss Renée," he said as I picked at my duck. "I believe Breaker Chasm is in the part of the lake country that many people believe is haunted."

"Haunted?" I repeated.

"I believe so."

That's when I felt it. At first it was subtle. Just a slight chill tickling my ankles. And then it moved, travelling up beneath the table to my arms, my shoulders, my neck.

I dropped my fork. It clattered against my plate and fell to the floor. The air around me seemed to rearrange itself into his name: Dante. But it couldn't be. He wouldn't be here; it was too dangerous.

Dustin stared at me. "Miss Renée, is everything all right?"

Shaking myself to attention, I nodded and reached under the table to pick up my fork. A draught must have snuck in through an upstairs window. Except we were deep into the Massachusetts winter; none of the windows were open. Could he really be here?

It was too dark to see anything out the window, except for the snow collecting on the panes, but I could still feel him.

"I'm finished," I said, picking up my plate. I had to go outside and see if he was there.

"But you've barely touched your food," Dustin said,

concerned. "Come, just a few more bites?" He must have seen me glance out the window, because he continued. "Is there something outside?" he said, following my gaze. "I can call the gardener to fetch it for you."

"No," I said quickly. "I was just admiring the snow," I said, and sat back down, not wanting to draw his attention to Dante.

After dinner I stayed up with Dustin, watching late-night talk shows until he nodded off, his head in his hand as he leaned on the arm of the sofa. Tiptoeing across the room, I turned off the television. The room went dark, save for the twinkling lights on the Christmas tree. I crept out, up the stairs, and into my room.

Before I could turn on the lights, a cold hand covered my mouth and pulled me inside, the door clicking shut behind me.

"I didn't want you to scream," a deep voice said.

My body went rigid. Dante. He was here, in my bedroom, his chest expanding against my back as he breathed. I could smell the sap on his clothes; I could hear the branches tapping on the windowpanes in rhythm with his heart.

When he released me, I backed away from him. Framed in the doorway of my closet, he looked like a mannequin. Tall, pale, and too perfect to be real, his broad shoulders stiff beneath his sweater.

He pushed a loose lock of hair behind his ear. "Why are you looking at me like that?" he said, his voice gentle. He moved towards me, but I stepped away.

His smile faded. "What's wrong?"

"Where have you been?"

"I was moving around," he said, offering me the same answer he always did.

"But where?"

He frowned, his forehead wrinkling into delicate lines. "Why does it matter? I'm here now."

"Why does it matter?" I breathed. "I've been trying to find you for months. I've been waiting for you, not knowing where you were or what you were doing. You know everything about me, but I know nothing about you. Do you know how that feels?"

"Don't say that," he said, hurt. "You know me better than anyone."

"It doesn't feel that way."

"I'm sorry," he said, his eyes a soft brown. "I was in Vermont. A town called Breaker Chasm. I haven't been telling you because I thought it would be safer if you didn't know."

I leaned against my bedpost. "Breaker Chasm?" I said miserably, the words deteriorating as they left my mouth.

He nodded. "Do you know it?"

"No," I whispered. "What – what were you doing there?"

Dante hesitated. "I was in hiding," he said. "Like I told you I was."

My lip began to quiver. I bit it and turned away, hoping he hadn't seen. "What do you do when you're in hiding?"

"I've been searching for an answer for us," he said, beginning to grow worried. "You know that."

I gripped the bedpost. "Searching where? In mailboxes?"

A flash of recognition passed over him. "Mailboxes?"

"Eleanor's mother is dead," I said.

"What?" he said, confused. "How do you know?"

"Don't pretend like it's a surprise," I said. "You went to a farmhouse and took a piece of paper from the mailbox. It had Cindy Bell's name on it."

"It's not what it seems," Dante said, guilt etching itself into his face as he stepped towards me. But when he saw me grow rigid, he stopped.

"What was it, then? Why did you go there? What did you do with that slip of paper?"

Dante gripped the edge of the dresser. "Please," he said. "Don't ask me these questions."

"Why not? I have a right to know."

"You don't understand," he said. "If I tell you, I'll be putting you in danger."

"Why?" I closed my hand into a fist to stop it from shaking. "What kind of danger?"

Dante searched for an answer. "I can't—"

Suddenly I was crying. "Did you kill her?" I said, so softly I wasn't sure he heard me. "Did you kill Eleanor's mother?"

"No," he said, his voice wavering. "Of course I didn't. You know I couldn't."

"You're lying," I said, studying him in horror, and backed away until I was against the wall. "And Miss LaBarge? Did you chase her boat in Lake Erie? Did you take her shovel and then follow her to the island and kill her?"

Dante's expression widened with bewilderment. "I – I never killed her," he asserted, though his voice cracked when he said it. He didn't deny the rest.

"My visions," I whispered. "They've been yours the entire time. You were looking for the secret of the Nine Sisters, and you never told me. Why? Why didn't you just tell me the truth? What's so bad about what you did that you had to keep it from me?"

"I wanted to tell you. I wanted to tell you more than anything."

I waited for him to go on, to give me some explanation, but instead he seemed to shrink into the shadows.

Downstairs, the clock chimed midnight. "I don't understand," I said, my voice wild with desperation. "Tell me why you chased her. Why you took Cindy Bell's name from a mailbox. Why you kept it a secret from me."

Dante raised his hand to me, and then let it drop, as if he were apologizing. "Please," he said, pleading. "You have to trust me."

"Why?" I cried. "Why should I trust you? I don't even know who you are."

Dante's eyes darted to the door, worried that I would wake someone up. "Of course you do," he said in disbelief, his shoulders sinking as if I had wounded him.

I moved away from him to my bed, suddenly frightened. "You're a murderer. I have the soul of a murderer." He sucked in his breath like I'd slapped him, but I didn't care.

"Don't say that," he said, shaking his head.

"What do you want from me?" I yelled. "Why are you here?"

"Because I wanted to see you," he said. "Because I love you."

Outside my bedroom window I noticed a downstairs light turn on, casting a long yellow rectangle across the snow on the front lawn. Dante froze when he saw it. Dustin must have woken up.

"I don't believe you," I breathed.

Dante blinked, his chest collapsing as if there were nothing left inside him. And for a moment I could see him the way he used to be – the Dante who ran with me through the rain and pressed me against the blackboard, kissing my neck, my arms, my hands. The Dante who carried me through the field of flowers behind the chapel and gave my soul back to me.

And for reasons I can't explain, I wasn't scared when he came towards me, his hand gentle on my waist as he lowered his face to mine. This is it, I thought as he studied me. He is going to take my soul, and I am going to die. I closed my eyes, not wanting to see him when he did it. I felt his weight pressing against my body, his breath cool against my skin...and then, delicately, he kissed my cheek.

"I would die for you again if you asked me to," he said so softly that I wasn't even sure if I had actually heard him.

From down the hall, I heard footsteps. Surprised, I opened my eyes just as Dante vanished into the shadows of my room.

There were three soft raps on the door. Confused, my eyes darted about the darkness. What had just happened?

"Renée?" Dustin's voice was muffled through the door. "I...heard something. May I come in?"

I rubbed my cheeks with my palms. "Just a minute," I said, and, wiping the tears from my eyes, I opened the door.

Dustin looked a bit groggy, the left side of his face red from sleeping on his hand; but his eyes were sharp as they darted around the room.

"Is someone here?" he said, his voice more stern than I had ever heard it before.

"No," I said, steadying my voice. "I was only reading."

Dustin followed my gaze to my nightstand, where one of my textbooks was resting. "I'm going to go downstairs and clean up a bit. If you need anything, I'll be in the kitchen."

"I'll help you," I said, eager to take Dustin's attention away from my room. "I wanted a glass of milk, anyway."

Turning off the light, I closed the door, my eyes lingering for the briefest moment on the spot where Dante had just been standing.

Downstairs, I helped Dustin with the dishes in silence. When we were done, I poured myself a glass of milk and went upstairs. I entered my room cautiously, a gust of cold air enveloping me as I opened the door. But once inside, I realized that it was just an open window. Dante was gone. It was just cold air now. Pushing the window closed, I looked down to the lawn, where his footprints were already being filled in with snow.

CHAPTER 12

THE ICE FARM

"RENÉE?" MY GRANDFATHER'S VOICE CALLED from outside my bedroom door. "It's time for lunch." He paused. "Renée?"

"I'm not hungry."

"You've barely eaten anything all week." He turned the knob, and when he realized it was locked, he rattled it. "What are you doing in there?"

"Nothing," I said, dragging a chair into my closet, which was still filled with my mother's childhood things from when it was her room. "Go away." I propped it against the wall, and when I thought my grandfather was gone, I climbed on top of it and patted around the top shelf until I felt a long leather case. Tugging it out, I pulled it onto the floor, where it landed with a thud.

"What was that sound?" my grandfather called. "Are you almost packed? We're leaving in an hour."

"Yes," I yelled, opening the clasps on the case. "I'm fine. Just leave me alone." Inside was a shovel, its wooden sheath dark with oil from my mother's hands; its head speckled with rust. My fingers grazed the metal. It was surprisingly heavy when I lifted it from the box and held it upright. I gazed across the room to the mirror, trying to see myself for who I was. A Monitor.

I pulled down the back of my shirt and stared at the reflection of the mark on my back, watching the way it subtly changed from white to pink as I rolled my shoulders, the way its shape seemed to transform when I moved my neck, distorting from an oval to a skull to the silhouette of Dante's face.

"There's nothing between us," I whispered, my eyes dark and heavy. And quickly, before I changed my mind, I tore a Band-Aid out of its wrapper and pressed it over the spot, covering him, embalming him, deleting him from my life.

Montreal was a metre deep in snow when I arrived later that evening. The wheels of my suitcase left two wobbly

354

trails in the street as I pulled it down the alley that led to St. Clément. Just before I reached the gates, I stopped. My suitcase had gotten stuck in a ridge of ice. Turning, I tugged on the handle, when I noticed that it wasn't just a ridge. It was a shape: a giant letter drawn into the pavement. I stepped back, pushing my hood from my face as I realized there wasn't just one letter, there were many letters. Carved deep into the snowy ground beneath the street lamp was a message written in Latin.

FORGIVE ME, it read.

I let go of my bag as I spun around, searching the alley and the buildings for any trace of Dante. A doormat slung over a fire escape flapped in the wind. Otherwise, all was still. Pulling my coat closer, I stood over the message, my cheeks stinging from the cold as I watched the falling snow slowly fill in the letters. Forgive him? How could I? He still wasn't being honest with me about what he had been doing.

After dropping off my suitcase, I went straight to Anya's, where I knocked on the door and hovered by the broom closet across the hall, fidgeting with my skirt while she yelled through the door that she would just be a minute.

She answered the door in a silk robe. "Renée, I didn't know you were back."

"We have to go to Vermont," I said.

355

She gave me a steady gaze. "Come inside."

Her room was cluttered with clothes and shoes and lacy underwear. She pushed them off her couch and sat down next to me. "You had another vision."

In her upper ear was a new piercing, which she rotated as I told her about the farmhouse and Cindy Bell's name, about taking my mother's shovel with me. I wavered before mentioning Dante. I wanted to tell her about him more than anything; the burden of it had been weighing down on me for so long that it seemed only natural to let it go. But for some reason, I couldn't.

That was the first time I realized that I really wasn't a great Monitor. If I were, I would have turned Dante in. I would have stopped him from leaving my room that night. I would have told my grandfather about him the next morning, and helped them hunt him down. So why hadn't I?

When I was finished, Anya frowned. "But Cindy Bell wasn't killed in Breaker Chasm. She was killed in Colorado. So what exactly did you see?"

"I don't know. That's why I have to go. I have to find out. Something could be hidden there. The last piece of the riddle, even." What I didn't tell her was that it wasn't just the prospect of finding the riddle that was pulling me to Breaker Chasm. I needed to understand what Dante had been doing.

"So what do you think?" I said. "Will you come? I was thinking we could go on Saturday. We could take a train."

"The day after tomorrow? I can't."

I gave her a puzzled look. "Why not?"

She stood up and went across the room to light a votive. "I have to help my dad at the store."

"Can't you take one day off?"

"No. It's really busy this time of year," she said, and blew out the match.

"It's the middle of January in Montreal," I said slowly. "Nothing's busy. You can barely walk outside without getting windburn."

"You haven't been wearing the necklace I made you."

I shook my head in confusion. "What?"

"You don't like it?"

"The one with the beans?" I said. "It's...not really my style. But why are you dodging my invitation? Do you just not want to go? Because you can tell me."

"Fine," she said. "I just don't want to go."

"Because you're scared?" I pressed.

"Because I just don't want to go," she repeated. "And I don't think you should go either."

"Why not? Since when are *you* the voice of reason?" I said, picking up a wishbone charm adorned with feathers.

Anya's face went taut, her lips parting as if she were

357

about to snap at me, but instead she sank back into the couch. "Why don't you take that?" She gestured at the charm. "You might need it."

I stood up and tossed it on the couch. "Thanks, but I think I'll manage on my own," I said, and slammed the door.

Maybe she was right, I thought as I walked back to my room. Only an obsessed person would want to follow a dream to a strange farmhouse in Vermont. But what else could I do? Everything had already been set in motion; I couldn't stop now.

Through the window, I could see the boys' dormitory across the courtyard, its windows lit up. One of them belonged to Noah. He would understand that I had to go. He wouldn't even need an explanation. And without thinking, I stood up and threw on my coat.

It was a frigid and still night, the trees white and motionless, as if the entire campus had been frozen over. I was halfway across the courtyard when I noticed a tall, huddled figure walking towards me. We crossed paths in front of the fountain, which was covered in a glossy layer of ice. I tightened my hood around my face.

"Renée," a voice said.

I stopped walking and spun around. "Noah?" I pushed back my hood to get a better look, my hair prickling with static.

Noah was wearing a heavy fleece coat and leather boots. Snowflakes caught on his hair. "I saw the light in your window and wanted to say hi."

"You know which window is mine?" I blurted out. The thought made me happy.

"But you're going somewhere, I guess?"

"No," I said, unable to stop the smile spreading across my face. "I was actually going to see you."

"Do you know which window is mine?" he said, flattered.

I shook my head and stepped closer to him, hugging myself in the cold. "No. I guess I didn't really have a plan."

"Me neither," he said. Unwrapping his scarf, he looped it around my neck.

"So how was your holiday?" he said, studying my face. His lips were pale red, the fog of his breath dissipating into the night just before it reached me.

"Can we go somewhere?" I said.

He motioned towards the back of campus. "This way."

The lights in the gymnasium buzzed as he flipped them on. It was dark, empty, and the only sound was the trickling of water coming from somewhere in the locker room. Chlorine, I thought, trying to remember the way pools smelled, trying to will my senses to life. But it was no use. My shoes squeaked against the wooden floor as we ran through the basketball court and down the stairs, until we reached the pool. The water was blue and so still that I could see the ceiling's reflection in it, making me feel like I had entered some back-to-front, alternate world.

We took off our shoes and sat beneath the diving board, dipping our feet into the water as I told him about the farmhouse in Vermont, about the slip of paper with Cindy Bell's name, and how I thought the last piece of the riddle could be there.

"Let's go," he said immediately. "Classes don't start till Monday. It's too late to go now, but we could leave tomorrow. What should we bring?"

We sat there talking and laughing and planning our trip, our shadows melting together as he fell asleep by my side in a pile of towels. I watched him, his chest rising and falling, and wished that I could fall asleep in the crook of his arm; that a single word from his lips could remind me of how beautiful it was to be alive; that a touch from his fingers could inspire me to breathe deeper, to live slower, to be better; that I could fall in love with him.

On Saturday morning, Noah was waiting for me by the school gates, holding two coffees and a brown paper bag.

It was a cold, yellow day, the sun partially obscured by clouds as we took a taxi to a boat station in lower Quebec, where we boarded a ferry.

The boat travelled slowly across Lake Champlain, the drone of the motor churning beneath us as we sat by a dingy snack bar near the window. Noah opened the paper bag and took out two dry brioches. "Chocolate or almond?"

I took the chocolate one and smiled. "Thanks."

The boat was empty save for a few people loitering on deck, their parkas bloated with wind. Leaning over, Noah wiped a flake of pastry crust from my lips, his fingers lingering there for a moment too long.

The loudspeaker hummed and then amplified the captain's voice. He spoke with a rural French-Canadian accent. "We are now leaving Canadian waters and entering the territory of the United States of America."

"We're in between worlds now," Noah murmured, gazing out the window.

The water was a deep blue and extended as far as I could see, the sky reflecting off it as if there were no beginning or end to the horizon, and we were suspended somewhere in the middle. Just like I was suspended somewhere between life and death, between my world and Dante's.

It was late in the afternoon when we disembarked on a

desolate dock on the northern tip of Vermont. The sky was streaked with red as the sun sank behind the mountains in the distance.

Three taxis were waiting in the parking lot. Noah and I approached the closest one. The driver was asleep, his head perched on his fist. A newspaper was spread open over the dashboard. Hesitantly, I knocked on the window. After jolting awake, he rolled down the glass.

"Where are you headed?" He was a gaunt man with grey stubble and wild, overgrown eyebrows.

Unfolding the scrap of paper from my pocket, I read him the address from my vision. With a grunt, he motioned to the back seat. As we climbed in, he pushed the newspaper to the passenger's seat and drove off.

Unrolling the window, he lit a cigarette. A cherry air freshener swayed beneath the rear-view mirror. "How far away is it?" I asked, leaning in between the seats, when a bump sent me toppling into Noah's lap. His warmth caught me off guard, and I jumped, surprised at how outside of me he felt. Is that what it would feel like to touch Noah, to kiss Noah, to be with Noah – a shock of the unfamiliar? The driver mumbled something back that sounded like *twenty minutes*, and turned on the radio to easy listening.

The landscape was frozen and glassy, the trees coated in a delicate layer of ice as we drove past dimly lit farmhouses and snowy fields protected by wooden fences. Just before dusk fell over the treetops, we passed a familiar sign. BREAKER CHASM WELCOMES YOU!

"We're close," I said, gazing at the street lights, the closed shops, the gas station; each looking exactly as they had in my vision. With a finger, I wrote the phrase *Fait accompli* in the fog of the window.

"*Irreversible action,*" Noah translated. "Why did you write that?"

I stared at the phrase. "I don't know," I said, before wiping it away with my palm.

The road was potholed and slippery as we rolled past a crooked tin mailbox standing at the entrance of a long driveway. I turned around and watched it through the rear window, remembering the way it had looked in my vision, buried in snow.

"Wait, stop!" I said, pointing to it. "That's it."

Putting the car in reverse, the driver looked over his shoulder, his face impatient as he backed up over the ice. Before he stopped, I opened the door and jumped out to read the side of the mailbox. It was printed with the same address as the one in my vision. Beyond it was a yellow farmhouse and barn.

We paid the driver to wait for us for an hour. "Any longer, and I'm gone," he said, and pulled over to a flat spot beneath a tree, where he turned off his headlights.

Just as they went out, a thin breeze blew through the trees, wrapping itself around my neck.

"Do you feel that?" I said, turning to Noah.

"Feel what?"

I held a finger to my lips, trying to feel it again, but when I closed my eyes, the air was still. "Never mind," I said.

"Look," Noah said, pointing to a patch of land on the side of the farmhouse, where dozens of little headstones poked out of the ground. "There's a family plot here. That's probably what you're feeling."

I let out a breath of relief. Setting down my bag in the snow, I bent down and pressed the hinges of the mailbox, just as I had done in my vision, so they wouldn't squeak. Quietly, I opened it. But to my dismay, there was nothing inside.

"Empty," Noah said, peering in. "I guess there's only one other place to go."

We gazed up at the farmhouse, which was surrounded by a sagging porch. Its darkened windows gave me solace. Picking up my bag, I followed Noah along the edge of the driveway, staring at the footprints embedded in the snow in front of us.

"It doesn't look like anyone's been doing home improvements," Noah whispered, testing the porch boards with his foot before approaching the front door. "I mean, look at this place. It's falling apart." Yellow paint was peeling off in huge strips, and most of the windows were either broken or boarded up.

A breeze made the shutters creak, and I pulled up the neck of my coat and crossed my arms. "Okay," I said, glancing behind us at the sun setting behind the trees as we slipped through the door.

The foyer was cold and stale, with dust suspended in the air, thickening it. Work boots covered in cobwebs sat on the floor, and greying paper hung off the walls. Noah flipped the light switch, but nothing happened.

The hallway was dark, and as we made for the next room, I bumped into him while trying to avoid a side table.

"You go ahead," he said.

"Thanks," I murmured, hoping it was dark enough that he couldn't see me blushing.

Although the farmhouse was covered in a film of dust, it seemed somehow lived in. The sofas and love seats were antique and dilapidated, but the pillows were all out of place, as if they had just been rearranged. And the imprints in the cushions looked almost like they were fresh. I bent down to touch one, half expecting the spot to still be warm. To my relief, it wasn't.

On the wall hung a picture of three men. They were each holding a large block of ice up to the camera.

"This was an ice farm," Noah said, skimming an article framed on the wall. There were dozens of them, all yellowed and faded, dating back to the 1800s. "It says they cut blocks of ice from the lake, insulated them with hay, and trucked them around to houses in local towns to use in ice boxes before the refrigerator was invented."

"That must be it," I whispered from behind him. He followed my gaze out the window. In the distance was a large frozen lake speckled with a flock of blackbirds gathered on the surface.

"An ice farm," Noah said, deep in thought. "I wonder how this place fits in with the riddle."

"I don't know," I said, though what I didn't understand was what this place had to do with Dante.

"Should we explore?" Noah said. "Where do you think it would be hidden?"

We went through each of the downstairs rooms looking for the last piece of the riddle, under furniture, behind paintings, and beneath rugs, until we found ourselves on the first floor, in a large bedroom.

"Welcome to the master suite," Noah said, holding the door for me with a grin. It was a puritanical old place, plain for the most part, with sturdy wooden furniture and a beamed ceiling, save for a canopied bed with yellowed lace fabric cascading down the sides.

There was a simple chandelier in the centre of the

room, but when Noah pulled the chain, nothing happened. "I don't think anyone's been here in years," he said, opening the closet doors. He glanced around inside to check for anything inscribed in the wood, but the walls were bare.

We scoured the room, looking for a plaque or engraving. With the sky darkening outside, and the overhead light out in the room, it was difficult to see, so we used our hands instead, running our fingers beneath the dresser, the nightstand, the armchair, along the grainy wood of the floor and the uneven plaster of the walls. We knew it wouldn't be on furniture, because the ninth sister would have been smarter than to leave the last clue to immortality on a disposable object. But after checking everywhere, we found nothing.

"There's only one place left," I said, brushing off my knees.

We stared at the bed. I had found the first part of the riddle beneath a hospital bed.

"After the lady of the house," Noah said, giving me a little bow as he lifted the lace of the canopy to let me under the bed.

Ducking beneath it, I dropped to my hands and knees and reached beneath the bedskirt. But no matter how many times I ran my palms over the crevices in the wood, I couldn't find anything.

"I don't feel anything." I inched closer, trying to reach deeper, but stopped when I felt something sharp jab my ankle.

"Ow!" I cried out, and squirmed out to see what it was.

Immediately, Noah was kneeling by my side. "Are you okay?"

"Yeah," I said, looking at the thick sliver of wood sticking out of my stocking. "I think it's just a splinter."

"A big one," he said. "Here, let me. I get them all the time." With a pinch, he pulled it out, leaving behind a hole in my stocking that quickly ran all the way up my leg.

Embarrassed, I shifted, trying to cover it with my skirt.

"Your legs," he said, staring down at the thin line of flesh peeking through the black nylon like a seam. "I've ruined them."

"Just the stockings," I whispered. "Not the legs."

We both moved to stand up at the same time, our fingers tangling together on the floor. Startled, I jumped back, only to knock the bedpost, sending a shower of dust onto our faces.

I gasped, and for a moment, everything went still as the dust coated our hair, our eyelashes, our shoulders. Blinking, I opened my eyes to see Noah, covered in grey powder as if he were the ghost of the farmer who'd owned the house. "I'm sorry," I tried to say, but instead let out a cough, and we both collapsed onto the floor, laughing.

"It's in my eyes!" I cried, tearing as I pressed them shut.

"Here, let me see," Noah said. I could feel him bend over me. He touched my eyelashes and wiped away the dust. My breath grew shallow as he moved down to my cheek, his hand gentle. And then I felt something graze my lips. It was warm and wet and soft. I hadn't been kissed in so long that I couldn't tell if it was a kiss or just his fingers running across my mouth. Except it wasn't just a touch. The time seemed to stretch, and I could almost imagine tasting him, smelling him, feeling his warmth against me.

As he pulled away, something trickled down my face. It might have been a tear; I couldn't tell. And then Noah's hand was on my cheek, wiping it away.

Neither of us said a word. The room was so silent I could hear my heart beating. When I opened my eyes, everything was just as before: Noah kneeling in front of me, his hair coated in dust.

But before either of us could speak, the temperature in the room seemed to drop, and I felt something descend on us, as if frost were creeping through the entire house. A cool stream of air coiled up through the heating vents. Noah had felt it too, and was staring at the doorway, his eyes suddenly alert.

I gazed out the window. The water that had been

dripping off the edge of the gutter had now hardened into icicles. I'd felt this before. The Undead. But this time, it wasn't Dante.

Soundlessly, I stood up and watched, as Noah did the same. We didn't need to speak; we were thinking the same thing. We crept along the side of the room. When Noah thought I wasn't watching, he wet the edges of his lips. Had he kissed me? Had it been real? Averting my eyes, I looked at my face in the mirror. It was dusty and hollow, as if it were an older me, an ancient me from a past life. If it had been a kiss, it must have happened in a different world, when we were both different people.

Once in the hallway, I could hear voices coming from downstairs. Closing my eyes, I tried to count how many there were. One by the window. One by the door. Another two at the kitchen table. Four more outside, by the barn. A handful more in the field. The only way to go was left, down the hallway.

Cautiously, I took a step, and then another, and another, until we reached a room on the other side of the house. Turning the knob, I pushed the door open and went inside, Noah at my heels.

We found ourselves in a narrow, dank room, with low ceilings and a narrow staircase going down the side. The maid's room. Except, instead of being furnished like a proper room, it was filled with toys. Worn toys, chipped and broken, as if they were lifetimes old. Plastic trucks and Matchbox cars and marbles and jacks were scattered across the floor. I stepped around them carefully, gazing at the room. What was this place?

I was about to lead us down the narrow staircase and out the door, when we heard more voices. They seeped through the heating vent like frost. I crouched down and listened. There were dozens of them, talking and laughing and fighting, their voices high-pitched and playful, almost whiny. They were children; boys, no older than twelve, for their voices hadn't broken yet. I tried to make out what they were saying, but it was all chatter.

I was about to turn away when a deep voice cut through them, speaking in Latin. It sounded like a boy – or rather a man – around Dante's age, maybe older. The room went silent. My lip trembled as I waited, but when he spoke, all I could make out were words here and there:

"The Nine Sisters."

"Name in the mailbox."

"Hold her and wait for us to come."

"Serve the Liberum."

Soundlessly, I stood up, willing my heart to beat softer. My eyes darted about the ceiling. The Liberum. Was the deep voice one of the Brothers? Were they employing Undead children to help them find the secret of the Nine Sisters?

I glanced out the window to where the taxi should have been waiting for us, but it was gone.

"What is he saying?" Noah mouthed.

"We need to get out," I whispered, so softly that I wasn't even sure Noah heard me.

But how? We were far away from civilization. Without realizing it, I backed away from the wall, trying to distance myself from the voice, but I had forgotten that the floor was cluttered with toys, and lost my footing on a train set that wound around the room.

It happened too quickly for me to catch myself. I stumbled, my arms flailing as I reached out for a desk. I was too slow, and fell to the floor with a loud thump, the toys beneath me scattering across the room.

I didn't move until everything had settled. The house went still. Noah's eyes were wide as they travelled from me to the open door and the shadowed hallway beyond.

From somewhere in the distance, I heard the light pitter-patter of footsteps. They seemed to be coming from nowhere and everywhere, like rain falling on the roof. The sound was low at first, and then grew louder, like dozens of tiny feet running up the stairs.

I felt them before I saw them: a rush of cold, as if I had just fallen into an icy lake. Goosebumps rose over my skin as they got closer, closer; the cold air enveloping me, wrapping itself around my throat until it was so tight I could barely breathe.

A pale figure emerged from the darkness at the end of the hall, running towards us. Another followed behind him – a flailing white thing – followed by another, and another. They were moving so quickly and so strangely, their limbs thrashing as they ran.

Noah's voice boomed across the room. "Come on."

Taking his hand, I pulled myself up.

We clambered down the narrow back stairway, my feet so close to Noah's heels that I thought I was going to knock him over. At the bottom was another long hallway, lined with family photographs and doors. At the other end I could see the windows of the kitchen, and beyond that, a back door.

We began to run for the door when I saw a white blur moving towards us from that direction.

Noah skidded to a stop, the oriental carpet bunching beneath our feet as I slid into him. He turned to me, his breath quick. Above us, I could hear the boys running through the maid's room, the ceiling sagging slightly beneath their footsteps. They were getting louder, closer.

"What now?" I said, searching the hallway, looking for a way out.

Noah ran to me just as an Undead child emerged from the stairwell, his eyes a cloudy grey. They didn't move as he turned about the room like a dizzy child listening for our sound. He couldn't have been older than six. I watched him, taking in his worn trousers, his bare feet, his wild hair; then I realized that he was blind.

Two others stumbled down the stairs behind him. Their eyes were clearer, more focused, tilting their heads as if trying to figure out what I was.

I felt Noah behind me. "Why are they staring at us like that?" he whispered.

"They're just interested," I uttered, cringing every time their blurry eyes met mine. "They're only children, remember? They don't know who we are. Just don't let them see—"

"Shovel!" one of them said in Latin, pointing to the small trowel sticking out of the inside pocket of Noah's coat.

Slowly, I walked backwards towards the line of doors, hoping one of them led to a way out, when I felt a tiny hand on my leg, tugging at my skirt. Startled, I fell down, the carpet rough against my legs as the boy crawled on top of me, his small body smudged with dirt as he grabbed at my face. Arching my neck away from him, I covered his mouth with my hand, flung him off me, and stood up.

Noah was a couple of metres away, kicking off three small boys, all barefooted and shirtless. Pressing my lips together, I pushed through them, pulling them off Noah and dragging him out. They grabbed at our ankles as I turned the knobs of the last door. It was pitch-black inside, and dank. A basement, I thought, staring down at the cement staircase. Just then, an Undead boy wrapped his hands around my leg. I pulled Noah through the door, taking the Undead boy with me.

The boy clung to my legs, his tiny fingers pressing into my thighs as I stumbled underground. I tried to kick him off, but he grew breathless, desperate, grasping at my skirt, my arms, my hair. Before I could catch myself, I slipped, crying out in pain as I toppled down the stairs, the cement bruising my back.

I felt the boy's face close to mine, his breath cold against my cheek. And then we hit the ground. The unfinished floor scuffed my knees, and the boy's grip grew loose. Peeling him off me, I scrambled away and watched his cloudy eyes grow bloodshot. They rolled back in his head. I gasped as he twisted his neck one way and then the other, as if in pain; faster, faster, until he was writhing on the floor.

Noah grabbed my arm.

"Wait!" I said, staring at the boy's slim body, his button nose, his chubby cheeks smudged with dirt. "He's dying. We have to help him."

"Leave him!" Noah said.

"He's just a child!" I said.

"He isn't any more. He's a monster." Before I could say anything else, Noah took me by the waist and pulled me towards the back of the room. It was a long stone basement filled with bales of hay and rusty farm equipment.

"Maybe there's a ground entrance," Noah said, scanning the ceilings until he found a set of metal doors. Standing on a bale of hay, he pushed them open to reveal the night sky, blue and wild with stars.

He lifted himself up and then leaned over to help me, but I was right behind him. A vast field stretched before us, the snow packed into ice. We ran through it, the air sharp on my lungs as we headed for the lake and the woods beyond.

I skidded to a stop as we reached the shore, where the ice met the snow.

"Is it safe to walk on?" I shouted, my hair whipping about my cheeks as I turned. Behind us, the Undead boys were slipping out of the farmhouse, their skin pale in the moonlight, like moths.

"Of course it is," Noah said, slowing as he stepped onto the lake. "This was an ice farm. They had to have gotten it from somewhere."

I wavered as I listened to see if the ice beneath Noah was cracking. But all I could hear was the snow crunching beneath the feet of the Undead behind us.

The blackbirds nestled on the surface scattered as we

ran across the lake, our shoes slipping on the ice as the January winds numbed my lungs. When we made it to the woods on the other side, I saw the boys through the branches, their pallid faces a dim blue in the darkness. It looked like they were going to follow us, until a deep voice boomed behind them. "Enough," it said, as a dark figure appeared, tall and narrow like a scarecrow. I felt the Undead children gather and become still along the perimeter of the lake, their dulled eyes following us as we vanished into the night.

CHAPTER 13

OPHELIA HART

"ICE", THE GAS STATION ADVERTISED in neon.

It had taken us an hour to get there, trudging through the woods until our legs were numb and caked with snow.

"There was no riddle in there," Noah said, catching his breath. "What was that place?"

"I don't know," I said, bending over my knees. "A place where the Undead live. A place run by the Liberum." I looked up at him. "They're looking for the riddle, too. They're trying to find the secret."

"They said that?"

I shook my head, my eyes watering. "No. I can just feel it." Suddenly I regretted not looking for the last part of the riddle sooner. What would happen if the Liberum found it first?

"Why would you have a vision of that?" he asked, incredulous. "Why would your dream tell us to go there?"

"It's not my fault," I cried out defensively, and then covered my face, embarrassed.

"I never said it was," he said, and held the door of the gas station for me.

"I know." I stepped into the fluorescent lighting.

Noah nodded to the cashier, a greasy man sipping coffee. "Do you think they followed us?" He glanced out the window at the trees.

I closed my eyes, remembering the tall dark boy hovering behind the children as we ran away. "I can't feel them anywhere."

While Noah approached the cashier to ask about a taxi, I wandered to the side of the store, trying to calm my nerves. But as I pulled a bottle of water out of the refrigerator, all I could think of was Dante doing the same thing in my vision.

Had the dark figure by the woods been a Brother of the Liberum? Had Dante been working with them to find the secret of the Nine Sisters? Is that why he had gone to the farmhouse and taken Cindy Bell's name from the mailbox?

"Renée?" Noah said. "Are you okay? You look sick."

I swallowed, realizing I was hunched over a counter, my stomach queasy. I knocked over a cup of plastic lids as I picked myself up. "Sorry, I'm fine," I said, and bent down to collect them.

"Here, let me do that," Noah said, helping me. "The cashier told me there's a late ferry, but we might have already missed it. He said he'll call a taxi to come pick us up, if we want to try and make it. What do you think?"

I nodded. I wanted to tell Noah everything about me and Dante, but knew that I couldn't. How could I explain that I'd fallen in love with the person who might have killed Miss LaBarge and Cindy Bell; the person who could have killed my own parents? I didn't understand. Was he lying when he said he loved me? Did everything that happened between us mean nothing to him?

I listened to the gas station coffee trickle through the drip while we waited for a taxi, Noah pacing by the pastry shelf, gazing out the window. The fluorescent lights buzzed over the gas pumps, illuminating the snow as it fell atop the canopy above them. The horizon beyond was black. I knew we had escaped, that the boys from the farmhouse had stopped at the words of the tall scarecrow figure, but for some reason I couldn't shake the feeling that we were being watched.

Thirty minutes later, a blue car picked us up, its windscreen wipers squeaking against the snow as we wobbled through the icy streets. A faint light shone from the ferry station, but after we paid the driver and went inside, we realized that it was empty. The ticket counter was closed and locked with a metal cage. I followed Noah into the darkened waiting room. It was lined with rows of cheap plastic chairs and metal rubbish bins.

He checked a note on the wall. "The last ferry was cancelled due to inclement weather," he said. "The next one isn't till morning."

"Now what?"

"We wait here, I guess."

"What if they come?" I said, staring out the glass doors.

Taking an inventory of the room, Noah picked up a mop from a corner and barricaded the door handles. Joining him, I helped move two trash bins in front of the back door, and then locked all the windows. "At least now we'll hear them," Noah said, and sat at the end of a row of seats.

Using my scarf as a pillow, I lay down on the chairs across from him. And as the rush of the night wore off, the air between us grew tense.

"It's different now," Noah said, staring at the pipes on the ceiling. His eyes were melancholy. "We're different."

"No we're not," I said, but my voice fell flat. Should I have pulled him towards me in the farmhouse? Should I have kissed him back? Part of me wanted to, but the rest of me had screamed *no!*, as if I were betraying something buried deep within me.

"Who is he?" Noah said. "What's so great about him?"

I felt his eyes on me, pleading to tell him something. But what could I say? I didn't know where love came from or why it attached itself to some people and not others. Despite everything that had happened with Dante, I couldn't bring myself to leave him behind.

"Do you believe in soulmates?" I whispered.

"You mean a human who has the soul of an Undead?"

"No. The idea of a soulmate. That there's only one person that's really right for you in this world."

I could hear Noah breathing as he thought. "No."

"Why?"

"Because it gives us no choice. It means that some cosmic force has already chosen the person I'm supposed to love. But that's not how it works. I don't want to be with someone who completes my soul; I want someone who will open it. I want to be able to choose."

I closed my eyes. "What if the choice isn't that easy?"

"Choices are always easy," Noah said, a hint of spite in his voice. "It's our heads that get us confused."

"What do you mean?"

Leaning forward, he reached into his pocket and took out a penny. "If it lands on heads, he's your soulmate." His voice hardened on the last words. "If it lands on tails, soulmates don't exist." He gave me a level look. "Okay?"

Confused, I shook my head. "It doesn't work like that—"

"Give me a chance," he said, and then looked away, embarrassed. Before I could say anything more, he threw the coin in the air. It landed on the ground with three clinks. Bending over, Noah picked it up. My shoulders went taut as I waited, surprised at how involved I was in something as meaningless as a coin toss.

Noah opened his hand. As he said, "Heads," I felt tears prick my eyes.

"Now be honest," he said. "Do you wish it had fallen a different way? It could have, you know."

I hesitated, too ashamed to admit that I didn't think it could.

"See?" Noah said, his lids growing heavy as he watched me. "You already made your decision. You just haven't accepted it yet."

I couldn't sleep that night. I had nightmares of fingers scratching at the windows, of the tall shadowy figure lowering his face to mine, his skin riddled with veins as his cold breath lapped against my lips.

The next morning, the ferry manager woke us up by

banging on the door. The white winter sky was bright as I rolled off the plastic chairs and let him in, gazing at the empty streets beyond, unable to shake the feeling that the Undead were watching us.

"I'm sorry," I said to Noah as we waited for the boat to leave.

"You don't have to apologize," he said, and gave me a meagre smile, pretending it was easy for him, even though I knew it wasn't.

When we arrived on campus, we walked through the St. Clément school gates as real Monitors. We had killed an Undead in the farmhouse; I had watched him writhe on the basement floor. But as I made my way with Noah down the snowy path, I couldn't help but feel like I was taking steps backwards. The more I learned about myself and the people I loved, the more I found myself looking back, trying to reread the past and see where it had gone wrong.

"Where are you going?" Noah said as I walked towards the girls' dormitory at the fork in the path.

"Back to my room."

"We have to go to the headmaster's office. We have to tell him that we found a house full of the Undead and maybe a Brother of the Liberum."

"No," I said quickly. "We can't."

"What? Why not?"

"Because they'll ask us how we found the farmhouse, and I'll have to tell them about my visions, and then..."

Noah waited for me to continue. "And then what...?"

"And then..." But the more I searched for an answer, the more I realized I didn't have one. I let my arms drop to my sides. "I don't know."

"It's not your fault that you're having these visions. If anything, the headmaster should be grateful. It's because of you that we found the Undead in the first place."

Feeling all the more miserable, I gave him a slight nod.

The windows of the headmaster's office gave off a warm yellow glow as we walked towards them. The cobblestones were packed with snow.

An older woman wearing a heavy sweater and a brooch answered. His secretary. She surveyed the state of our outfits, which were stained from the night before. "Out late practising?" she asked.

"We need to speak to Headmaster LaGuerre," Noah said.

"I'm afraid he hasn't arrived back yet from the winter holidays. Is everything all right?"

Noah glanced at me. "Do you know when he'll be back?"

"He'll be in the office tomorrow morning. Do you want to leave him a message?" she asked, and took out a pen.

"No," I said firmly. "We'll come back tomorrow."

After we made plans to meet before class the next day, Noah walked me back to the dormitory. The snowflakes caught in my eyelashes as I stood on the stoop.

"Thank you," I said.

"Please don't say that," he said softly, though there was an edge to his voice. "It makes me wonder if I could have changed your mind."

I pushed a lock of hair from my face. "No – I—"

But before I could say anything more, he backed down the stairs. "Keep safe, Renée."

I was so dazed when I got back to my room that it took me a few moments to notice the closet door was ajar. "Strange," I said, flipping on the lights and glancing inside, where nothing seemed wrong. But as I went to my desk, something crunched beneath my feet. A few pieces of broken glass were strewn in front of my bed; the remainder of a water jug I kept on my nightstand. Bending over, I picked up a shard and then checked the trash bin, where I found the rest of the glass. Someone had been here.

Throwing my stuff down, I burst through the bathroom and banged on Clémentine's door.

To my surprise, the headmaster opened it.

"Renée," he said as he put one of Clémentine's bags

386

down. He was wearing a coat and hat, his shoulders dusted with snow. Clémentine was standing behind him in tall fur boots and earmuffs.

"Headmaster LaGuerre," I said, my shoes squeaking against the wood as I stopped short. "You're here."

He gave me a bemused smile. "Yes I am. Were you coming to say hi to Clémentine?"

A smirk spread across Clémentine's face.

"Oh, um – yes. I'll come back later. Sorry to intrude."

"Well, don't leave on my behalf," he said. "I'll be gone after I help Clémentine carry her things in."

"Oh, that's okay," I said, and made for the door, when Clémentine stepped forward.

"Did you want to ask me something?" she said, taking off her gloves. "You can do it now. No need to be shy."

I glanced at her, and then at her father. He blinked, waiting. "I just – found something in my room. A broken water jug. And the closet door was open, but I'm certain I closed it before I left. I was wondering if you saw anyone go into my room while I was away?"

Clémentine raised a delicate eyebrow. "But I only just got back. How would I know?"

The luggage by her feet was wet from snow. Maybe she was telling the truth. But then who had been in my room?

* * *

I slept on Anya's couch that night, beneath a coarse patchwork quilt that her grandmother had made, with the sign of the cat embroidered on it for good luck. Anya lit candles around the room while I told her about the farmhouse and the dark figure that had been standing behind the children as we'd run into the woods. Even long after she fell asleep, I stayed awake, the candles around me flickering as the clouded eyes of the boy I'd left writhing on the basement floor blurred into Dante's, haunting me until I drifted into dreams.

Anya shook me awake the next morning. The candles had all burned out, and the January day was peeking in between the curtains. "We slept through Strategy and Prediction," she said, throwing clothes on. Our class was supposed to have been held at a location outside of the city. By the time we made it out the door, class was over, and the van was already parked near the school gates. I spotted Noah by the kerb, holding his gear.

"What happened?" he asked. "We were supposed to meet the headmaster this morning."

"I'm so sorry," I said, lowering my voice when I noticed Clémentine watching us. "I overslept."

Noah studied me, as if trying to figure out if I was telling the truth. "You didn't not show up because of—"

"Of course not," I said, before he could finish.

The headmaster was carrying the last of the supplies

out of the van when we approached him.

"Headmaster?" I said, tapping him on the shoulder.

He jumped. "Oh, Renée. And Noah. What can I do for you?"

"We need to talk to you," I said. "In private."

Shutting the door, he rubbed his hands together in the cold. "Is everything all right?"

I nodded. "It's about the Liberum."

The smile faded from the headmaster's face. "Excuse me?" he said, bending over us.

Down the path, Clémentine watched us.

"We know where they are," Noah said. "We saw them."

The headmaster looked in either direction and then buttoned his coat. "Come with me," he said.

Inside his office, he cleared stacks of paper from two chairs and motioned for us to sit. Then he settled himself behind his desk and crossed his hands. "Now tell me."

"It started with a vision of a farmhouse," I said, and told him about our trip, the nightmarish house, and what I'd overheard through the heating vent. Noah finished the rest of the story while I stared at the plants on the window sill, trying to push the image of the boy in the basement out of my head.

"You're certain the person you saw was a Brother of the Liberum?" the headmaster asked when we were finished.

I hesitated. "Not certain, but I heard him speak in Latin when he was talking to the children."

"You knew this last night and you didn't tell me?" he said, staring at me.

"We went to your office, but you weren't there," Noah said, not knowing what the headmaster was referring to.

"Did they see you?"

"Yes," I said.

"But most of them were blind," Noah interjected.

The headmaster's shoulders slumped in relief. "And they had no way of identifying you?"

"No," Noah said, just as I blurted out, "Maybe."

The headmaster glanced between us, his eyes wide as he waited for a clear answer. "Did they follow you here?"

I swallowed as he turned from Noah to me. Someone had broken into my room, and it hadn't been Clémentine. Could it have been the Brother of the Liberum? "Maybe."

The headmaster's face seemed to drain of its colour. His eyes darted to the window, and without warning, he stood up and closed the shades. "Then you need to prepare yourselves."

But how?

I skipped the rest of my classes that day and ran to the waterfront, the wind chapping my cheeks as I slowed and stared at the icy waters of the St. Lawrence River. Across the water on the opposite bank, the rounded peaks of the grain silos stuck out of the snowy gust like mountaintops. I walked towards them, my feet making fresh footprints in the snow as I approached the railing.

The wind swirled through, making my eyes water as I leaned over and spoke to Dante. "If I don't see you again," I said, swallowing, "I wanted to say goodbye."

Bye, bye, bye, bye... The sound sent a chill through my bones as it echoed back to me.

Wiping my cheek, I was about to turn away when I noticed a message scratched into the metal of the handrail among the rest of the graffiti. Except this one was written in Latin. *I'll come for you*, it said, as if he had heard me and spoken back.

"Being on the defensive isn't enough," I said to Anya over dinner late that week. Four guards were manning the doors of the dining hall; otherwise, everything seemed to carry on as normal. No one else knew about the threat of the Liberum.

"Are you suggesting we go out and find the Liberum before they find you? Because I don't want to do that." Anya slid down in her chair, sipping a glass of milk. Noah was nowhere to be seen. He had barely said a word to me after our meeting with the headmaster, and after classes he had just disappeared.

I lowered my voice. "Of course not. The Liberum are looking for the secret of the Nine Sisters. The last part of the riddle – that's what they really want, right? But we can't let them have it. You should have seen what he was like..." I said, remembering the dark figure, his body thin and somehow sunken.

The table behind us erupted in laughter. Probably from some stupid joke.

"We need to find the riddle," I said. "We need to find it before they do."

Anya glanced over her shoulder. "But how?"

I chewed on my straw. "I don't know."

And then from somewhere behind me, I heard one of Clémentine's friends say, "Gottfried should be shut down. It's just breeding the Undead."

"That place is cursed," another girl said.

"Gottfried," I repeated. "Curse."

The Gottfried Curse. I had almost forgotten about it. Pushing my plate aside, I turned to Anya, my face flushed. "Did you hear that?"

"Hear what?" she said.

"I have to go." I stood up.

"Wait!" she called after me. "Where are you going?"

"I'll tell you later." And I was gone.

Back in my room, I rummaged under my bed until I found the book I'd bought last year on Grub Day, our school outing to the town of Attica Falls. Its binding was a worn cream, with the title *Attica Falls*. I wiped it off with my hand, sneezing from the dust. I flipped through it until I found the article called "The Gottfried Curse", the same one I'd read last year.

I skimmed the pages. *Since its founding in 1735, Gottfried Academy has been plagued by a horrific and inexplicable chain of tragedies, including disease, natural catastrophe, and a string of accidents of the most perverse and bizarre nature...*

I flipped ahead, scanning the paragraphs about how Gottfried was founded first as a hospital for the Undead, until the head doctor, Bertrand Gottfried, died, and the school closed its doors. That's when I found what I was looking for.

Yet, just as suddenly as the hospital closed, it reopened. This time, as a school. The head nurse at the time, Ophelia Hart, ascended as the first headmistress. She named it "Gottfried Academy", after its founder.

Ophelia Hart. Or Ophelia Coeur? Coeur meant "heart" in French. Could they have been the same person? This was where I'd recognized her from. Ophelia Hart was the first headmistress of Gottfried Academy. She was the nurse who had turned it into a school, and who seemed to preside over it while all of the strange tragedies were occurring. And then in 1789, the tragedies mysteriously stopped. I flipped ahead, trying to figure out if they had anything to do with Ophelia Hart leaving the school, but there was no other information.

I leaned back on the carpet, deep in thought. Ophelia could have changed her name to "Coeur" to keep her real identity a secret. But it was easy to see through. Why didn't any of the books about her scientific work mention it? Why hadn't Noah's father, a celebrated historian, considered that Ophelia Coeur could have been the first headmistress of Gottfried? The names seemed far too similar to be coincidental. He hadn't even mentioned anything about that.

And then I realized: the Ophelia that Noah's father had told us about had done all of her water research in the early 1900s.

The Ophelia on the page in front of me, the one who was the first headmistress of Gottfried, had been alive in the mid-1700s, which was right around the time when the Nine Sisters had been killed.

It seemed impossible that there were two Ophelias in the Monitoring world, and each with a variation of "heart" as a last name. But did that then mean that these two Ophelia Harts – one a nurse in the 1700s, the other a nurse and scientist in the early 1900s – were the same person?

We were right, I thought, piecing it all together. Ophelia was the ninth sister. That was the only explanation for how a woman could stay alive for two hundred years, maybe more. She *had* used the secret of the Nine Sisters to become immortal.

"It's true," I said out loud, even though there was no one else in the room to hear me. I stared at her name in the book, unable to believe that I had finished what my parents had started, that I had actually found her. I was one step closer to discovering eternal life, the secret that everyone had been searching for. But as I traced the *O* of her name, my excitement faded to fear, and I realized that I now had exactly what the Liberum wanted, and that soon I would have to face them. Life *and* death, Zinya had predicted. I was one step closer to that, too.

CHAPTER 14
ÎLE DES SOEURS

SHUTTING THE BOOK, I THREW it in my bag and went to the closet to get my mother's shovel, not sure where I was planning on going, just that now I knew I had to take protection with me everywhere I went. The only person I wanted to tell was Dante, but the mere reminder that even after everything I was somehow still in love with him, made my chest ache. What was wrong with me? Why couldn't I let him go?

I was about to shut the closet door, when I realized something was wrong. I hadn't noticed it the night I'd confronted Clémentine and her father, but now a wave of unease overcame me. I pushed through the mess of hangers, throwing shoes and clothes out onto the floor until I had a clear view of the back. The long rectangular case was there, but the shovel I kept inside it was gone.

But how? Hoping I was somehow mistaken, I pulled out the case and checked behind it, but found nothing. All the while, my own words echoed in my head. "Just don't let them see your shovel," I'd started to tell Noah in the farmhouse. Could the Undead have followed me here, to my own room, and stolen my shovel? Feeling faint, I glanced at the window, and then at the door, wishing there was a lock on it, when I realized that there was a far simpler explanation.

Furious, I stormed through the bathroom and burst into Clémentine's room. She had just gotten back from dinner and was chatting with two of her friends by the door.

"Did you take it?" I demanded. "Did you go through my room?"

Clémentine turned to me. "Take what? What are you talking about?"

"My shovel. It's gone. Where is it?"

And barging towards her closet, I flung open the doors. Clémentine yelled at me to stop, but I didn't care. I pushed her clothes aside and fumbled through her shoes and bags, but nothing was there.

"It's here somewhere. I know it is," I said. Ignoring her protests, I checked behind the door, beneath her bed, beside her bureau. All I found was her shovel, which was made of a dark metal and smooth, oiled wood.

"I didn't take your shovel," she said firmly. "And I didn't go through your room before, either."

"Then who took it?" I demanded. "You've already gone through my things. You waited in my room for me when I wasn't there. It was you. I know it was you."

Clémentine hesitated. "It wasn't me."

Before I could stop myself, I grabbed her slender wrist and dragged her into my room. "Then why is the case empty?"

She squirmed out of my grasp and parted her lips to respond, when her face gathered in a wince. "What is that smell?"

I shook my head. "What? What are you talking about?"

She covered her nose with her hand. "How can you not smell that?"

"You're trying to distract me," I said.

"I'm not!" Clémentine insisted, and stepped back into the bathroom. "It smells like something rotting."

I must have looked confused, because she pointed to the radiator below my window. "It's coming from over there."

I glanced at her once more to make sure she was telling the truth, and bent down. I sniffed at the air, trying to smell what she did, but my senses were so dull that I could only detect a vague stale odour, like something left in the fridge for too long.

Slowly, I reached beneath the vents and patted the floorboards until my hand met something soft and wrinkled. With a gasp, I pulled back my arm.

"What is it?" Clémentine said from the door.

"I don't know," I said, my lips trembling as I crouched low to see what it was. Something knotted and white.

Clémentine picked up an umbrella that I had thrown from the closet. "Use this," she said.

Taking the umbrella from her, I stuck its curved handle beneath the radiator and pulled the thing out. It was a thick, gnarled root, like a carrot, except it was white and rotten. I touched it with the tip of the umbrella. It was soft and shrivelled from age, the bottom side brown and blistered from sitting on the floor in one position.

"I think it's some sort of vegetable," I said.

"Why is it here?" Clémentine demanded.

"I don't know," I said. "I don't even know what it is. Someone must have put it here."

"Why would anyone do that?"

If it hadn't been Clémentine, then who could it have been? There was no one else who would have wanted to come into my room. Except...the Liberum, I thought.

I ran down the hall to Anya's door, carrying the root by

its tip. If anyone would know what it was, it was her. But just as I raised my hand to knock, the door opened.

"Renée!" Anya said with a gasp. "I was just about to go to your room," she said. "Why did you run away like that?"

The white root went flaccid when I held it up, pinching it by its wiry tip. "I found this in my room, beneath the window. Do you know what it is?"

She froze when she saw it. "It's a parsnip," she said slowly, gazing at its wrinkled skin.

"Why would someone put it in my room?"

She hesitated, as if she knew something but didn't want to say it.

"Tell me!" I said, exasperated.

"A white root that rises from beneath the earth. It's a symbol for the Undead."

"What?" I said, my mind racing. Did that mean that the Undead had entered my room and left it there? Had they taken my shovel, too, to disarm me? "It doesn't make any sense. Why would they take my shovel and leave this here to announce themselves, when they could have just attacked me? Why wait?"

Anya sniffed the root and winced.

"Do you think they were waiting for me to find the identity of the ninth sister so that if they take my soul they'll have more information?"

"That would be stupid," Anya said. "We might never find her."

"That's not completely true."

Anya squinted at me, reading my expression. "Wait. Did you find her?"

We retreated to my room, where I showed her the article about the Gottfried Curse. "This proves that there was a Monitor named Ophelia Hart alive in the 1700s. And according to Noah's dad, there was another Monitor named Ophelia Coeur who was alive in the 1900s. *Coeur* means 'heart' in French. It has to be a pseudonym. It's too strange to be a coincidence – they have to be the same person."

"But that means she would have been alive for over two hundred years. That's impossible."

"Exactly," I said. "Unless you're the ninth sister, and have the secret to immortality. It was her all along," I said. "I'm sure of it."

"I thought we already crossed her off," Anya said slowly, the pages of the book fanning open as she loosened her grip. "The ninth sister died. That's why she hid the secret. You went to her headstone."

"Maybe she never died."

Anya frowned. "Then why would she have a headstone?"

"I don't know, but everything else matches up. She was

alive in the early 1700s, during the time of the Nine Sisters. She was incredibly smart, had ties to the Royal Victoria, and to salt water, from her later research in water and lakes. It fits, it all fits."

I watched Anya work it all out in her head. When she looked up at me, her eyes were wide with wonder. "It could be. So now what?"

"We figure out where she would have hidden the first part of the riddle."

"How?"

"She probably hid it in a place that was important to her, right? So all we need to do is find out more about Ophelia's life."

"But how?" Anya said, exasperated. "She could *still* be alive. Where do we even start?"

My mind skipped back to the last time I'd heard about Ophelia Hart. "Noah."

We ran outside, through the snowy campus towards the boys' dormitory. Asking one of the boys on the stoop which room was Noah's, we raced upstairs, winding through the maze of hallways that were arranged exactly as ours were, except the wallpaper was brown. When we reached his door, I smoothed out my hair and took a breath before knocking.

"Renée?" Noah said, adjusting his glasses as his tall body filled the doorway. "I – I'm sort of busy right now—"

"I know you probably don't want to see me right now," I cut in. "I don't blame you. But we found her," I whispered. "We found the ninth sister. And we need your help."

Noah went rigid as he took in what I had just said. And glancing over my shoulder at Anya, he pushed his door open. "Come in."

And just like that, we became friends again.

Noah's father had an office in the history building at the university. "There's an entire library of archives in the basement; I go down there with my dad when I help him do research. They have stuff going all the way back to the founding of Montreal."

So the three of us piled into a taxi and set off. I turned around and stared out the rear window as we wound through the city, my eyes glued to the pavements, searching for any sign of the Undead. Even though the streets were empty and motionless, something about the pressure of the air made me nervous.

The university campus was white and slushy as we ran through it, the quadrangles peppered with statues sculpted out of a dark bronze.

"Do you feel that?" I said, slowing to a jog as a prickling sensation climbed up my legs, as though a cool wisp had wrapped itself around me.

"It was probably just the specimens in the biology lab," Noah said, glancing at the building to our right. "Come on."

But it wasn't just the biology lab. It was a familiar feeling; the kind of chill that made the air seem thinner, staler, as if it were rearranging itself into a path.

"Come on," Noah said. "We're almost there."

But just as I started walking, I saw a flash of white. And then again.

"There," I said, pointing to the thicket of trees. "They were right there."

If Anya and Noah heard me, they didn't let on.

I slowed, letting them walk ahead, and quietly, I approached the statue. "Dante?" I whispered, hoping it was him I had felt, though the cold, odourless air told me it wasn't. I blinked into the night.

Someone laughed behind me; a child. I whipped around, but no one was there.

"Renée?" Noah shouted from up the path.

Before I could respond, two boys, short and pale, emerged from the trees, their faces round and chubby. They ran towards me from either side, their bodies so light they didn't even sink into the snow. "No," I whispered, but the words never left my mouth. And then they were touching me, grabbing at my legs, my skirt, my coat.

Jerking around, I flung them off, the shadows parted, and a thin figure stepped through the air, his face a streak of white against the sky. My breath got caught in my lungs as I fell backwards, staring at his limbs, long and stiff like a scarecrow's.

I tried to stand up, but the two boys were grasping at my arms, pressing me deeper into the snow. But as I struggled, my fingers digging into the ice, all I could think of was Dante; of how I wished I could see him one last time.

And then I heard a girl's voice whisper in Latin. It was so soft, I could barely hear it, but slowly, the Undead around me seemed to become calm, their grip weakening until they slinked back, retreating into the shadows.

"Go," she said to me, in a voice I recognized.

"Anya?" I whispered, as she pulled me up.

"Go!"

Before I knew it, I was running, Noah by my side.

"What about Anya?" I said, looking wildly behind me, but Noah pulled me on.

"She's fine," he said. "She's taking care of it." Grabbing my wrist, he led me off the campus to the street, where he hailed a taxi. It screeched to the kerb.

"We can't just leave her," I said, but Noah took my hand and pulled me in, slamming the door behind us.

"Drive," Noah said over the front seat.

"What are you doing?" I demanded. "Anya is back there, alone."

"She's fine."

"How do you know?" I said, incredulous. "Haven't you seen her in class? She can't take them on her own."

"She can," Noah said firmly. "She's a Whisperer. A rare kind of Monitor. One that can speak to the Undead; persuade them, manipulate them."

"What?" I said, confused.

"Didn't you hear her just now? She was speaking to them. She has it under control. They're looking for you, anyway, not her. We can lead them away from her. So focus. Where should we go?"

I glanced out the rear window at the pale children in the distance. "Île des Soeurs," I blurted out, before I realized what I was saying. The taxi slowed, and with a jolt, we made a sharp right turn.

As we wound through the Montreal streets, I wiped the water and dirt from my face and caught my breath. Every so often I glanced through the rear-view mirror, expecting to see flashes of white trailing behind us, but the streets were empty. I don't know why I had an impulse to go to the Île des Soeurs. Maybe it was because the convent on the island was the one place the Undead feared, though I hadn't thought of that till after. No, it was a feeling I had, a feeling I hoped I could trust.

We drove until we reached a long bridge leading over the St. Lawrence River. On the other side was a tiny island pinpricked with trees.

"Can you drop us at the convent?" I said to the driver. He nodded beneath his cap.

Île des Soeurs was a small island with neat rows of houses, the glow of televisions flickering through the windows. Driving through the streets, I felt somehow calmed, as if everything here were visible. The driver parked in front of a gated building that looked like a junkyard. The pavement was covered with loose trash and scraps.

"This is it?" I said, as a grey cat darted out from behind a garbage bin and scampered across the road.

"Yep," the man said.

We paid him, and the rumble of his car's exhaust muffler faded away into the distance. Behind us, the setting sun was bleeding red all over the St. Lawrence River. Pulling up my scarf, I ran towards the plain rectangular building looming behind the iron gates. It was cream with brown trim and thin bars over the windows.

Parked in its driveway, hidden in the shadows, was a grey Peugeot.

"It can't be," I said. "It's the same one I saw Miss LaBarge in a few months ago."

"Come on," Noah said, and led me to the tall gates. The iron bars twisted and coiled towards the centre to form the words: COUVENT DES SOEURS. In the middle of the gates, the bars were lashed together with a chain, and locked.

"Do you think she's in there?" I said.

As if in answer to my question, a light turned on in one of the windows on the second floor. I jumped, bumping into Noah, who caught my arm.

"There's only one way to find out," he said.

Before I knew what was happening, Noah grabbed the top rung, and in an elegant swoop, lifted himself up and over the gate, landing on the other side.

Wiping his hands on his trousers, he let out a breath and stood up. "Now you."

He braced himself to help me climb up, but instead, I grabbed the bars and stuck one leg through, and then another, contorting my body until I had squeezed through to the other side.

There were stray cats everywhere. Creeping between the crevices of the foundations, crouching beneath the bushes, peering out from underneath the front stoop as we approached the front door.

"Are you just going to knock on the door?" I asked.

"Do you have a better idea?"

I didn't, but something about it made me feel uneasy.

A cat darted across the lawn in front of my feet. I covered my mouth before the gasp came out.

Noah took my hand and squeezed it, and together we climbed up the steps. I braced myself against the railing as Noah pressed the bell.

Somewhere inside, a chime sounded, but no one came to the door. A calico cat rubbed its head against my ankle; I nudged it away. Just as Noah held his finger up to the buzzer again, we heard footsteps thud inside. The sound of locks being unlatched. And then the knob turning.

The door opened a crack, and a woman appeared, peeking through the chain bolt. She was holding a shovel, its tip pointed at us through the gap. The hall behind her was dark.

When I saw her face, I froze. "Miss LaBarge?"

She paused before answering. "Who are you?"

The calico cat slipped inside through Miss LaBarge's legs. "It's me," I said, unable to comprehend why she didn't recognize me. "Renée. From philosophy class last year?"

"How did you get in?"

"I squeezed through the bars," I said, putting my hand on the door frame. Miss LaBarge jolted at my advance.

"What do you want from me?" she asked, wedging the tip of the shovel deeper into the gap.

I searched her face, baffled. Maybe she had lost her memory. Maybe that's why she was acting this way. "I don't want anything. I – I didn't know you were going to be here. But now that you are, I just – I'd like to talk to you. Everyone thinks you died." I lowered my voice. "It was on the news. I went to your funeral. I watched my grandfather bury you in the ocean. But now you're here."

She looked at me, and then at Noah. "You're both students at Gottfried?"

"Lycée St. Clément," Noah said.

"What are your names?" she asked.

"Renée Winters," I said.

"Noah Fontaine."

Miss LaBarge squinted at me, as if trying to see something she hadn't seen before. "Winters? The daughter of Lydia and Robert?"

I loosened my grip on my bag. "Yes," I said, confused. "You knew them."

Without warning, she receded into the darkness.

"Wait!" I yelled, but it was too late. She had already shut the door.

I rang the bell again and then collapsed with a sigh on the edge of a cement pot by the railing. A black cat that had been sleeping inside hissed and jumped out. "I don't understand," I murmured, looking up at Noah.

He put a finger to his lips. On the other side of the door, I heard something clicking, and then just as abruptly as it had closed, the door reopened.

"Get inside," she said, her eyes darting about the quiet street behind us as we shuffled past her.

The convent was dark and draughty. After bolting the locks, Miss LaBarge gave us a quick glance. She led us through a series of rooms, each one sparsely decorated with little more than a table and a few chairs. There were cats everywhere – curled around the banister, stretching on the window sills, yawning from beneath the radiators. A Persian jumped down from a mantel and followed us until we reached the kitchen. Miss LaBarge turned on the overhead light bulb, which bathed her in a dingy yellow glow.

There she was: her plain brown hair, small nose, and ruddy cheeks that made her look like a farm girl. Leaning on the back of a chair, she opened her mouth to say something, but then changed her mind and walked to the stove.

Arrested at the sight of her in the light, I shuddered, my entire body growing cold. Something wasn't right.

This woman looked exactly like Miss LaBarge, but at the same time she didn't. Her features were the same, yes, but the angles weren't correct. Her cheekbones looked a little higher; her jawline looked a little heavier; the wrinkles around her eyes looked a little less defined, as if she were a grainy photocopy of the real Annette.

She removed the lid from a dented kettle, crossed to the sink, and filled the kettle under the tap. "Tea?"

I must have been staring, because Noah nudged me with his elbow.

"Yes, thanks," I said.

Miss LaBarge moved too briskly about the room. I watched, horrified, as she sliced a lemon and squeezed its juice into her tea. Miss LaBarge always preferred cream.

"You're – you're not Miss LaBarge at all."

The impostor put down the lemon and gave me a sad sort of look, like she pitied me. Wiping her hands on a tea towel, she pulled out two chairs at a plain wooden table. "Please, sit down."

Noah sat down at the end of the table, but I didn't move. I couldn't. I felt paralysed and confused and angry, so angry. Who was this woman pretending to be Miss LaBarge?

Setting two mugs of tea on the table for us, she took a seat across from Noah. "My name is Collette LaBarge," she said. "I'm Annette's younger sister."

I nearly spilled my tea. "What?"

"Annette is dead. She died in August. I'm her younger sister."

All at once, everything suddenly made sense. I hadn't been seeing Miss LaBarge this year; I had been seeing her sister. It seemed too easy and too dreary to be true.

She frowned. "You look disappointed."

"I thought—"

"You thought she was still alive. You wish I were

someone else." Collette's eyes had a coldness to them, and her hands were balled into fists, as if she were ready to fight. She leaned back in her chair. "I'm sorry."

"So there's no way she's still alive?" I uttered, only realizing then that somewhere within me I had reserved the smallest hope that Miss LaBarge had survived.

Collette lowered her eyes. "No."

"But then why are you here?" I asked. "Why are you in hiding? No one knows about you. You didn't even come to her funeral."

"I did attend."

"I saw you, then," I said, realizing that it was Collette on the coast that day as we sailed away. "But you weren't on the boat. You were on the shore."

"Annette and I weren't close."

I shook my head, trying to understand. "But every time I saw you on the street you acted like you didn't want to be seen."

She put down her mug. "When have you seen me?"

"The first time was at Miss LaBarge's burial. The second time was when your car stopped at a crossing. I wanted to talk to you, but you vanished. The third time, I was with Noah at a bakery in the old port, when you walked by. We followed you downtown, where you took an elevator into the underground. When we made it to the tunnels, we couldn't find you anywhere."

Collette didn't say anything for a long time, her eyes darting between us. Finally, she spoke. "Why have you come here?"

Noah's eyes met mine, but neither of us answered.

"Was someone chasing you?" she said, her eyes wild.

"We were looking for the secret of the Nine Sisters," I said finally.

Collette coughed.

"You know it?" I said, studying the way her eyes widened, the way she shifted her weight.

"You're asking a dangerous question," she said softly. "Looking for the secret of the Nine Sisters can only bring death – just like your parents', my sister's, Cindy Bell's. Or you'll become like me, living in confinement, waiting for the Liberum."

"It's too late," I said. "They already found us."

As my words sank in, a flicker of understanding passed over her face. Her body grew tense as her eyes moved from us to the window. "Did they follow you here?"

"What do you know?" I said.

"Did you bring them here?" she said, growing panicked.

"It's possible," I admitted. "Please, tell us what you know. There isn't much time."

She pushed her tea across the table and gave me a level look. "I'll show you."

We followed her down a corridor and one set of stairs, until we were in an old cellar.

"We all became friends at Gottfried – your mother, Annette, Cindy, me. That's where we first heard about *les Neuf Soeurs*. Like everyone else, at first we were just intrigued, but as we did more research, we started to believe that the secret still existed, hidden by the mysterious ninth sister. And what started as a hobby turned into an obsession.

"We travelled all over Europe – France, Italy, England – looking for any kind of information that might identify her. We searched through all of the French Monitor archives, looking for a talented girl of seventeen who had lived around the time of the Nine Sisters. Of course we didn't find anything. The problem was that we had focused our entire search on France, since that's where the Nine Sisters had come from. It never even crossed our minds to look in Montreal, where they sent their youngest member for schooling."

Collette walked to a hutch in the corner of the cellar. She opened one of the drawers and took out what looked like a box of loose leaf tea. Lifting the lid, she removed an envelope, yellowed with time.

"Annette gave this to me before she was killed. She said your parents had given it to her, and that it was incredibly important I keep it safe."

With that, she handed it to me. The paper was so worn it was almost transparent. It was addressed to Alma Alphonse in France. I remembered the name from Madame Goût's lecture: Alma was one of the eight Sisters who was murdered. Gently, I opened the envelope and removed the paper, flattening it on the counter. It was faded and creased and smudged with oil, as if it had been folded and unfolded dozens of times. The right-hand corner was embossed with the crest of a canary.

April 2, 1732

Chère Alma,

I fear we have made a grave mistake with Ophelia. Her doctor at the Saint-Laurent says she is responding well to treatment; however, after visiting her in Montreal, I am quite worried. She seems rash and unable to control her urges. In confidence, she confessed to me that she often desires to kiss people, and her mood fluctuates between rapture and severe melancholy, in which she complains of the world clouding to tedium. She is resistant to the treatment we give to her kind, and speaks of suffering from a moral crisis and lovesickness, though it is unclear with whom she is in love. The only person she seems fond of is her doctor, Bertrand Gottfried.

She has taken an unusual fancy to water. Her

nurses say she studies it day and night, staring at the basin in her room or sitting by the fountain, a practice which is in stark contrast to the vigour and discipline she held as first rank Monitor. No doubt this is a reaction to the fire; however, I have asked them to remove her from St. Clément for the safety of the other students. Doctor Gottfried expressed interest in taking her to the American colonies, where he plans on opening a new hospital for the Undead, though I wonder if it will help. I implore you to consider the safety of our discovery. Ophelia Hart has changed too much. We cannot trust her, and I beg of you to consider the option of putting her to rest.

Votre soeur,
Prudence Beaufort

I looked at Noah. "Ophelia Hart was a student at St. Clément when she was in a terrible fire?" I said, my mind racing as I scanned the letter once more. *The world clouding to tedium. She often desires to kiss people. Unable to control her urges. Reaction to the fire.* Those could only mean one thing. "She became Undead?" I said in disbelief. "Is that why she used the secret and then preserved it?"

Collette gave me a slight nod. "I think so. Your parents were the ones who first discovered that Ophelia Hart was the ninth sister. Your mother found this letter buried beneath a birdbath in Alma's old house. They retraced Ophelia's life and found the second part of the riddle in the hospital, in the same room where she first reanimated as an Undead."

"She must have planted it when she worked as the head nurse there over one hundred years later," Noah said, his eyes trained on mine.

"And then she created the headstone," I said. "She must have erected it in honour of her teenage life. She etched the last part of the riddle on it."

Noah nodded, his expression almost sad.

My hands trembled as I held the letter, imagining my parents holding the exact same sheet of paper, just two years ago. "And Miss LaBarge and Cindy continued the search, assuming the next riddles were hidden somewhere having to do with her research on water," I murmured. "That's why they were found near lakes."

Collette nodded. "I'm the only one of us left. I've been finishing their search but still haven't found the last part of the riddle."

Ophelia Hart had gone to St. Clément, just like me, and at some point while she was there, she had died. What could be more meaningful than that? "But they were wrong," I said. "The part of the riddle we're missing is the first part, not the last. And before Ophelia was a scientist, before she was a nurse, she was a student at St. Clément.

She might have even died there." I turned to Noah. "Didn't your father say that she'd worked briefly as a nurse there?"

Too surprised to speak, Noah gave me a slight nod.

"What if she went back to work at St. Clément because she wanted to plant something there?" I said.

"The beginning of a riddle," Noah said, completing my thought.

And together, we turned to Collette. "We need to go back to school."

CHAPTER 15

THE BROOM CLOSET

WE FOLDED OURSELVES INTO THE back seat of Collette's car and waited beneath a blanket as she drove us back to school. "I think it's safe," Collette said, turning the ignition off. She had parked in an alley a few blocks away from the entrance.

I closed my eyes, feeling for the vacant presence of the Undead. "They're close," I said. "But not here."

Noah and I slipped out of the car and down the alleyway, giving Collette one last nod before we disappeared into St. Clément.

The buildings surrounding the courtyard blinked with

lights, turning on in one window, going off in another. We knew the first part of the message had to be in one of them, but we weren't sure where. The school was huge, with oddly shaped rooms and an endless maze of narrow hallways and dark crevices. It could be anywhere.

"Where would she have hidden it?" Noah said as we stopped in the shadow of a building.

In my pocket, I could feel the letter Collette had given me. Ophelia had left her home to go to school at St. Clément. She'd been sent here with a secret, just like I had been.

So if I were Ophelia Hart, where would I have hidden the first piece of the riddle? It had to be a place that was private, where no one would find me while I hid the clue; but it couldn't be too private, or else I risked the chance that no one would ever find it again. Most importantly, though, I would only bury my deepest secret in a place that had personal meaning to me when I attended St. Clément.

Suddenly I stopped walking, tripping Noah, who was a step behind me. "Her room," I said, as he pulled himself together. "It's in her old dorm room."

We went to the library. There, we rifled through the card catalogue until we found the location of St. Clément's old school files. It was upstairs on the fourth balcony in a dim, dusty corner that looked like it hadn't been visited in decades.

I started from the right side, Noah started from the left, and, moving towards each other, we scanned the books, looking for a volume that contained all of the old housing assignments. Each book was at least a few centimetres thick, full of bound school documents, and most were poorly labelled. I was about halfway through the top row when Noah called out to me.

"I found it."

Pushing a volume of old admissions tests back onto the shelf, I jumped off a step stool and ran over to him. Noah was trying to extricate a thick book from its neighbours. Giving the book a firm tug, he stumbled back, and it fell to the floor with a thud.

We set the book on a window sill and flipped through it. The paper was thick and brittle, the words written in a small, slanted hand. Each page contained nothing but a long list of names and their corresponding room numbers. And it went on for hundreds of pages. No wonder no one came up to this section of the library.

And then we found it. The year 1730. Using my finger, I scanned the list until I found it: *Hart, Ophelia. Room 22.*

"Room 22. Do you know where that is?" Noah asked.

It was on my floor. Closing my eyes, I mentally counted off the doors, starting at the stairway and working down, down, down...and then I stopped. It couldn't be.

I counted again, this time from the other direction, but I was right the first time. "Yes," I said, opening my eyes. Noah was bent over the book next to me, his face centimetres from mine.

"Who has that room?"

"No one," I said, amazed that I hadn't realized it earlier. Anya's room was number 21. And Arielle's room was 23. The room in between them was Ophelia's. I must have passed it dozens of times this year without giving it a second glance. Except I never knew it had been a room. "It's a broom closet."

Just to make sure, I flipped ahead to the next year and found her name. And then to the next year. Ophelia had lived in the same room for the entirety of her stay at St. Clément.

But strangely, in the years that followed, room 22 wasn't listed at all.

"She was the last one to live there," I said, turning to Noah.

As if reading my thoughts, he said softly, "We found it, then."

Picking up our things, we hurried down the stairs and through the double doors into the cold February night.

The warm lighting and rose wallpaper of the girls' dormitory greeted us as we burst through the doors. We quickly composed ourselves when we noticed a group of girls staring. Once upstairs, I peeked around the corner to make sure the hallway was free of Clémentine and her friends. And after waiting for a girl to disappear into her room, Noah and I slipped through the corridors until we were standing in front of Anya's room, number 21.

Just beside it was the broom closet.

Up close, I could see the layers of paint that coated the door. It was so thick that it filled the seams between the door and the knob, sealing it shut. Still, Noah tried the knob. It wouldn't turn. After watching him try it a few more times, and giving it a series of firm, frustrated pushes that made more noise than I would have liked, I grabbed his arm.

"It isn't moving," I said. "The only way would be to break down the door, which would probably arouse some suspicion."

Noah wiped his brow, looking dejected for the first time today. "So now what?"

I bit my lip, trying to think of some solution, but I was all out of ideas. The room had obviously been sealed on purpose, which meant that someone didn't want anyone getting in here.

From somewhere behind us, I heard the muffled sound of things clattering to the floor. Noah and I exchanged puzzled looks and turned around. It had come from Anya's room. Beyond the walls I could hear her cursing at something in Russian.

Abandoning the broom closet, I knocked on her door. Something shuffled inside, then stopped. The door cracked open, and one large eye peered out at me, its lashes thick with mascara.

"Oh, Renée!" Anya said.

"You're okay," I said, relieved.

"I got them to tell me their names and where they lived," Anya said proudly. "I think one of them might have even liked me—" but she cut herself off when she saw Noah behind me.

"Can we come in?" he said. "We need to use your bathroom."

Dozens of candles were lit about her room, making the atmosphere hazy. Noah tripped over a box of incense and knocked a set of metal charms as he steadied himself on a bedpost. They clinked together like chimes.

"What do you need the bathroom for?" Anya asked, picking up a pile of dirty clothes.

"Ophelia Hart hid the first part of the riddle in her dorm room—" I began to say, when I noticed that Anya's closet door was ajar. A worn wooden handle was sticking out from between her clothes.

"What is that?" I said, gazing at the handle, and then at Anya.

Her face seemed to grow pale. "Just a broom," she said quickly, and ran to shut the closet door, but I made it there first. Grasping the handle, I pulled it out of her closet, knocking the hangers from the rod.

"This is my shovel," I said, and turned it around to inspect its rusty head. Baffled, I turned to Anya. "Did you take this from my room? Did you go through my things?"

Anya backed against the wall as I held the shovel up, not even realizing I was shaking it at her. "Did you – did you put that parsnip beneath my radiator?"

"It was for your own good!" Anya said quickly, staring at the tip of my shovel as it hovered centimetres from her face. "If you put one beneath your window, they're supposed to keep the Undead away. I accidentally knocked your water jug over on my way out," she admitted. "And it's bad luck to use a shovel that belonged to someone whose soul was taken. I couldn't let you use your mother's shovel, but I knew you wouldn't believe me if I told you, so while I was there, I took it."

I felt my mouth move as I tried to form words that would express how equally disturbed and relieved I was to discover that Anya had been the one who broke into my room.

"You're angry," Anya said, fidgeting with the end of her braid. "I know. I shouldn't have lied to you—"

Before she could finish, I jumped towards her and gave her a hug, her bony shoulders relaxing beneath my grip.

"Thank you," I said, giving her an understanding smile as I stepped back. "But please don't ever do that to me again."

"I won't," Anya said. She began to twist one of her earrings. "There's one more thing."

My smile faded.

"I never told you my fortune."

Slowly, I lowered the shovel and waited for her to continue.

"For my past, Zinya told me that I had thought myself worthless because I never had any Monitoring talent. For my present, she said that I was developing a new rare skill that a friend would bring out in me."

"You're a Whisperer," I murmured.

Anya nodded, but didn't meet my eyes. Her face grew sombre.

"And your future?" I asked. "What did she say about that?"

Anya fidgeted with her fingernails, unwilling to meet my gaze. "That I was going to lose that friend."

I lowered the head of the shovel to the ground. "But – what?"

Her words hung in the air between us as I stood there, unable to move. "Did she mean me?"

Anya's eyes drooped. "I don't have any other friends."

"But it can't mean that," I said. "Zinya told me that I

would meet life *and* death at the end of my search." And then it dawned on me: maybe I would die, and Dante would live. "Maybe she meant that I would just go away," I said. "Lose doesn't necessarily mean death."

Anya nodded. "You're right. That's probably it."

But I barely heard her. "Why didn't you tell me before?"

"Because it's bad luck. I was hoping it wouldn't be true. That I wouldn't become a Whisperer. That you wouldn't find the clues to the riddles, or discover the ninth sister. But all of that happened."

I blinked.

"Renée!" Noah called from the bathroom. "I think I found it."

I glanced over my shoulder at Noah's legs in the bathroom.

Anya met my gaze. "If Zinya knew you were going to die, she would have told you. But instead she said life *and* death. Nothing's certain."

I bit my lip, not sure if she was saying that to make me feel better, or because she really meant it. But no matter. There was only one thing left to do. Dropping the shovel, I ran to the bathroom.

Noah was standing in front of the full-length mirror, positioned in the same place the door leading to Clémentine's room was in my bathroom. "I think this is it," he said, speaking to my reflection. "Feel this."

He guided my hand to a tiny hole near the corner of the mirror. Pulling open Anya's bathroom drawers, he rummaged through them until he found a pair of tweezers. "Look for another pair," he said as he kneeled in front of the mirror and inserted the tweezers into the hole. Rotating them slightly, he looked up at me and grinned. "It works. It's a screw."

As Noah made his way around the perimeter of the mirror, I went through the rest of her drawers.

"The bottom left," Anya said from the doorway. Following her direction, I rifled through her toiletries until I found another pair, peered into one of the holes, and began unscrewing the tiny bolt within.

Noah had already finished the penultimate screw, and was placing it into a soap dish by the sink, when I felt the final screw wobble in the hole. I pulled out my tweezers, and a little piece of metal fell through my fingers and onto the floor.

The mirror trembled.

Noah grabbed my arm and pulled me towards him. Anya screamed.

And with a loud swoop, the mirror fell to the ground, shattering across the tiles.

When everything had settled, Anya was crouched in the doorway, covering her head. Noah was kneeling beside me, asking me if I was hurt. And where the mirror used to be, there was now an old wooden door.

"I'm fine," I said, and stepped over the shards, the glass crunching beneath my shoes.

The door was a dark brown, with peeling varnish and slanted slats like the kind you see in psychiatric institutions. Little wormholes dotted the centre.

I shook the knob, which was loose. The door rattled in its frame but didn't open.

"Move out of the way," Noah said, backing up. And with a determined look, he ran at the door, hitting it with his shoulder and bursting through to the other side.

There was a loud crash, the sound of wood cracking, and then a groan.

"Noah?" I shouted into the darkness.

No one answered for a long time. I looked at Anya, who was squinting into the room. I was about to repeat myself, when Noah's voice echoed from inside. "You have to come in here."

I stumbled over the splintered fragments of the door and into a dark and musty room. A long rectangle of light from the bathroom shone across the ground.

Behind us, Anya held up a flashlight and pointed it around the room, illuminating the interior in a slow sweep as if we were exploring the remains of a sunken ship.

The windows were shut and coated with a thick layer of dust and grime. Sheets were draped across the room, protecting candelabras and piles of books and linens. The furniture all looked antique, the armchair standing on curled claws, the bookshelf plated with glass doors, the desk inlaid with lovely layers of wood. And the bed – a beautiful bed engraved with vines that looked much too small for any person born in this century.

All of it was blackened with smoke stains, including the walls.

"There was a fire here," I said to Noah, touching the dark billowing patterns on the walls, the dust tickling my nose. "This was the fire she died in. That's why the room was closed off."

I gazed out the window, trying to imagine what the courtyard looked like when Ophelia lived here.

She must have been just around my age when she'd died. If I were her, and came back to this room to plant a message, where would I have put it?

Anya had opened the French doors of the closet, and Noah was scouring the walls, but I knew they were wrong. I wouldn't leave a message anywhere that could be easily painted or papered over or burned away.

With sudden conviction, I spun around. There, on the far wall, was a sturdy brick fireplace, the red darkened to a smoky brown hue from the fire. This must have been the fire Dustin had told me about that led the school to ban the use of the fireplaces. It was the only part

431

of the room that wouldn't be torn down or changed in any way, unless the entire building was demolished.

Kneeling on the floor, I flung off my coat, rolled up my sleeves, and reached my arm into the chimney. It was soft with spiders' webs and ash. I brushed all of that away. The flue was shut and locked in place, so I patted around below it, tracing the lines of the brick until I felt something cool and smooth, like metal. I went over it again, this time slower, passing my palm across it. There were lines etched into it. I was so shocked that I pulled my hand out and glanced around the room. Anya and Noah were busy searching the far wall. When I put my hand back, I half expected the metal to have disappeared, a figment of my imagination, but instead, it seemed even more real, the lines carved into it forming letters beneath my fingertips.

"I think I found it," I said, my voice cracking. But no one seemed to hear me. "I found it," I repeated, this time louder. Noah froze, his face softening to a smile.

"Can I borrow your flashlight?" I asked.

He handed it to me, and I ducked into the chimney. Dust sprinkled from above, making me cough as I shined the light on the inner wall. And there, cut neatly into the metal, was a message.

If you wish to find what the nine have kept,

from the highest rank to the lowest depth,
you must be schooled in my grief;

I read it out loud three times, until I was sure I had it committed to memory, and then climbed out, shaking the dust from my hair. "We found it."

"What do you think it means?" I said, writing the full riddle on a piece of paper and spreading it in front of us on the carpet in Anya's room.

If you wish to find what the nine have kept,
from the highest rank to the lowest depth,
you must be schooled in my grief;

to arrive there
follow the nose of the bear
to the salty waters beneath;

here it is laid to rest
where to only the best
of our kind it shall be bequeathed.

"The first verse doesn't tell us anything," I said, reading it all again, even though I knew it by memory.

"Highest rank? Schooled in grief?" Noah said, tracing the second and third lines. "Clearly, the hiding spot has something to do with a school."

I bit my lip. "But not this school. She couldn't have hidden the secret at St. Clément. Ophelia would never have hidden the secret in the same place as the first part of the riddle. That would defeat the purpose."

Anya sat down between us and pushed the riddle aside. "You're going about it the wrong way. I think the last few lines mean that Ophelia hid these riddles for only a very specific kind of person to find the secret. Probably someone like her. Top rank."

Noah and Anya both slowly turned and looked at me.

"The riddle gives us half the information," she said. "It tells us that the secret is submerged in salt water, beneath a bear. And that it might be associated with a school. But it isn't enough. I think in order to find the secret, we have to *think* like her."

Closing my eyes, I tried to imagine what it would have felt like to have a secret so big you couldn't tell anyone. It wasn't hard; all I had to do was think of Dante. So if I were going to write down the story of our relationship and hide it, where would I put it?

Where we first met.

I opened my eyes. "If I were her, I would have hidden

434

the secret where I had first *used* it. That seems lucky. So let's just consider what we know." I looked at Anya. "Ophelia Hart died here, in this fire, in her dorm room at St. Clément. She was sent to the Royal Victoria, where she reanimated into an Undead."

Noah adjusted his glasses, deep in thought. "Then she went with her doctor to his hospital in the American colonies."

"Gottfried," I said, deep in thought. "When she was there, she somehow transitioned from patient to nurse and headmistress. But she couldn't have survived long enough to be either of those as an Undead. They only have twenty-one years to find their souls." The lines of the notebook paper blurred as the dates swirled in my head. The realization came to me before the words to articulate it did, and I let out a strange squeak that halted conversation. Anya and Noah stared at me, waiting. My back went rigid as I looked up. "What if she used the secret while she was there?"

Noah held a finger to his lips in thought. "Isn't there a lake there?"

"A salt lake," I murmured, still unable to believe what I was saying. "With the Ursa Major statue looking over it."

"A bear," Anya said in awe.

"Yes," I said, my pulse racing as I realized that the

answer to my soul, to Dante's soul, had been at Gottfried all along.

Noah looked up at me with a small smile. "So when are we leaving?"

Chapter 16

Gottfried Academy

It was that witching time between four and five in the morning when Noah and I boarded a train to Maine. The cars were rickety old things, mostly empty, as we walked through them and took two seats near the back. I wedged our shovels by the window, Noah's and mine. Anya wanted to come, but I hadn't let her. Someone had to stay behind in case we didn't come back.

With a groan, the train heaved forwards, hurling us south, though I wouldn't have known it from the view. It was all black to me. Noah fell asleep almost immediately, his head slumping until it was resting against my shoulder.

Gently, I shifted beneath his weight, trying to nudge him awake.

This whole search had started with something simple, just Dante and me; but now I was on a train, crossing the border in the middle of the night with two shovels and Noah, the weight of his head pressing me deeper into the seat. I felt so far from where I had started that it seemed I would never be able to find my way back.

A conductor sauntered down the aisle in a black uniform. "*Billets,*" he said.

I reached into my sweater pocket for our tickets and handed them to the conductor. He stamped two of them, and studied the third before handing it back to me. "*Ceci n'est pas un billet,*" he said.

Taking it from him, I turned on my overhead light and gasped.

It was a worn photograph of a small stucco house with an overgrown garden that was overexposed with yellow California light. I knew that door, I thought, tracing its edges. I knew the carpet behind it, the way it felt plush between my toes. I knew the rooms beyond: the living room, the den, the stairs with the creak in the third step. Through the front window I could see a man and woman standing over the counter in the kitchen. It looked like they were laughing. My parents. My kitchen. My life.

I gripped the photograph, staring at the blur of their

faces. I had never seen it before. How had it gotten into my pocket? Where had I been when it was taken? The longer I stared at it, the more agitated I began to feel. My eyes darted about the train car to the other passengers, slumped in their seats. They didn't know, I thought. No one knew except for me. I gazed at the photograph, overwhelmed with regret. I was the only one who could have warned my parents. If only I had gotten there sooner. I could have saved Annette LaBarge, too. I could have saved all of them.

My eyes grew wet. I blinked. A tear fell onto my lap.

I blinked again, my eyes growing heavy, and the sky outside seemed to brighten.

A third time, and the leaves budded on the trees, as if it were spring. Exhausted, my head fell back against the leather of the seat, and my world disappeared.

Then it was morning. I was walking on a muddy road surrounded by a green birch forest. I saw no sign of life other than the twin ruts of tyre tracks caked in the dirt. I didn't stop until I was in front of a log cabin hidden behind the weeds. A mailbox stood outside, labelled with the number 66. Beside it hung a sign that said: BEWARE OF DOG.

Crouching low behind the bushes, I waited until a car drove up the road where I had come from. From the bottom of the shrubs, I could only see four feet as they stepped out of the car, but I already knew who they were. Two Brothers of the Liberum. "How did you find this woman?" one of them said in Latin, his voice smooth and easy, like a teenager.

"I followed her through Europe," the second brother said in a low baritone. "I think she found something that might lead us to the Sisters."

"They never find anything," the other one said, kicking a rock. It landed centimetres away from my face. And without saying anything more, he opened the mailbox and placed a slip of paper inside. Looking in both directions, they got back into the car and drove away.

At first I didn't move. I stared at the cabin windows, checking to make sure no one had stirred inside. When I thought it was clear, I opened the mailbox door. It made a loud screech. My eyes darted to the cabin, where I heard the sound of little footsteps. Quickly, I took the paper and vanished into the woods, just as a swarm of Undead children burst through the front door.

Before I knew it, I was on a train travelling south. In my lap was a photograph of a small stucco house with a garden. Through the window was the blur of two people. I flipped the photograph over. All it said was *Lydia Winters*.

"Costa Rosa, California," a man announced over the intercom.

440

I got off and hailed a taxi outside the station and told the driver the address. He drove me through the tree-lined streets and neighbourhoods coloured with little square houses until he stopped in front of a stucco house. I took out the picture to compare it. It was the same.

I paid the driver and stepped out. There was a sprinkler on in the front yard, which skipped in a semicircle and then back again. I hesitated, and then jumped through it just before it splashed my ankles.

But before I could approach the house, the screen door opened. Startled, I jumped back and hid behind a bougainvillea as a girl stepped out. She was young, maybe sixteen, and looked fearless and carefree. Her long caramel hair was tangled and unkempt. Freckles spotted the bridge of her nose. She raised her chin in the air, as if sniffing something, and then turned to me, her eyes out of focus as she stared at the leaves that blocked me from view. She was wearing cut-off shorts and a baggy T-shirt. Her feet were bare as she stepped towards me.

"Renée? Who's there?" her mother called from inside. Music floated out from the open window.

She gave the bougainvillea one last look before turning. "No one," the girl said, her voice deeper than I had expected. Crisp. "I'm going to meet Annie now. I'll be back by dinner." With that, she slipped on a pair of sneakers from inside, and picked up a bicycle leaning on the side of the house. I watched as she hopped on and pedalled down the street.

After she left, I snuck out from behind the bush and darted along the side of the house to the back door. Lydia Winters was in the kitchen. The tap was running.

I approached slowly. They were Monitors, after all. I didn't want to scare them.

"Robert, do you feel that?" Lydia said.

"Feel what?" a man called out from somewhere in the house.

A bee buzzed around my head as Lydia turned off the tap. I swatted it away as the back door slid open. Lydia stepped outside, gripping a garden trowel in one hand, and before she could scream, I put a hand over her mouth and pulled her against the side of the house.

She kicked beneath my grip, trying to hit me with the trowel, but I was stronger than her. Slowly, I twisted her wrist until the trowel dropped to the grass. Squirming, she yelled something, but it was muffled beneath my hand.

"Don't scream," I said. "I'm not here to hurt you."

It just made her thrash more. "Stop moving," I said. "I don't want to break your wrists."

A flash of fear shot through her eyes, but quickly transformed to rage.

"You're being followed by the Liberum," I whispered. At the mention of the brotherhood, she grew still. "I've been following them. I intercepted a note with your name on it and a photograph of this house. They know you found something in Europe. You have to hide it."

She had now grown totally still. Carefully, I removed my hand from her mouth.

"Lydia?" her husband called.

"They're coming for you," I said in her ear, just before I let her go. "Prepare yourself."

I woke up to Noah shaking me. "Renée," he said. "Renée." With a start, I opened my eyes.

"You were talking in your sleep," he said. "You were saying something about them coming. About preparing yourself." His hand was wrapped around mine. I slipped my hand out and held it in my lap, opening and closing my fingers as he touched my cheek and wiped it. "You were crying," he said.

"Was I?" I said, but I was still miles away, years away. Crumpled in my fist was the photograph of my home. I held it tighter, trying to hold on to the sound of their voices, to the feel of my mother beneath my grip. Dante's grip.

"He was warning them," I whispered, my voice cracking as I realized what Dante had done. He was an Undead, they were a pair of Monitors; they could have buried him in an instant, but still he risked his life to try to save them. "The whole time, he was warning them."

"Who?"

I glanced down at my sweater, the same one I had been wearing when Dante had showed up at my grandfather's house. He must have slipped the photograph to me when he had put his hand to my waist and kissed my cheek. Reaching over my shoulder, I touched the bandage covering the mark on my back and suddenly felt lonelier than I ever had before. "Someone from a dream."

When Noah turned to the window, I opened my fist and flipped the photograph over. A name was written on the other side. *Lydia Winters.* Below it was a message scrawled in a different hand; one that I recognized, one that pulled me back in time, until I could remember how the rain smelled on the muddy paths as we ran across the Gottfried campus; how delicate the water sounded as it dripped from his hair while he guided my chalk across the blackboard; how my skin tingled beneath his lips when he kissed my neck, my collarbone, my shoulder:

It was all for you.

The sky was a dull grey when the train arrived at the station in Maine. The rain came down in a damp mist as we walked to the parking lot, where a line of black taxis were waiting. The driver of the first rolled down his window.

"Attica Falls," I said, and climbed into the back seat. The seats were made of cheap upholstery and the windows were tinted, which coloured the snowy landscape outside in sepia, as if we were travelling through an old photograph. And in a way, I was.

Attica Falls looked exactly the same as it had last year, the potholed roads lined with dilapidated houses and little shops that might have been cute fifty years ago, but now just looked dreary. The snow flanking the street was dirty, and the stores all looked closed, save for Beatrice's diner and a souvenir shop. As we passed the boarding house where Dante used to live, I closed my eyes, trying to see if I could sense him, but I couldn't feel anything.

When I opened my eyes, we were almost all the way through Attica Falls. I saw an old man carrying a bag of ice from the gas station to his truck. He watched us as we passed, black water splashing onto the windows of the truck as we rounded the bend to the main entrance of Gottfried Academy.

I was suddenly overwhelmed with the vacant feeling of the Undead. A plastic bag kicked around the street in front of us and then floated up into the sky. At my direction, the driver pressed on, dropping us at a snowy field at the edge of town.

Slinging my shovel over my shoulder, I led Noah to the well shaded area by the crab-apple trees in the back of the field. The same place Dante had taken me last winter.

"What is this?" Noah said as I brushed the snow off the cover of the well. The air inside groaned as I lifted it off, letting out a burst of warmth.

"Maine has a tunnel system, too," I said, and lowered myself into the earth.

I led Noah through the tunnel, my muscles remembering the turns as if I had just woken up from spending the night with Dante and was running back to the girls' dormitory to shower before class. We surfaced in the chapel, behind a corroded vent. Everything was still, the light filtering through the rose-coloured windows like a kaleidoscope.

"No one can see us," I said as we crept through the pews. We pushed with all our weight against the chapel doors until they opened against the wind.

The rain was a cold mist when we stepped outside. A few metres away from us, a man in coveralls was chopping the trunk of a tree into pieces and throwing it into some sort of furnace. Noah and I both froze, thinking we were revealed, but he just tipped his cap and kept working. He must have thought we were students. Giving him a slight wave, we walked off, keeping within the shadows of the buildings. But as I gazed around at the campus I thought I knew, my pace slowed.

Everything looked the same, yet wholly different, like a piece of fruit that had become rotten from the inside out. The green was covered with ice and slush. In the middle, where the great oak used to be, now stood a pathetic skeleton of a tree. All of the branches on its right side had been amputated. In fact, most of the trees that used to line the walking paths had now been cut down, leaving severed stumps peeking out of the snow like headstones.

"What happened?" I said, and glanced at the stump beside us, which was tied with a tag. BEETLE PESTICIDE, it said.

"It doesn't matter," Noah said. "Come on."

It's amazing how quickly some things return to you. As I ran across the snowy green to the lake, the sun a glazed red over the trees, it almost felt like I had travelled back in time to last winter. I stopped in front of the dismembered oak, breathing in the cold air and imagining that I was running back to the dorm after meeting Dante. What version of the past was that? Had I known then that Dante was Undead? That I was a Monitor? That we had the same soul?

Dusk fell over the trees as Noah and I ran towards the lake. It was completely frozen over, my feet slipping beneath me as I slid across its bumpy surface. I stared down at the striae in the ice, which looked like thick blue ribbon candy, but I couldn't see to the water below. I didn't know what I was looking for; I could only hope that I would feel it.

I had almost made it to the statue of the bear on the other side of the lake when I heard a soft crack. I wasn't even sure I'd heard it; it could have been a tree creaking or a window closing in the distance. So I pressed on, my breath coming out in quick, shallow clouds, until something beneath me quivered. And before I could move, before I could even take one last breath, the ice broke.

Just before I could fall in, Noah grabbed my waist and pulled me to the shore, where I landed beside him on the crest where the snow met the ice. Lying back in the snow, I stared at the grey sky and was about to say thank you, when I felt it. A tug so slight it could have been nothing; except it wasn't. I had felt it once before, during my placement exam.

Digging his heels into the snow, Noah stood up, but I didn't move. Instead, I closed my eyes and let the thread of air wrap itself around me, leading me down, down into the depths of the lake.

Suddenly I knew what to do. I threw down my bag. Sitting up, I unbuttoned my coat and pulled it off.

"What are you doing?" Noah said as I approached the hole in the ice.

"It's down there. I can feel it," I said, taking off my scarf. "About three metres below, a little to the left."

"You can't go in there," Noah said. "It's too cold. You could die."

"How else are we going to get it?" Turning from him, I stepped off the shore and onto the ice. The hole was about a metre away. "Besides," I said, trying to control the shiver in my voice, "it's in the shallows. It won't be that bad," I said, my words turning to fog in the winter air.

"Renée, let me go first," Noah said from behind me. And before I could stop him, he threw off his coat and blazer and strode past me onto the ice.

"Wait!" I said, trying to stop him, but he had already reached the edge of the hole. And glancing at me over his shoulder, he jumped in. He broke the water with a gasp, and, his arms thrashing once against the ice, he sank into the water below.

"Noah?" I said, searching for any sign of him. "Noah?" I shouted again, and leaned over the hole and reached my hand in. The sharp pain of the cold shot through my fingers, making them numb. I gasped and pulled it back.

It had been almost a full minute. I was about to dive in after Noah when he burst through the dark surface of the water. He grasped at the edge of the ice, but it crumbled under his hands. Relieved that I hadn't followed him underwater, I grabbed his arms and pulled.

"Help me!" I said, but his body had already grown stiff.

His shirt was hardening around him. "Please, Noah. Help me."

From somewhere beneath his clothes, I felt the muscles stir within him. I heard his legs kick in the water, pushing against the ice. Using all my strength, I heaved, dragging him out of the lake and onto the snow.

I rolled him over, rubbing his face to warm it, when I noticed that he was clutching a small iron box to his chest, its sides held shut with clasps, its lid engraved with the worn crest of a canary.

"You found it," I said, wrapping his blazer and coat around him. His hair was hard with ice. "You actually found it."

Noah gave me a weak smile, which deteriorated into a shudder. His face was losing its colour, and his lips were turning blue. Without thinking, I leaned over and kissed him.

When I pulled away, he gave me a sad grin. "I like this."

I laughed and rolled my eyes. "Okay," I said, taking his hand. "Do you think you can walk?"

He gave me what I thought was a nod and put his arm around my neck.

"Where are we going?" he said, as I crouched low. Once I was sure the path was empty, I led him across the green.

"Inside, so you can warm up."

The closest building was Horace Hall, which would be

empty now that classes were over for the day. Taking a chance, I walked towards it, Noah leaning on my side. We were almost at the entrance when I froze. The doors of the building opened and my grandfather stormed out, tapping his shovel beside him like a cane. His white hair was thin and matted to the sides of his head in the misty air. Thinking quickly, I pulled Noah to the ground behind a pile of snow. We waited, and when the doors to Horace Hall swung closed behind my grandfather, I helped Noah up and walked him inside.

The foyer was dark, the windows shaded by thick blue curtains. Beneath them, the radiators crackled with heat, the red carpet plush beneath my shoes as I set Noah down, holding his hand against the small of my back to make it thaw. Noah closed his eyes as his muscles relaxed. From the upstairs balcony, a pendulum clock chimed seven. Its low, lethargic sound reminded me of my grandfather's house in Massachusetts.

With a groan, Noah hoisted himself up.

"No," I said. "Rest."

But he shook his head and held up the box from the lake floor. "Open it."

I hesitated.

"Go on," he said, thrusting it into my hands. It was surprisingly heavy, its dark metal carved with ornate shapes that covered its sides. Engraved on the top was the crest of a canary. I traced the wings of the bird, which were still lined with mud. Jiggling the clasps loose of the dirt and rust, I slid them down and opened it.

The inside of the chest was perfectly dry. Pinned to the inside of the lid was a preserved canary, its pale yellow wings spread open as if it were in flight. Only then did I realize what the riddle had been referring to. *The best of our kind.* Only the best Monitor could sense a canary, especially one submerged in water.

Beneath the canary was a smaller metal case, etched with a strange shape that almost looked like the outline of the canary with its wings spread. Drawn across it were dozens of lines and dots and triangles, swirling together to form a landscape. Carved in the centre was the following phrase: *Pour l'amour vrai.*

"For true love," I whispered, finally understanding why Ophelia had decided to defy the pact her Sisters had made to let the secret die with them. She had been in love, just like me. Like Dante, she wasn't ready to die. Picking up the small box, I tried to lift its lid, but couldn't.

"It's stuck," I said, turning it upside down, looking for a seam. But before I could do anything more, the front doors of the building blew open, banging against the walls as the room grew cold.

"What was that?" Noah said, but I already knew. I could feel it.

Putting the small case back into the chest, I closed the clasps and tucked it into my bag. "Stay here," I said, and ran outside to the stoop.

The campus was vacant as night closed around it like a curtain. In the distance, I thought I heard the sound of snow crunching beneath feet, but then it stopped. Sliding my hand down the railing, I waited, listening. My eyes darted to the left at a flash of movement. And then to the right. The wind swirled past me as something on the horizon seemed to flutter. And then the air pressure changed, compressing in on me.

I felt them before I saw them, their name whistling through the branches: the Undead. I heard a pitter-patter in the snow; soft, like the wings of a moth beating against a porch wall.

I backed up the stairs and into Horace Hall, where I took Noah by the arm. "They're here," I said. "They're coming for us."

But as we stepped out the door, I realized I was too late. They were already running towards us, their small bodies zigzagging randomly across the green, stumbling and then picking themselves up as they followed each other, building momentum like the beginning of an avalanche tumbling down a mountain. The professors must have felt it too, because slowly they came out of the buildings, some in suits, some in pyjamas, their expressions distorted in confusion as they watched the Undead descend on the campus.

I reached for Noah's hand to pull him to the basement, but he was already outside, running towards the Liberum, wielding his shovel over his head. "Noah, wait!" I screamed, even though I knew he couldn't hear me. "The tunnels!"

The Undead boys closed in on him, their tiny white hands grasping at his face. Picking up my bag and shovel, I ran after him. By the time I caught up, Noah had led them onto the lake, fighting them off with his shovel as he slipped across the ice. When I called his name, he hurled a child off his back and turned to me.

That was the moment.

He blinked, his gaze meeting mine, and the shovel slipped from his hands, its tip stabbing the ice by his feet. A jagged gash splintered through it, and just as his lips parted to call out to me, he fell.

The lake swallowed him, the water sloshing as he grabbed at the edge of the ice. But it only crumbled beneath his fingers, making him sink deeper.

I gasped as the Undead boys followed the sound of the water as it sucked him below, their bare feet sliding across the ice as they surrounded the hole. I was about to dash towards them when a palm pressed itself against the underside of the ice, only a metre from the hole. I jumped back when I realized it belonged to Noah. Crawling towards it, I began to bang on the ice, trying to break it, but the ice was thicker here, and even under my sharp shovel, it wouldn't split.

"Noah?" I screamed, pounding at the ice. "Noah?"

My breath grew ragged as I kept trying, using my heel to kick the blade, but to no avail. There was nothing I could do except stand and watch as Noah's hand slipped away from the ice and grew distant as he sank into the depths.

I didn't even fight when they came for me. I heard the hush of children's voices in the night. Two tiny hands closed over my eyes. Two more covered my ears, and another my mouth. Still more over my arms and legs, until I collapsed into the snow. It was all I could to do to rip the bandage from my back and touch the mark between my shoulders. "Dante," I whispered, pain reverberating through my spine. "I'm sorry." His voice spoke back to me. *I'll come for you.*

The moon was a white hook in the sky as they dragged me into the Dead Forest. The decaying stumps poked out of the snow like toothpicks. I could feel the weight of the dead beneath us, the air vacant, totally absent of life.

A tall, thin figure walked towards me through the snow, his face a sliver of pale beneath his hood. A Brother. Crouching down, he picked me up by the arm and lowered his face to mine, ready to take my soul, my secrets. I closed

455

my eyes. I could smell the bitterness of his breath. I pressed my lips together and thought of Dante, imagining it was him.

That's when something strange happened. I didn't feel scared or angry or even weak. I could barely feel anything except cold. I shuddered as I felt a prickling chill hurtling towards me.

Dante, his skin as white as the dead trees around us.

He dived between the Brother and me, his lips brushing past mine as he shoved the Undead onto the forest floor, knocking him out with a swift kick to the head. Dante whisked me off the ground and took me into his arms. Our bodies fitted together, my limbs tangled with his until I couldn't tell which were mine and which were Dante's, and I began to melt, the warmth seeping through my palms and travelling higher, higher, through my hands, my arms, my throat, my lips, until I was crying. The chest from the lake bounced up and down in my bag as he ran. My fingers tightened around his shoulders, and I closed my eyes, smelling the sweetness of pine in the air; hearing the symphony of the trees creaking in the wind, the crows crying from branches, the snow crunching beneath Dante's feet, his heart beating an irregular staccato as we vanished into the woods, until there was nothing left of us but a swirling, snowy gust.

ACKNOWLEDGEMENTS

Ted Malawer, for making the impossible always seem possible. Abby Ranger, for asking all the right questions, and for forcing me to be a better writer. Laura Schreiber and the team at Hyperion, for taking such good care of me. And Ari Lewin, for teaching me how to write a book.

Nathaniel, Lauren, Bec and Katherine, for making the friendships in this book come to life. Brandon, for keeping me updated on everything zombie. Paul, for giving me a Montreal education, and for designing my whimsical website. My family, for feeding me when I was on deadline, and for being my most enthusiastic fans. And Akiva, for colouring every page.

Thank you.

For more breathtaking discoveries, go to
www.usborne.com/lifeeternal

Just one *kiss* will take your breath away..

DEAD
BEAUTIFUL

YVONNE WOON

DISCOVER THE DARK SECRETS OF
GOTTFRIED ACADEMY IN THE FIRST
MESMERIZING MYSTERY...

DEAD
BEAUTIFUL

DESIRE. DANGER. DESTINY.
Little did I know that this is what
I would find at Gottfried Academy.

Coming from sunny California, the mist-shrouded
Academy was a shock, with its strange customs,
ancient curriculum and study of Latin – the language
of the dead. Then I discovered that the school
has more than one dark secret...
I also discovered Dante. Intelligent, elusive and
devastatingly gorgeous, most people can't decide
whether they love, hate or fear him. All I know
is that when we are together, I've never felt
more alive – or more afraid.

"Riveting and different...a real page-turner." SLJ

ISBN 9781409530244

For more intoxicating reads, go to
www.fiction.usborne.com